We Three

We Three

Kerry Ames

We Three

Copyright © 2023 by Kerry D. Ames

Historical Fiction
Biblical Fiction
First edition

Cover design by Paul Ruane
Paperback ISBN: 978-1-0881-9869-8
Ebook ISBN: 978-1-0082-1425-1

Scripture taken from the Holy Bible, King James Version, public domain.

Independently published.

Based on the account of the Nativity found in the Holy Bible, KJV, Matthew 2:1-14

Now when Jesus was born in Bethlehem of Judaea in the days of Herod the king, behold, there came wise men from the east to Jerusalem, saying, where is he that is born King of the Jews? for we have seen his star in the east, and are come to worship him.

When Herod the king had heard these things, he was troubled, and all Jerusalem with him. And when he had gathered all the chief priests and scribes of the people together, he demanded of them where Christ should be born. And they said unto him, In Bethlehem of Judaea: for thus it is written by the prophet, and thou Bethlehem, in the land of Juda, art not the least among the princes of Juda: for out of thee shall come a Governor, that shall rule my people Israel.

Then Herod, when he had privily called the wise men, enquired of them diligently what time the star appeared. And he sent them to Bethlehem, and said, Go and search diligently for the young child; and when ye have found him, bring me word again, that I may come and worship him also. When they had heard the king, they departed; and, lo, the star, which they saw in the east, went before them, till it came and stood over where the young child was. When they saw the star, they rejoiced with exceeding great joy. And when they were come into the house, they saw the young child with Mary his mother, and fell down, and worshipped him: and when they had opened their treasures, they presented unto him gifts; gold, and frankincense and myrrh. And being warned of God in a dream that they should not return to Herod, they departed into their own country another way.

And when they were departed, behold, the angel of the Lord appeareth to Joseph in a dream, saying, Arise, and take the young child and his mother, and flee into Egypt, and be thou there until I bring thee word: for Herod will seek the young child to destroy him. When he arose, he took the young child and his mother by night, and departed into Egypt.

To Donna

CHAPTER 1

Any vacant space inside Topur's substantial home now served as temporary storage, accommodating the bounty accumulated from his most recent trading odyssey. Through the exertions of his wife, Atarah, and their four daughters, order and comfort were restored. What were once haphazard piles were now orderly stacks. Rugs, vases, amphorae of oils, and chest-high columns of silver plates lined the hallways. Piled bags of spices competed to perfume the home, with coriander the current winner. Statuettes found safe placement upon wooden crates housing dried fruit, dyed cloth, and gems.

Within the largest room, Topur admired his trove. He stood behind his favorite chair, patting and stroking the furs draped over its back. He had never touched pelts this soft and smooth. The pale-skinned trader at the bazaar in Damascus enticed him, declaring no fur was more luxurious. According to the seller, men would clamor to give their wives such a gift. Topur believed him and purchased every one.

Atarah had organized the items in the room into sensible groups—glass, goblets, urns, plates, and vases in one corner, tools and cookware in another. For the first time in his many years of trading, Topur bought bolts of silk and, in his glee, traded for the four jade chests they lay in. How many, he wondered, would be affluent enough to pay the price he would command? He vowed to keep one pale green chest for himself.

He had paid his investors. Every item that remained in the

house was his to sell, to trade, or enjoy. Without question, this had been his most successful trip. The profits he would realize would maintain his family's prominent status within this trading city. Prosperity was theirs, though Topur knew his being Jewish here meant there were limits. To keep their tenuous hold on this level of comfort and stability, Topur had to remain active. But this latest trip may have rewarded him with the most treasured commodity of all: rest.

He needed respite, a pause from the harsh demands surrounding a successful trading venture. He was weary, but that was true after every journey. Any trading mission meant dealing with the inescapable companions of loneliness and discomfort. The handsome earnings always compensated for the tribulations.

Though now, he had doubts.

Accompanied by a long groan, Topur settled into his chair. On recent trips, his unease was escalating. The reasons were hardly a mystery. In his youth, the travel, the suspense, and the frenzied pace of the lively bazaar had been a welcome and exciting change from the slogging marches. There was a fervor in the trading circles that could not be replicated elsewhere. It fueled and stimulated him. He sought the challenges of bargaining, and successful trades were thrilling. And, throughout his experience, he'd established relationships, even made friendships. He delighted in repeated visits to those he'd come to like, respect, and depend on.

Many of those men were gone, replaced by strangers, foreigners, occupying markets teeming with a cacophony of languages. The new bazaars were dins of shouting and shoving among sweaty traders who smelled of their animals and the burnt flesh roasting nearby. He had never liked the elbowing, the jostling—the touching—market trading required, but it was bearable. Now, contact with rough, unintelligible strangers repulsed him, affecting his abilities and probably his profits.

The rare bands of robbers had always been a threat, but

what was once the occasional nuisance was now a grim likelihood. Worse than the thieves were the soldiers. Romans. Armed and angry, they were eager to impose their individual interpretations of the Perfect Order they were charged to defend. Innocent traders were killed on the spot for imagined infractions, victims of a legionnaire's violent impulses, or a bad hangover. He'd seen it happen.

Thoughts of quitting were useless. But the gains from this last trip meant he could afford to pass on the next two, maybe three, projected caravans. He could maintain his family's standing for a year, perhaps longer.

Topur rested his neck against the soft fur. He crossed his arms over his chest and smiled. Soon, even though sunlight still filled the room, he was fast asleep.

A loud rap upon his heavy wood door snapped Topur out of his slumber. Hearing it again, he felt in no rush to answer.

"Will you see to the door?" Atarah called from a back room. "I am not done with the girls." She was correct to be cautious.

Topur heard the rustling.

Atarah was likely removing any evidence suggesting she was teaching their four daughters to read. Her initiative was stepping outside custom and could lead to community rebuke. Daughters were the only available students in this family, and Topur wanted his daughters to be as capable and competent as their mother. Topur loved each of his daughters independently and dearly and understood they would need to find their own ways to cope with the impairment of being Jewish women outside their homeland.

He had limited input. His livelihood demanded he be absent from home often—too often. Atarah was the clever one. Topur had come from a line of merchants who spent their lives in markets with pack animals and their unscrupulous owners. Atarah's family was overflowing with scribes and rabbis. She benefitted from their unconventional ideas about literacy. Eventually, her parents chose financial security over a contemplative companion for their precocious daughter. Any concerns that the union might not last were extinguished long ago.

"Are you ready? I will answer," said Topur. "That voice sounds like Faddey."

"Girls, hurry," Atarah implored. "Faddey? What would Faddey want with you?"

Topur didn't respond. He wondered the same as he approached the door. The next knock was more urgent.

As he reached for the door, Topur shouted, "Yes, yes!" He lifted the black iron latch. The door creaked upon opening, but only a slit of light broke into the home's stone floor. "Who is this?"

"Topur, open up! These are prominent men!"

"Is that you, Councilman?" The door didn't budge. "It sounds like Faddey, but it wouldn't be likely that he would come to this house." Topur snickered. Opportunities to frustrate the imperious councilman were rare.

"Topur, open this door immediately! You don't realize who is standing with me. They say they must meet with you."

Topur eased the door by tiny increments. When able, he popped only his head through the opening. "Faddey, does someone have an issue?" Peering out, Topur held fast. He cocked his head. His smile vanished.

Before him stood Faddey, scowling, dressed in his finest red-and-green-striped kaftan. On either side of him were two men. The first was tall, effortlessly plumb, a brunet, decidedly handsome. The other was shorter, stocky, with powerful limbs, and armed with an intense glare. Behind them, astonishingly, stood a glut of Topur's fellow city dwellers, stuffing the narrow confines of the street outside his home. Packed shoulder-to-shoulder, men, women, boys, and girls gaped in uncharacteristic silence, suspecting they would repeat their memories of this moment to their grandchildren many times.

The stocky man spoke. "You are Topur, the merchant?"

Topur blinked. "Yes."

"Then I will introduce myself." The crowd inched forward. "I am King Xaratuk." He straightened, then glanced to the side. "With me is my friend, King Mithrias. We wish to speak with you privately."

Behind Topur, a clay pot crashed to the floor.

The men before Topur weren't dressed like kings. Their trousers, boots, and fitted shirts were foreign, but they could have passed for any of the myriads of other travelers on the Trading Road passing north of the city.

Topur scanned his tunic, wondering if the others noticed his pulsating heart. Atarah picked up the remnants of the pot and sent their four daughters scurrying to do what little they could to prepare the home for unexpected guests.

"Welcome?" Topur's greeting sounded more like a question than an invitation. In his confusion, his feet remained fixed, refusing to move aside. His quivering hand pointed the way.

Faddey's thin chin rose as his eyes narrowed. He thrust his hand before the kings. "You asked me, as head of our city's council, to take you directly to the home of our esteemed merchant, Topur. I have fulfilled that request. May I suggest that if Topur is unable to satisfy your wishes, you return to me, to Faddey. I will, of course, meet any and all of your requirements. Even now, I can remain with you. Perhaps my presence will—"

"Not necessary." Xaratuk stepped toward the open door. Faddey's sweeping arm blocked the king's progress. Faddey turned, glaring at Topur.

"Topur, these men are kings," he hissed. "If you feel you are insufficiently prepared for such nobility, and seeing as I am the head of our council—"

"Out of our way." Xaratuk pushed against Faddey's arm.

Faddey attempted to place a conciliatory hand upon the king's shoulder, but Xaratuk grabbed his wrist, throwing it to the side.

Faddey let his hand continue to sweep, then bowed,

rendering the snub less potent.

"A most tiresome man." Xaratuk passed into the house. The taller, elegant King Mithrias followed. Topur offered the crowd a weak smile, then turned and closed the door.

Inside, Atarah and the girls had achieved hasty improvements. Topur directed the kings to the home's largest room, still overrun with his trading surplus, but all of it orderly, as if on display. There was ample room to seat the guests. He offered the kings the low pillowed chaises. The daughters raced to place cushions at their feet. Topur moved a wooden table between the kings, then excused himself to retrieve some wine.

He passed Atarah, who entered the room with three silver trays, each loaded with fruits, figs, dates, and nuts. She had changed into her finest beige dress. A golden sash belted her waist, hinting at a trim figure, remarkable for a woman with four children. A silken scarf covered her head. Thin silver bracelets girded each light-umber forearm.

Topur returned and poured wine into the home's best chalices, though his hand shook. The kings smiled.

"I recognize those pelts," said Mithrias, selecting a date. "Fine fur. Luxurious. Far more common where I live." He scanned the gathered goods. "You display your prosperity with elegance." He raised his cup. Topur nodded without comment, made a half-hearted bow, and sat in the fur-draped chair directly across from the kings.

"Yes, this is a gracious home, Topur," Xaratuk added, inspecting the room's inventory. "We haven't experienced this kind of comfort for a long, long time." He inhaled. "Ah, the scent of saffron. I have missed that."

After sending the girls away, Atarah returned and sat in the remaining empty chair. Only Xaratuk showed signs of surprise.

"We realize we are an intrusion," said Mithrias. "That was unavoidable because our entrance into your city was to have been quiet and anonymous. We planned to avoid attracting attention, specifically the attention of an entourage like one that followed us to your door."

"Your councilman has difficulty keeping secrets," said Xaratuk.

"Yes, we requested our anonymity be protected." Mithrias sighed, then swept his hand over his torso. "This is not our normal wardrobe. It was part of our plan to be inconspicuous, in case you think we are misrepresenting ourselves."

"No. No, no." Topur wondered if the kings could see his trembling hand as he brought his wine to his lips. "No. No one thinks that." He was so confounded he could do little more than stutter. To avoid spilling, he placed his cup on the floor.

"Being unfamiliar with your city, we didn't know how to find you," said Mithrias.

Topur sat upon the edge of his chair, unable to look his guests in the eye. Kings didn't seek men like him. He reasonably assumed he had done something to offend them, something awful.

He stopped listening. His gut felt like twisted rope. He would have swallowed if only he could. He reached for his wine but recoiled upon seeing his hand still shaking. Atarah came to his aid, filling the silence with small talk.

"We are so honored by this visit," she said. "Imagine our astonishment at seeing men such as you at our door. Excuse us if we seem overcome. We never anticipated—"

"We are camped by the Trading Road," Xaratuk interrupted. "Topur, your name is mentioned often as it relates to our interests. Over and over, it was the same." His eyes narrowed. "I said, 'We must find this man.'"

To Topur's ears, Xaratuk's statement insinuated threat. Surrendering to his frayed nerves, Topur burst, speaking before he had command of his thoughts. "I can't think of anything. That is, I—I don't recall anything," he stammered. "Is it the jade chests? Some statue? I can't begin to imagine. I am merely a merchant. I buy things. I trade. If I have done something wrong, have unwittingly acquired something you believe—"

"I'm not sure of your meaning." Xaratuk grabbed for some almonds.

"Anything I might have handled was unintentional, I assure you. I will do anything necessary—"

"Topur." Mithrias leaned forward in his chair. "We are not here to settle some score. You've done nothing wrong. Please put your mind at ease."

Topur sank within his chair. Tension ebbed through his slumping shoulders. As her husband reclined, Atarah smiled.

"Wrong? No, of course not," said Xaratuk. "Topur, we need your help but also offer you an opportunity." He cleared his throat. "We are here to invite you to be present with us as we investigate the most important event in generations." His voice rang as his excitement rose. "Maybe the most extraordinary event—ever."

From that moment, Xaratuk strode about the room as if acting in a Greek play, complete with melodious oration, sweeping gestures, and dramatic pauses.

"We are not lost," Mithrias added, "Not yet. But we are farther from home than planned. We are no longer in familiar territory."

"Word reached us that there is no better guide from this region than Topur." Xaratuk stood imperiously over Topur. "We heard this from traders, travelers, foreigners, even your neighbors—everyone except that loathsome councilman. Everyone agrees you're the man most suited for this task."

Topur smiled. It was true. Few, if any, in the region could match his experience. "I am humbled by your comments and the high opinions of those around me." He paused, looking to Atarah. "I am away from my home more than I am here. I have seen much." Glassy-eyed, he sighed and reached for his cup. "Tell me, where will we find this momentous event?"

Xaratuk positioned himself directly in front of Topur, hands on hips. "We don't know."

Topur's chin retreated beneath his beard. "You... don't

know?"

Xaratuk strutted away, restless, gesturing toward the window. "Topur, you've seen it. A man like you pays attention to the night sky." He smoothed his broad mustache. "You've seen it. The star!"

"I'm not sure I understand." Topur glanced away, avoiding Xaratuk's glare. "A star?"

"Yes."

"A star? If you mean that bigger one, the bright one—yes, but—"

"That's it!" shouted Xaratuk. "That's the one!" He pointed a finger directly at Topur's forehead. "You have seen it, of course!"

"Perhaps we refer to the same one. There is one considerably larger than the others."

"Topur, you're a merchant, a traveler. You read the stars. You see their movements. You rely upon them for direction. Have you ever seen a star act like this?"

Topur hadn't given it much attention, though this was not the time for that admission. Yes, he had seen a large star, but what of it? Rather than admit such nonchalance, he encouraged Xaratuk to move ahead with his interpretation. "This star is so different, so unusual?"

Xaratuk retreated to his chaise. He filled his cup, gulped the contents, then refilled it. "Yes, oh, yes. Topur, tell us, how long do you say this unexpected star has appeared in our evening sky? A week? Two weeks? A month? Forever?"

"I can't say exactly. Months, perhaps, but—"

"It appeared,"—Xaratuk slapped the tabletop—"like that! One night, no star. The next night, there it is. Am I right?"

"I suppose that—"

"Of course I'm right. Stars don't do that. They don't suddenly appear. In all your life, in all your observations, have you ever encountered such a thing?" Xaratuk did not wait for a reply. "No, you haven't." His urgent voice surged. "This is different. In my court, I am surrounded by advisors who immerse themselves in studying the heavens. Two of my best are with us. They tell me this star differs from anything our fathers or our fathers' fathers experienced. They assure me we stand at the threshold of something marvelous." He paused. "They are never wrong."

Topur glanced at Atarah but found her attention was focused on Mithrias.

"And you, Topur," Xaratuk continued, "will take us there."

"And this star, you believe it signifies... what?"

"It is a beacon, a heavenly guide," said Mithrias.

"Its light," Xaratuk interrupted them by saying, "will reveal the most significant event of our lifetime—or for generations, who knows?" Mithrias slunk into his chaise.

"But you can't say where," Topur drawled.

The lingering pause amplified Xaratuk's sneer. "If we could, why would we need a guide?"

The silence was awkward. Topur frowned. He had never been asked to guide anyone to an undetermined destination.

Mithrias broke the uncomfortable lull. "Topur, we trust there is a conclusion to our journey. We believe the rewards will outweigh our efforts. Admittedly, at this moment, we can't offer details. Including you on our journey will increase the certainty of success. And for me, there are other benefits. I might better understand you and the people we'll meet. Your cooperation will give me that opportunity. Who knows what advantages might ensue? Developing understanding is never a waste of time or effort."

Topur nodded.

Mithrias expounded upon the importance of building friendship while Xaratuk squirmed in his chaise. "Ever, I say!" Xaratuk pounded a fist into his hand, interrupting. "This is the Discovery of the Ages! The most extraordinary event ever! And you'll be wise to understand that!"

Mithrias stared into his lap. A look of stony melancholy replaced any earlier show of enthusiasm. Either Mithrias did not share Xaratuk's excitement, or he'd witnessed these theatrics too many times. It was clear which king was more invested in this mission.

Xaratuk's melodrama lacked what Topur wanted most: specifics. With no clear destination, it was evident that no one knew what this "Discovery of the Ages" might be. All the embellishment felt like artifice.

Head up, his nose in the air, Xaratuk asked, "So, Topur, we can count upon you?"

Mithrias straightened to see Topur's response.

It wasn't exactly a laugh. It wasn't derisive or mocking. But judging by the look of horror on Atarah's face, Topur's nervous snicker had the trappings of insolence. His reaction was involuntary, the product of his many confrontations with unscrupulous traders looking to promote items they knew had little value. Topur's senses, tuned to identify shams, warned him this might be one.

Of course he'd noticed the star. But proceeding in its direction meant more hardship and danger than these men realized—it might mean their collective doom.

"I—I might..." Topur stammered through an embarrassed smile. "That is, I could offer you better service if I had more details, such as how far and how—"

"I've said all I'm willing to say." Xaratuk rose, scowling. "It is late. Where do you propose I sleep?"

Atarah rose as well, making certain Topur could recognize her look of disapproval. "Please, Your Excellency, follow me," she said. "Your room is prepared."

Silent, Xaratuk brushed past Topur.

Mithrias sighed as he rose from his chair. His perfect smile had retreated. Stepping close, he placed a hand on Topur's shoulder. "Please excuse my friend. He is excited, but he is also tired. We have been on this excursion for too long and still don't know how much farther we must go. If that is frustrating for you, imagine how frustrating it is for us. But he has the energy of a thousand men, and he'll be certain we arrive—somehow—wherever that may be."

He drew his hand back. "What I say about building relationships is true, however. If you come, even if, at its conclusion, you feel you were not a part of the greatest event ever, you will have no regrets." A weary smile emerged. "Now, where are you putting me for the night?"

CHAPTER 2

The kings had retreated to their rooms. Topur retreated to the refuge of his flat roof. The moonless evening was cool. The sky glistened. Small groups of people still milled about the street outside his home. Topur gulped the crisp air, but he could feel his heart pounding with the same intensity as when he first answered the knock. Any temporary relief he felt when the kings assured him they weren't seeking retribution was replaced by a knotted stomach again.

These kings weren't vindictive. They were deranged!

Topur placed damp palms upon the waist-high clay walls girdling his roof. His gaze shifted from his feet to the sparkling firmament.

There it was: the star.

"A star? So, it's brighter. Yes. Who doesn't see that? Larger, too." But the kings' assertions were preposterous, their claims unsupportable, their mission absurd. Yet they expected him to be eager, even grateful, to be complicit in their madness. "No." He shook his head. "I must consider this with great care."

The ladder creaked, signaling that Topur's fragile reprieve was over. He turned to the square hole through which the unwelcome intruder must emerge.

The silver bracelets around Atarah's wrist appeared first, then her covered head.

"Atarah, what are you...?"

Topur's wife rarely visited the roof. Her domain was within

their comfortable home's walls. He rushed to assist her up the last few steps. She gripped his hand and leaned against him, steadying herself on the flat clay rooftop. Her eyes made inquiries of the night sky, then of her husband.

"What are you doing up here, Atarah? You don't like the roof."

"You're right. I don't. I don't see why you do."

"Is something wrong? Are the—"

"I thought you needed someone to talk with." Her stern, dark eyebrows showed no evidence of empathy. A long, tense silence followed.

Topur knew his behavior had been questionable, even inhospitable. It was clear Atarah had not climbed to the roof to soothe. She was there for an explanation.

"I'd prefer someone who'd listen to me," Topur finally mumbled. "Those men were not inclined to do that."

"Listen to you? Listen to you? Topur, these are powerful men." Atarah's words were hushed but urgent. She patted his chest. "You will meet no one—ever—more important than the men who lie in those rooms below. You saw how the city reacted to them. Any man would give an arm to be in your place. And you laugh at them! Topur—"

"Yes, I..." Topur hung his head. "I didn't mean to laugh. I didn't. I felt relaxed after they assured me their visit wasn't to punish me. Maybe I was too relaxed, too relieved. King Xaratuk was waving his hands, wide-eyed, like some Greek dancer. His pronouncements were preposterous! 'A star—some beacon—guiding them to the most important event ever!' You heard him."

"Shhh. They may not be asleep."

"Who wouldn't laugh?" whispered Topur. "These men want me to help them chase down starlight, Atarah. *Starlight!* You know our teachings far better than I do, so, when has anyone accomplished such a thing? When has a star been anything but a star?"

"We should doubt Moses heard a voice from a burning bush? Don't presume to put your limits on what God chooses to do. Events beyond our comprehension have happened and will happen again. No one can challenge that."

"I respect those men. Of course I do. You must believe that. I didn't intend to be impolite. It just burst out." His expression turned sour. "Perhaps I should apologize."

"I don't know, Topur." Atarah grimaced. "I do know tomorrow you greet them with a different attitude. If they sense any more reluctance, they'll find someone more agreeable. You heard Faddey. He told them to find him if you can't satisfy their wishes."

"Faddey couldn't guide a falling man to the ground."

"You follow my meaning. It won't be Faddey, and it won't be you. It will be another, and that man will reap the benefit—not you."

"I have been home, what, four days? I'm not ready to head back through the desert. There is nothing to trade. How long would this take? Can they tell me? No. Can you tell me? Can you and our daughters manage for weeks, months without me—on some trip I'm expected to guide for who-knows-how-long? And what is in it for me?" His whispered voice mocked, "Oh, but there will be something wondrous underneath that star—something astonishing." He rolled his eyes. "I admit it; that still makes me laugh." His smile drained, a stern frown rushing to replace it.

He had invited none of this. The kings' arrival happened so unexpectedly. Why should this intrusion fall upon his shoulders? Why had two such powerful, prominent men come to his doorstep asking for his help? And why should they expect him to change his life and leave home at their mere suggestion?

"Atarah, what did they say tonight that you found convincing? What claim did they make that had the least hint of merit?"

Atarah's lips tightened. She folded her arms.

"It's a fool's undertaking." Topur studied his wife, still waiting for her response. "If that star signified something so astonishing, wouldn't word on the Trading Road have reached us by now?" His head twitched. "I don't offer my services to those who chase clouds—or stars. Isn't my time more important than that?"

His objections were reasonable, though his reluctance was also based upon one significant reason he could not share with Atarah. Not yet.

How could he explain he found his livelihood frightening? A man doesn't confess that to his wife, or to anyone. Such an admission was cowardly and irresponsible. But leaving home was agonizing. Apprehension saturated every journey. The odious, alien presence of the Empire confronted him most anywhere he could productively trade. To make a living meant doing so under Roman surveillance and Roman rules. Though the Romans encouraged trade, such promotion extracted a horrible human price, a reckoning he would confront every trip.

Encountering repeated instances of subjugation had changed him. Quite unlike his earliest expeditions, he now felt vulnerable, exposed. He was convinced his continued existence was due more to luck than skill or foresight. His father and grandfather taught him to anticipate and avoid disaster, but when would probability work against him? How many times could a man thrust his hand into a basket of snakes and not get bit? It only took once.

He didn't want to die alone, apart, away.

Any future trip might easily be his last. The thought of not returning to his wife and four lovely daughters nauseated him. Imagining them having to continue without him could trigger tears. So, even though the kings' regal invitation impressed his wife, he desperately wished to remain home.

Topur studied Atarah's face, the lines of concern etched across her forehead. Her dark eyes reflected the mystical charm of the celestial show. He felt his chest swell without inhaling the night air. Atarah's loveliness was fit for the eyes of royalty. Why leave such beauty behind unless survival demanded it? Someone else could guide those kings.

"These men can help you," said Atarah. "Think of the benefits they could bring to your business."

"I didn't think business was bad." Topur struggled to hide the hurt. He'd considered himself a prosperous provider, especially considering the occasional impairment of being Jewish. Their comfortable circumstances were no accident. "What do you lack, Atarah?"

"Dearest..." Atarah's dark eyebrows finally relaxed. "Because of you, I lack for nothing. We have everything we want. But every time you return home, you complain about the Romans. They're here, they're there, they're beasts, they're murderers. I'm only repeating what you say. These kings are from the east. If you gain their friendship, you'd have new markets, away from the Romans. They could use their influence to give you access to more tranquil and productive areas." Her voice softened. "You won't get that chance if you provoke them. Your questions are thinly veiled criticisms, and they know that."

Topur took his wife's hand and moved toward the roof's walled edge.

"Not too close," Atarah admonished. They halted.

"I have always trusted your advice. I don't disagree, Atarah. Yes, I would prefer to trade without some Roman looking down his nose at me." Though conceding, there was the gnawing pang that the time he might spend with those he loved most was dwindling. He'd leave home only when he must, and thus far, these men had presented no evidence to persuade him, benefits to business or not.

"Atarah, what I asked was not difficult to answer." Topur pulled at his beard, then pointed to the large star. "You know that, and they know that, but did they ever give me an answer?"

Atarah shook her head.

"What is so difficult? Is it too much to ask where I'm

expected to take them?"

The star glowed lustrous in the western night sky, giving no more hint of any ultimate objective than the kings. Should he prepare for Alexandria or Tarsus? Was it Rome? If it were Rome, he'd stay home—no matter what. Hadn't anyone considered that traveling in that direction might be disastrous?

Topur agreed with one thing: this star had an allure. He gestured with his raised arm. "It is different, I'll agree. It does beckon. Could the kings be right? Could this single, strange star be so unique?"

Atarah did not answer.

"Or is it merely unusual? Rainbows and sandstorms are unusual, too, but they're never omens. This might be worthy of investigation, but not necessarily by me. I have a family to consider. I have my safety to consider. And, after meeting the man, I don't relish the idea of traveling alongside King Xaratuk."

"Maybe your questions don't need answers." Atarah turned toward the ladder, stopped, and looked back at her husband. "It doesn't matter where the kings are going. Knowing such important and influential men, standing with them, being recognized, and being in their confidence will improve your stature and give access to new markets away from ports and cities you're currently constrained to, ones under the feet of the Romans. Besides," she added, "what will our neighbors, your customers, your friends think of you if you reject such eminent men and refuse their bidding? Who would turn away from such an offer?" Atarah finally paused for a breath. "It is vital you become a friend to these men, and this is the perfect opportunity."

Atarah reached for Topur with outstretched hands. "I am so proud of you. I have always been proud to be your wife. Your daughters are proud of you, too. We have good reason." She licked her lips. "I've been wondering why these great kings came to our doorstep. The answer came in a moment of clarity, and I want you to consider this seriously."

Topur braced himself. At her most serious moments, Atarah was unfailingly insightful.

"God is behind this," she said. "I'm certain. That two such powerful men seek you, and only you—by name—is a divine act. There is no other explanation. Don't you see? It isn't the kings asking you to go—-it is God. This is God's will."

"God's will? God's will? And for what purpose?"

"I don't know, my dear. That... that is what you must discover."

Topur stopped breathing. Successful challenges to Atarah's convictions were as rare as this star. He had no response to counter her this time, either. She brought God into the mix. Who challenges God?

Nonetheless, he wanted to be clear: his reluctance was not born out of thoughtlessness, or stubbornness, or fear, or indifference.

"Dear wife," he began, "what heavenly light has ever shone upon one city, one palace, one person? The far larger moon shows its light upon us all. I join the kings and chase this light, stumbling in the desert for months, never reaching our destination,"—he paused—"because there isn't one! The star's light shines everywhere! And while we drift, we'll likely encounter cities or kingdoms that will not welcome these men. Some—I guarantee it—will be dangerous." His voice fell to a whisper. "And during that time, I'll be away from you, away from our daughters, away from my home, away from all I hold dear. Gone. And for what?" He cupped his hand around Atarah's cheek.

Atarah placed her hand upon his and whispered a single word: "Go."

Air hissed through Topur's nostrils. He was defeated. "I'll have to gather some things. I'll need your help." He grimaced, dreading the thought of leaving his home so soon. "I'll take Najiir with me. You don't need him for anything, do you?"

"What you do with that boy is none of my affair," Atarah

replied.

"I haven't seen him for days. I will make inquiries. He'll enjoy this futile chaos. At least I will have some company."

Topur, alongside two smiling kings, left his home the following afternoon.

CHAPTER 3

Topur floundered in the soft sand. The sandals on his feet and the burdensome bundle of supplies upon his back made the uphill trudge grueling. Each step was an independent test of will. With his eyes puckered shut to battle the gritty wind, he could only guess how far he'd advanced up the long, torturous slope.

"Enough," he sighed. "This should do."

Topur halted, then turned, dumping his wearying pack. His grateful back immediately registered relief. He felt, momentarily, as though he might float. His hood and sleeves slapped about his hunched frame. The stinging wind now beat from behind, rendering his eyes useful once more.

He blinked the scene into focus. From this modest elevation, he scanned the imminent dusk across an empty desert. His view ranged so far over the endless sand it was as if he was beholding the very edge of the world. It wasn't the edge of anything. He knew that. But beyond that desolate horizon lay a vastly different world. He'd been there.

Gripping the bridge of his nose, Topur scratched at the crust surrounding his eyes. He moved his hand to his grimy forehead. He rubbed along its hollowed lines, hoping to offset the pounding within his head.

"Why? Why, God, why? There's nothing for them there," he murmured. His untethered donkey, standing dutifully at his elbow, twitched one ear. She was his only audience. Her patient, sympathetic eyes studied him closely, though there was little else to offer distraction.

Their silhouettes stood in stark contrast to the bleak hill looming behind them. Not a tree, not a bush, not a single plant emerged to compete with their footprints, the only impressions upon this barren canvas. This desolate portion of the desert was unremarkable but not unfamiliar. Topur knew this region. He'd made this same trek, or ones nearly like it, twenty times—maybe more—but always as a merchant, never as a guide to foreign men.

Absent any landmark, Topur focused on a distinct segment of the sunset horizon, waiting for the caravan's true guide to rise. The star alone held ultimate authority. The expedition assented to its influence entirely. And that was nonsense. Could no one else see the risk of adhering to a transient, non-communicative, unintelligible spot of light? The star's unexpected appearance implied that predictability and permanence were not inherent. At any moment, it might disappear forever, just as quickly, just as incredibly, as it materialized. What then?

If it rose again tonight, this star would confirm his suspicion. To Topur, the star's gleaming directive was becoming apparent. If he were correct, there would be no mistaking their route, and maybe—finally—they could decide, or at least discuss, where this group was going.

But, please, God. Not there.

"You and I would blend in." The donkey's ear flicked again. This time she averted her gaze, protecting her own eyes. "Not these men." Topur untied the ropes holding a stack of kindling to the donkey's back. "Their renown will provide no advantage. Their pointed hats, their baggy trousers. They are the strange ones, not me."

The load dumped to the ground with a startling thump, but the donkey stood unfazed. Unburdened, she shuddered, her hide rippling with the newfound freedom. Topur patted her, then began to rub the base of one ear using his thumb and forefinger. A butting head, lifting him off his feet, assured Topur of her approval. "Isn't that better?" He smiled, continuing to pet and soothe. "Stay close, my friend."

The kindling massed in a tangled heap. "Sticks? That is all?" Topur's voice was thin and high. "You and I are only good for moving sticks?" He inhaled sharply. "They came to me, you remember. It was they who begged me to come. I didn't ask to do this. When they first told me about it, I laughed. How could they be serious?" He kicked some stray kindling across the wind-whipped sand back into the pile. "I shouldn't have laughed." His sneer defied suppression. "But you and I, we come, and what do they have us do? The kings rarely speak to me. They don't ask questions or seek my opinion. No, we haul sticks. So why do they need us to help them chase that light?"

They hadn't.

After all their heavy-handed persuasion, the kings had been content to ignore him. They were cordial since first adding him to their journey but had yet to approach him for advice or direction. With—or despite—his inclusion, the expedition continued to move as it had all along: heeding the directive of the star's light, trudging along established routes, and sticking to the ordinary. As of tonight, he had done nothing of consequence. He felt neglected and insignificant.

Topur stared down the slope as the caravan's first dozen members lumbered into view. Behind them came lines of donkeys, mules, wagons, carts, and more men. He'd left his cart on the vast flat area as a marker, placed at the location best suited for assembling camp, considering the available firm ground and bracing wind.

Tonight, for the first time, he would set his tent apart from the others.

"Have they never been in the desert? If I hadn't suggested we collect kindling days ago and save it for a night like this, those cooks would have no fire, and the others would find it too cold to sleep." His gaze returned to the donkey. "And that is the extent of my contributions? They need some guide to tell them they must gather sticks?" He groaned in disgust.

The waning light fostered a chill. Topur placed his hood over his head and cinched his robe's belt tighter. He reached for the dagger belted to his left side. Its smooth bone hilt offered comfort and reassurance. Only he knew exactly where they were, and he alone knew that continuing to head directly toward the star would call for a dagger to be within reach.

His weary legs buckled, and he dropped to the sand. This was precisely the region he had hoped to avoid. Had he known from the beginning the star would beckon them here, he would have emphatically declined the kings' offer, even if that meant enduring ridicule from his wife and neighbors. But, defying his better judgment, here he was, waiting for the star to rise tonight and prove this group was in more danger than it understood. His tight stomach reminded him of how trapped he felt being among them. "After tonight, it's more than picking up sticks," Topur huffed. "It's more than that."

With a groan, he rose and stepped to the donkey, giving her a last pat on the head. From the tangled wood, he delved through the gnarled kindling. Once he found firm footing on the windswept surface, he kneeled to arrange the tinder into a pyramid frame. Satisfied, he staggered to the bundled tent supplies. He rummaged among the items to retrieve his fire-making kit, a customized collection of stones, flints, rubbing sticks, and dried grasses.

On hands and knees, Topur chipped tiny sparks of fiery flint into the bundle of kindling, igniting the grasses at the base. With the chill wind, tentative flames eagerly grew. Topur scanned the horizon, squinting. Threats may already be present. His footprints, along with the donkey's, were the only suggestions that life had found this sandy rise, satisfying him that he alone occupied this hill.

Topur had neglected to look behind, into the wind, to the

summit of the great dune where three ominous human shapes stood in the dim distance. One turned, separating from the others, and began trotting directly toward the developing fire.

Three hundred paces at the bottom of the sandy dune, the expedition's soldiers, ox carts, livestock, supply wagons, feed wagons, slaves, and servants gradually assembled on the flat area. The rushing and bustling began. Fires sparked and sparkled. The cooks and their helpers would be the first to need the heat. After that, the caravan's entourage would arrange their tiny tents like spokes from a glowing hub to take advantage of the warmth. Topur preferred the greater concealment of a fireless camp, but the coldest evening to date prohibited that option.

Crews of men strained at ropes hoisting the expedition's three largest tents. The oversized, bulky center poles routinely defied placement. Urgent commands and their equally clamorous responses were audible even from this distance.

The stick in Topur's hand was meant for the fire. He stabbed it into the soft sand instead. Those tents. Traveling time was sacrificed at both ends of daylight while crews devoted themselves to the tasks of assembly or disassembly, packing or unpacking the comfort the kings insisted upon. Some days, the expedition didn't take a forward step until mid-morning. Once moving, progress was dreadfully slow, driving so many people, the animals, and the rolling supplies. Topur had once made this same trip in eleven days. As of tonight, it had been nearly three times that. He had not planned to be away this long.

Topur rose, then followed his footprints back to his bundle of supplies. In contrast to the kings' tents, his was simple: six straight, hand-smoothed sticks—two long and four short. The black goat-hair hides, woven and stitched together, provided adequate shelter. His tent rose only as high as his hip and had an open front. Once assembled, it would sleep three men cozily, if not comfortably. A king's tent could hold ten or more, but usually slept one or two.

The fire required his immediate attention. "This foolishness is taking too long," he mumbled as he replenished it. His pounding head had not improved, as he could think of little besides those he'd left at home. He dropped into the sand, massaging his temples. "I said it, didn't I? I said we'd stumble about for months." The donkey, dutifully attentive, swung one ear. "And it will amount to nothing." Topur poked with his stick, encouraging the fire's toddling flames, then spat. "Who listens to me?"

Fresh with fuel, the fire grew, as did Topur's feelings of doom.

Topur felt a hand grip his shoulder. He stiffened, shrieking an unflattering falsetto, then sprang, groaning in pain as his shoulder was the first to hit the dense, quaggy sand. From there, he was a jangle of knees and elbows. He tumbled downhill from the unassembled tent, grasping for his dagger. He rolled, then rolled again, striving for separation. Crouched, dagger in hand, he lunged upward, stabbing and swinging at the empty air as if battling an onslaught of wasps.

"It's me!"

Dizzy and wobbling, Topur tried to stand, fell, then tried again. His outstretched hand still brandished his dagger. He grunted, struggling to identify the figure before him.

"It's only me!" Najiir repeated, backing up. "I didn't think I would startle you!"

Topur's shoulders slumped as he exhaled, still clutching his dagger's hilt. He groped his chest. "Startle... yes, Najiir." Between gasps, he returned the dagger to his belt, inhaled deeply, then brushed the sand from his knees. "The wind. I never heard you." Panting, he stepped to Najiir, placing his hand on the boy's shoulder. His other hand, upon one knee, propped his bent frame. "Where did you...?" He puffed. "I looked to camp. No one." Still struggling, he straightened. "I was certain you were a bandit or, worse, some Roman."

"I didn't come from camp. Some of our soldiers let me come

with them to search the area, and I saw you up here by yourself. I didn't mean to scare you." Najiir gazed at the purple horizon. "Are we that close?"

"Close enough, close enough," said Topur.

"Why are you up here? Why is our tent away from the others?" Topur understood this separation violated Najiir's inherent and inveterate compulsion to gather. Though he was still a boy, Najiir was remarkably open, inclusive, and inviting, making and keeping friends with uncommon ease. Topur, on the other hand, was accustomed to the harsh realities of being an outsider. He lived his life on the periphery, and this journey was no different. He was reluctant to respond, hoping, in part, the answer was obvious.

"Shouldn't we be with the others?" Najiir pressed.

Topur flipped a branch into the fire and returned to his bundled tent. He kneeled beside it, picking at the knots. His nervous hands limited any progress. "Help me unpack."

Najiir kneeled beside him.

"Uphill, I can evaluate the star clearly. I have a bad feeling. I've had it for a while. I must know if it is justified. From here, I can judge where that star intends to take us. Since no one tells me where we are going—apparently no one can—I'll have to figure this out on my own. And..."

"And?"

"Najiir," Topur began, "if this star demands we go where I assume it will, I will tell our kings they must turn back. "

"Turn b-back?" Najiir sputtered. "But—"

"You act surprised."

Najiir's enthusiasm for this adventure outpaced Atarah's.

"For such important and sophisticated men, none of them realize where they are. No one in this group knows but me. But you might know." He paused, frowning. "You should."

Najiir fumbled, "But I thought—what is different? But aren't we—? Why?"

Topur stared downhill, past the camp, across the vast,

blank sameness. The horizon's unbroken line was still separate from the livid hues of a waning twilight. But the sky revealed stars, tiny specks of glimmering light offering faint challenges to the dominion of darkness.

"Why? You ask why?" Topur sighed. He stretched his arm. "That's why."

Najiir's gaze followed Topur's hand. The star had emerged, edging above the dusky horizon. It was distinctly larger, brighter, and more prominent than any other heavenly body except for the far larger moon.

"The star?" Najiir whispered. "What? Has something changed?"

"Their star is a stubborn star. It would be healthier for us if that star appeared elsewhere." Topur's eyes smoldered. "Wishing for that has not been persuasive. From the very first, I dreaded this possibility. Arriving here is exactly why I wanted no part of this—chasing some fantasy into a place like this." He rose, stepping to the pile of dry kindling. "Najiir, come here."

Topur grabbed the straightest stick, then moved downhill. With the fire's light behind them, he pointed directly at the star. "Follow the direction of this stick and tell me where we are headed. You know, don't you?"

"I think so," Najiir said tentatively.

"Yes, you should. I don't take you this way as often. I find almost any reason to avoid it. But you have been this way and should be familiar with this region. If we follow the direction of this stick, where will we be?"

Najiir bit his lip, tracing the aim of Topur's arm. "Jerusalem, I think?"

Topur thrust his stick into the fire. Embers fluttered upward, glowing feathers riding hot air into the inky sky. "Jerusalem," Topur whispered. "Correct. And those kings must never set one foot in Jerusalem."

CHAPTER 4

Spinning clusters of luminous ash still fluttered from the fire. Najiir, hands upon hips, remained fixed, gazing at the star as it resumed its recurring position in the night sky. To be heard above the wind, Najiir shouted, "I hadn't paid attention, but it's true."

"Of course it's true. You're right. You pointed to Jerusalem."

"No, no. It's true that we don't go into Jerusalem as often as we used to."

"If my business demands, I will go, but I would rather go almost anywhere else. Jerusalem has never been quiet, but it's far more dangerous now than when I was your age."

Topur pulled nervously on his beard. Over the years, he became friends with several local men he frequently encountered in Jerusalem. Now, those men were anxious. They spoke of ardent factions, brimming with anger and dogmatism, that vied for domination within the city. Each fractious bloc considered the views of its opponents—other Jews!—to be so mistaken, so corrupt, as to threaten their people's very existence. Jerusalem's citizens were keen to quarrel, eager to pick a fight. It was a city divided, then divided again—a cauldron of yelling, finger-pointing, and condemnation. The lethal consequences of soldiers enforcing Rome's "Perfect Order" were matched by the harsh fanaticism of Jewish brethren convinced God shared their intolerance.

"It's so risky, even for a Jew!" Topur added. "And so many foreigners. Good for trade, I suppose, but if it weren't for the Temple, Jerusalem would hardly feel like a Jewish city." He crouched, smoothing the sand with his fingertips. "Najiir, come sit by me."

The pair sat facing the fire, watching the busy camp. "Even with Jerusalem this troubled, you and I could walk about unnoticed. But entering the city would be a death sentence for our kings." Topur studied the boy, confirming he had his attention.

"Death sentence? Why?"

"Our kings are from the east, Najiir." Topur summoned his gravest voice. "Carrhae."

Topur's hood flapped in the wind. He put his arm around the boy. He pointed down to the fires, to the frenetic movement, and to a silhouetted man on horseback racing between tents and supply wagons, issuing frantic commands. "You may not realize how intimately that man is linked to those who crushed Crassus and his son. Those victors are among King Xaratuk's friends and allies. Some of his family fought there. Thirty thousand of Crassus's men would never return to Rome. I can't begin to comprehend that number. The Aquila was surrendered. That insult sickens the stomach of every Roman. To them, that man is a bitter, hated enemy. If they capture King Xaratuk, they'll wreak bloody vengeance."

"He must know that," said Najiir. "He must be afraid of what might happen. He wouldn't—"

"Afraid?" Topur paused. "I wonder if that man is afraid of anything—or anyone. His bravado and this small band of soldiers might deter the occasional robber, but they are no match for a curious Roman centuria. When I remind him of that, I can only hope he'll listen."

Najiir stiffened. "He respects you." His tone was not convincing. "Maybe we won't meet any Romans. Maybe we won't have to go as far as Jerusalem. Earlier, I overheard Merkis and Khartir. They said we are near."

"You can understand Merkis and Khartir?" Topur already knew the answer. Najiir possessed an uncommon talent for acquiring new languages. It was a remarkable skill, one exploited by Topur to his advantage.

Merkis and Khartir were advisors to Xaratuk. After joining the caravan, Topur understood that these mysterious men, with their equally mysterious tools, instruments, scrolls, and codices, were the wisest, most perceptive members of the expedition. It was they who had sparked Xaratuk's enthusiasm, and they who had the ultimate word regarding the caravan's direction. Like the kings, they maintained a cordial but distinct distance, always preoccupied in deep discussions.

"Their language isn't difficult for me," said Najiir. "It's often spoken on the Trading Road and is similar to others I already understand." He cocked his head. "Near. The advisors kept saying near."

"So we're near, you say. They'll have to explain that to me. No one can identify where we are going, yet Merkis and Khartir claim we are near. Near what, Najiir? Where? The star looks the same as always. Near? I can't say whether that star is near, but I know Jerusalem is. And the closer we get to Jerusalem, the greater our chances of being spotted by some Roman guard or legionnaire. They'll recognize these foreigners with their open tunics, their pointed helmets, and their trousers. Those things are peculiar and are bound to be noticed."

Despite the chill wind, sweat beaded upon Topur's forehead. "Our course has become obvious. I've known it for days. It's time to stop this nonsense. We're going back. I'll convince the kings––"

"But––" Najiir blinked in disbelief.

"Consider what we've done. You and I have ushered these kings to the empire's doorstep, kings from the east. If the Romans find us, they'll exact their brutal revenge on King Xaratuk. You and I will be standing next to his corpse. Do you imagine any Roman official will be interested in our explanations?"

"But... go back?" Najiir looked away. "They won't," he

whispered.

There was a long pause. "You don't think so? You don't think I can convince them, make them realize—"

"They won't. They won't stop. They won't go back."

"They must." Even now, Topur thought, they had journeyed too far—and in the most perilous direction possible. For days, he silently debated leaving, breaking free of the madness and any association with the kings. But after further consideration, that option vanished. If he abandoned the kings, they would blindly, inevitably, fall into the ruinous clutches of the Romans. Without his efforts to keep them hidden, the kings would be murdered in the most brutal fashion. News of the atrocities would spread, followed by the awful consequences.

"Listen to me, Najiir." Topur waved his hand to the camp. "I shudder when I consider what could happen should King Xaratuk and Augustus come to blows. The Romans aren't invincible. Carrhae proved that." After pausing, he shook his head. "He, or those seeking to avenge his murder, would be equal to the task. Losing our lives would only be the beginning. So many would die. Think of it. With Romans to our west, and King Xaratuk to our east, their armies would meet at our doorstep. A Kush trader once told me that when two elephants fight, it is the grass that is destroyed. Najiir, that grass is us— my family, our friends, our city."

"But they won't stop." Najiir was unmoved.

The wind spread fiery sparks downhill before they had the chance to climb. Topur placed a hand on Najiir's knee. "You are beginning to sound like my wife—finding ways to contradict me. She alone said the one thing that could convince me to accompany the kings."

"One thing?" Najiir slid closer to Topur's warmth.

"It's God's will, she said." Topur looked down at Najiir's head, resting his chin upon it. "Was the kings' appearance on our doorstep the culmination of amazing coincidences? No, Atarah claimed it was God's will. She can be convincing. So, lacking a persuasive response, I joined the kings. Now that we've reached Judaea, I see God's purpose. He requires me to keep these wanderers alive. That is my responsibility. As their guide, I can see those disasters that await. There is a trap, and I alone know what lies ahead. You agree?" Najiir offered no response. "I trust God will give me the gift to describe the peril and convince these men they must be saved from themselves. I'll show them this is futile. I'll prove this is madness, and they must stop before meeting their destruction."

"God's will?" said Najiir.

"Yes," said Topur, looking at the boy. "What?"

"You said this is God's will." Najiir's voice grew more confident. "The kings will go on—with or without you." Najiir pulled back and looked squarely into Topur's eyes. "The mistress was right. God brought these men to you, but not to be their guide. They have the star for that. You are their shepherd. They're determined to continue. They need you. It is you who stands between them and the Roman wolves. If you're not there..."

"*That* is what you see as God's will?" he snapped. "Staying with them to see this folly through? Do you understand what risk... our...chances?"

Topur didn't wait for any response. He rose, moving to the dwindling woodpile, kicking the kindling in frustration. He wished Atarah could whisper to him the most convincing arguments. It was likely that no amount of eloquence or evidence he could muster would dissuade those kings. Najiir was right. They would never go back.

Grabbing the straightest stick, he stomped beyond the fire's light and inspected the coarse earth. Over the wind-polished surface, he began to scratch a line. The dense sand willingly gave way.

"If I can't convince you, what hope have I of convincing the kings? But I say we're doomed!" Najiir didn't respond, looking as though he felt he had been punished. "Why would God send these kings toward Jerusalem? There is nothing there, and each step brings us closer to a Roman sword. And, I should add, it's not just the Romans. Herod is the equal threat of any Roman."

"King Herod?" Najiir sputtered.

"You know what an awful man Herod is, but these men don't have the slightest idea. Herod may have been given rule over Judaea, but he isn't the king of this Jew." Topur pounded his fist into his chest. "Every day, I thank God that I live far away from the clutches of that beast. Herod and the Romans are one and the same. If that fox found these kings within the borders of Judaea, he'd throw them to the Romans and reap the benefits."

He continued his scratching until he had etched a figure of curving parallel lines that diverged into a bloated middle, then resumed a parallel course again. It resembled a moving, headless snake digesting its meal of a mouse eaten three days earlier. He stepped back to critique his handiwork. He rubbed his brow, etched with its own deep lines, and squinted. "It will have to do."

Najiir remained silent, his head still bent toward the sand. His reticence was unusual. Topur sat next to the boy and ruffled Najiir's wavy brown hair. "Why would a star shine down on Jerusalem, Najiir? There is nothing there, no one so important."

"I don't see why not," said Najiir, clearing his throat. "Someone or something great might be within Judaea."

"From where, then? From whom? It couldn't be any of Herod's princes—the ones left alive. Why Jerusalem?" Topur looked over his right shoulder and pointed. "Why couldn't it be Tyre, or Byblos, eh, Najiir? Wouldn't it have been a greater adventure to go there—someplace more stable, more productive for us? Oh, how I wish it could have been Cyprus. The star over Cyprus!" Topur rose, spread his arms, and smiled. "The star should shine over Cyprus!"

He stared out over the stark desert, away from the star's shimmer. "I have never been on a boat. Why couldn't we be on some boat bound for Cyprus, where we'd be greeted as guests in the palace of some noble prince? Oh, but how Atarah would bellow! Me—on a boat!" After pondering the illusion, Topur sat down and put an arm around Najiir. "God's will? If it is what you say, I must devise some way to sneak this herd under the noses of the Romans and on to the place where all this will be explained."

Moments passed while Topur mulled over the prospects of continuing with the kings. He rose and stepped to the lines he had drawn in the sand earlier. "Come here, Najiir. This has become very important. You must see."

As Najiir stepped closer, he cocked his head as he considered the figure Topur had sketched.

"You say our kings will not agree to turn back?" Topur didn't wait for any response. "If so, I need to plan a diversion. Here is my solution." He waved his long stick above the sand. "This represents the pathway through the canyon."

"What canyon?" Najiir's expression shifted. He moved in for a better inspection. His look challenged Topur. "Scary. Canyons always frighten me. Are you saying we should take the entire caravan through a canyon?"

Topur placed his hand on Najiir's back. "This route gives us the only reasonable opportunity to follow that star but avoid Jerusalem."

"You're certain this is the only way?"

"There is no other. We can't afford to be spotted. If I can't convince the kings to turn back, I must convince them to remain hidden. God help me."

Najiir nodded, though his arched eyebrow suggested skepticism.

"Najiir," Topur continued, "it will be cold, probably the coldest night yet. I have extra blankets if you think you'll be sleeping here." Topur walked closer to the fire. He rubbed his hands. "I see so very little of you. How can it matter to you where I set our tent since you don't come to it at night?"

Najiir's boyish smile emerged. "I'm not getting into trouble.

I'm just talking. I enjoy getting to know people better," he added. "It's my chance to practice speaking their language. It's fun."

"I realize you don't look for trouble. You aren't that kind of boy—praise God."

Topur put his hand on the boy's shoulder and squeezed it. "I have missed your company. I'll admit it. You're always with someone else, keeping busy. But I am concerned about where you go and what you find." Topur shook his head as if to clear his thoughts. "You are always such help to me, so why should I worry?" He tried not to imagine the worst. There was no justification for it. "Do as you wish, but remember, from this point forward, things are entirely different. We are in Judaea. We must watch for both the Romans and Herod's men. If you spot either, you tell me, understand? Find me as quickly as you can. That information could save our lives." With one last wave of his finger, he added, "Should you or your new friends meet anyone, even if they seem friendly, be careful what you say about us."

Topur managed a half-smile but shivered inside. The night had turned even colder, but he didn't notice. Still, he shook, knowing he was inextricably bound to this caravan and its fate. There were no justifiable means of escape. His feet were inside the snare, and the rope was about to be pulled by some star insisting they come to Judaea.

CHAPTER 5

D own the hill, a tall, sleek figure had already begun his advance. "Isn't that King Mithrias—and he's headed toward our fire?" said Topur.

Najiir spun around. "Here? To this fire?"

"A king...coming to us. Finally." Topur smiled. "Tell me, quickly, before King Mithrias arrives, are you learning his language? What can you share?"

Frowning, Najiir shook his head. "Nothing," he said. "Nothing at all. I thought it would be easy. I would learn from his son. We're nearly the same age. But Prince Salnassar won't speak to me. He is only interested in following Captain Regulus."

"May as well be the man's shadow," said Topur. "He has offended almost everyone on this trip, including me. Either he doesn't realize he's rude or doesn't care. He barks orders at me like I'm some simple-minded servant. I've learned to ignore him."

"Why does he hate his father?" Najiir continued to study Mithrias's uphill trek. "He's alone. Everyone else likes King Mithrias. I do. He's friendly. He knows people by their name. But he stays so close to King Xaratuk that I never get the chance to learn his language. I've no one else to speak to."

As Mithrias ascended, he showed nothing of the floundering and wallowing Topur displayed during his march up the sandy slope. Mithrias's erect posture, broad, square shoulders, and effortless gait expressed regal elegance. He was clad in a luxurious white robe that seemed a source of light in the murky dusk. The fire's playful, dancing light intensified the enticing lines and angles on his sculptured face and shimmered in his dark, wavy hair. As he neared, he presented his characteristic smile, every one of his impeccably white, straight teeth aligned perfectly, like a row of shiny, marble soldiers at attention.

Topur whispered, "That. That is how a king should look."

"It is," was all Najiir could say.

Mithrias's smile lingered as he reached the fire. Topur and Najiir stepped to greet him. They ceased speaking their native Aramaic, addressing the newcomer in Greek. It was the common use of Greek that allowed the caravan to communicate. Alexander's exploits remained potent in a stark Judaean desert hundreds of years later.

"We've had a long day, Topur," said Mithrias, gently grabbing Topur's right forearm. "I wasn't sure I had enough energy to follow you up this hill." Continuing to smile, he turned to Najiir, "Greetings to you, too. Najiir, isn't it?"

"Yes," Najiir said politely. "Good evening, King Mithrias."

"You have prepared a pleasant fire, Topur. We'll all need to be by a fire tonight." He rubbed his hands together. "But why here, so far away from camp? Wouldn't it be better to be closer to the others? Wouldn't you be more comfortable down the hill?"

"Thank you, King Mithrias," Topur replied. "That may be so, but I need to observe this star tonight, and for that, this spot is better."

"I see. You need to watch our star? Is tonight so different? You'll see the star from camp just as well, won't you? Why be so far from the rest?"

"Tonight is different, yes." Topur's gaze drifted to the star. "From camp, I can look up to the star, but tonight I need to look past it." Topur narrowed his eyes as he turned to Mithrias. "No one will say where we are going, so I must use what hints the star gives to make my best guess. As your guide, I must alert you to some necessary adjustments."

"Adjustments? If viewing the star from here helps you draw your conclusions, I understand, but don't make this separation permanent, Topur. I never see you. We've spent almost no time together since we left your city." Mithrias paused, looking at his feet, then back up. "I believe I owe you an apology."

"An apology, King Mithrias?" Topur was stunned by the frank, though accurate admission, yet still felt subservient to the great king. "No. There is no need for you to apologize to me for…for anything. Sir, you are an important man. You have many demands, and I do not wish to add to them. I am on this journey to help in any way I can."

"You are the victim of my neglect. I encouraged you to join us and use this time to learn more about each other. Until now, I have not made one move toward that end. My actions are not matching my intentions."

"But, King Mithrias, I don't—"

"The truth is, Topur, I have been too lazy to break away from King Xaratuk." Mithrias looked away. He shifted his stance. "Allow me to be blunt. King Xaratuk prefers the company of those much like himself. For him, few confidants meet his requirements on this trip. Besides, we are old friends. So, it comes down to me to be the ear that listens, though I dread having to listen to more."

Arms folded, Mithrias began to pace while studying the fires about the camp. "Look at him."

The only stationary figures below were those near the fire preparing the meal. Every other body was racing from one spot to another, moving, tugging, hauling, hoisting, or heaving. A single figure conducted the actions of all the others.

"One of the big ox carts has wheel problems," Mithrias noted. "The man has two wheelwrights for precisely these circumstances, yet he needs to be in charge, directing those men. And he probably doesn't grasp the least thing about wheel repair."

Xaratuk's commands were audible even at this distance.

"His voice follows me—even to here."

Mithrias and Topur exchanged smiles.

"Of course, the oxcart with the bad wheel must be the one carrying our tent supplies." Mithrias sighed, turning back to the fire. "He won't tolerate any problems with that cart. Those center poles on it are his obsession. He never lets them out of his sight."

"Those poles are remarkable."

There were three. Each was massive and magnificent, stunning works of art. Stout, made of durable timber, they were carved with intricate, ornate geometric decorations meticulously outlined and colorfully painted. Shiny shellac protected the craftmanship, making the poles glisten. They were pretentious items for such an arduous journey.

"A rich and powerful king deserves to be surrounded by such beauty," said Topur. "I admire those who take special care of the things they value."

"Those are kind words." Mithrias nodded. "But the man has others who can care for those poles, or those wagons, or those wheels more capably than he." Mithrias's tone turned sarcastic. "He needs to feel needed. His hands must be upon every little thing."

"Begging your pardon, Your Excellency, but isn't that part of what makes a king great?"

"True enough, Topur. True enough. Very generous words. The man has ignored you for weeks, but you speak highly of him. Commendable of you." Mithrias sighed, then moved to grab a stick from the kindling pile. He gave it a reluctant shove into the fire and stared. "He can be boorish, I admit, but King Xaratuk is my friend, and I have needed his friendship lately...." Mithrias closed his eyes. "Very, very much." His chest rose and sank with each slow breath. After a pause, he gathered himself. "He is a good man. Don't mistake me. If I have led you to believe otherwise, it is an unforgivable lapse on my part."

Mithrias dropped to his knees, eyes sealed shut, one hand pinching the bridge of his nose.

"King Mithrias?" Topur scrambled to his tent and pulled out two blankets. He kneeled next to the king. "Please, sit upon these." He spread out his finest colored blanket of scarlet and gold and motioned to Mithrias. "Are you unwell?"

Mithrias opened his eyes. "This is kind of you," he said, moving toward the blanket. He sat upon it. "It feels good to hear someone else's voice for a change. I respect the man as much as the day is long, but it has been week after week listening to King Xaratuk congratulate himself." Mithrias laid back, pinching his eyes shut. "I feel unfaithful to him by loosening my thoughts. I have said too much."

"Please, King Mithrias, understand neither of us would say anything that would not reflect our highest esteem," said Topur.

With a groan, Mithrias sat back up. "I have done nothing to deserve your loyalty, and I must tell you I appreciate it. I find it quite pleasing to speak with you." Mithrias's smile supported his kind words. "You were far out ahead of us today. I meant to talk earlier, but I could not catch up."

"I was trying to encourage all the speed we can muster." Topur kneeled upon the blankets, a respectful distance from the king. "It is best to keep the group moving—as quickly as it will move."

Mithrias exchanged his smile in favor of a frustrated frown. "And we don't show the least ability to do anything quickly, do we?" he said, shaking his head. "We are a slow, slow group."

"Too slow," said Topur. "It makes us a tempting target. A group this size will surely draw the interest of any Romans nearby."

"Romans?" Mithrias twisted, grabbing Topur's shoulder. "The Romans?" he said, his eyes darting. "We've come that far?"

Topur nodded.

Mithrias released his grip. He shuddered. "It gives me chills. I never dreamed we'd have to come this far west. Romans. This can't be good." He looked to Topur. "We should share this with the others."

"Yes. I was hoping you'd say that." Topur exhaled in relief. "And not knowing our destination only complicates any plan."

Mithrias nodded. "Aren't we close? We must be. I spoke to Merkis and Khartir before coming up the hill. The king's advisors tell me we are near."

"Near. Najiir overheard the same word. Near," Topur repeated, still troubled by the word's imprecision. "King Mithrias, if I may… everyone must understand that unless 'near' means less than a half-day walk from here, this journey becomes much more uncertain, much more dangerous. We are in Judaea, and Judaea is part of the Empire. Until now, our challenge was negotiating the desert. That work is almost complete. I suggest a meeting—away from the rest—bringing you, King Xaratuk, Regulus, and the advisors together. Surviving the desert isn't your only concern from this point." Knees aching, he opted to sit as well.

"A meeting? You shall have it." Mithrias exhaled a long breath, his cheeks puffing out. "I have heard what Romans do to captured kings—putting them in chains, forcing them to Rome, parading them bound through the city, humiliating them, then brutally executing them. I want no part of that, of course. Thankfully, my kingdom has remained beyond the aims of their Empire. King Xaratuk is a different matter altogether."

"It is best for everyone—best for the world—that King Xaratuk and Augustus never meet."

Mithrias placed his hand to his mouth. "What will you suggest we do?"

Topur grunted. "What I would like to suggest will be ignored."

"Why? What do you have in mind?"

"Turn back. Go home." Topur quaked underneath his robe. "King Mithrias, is this worth it? We're taking such chances, believing we might, by some miracle, slip past the Romans. Why are you doing this? Who is out there? I'm familiar with this region, with Judaea, and I don't—that is to say, there can't be…" Topur stopped his stammering and resumed in a more deliberate voice. "It's merely a star. It probably means nothing. Why are you so willing to take these risks? What basis could there be for such a—do you honestly believe we'll find someone, something so special that a star is required as an announcement?"

"I don't know, Topur. I don't know." Mithrias bowed his head. "I don't know what I believe, or if I believe in anything. But what I believe is of little consequence." He gave a brusque wave to the camp below. "That man will see this through."

"I am not one to abandon my duty, sir." Topur halted. He felt traitorous, but there was so much at stake. "If the Romans find us, King Xaratuk will not be the only one to suffer."

Mithrias's face softened. "It is my good fortune to have made the climb to your fire tonight, Topur. I wish to know you better, and I would be bitterly disappointed if you left. But if you maintain you should, no one will stop you. No one will think less of you." He nodded to the camp without looking. "That man will never consent to anything but discovering who or what is under that star. He believes in this mission. He is convinced this star signifies someone uniquely special, uniquely powerful." He clenched his jaw. "He's counting on it."

Topur could not stop his hand from quivering as he stroked his brow. "Then we must consider our options because we have a problem. Our movements must be planned so we remain undetected, even though that star obliges us to move under the noses of the Romans."

"This is quite compelling. Given how long we've traveled, I should have expected this. But lately, my head has been muddled. I had never considered confronting the Empire." Mithrias stroked his trim beard. "How could it come to this? You shall have your meeting."

The fire's prosperity came at the expense of Topur's

kindling supply. "If we speak more about the Romans, the others should be with us," said Mithrias. He eyed the assembly below, then sighed. "But I'm in no mood to head to camp. May I remain here with you for a while longer?"

"I would like that," said Topur. "But we'll need more wood." He turned. "Najiir?"

"Of course." Najiir jumped up and brushed the sand from his tunic.

"Take my donkey," Topur added. "Feed and water her first. Ask Regulus for as much wood as he can spare. I want a large fire." Najiir nodded, trotting to the donkey. He grabbed the halter and pulled, but she held fast. Najiir pulled again. The donkey turned her head toward Topur, refusing any movement without his permission. With a wave of his hand, Topur broke the donkey's resistance. She stepped forward, following Najiir's lead.

Mithrias stared as the pair receded into the darkness. "He seems like a good boy. Always moving, isn't he?"

"Running, usually," Topur affirmed. "Always active, yes. Sitting still is difficult for him." He looked down the slope at the line of footprints. "So restless. Where does he find such energy? The boy doesn't sleep. I can almost assure you he will not come to our tent tonight. He'll be talking to the soldiers, or a servant, or anyone awake. He is drawn to people and activity." Topur fell silent. He was babbling about topics unworthy of royal attention, though he preferred this to the subject of Roman capture.

"A friendly boy, it seems."

Though puzzled by the king's continued interest, Topur went on. "Yes, uncommonly so. For him, friendships are made quickly, easily. I see it as a rare gift, one of his many. And, as you mentioned, he is a good boy. He has earned my trust."

"Topur, I am right, am I not, that he is not part of your family. He is not your son or relative, but your slave?"

This sudden shift stunned Topur. It felt intrusive. His

answer, as though it was shameful, was barely audible. "Yes. You are correct, King Mithrias."

"I don't mean to sound accusatory. At first, not having met him, I presumed he was your son. You treat the boy as though he were."

There was a pause. "I suppose I do. As I say, he is an especially good boy. My family and I are quite fond of him."

"Forgive my curiosity—and stop me whenever you don't wish to answer my questions. I know practically nothing about your people, Topur, but Jews aren't particularly noted for having slaves."

"Oh, there are slave owners among us. You are right—not many. We are too familiar with the other side of slavery. We have had to fight for our place on this earth, and at certain times, God has seen fit for us to be the slaves. If, as a people, you don't wish to be slaves, perhaps you understand others don't wish for such a life either. There is scripture about this," Topur added, sounding defensive. "It is not against the Law to have slaves, and there are provisions for their proper treatment."

"Do you have more than the one, more than Najiir?"

"No. Just Najiir."

"Well, you don't strike me as the normal slaveholder. What made you decide you needed a slave? Where did you get him?" Mithrias peered at Topur. "Oh, have I overstepped?"

Topur shrugged. "I have never spoken of it." He struggled to speak. "Only Atarah knows."

"Knows? Knows what? Why? Why such a secret?"

Topur rocked back and forth, arms crossed. "Well," he began, uncertain if he should, even now, tell the story. "I lost a great deal of..." His words formed a plug in his throat. "And much of it wasn't mine to lose."

"If I am prying—"

"No, no. Until now, there was no one I could share the truth with, so it was best to say nothing. It is a long story. You say your ears are tired?" It was a desperate effort to evade the subject.

"You don't need me to punish them as well."

"Topur, your voice is like music to me. I am grateful for a story that doesn't involve swords or soldiers or assassins—I presume. I beg of you, continue." Mithrias adjusted his blanket, laying back on his elbows to prepare for a welcome distraction.

"This is, even now, painful for me to recollect. God, give me strength."

"Painful?" Mithrias sat upright. "I am... intrigued... and surprised. Now you must go on."

Topur sat cross-legged, eyes focused on the fire. "It was nine years ago, on one of my trading trips. I was alone. For once, no others from my city accompanied me. I was returning from Gaza. It had been a very profitable outing. Flush with new goods and healthy profits, I stopped at a small oasis town to rest my animals and resupply some provisions."

Topur rose, putting nearly all the remaining wood upon the fire. He spoke through the burgeoning flames. "In the town, there was a small inn. I tied my animals there. Najiir must have been outside that inn holding on to some camels for an Arab trader, a man from Beersheba, who was his owner. That man had gone inside for some refreshment. In doing so, he trusted this five-year-old boy to protect everything on the backs of those camels. Najiir's restlessness became his undoing. While watching the camels, his attention was diverted. There was a dice game nearby, and a fight broke out. Everyone likes to watch a fight. Najiir was no different. Those unattended camels wandered off—or were stolen. No one knows."

"Trouble!" exclaimed Mithrias.

"Trouble," Topur confirmed. "I'd seen too many fights. I was almost alone tending to my animals when that Arab stumbled out of the inn and found no camels and no boy. Then he started screaming. The throng shifted its attention away from the quarreling gamblers to this bellowing man as he thrashed about, searching without success for his camels, and then Najiir. When he finally found the boy, he beat Najiir with his fists. The poor child simply stood there. He didn't scream. He didn't fight back. He didn't even raise his arms to protect himself. Blow followed blow until Najiir collapsed, but the awful man grabbed him by the arm, then dragged him over the stones toward the inn. The Arab pulled a whip from someone's pack and used it on Najiir. I couldn't believe it, whipping this child—as he lay face down upon the stones! That trader got one lash out over Najiir's back before I ran over, pushing my way through the crowd. I stood between the boy and his tormentor. Najiir was already bleeding terribly from his head and his back."

Topur drew a deep breath. He could feel himself quiver. His anxious legs buckled in as he seated himself next to Mithrias. Images coursed through his mind—images gratefully buried, now resurrected: elbowing through the thick swarm to confront the man; the boy's motionless body on the cold, stony ground; blood; the smell of stale wine on the Arab's breath; the man's crooked teeth; his awful, evil eyes; and everyone else standing—not one coming to the boy's defense. His throat tightened. The words that followed would be broken. "I'm sorry," he said in little more than a squeaky whisper. His head bent. He felt an arm around his shoulder.

"When you are ready, my friend, when you are ready."

Only after several halting, deep breaths could Topur continue. "I stepped toward the Arab and grabbed the hand holding the whip. I told him to stop. He scowled at me. He threatened to use that whip on me if I didn't move aside. Again, I told him to put the whip down. He stepped back, ready to put the next lash on me. All I could think to do or say was shout out, 'I'll buy him. I'll buy the boy!' That made him pause. The Arab looked at me suspiciously. I had made a startling offer. Gradually, he brought his arm down. I restated my willingness to buy the boy.

"At first, he rebuffed me, so I persisted. Being a shrewd trader, he realized I had given him every advantage. I wanted something only he could sell, and the cursed man set a horribly high price. He said he'd sell me the boy, but I would also have to compensate him for the goods he'd lost because of the boy's carelessness." Topur pounded the sand. "That was a devilish thing to suggest, and I protested, but he stayed firm. What choice did I have? I couldn't take back my offer. I had to pay his price. To get the boy away from that fiend, I had to pay all the earnings I had made from the trip and all the earnings I had made for my customers as well."

Topur's shoulders sagged. He put an elbow on one knee, propping his head on one hand. "It was a king's ransom, but I paid it. I believed I had to. The poor boy lay still on the ground. I wasn't certain he was even alive."

Mithrias looked aside. A deep, grievous melancholy settled upon his face.

"Oh, was Atarah mad when we reached home. Another mouth to feed. A slave we did not need. And I had spent all my money and our customers' money as well. And one more thing: a boy—one that wasn't a brother to the two daughters we had at that time. Worse, a Gentile. 'We are not slave owners,' Atarah protested, and she was right. What were we to do with him? Even more, in front of my customers, we had to act as though nothing had happened. It must appear that we planned to take on a slave and not let on I had spent their money. We paid all my investors, however. It emptied our fortune. No one knew a thing. They still don't."

"You still paid them? You paid them all?" Mithrias's head bobbed. "I now understand why your name commands such high respect in your city. Your reputation is uniformly without fault. I see you have earned every bit."

"Thank you," whispered Topur. "These are my friends, my neighbors. They rely on me to make good decisions for them. I could not expect their trust if I told them I spent their money to save a child from being whipped."

"Whipped? It was more than that. You saved the boy's life."

"Perhaps. But we mentioned no word of this to anyone. You

are the first to hear it. Everyone simply assumes I bought a slave to keep me company on my trips."

There was a pause. Gently, Mithrias asked, "What about Atarah?"

Topur allowed a slight snigger. "Najiir and Atarah began badly, but things are better. Being friendly is natural for Najiir, but Atarah is bound by her faith and her beliefs. I admire the foundation this provides her, but it is hard for her to have someone outside the faith living within her walls. Najiir can sense that. We feed him, clothe him, and he knows he can sleep in our home. But he spends most of his time, day and night, along the Trading Road. That is where he is most comfortable, and that is comfortable for Atarah, too. I can't make her realize the value Najiir has been to me and my business through the years. He has more than made up the difference from my initial losses."

"He has?" said Mithrias. "How?"

"Simply, he is aware of everything. He is, for me, a talented and effective spy."

Mithrias grinned. "A spy, you say?"

"He is a perfect combination of ability and cover. I'm sure you don't realize it, but that boy can converse fluently in at least seven languages and does capably well in about as many others. He is uncommonly gifted. I travel often and to many places, and I've never seen anything like it."

"Amazing."

"It is amazing, I assure you. He is getting to know King Xaratuk's tongue simply from speaking with his cooks and servants on this trip." Topur's tone was boastful. "So smart. Lately, I have been teaching him to read, too—parts of the Torah." Topur halted. "Please don't tell Atarah. She'd sell me into slavery if she found out."

Mithrias laughed. He placed his hand on Topur's knee. "I won't say a word. Your secret is one I will happily keep."

"Najiir is a familiar fixture on the Trading Road. He notices everything. He's friendly. He's helpful. He listens. No matter who they are, he encourages them to talk. Most are eager to comply. Where have they been? What is selling? Who is buying? What problems did they encounter? They'll be more forthcoming to some slave boy than they'd be with me. I'd only arouse suspicion. From his information, I can decide where to go or when is best."

Mithrias moved his hand and lay back, elbows propping his long frame. "Later," Topur continued, "when we are in the markets or bazaars, he blends into the background. This boy, idly biding his time, becomes invisible to the traders and money changers. They'll speak their native tongues, exchange gossip, and talk business, believing their information is secret, but there are no secrets around Najiir. He comprehends it all."

Topur chuckled. "He'll find me the best exchange rates. He'll discover who has a surplus, who needs to buy, and what they will pay. I make better decisions and make larger profits. And by the time we are ready to depart, he has become fast friends with everyone. They eagerly await his return. With his help, I bring more earnings to my customers than expected. I have been far, far more successful when Najiir accompanies me." Topur looked at his lap. "It turns out buying him was the best deal I have ever made."

Topur blinked through his moist eyes. He felt remorseful about describing his affection only in terms of money. "Please forgive me, King Mithrias. I am so sorry. I must appear weak to you. When I think of the poor boy being beaten so savagely, I become overwhelmed. In a way, I am fortunate I haven't had to tell this story. I knew it would be difficult, and it's not for every man's ears." Topur's throat ached. "The incident affects me— even now. No mother to turn to for comfort. No father to offer protection. A defenseless little boy. It infuriated me to believe a child might believe the world is fraught with men like his master, that this is how things are. Aren't we members of a better world?"

Topur slowly raised his head, finally able to look at Mithrias. The king's clenched jaw, tightening, loosening, tightening again, betrayed the tension underneath his stoic gaze.

"I am not certain, my friend." Mithrias's voice was raspy and cracked. He sat up. "Maybe not. Beautiful deeds. I ache to hear such things. I hadn't expected such a story. Not at all."

At camp, the fires were tamed, and only embers glowed. A brief change in the breeze brought the satisfying smell of cooking meat. People still darted about, performing the final tasks of assembling and preparing the evening's meal. Mithrias grabbed Topur's arm, staring at the movement below. "No," he murmured. "No, I don't think you are weak—hardly. I admire you and what you did for a boy you did not know. I don't get to talk about things like this, about people, kindness, and concern for others and their lives. Kings are meant to attend to... other...." His voice faded. It didn't return.

"King Mithrias?" Topur sensed the despair. "May I get you something? I have upset you."

Mithrias blinked forcefully and regained his composure. "I am fine, Topur. I only wish I had come to you sooner." He rose from the blankets, and Topur rose with him. "I hope we can talk more—much more. I realize we put pressure on you. This is not a waste of your time. It isn't. I am grateful you are with us. Please stay. I assure you, we will properly reward your efforts."

"There is undeniable value for me simply being with two great kings," said Topur, echoing his wife's assertion. "I never expected this to be an opportunity to trade. Without a clear destination, how could it be? I packed some extra myrrh I had been saving. It trades easily, no matter where we go."

"Well, now more than ever, I am glad we convinced you. You are crucial to us. Our safety—our success—rests with you." Mithrias held his head high and looked to the west. "Judaea, then? Is Jerusalem far?"

"No," said Topur softly. "Jerusalem is not far. If your

original invitation had been to join you on some trip to Jerusalem, I would not have come. I apologize, but that is true. All this time, I had hoped the star would have guided us to another city—anywhere other than Jerusalem. Things are so..." He stretched an arm, pointing to the western horizon. "Before you came up to our fire, I told Najiir how I wished we were headed to Byblos or were on our way to Cyprus on a boat. I have never been on a boat, and I—"

Topur stopped short when he heard a thud. He turned. The kind man who had been standing beside him was now on his knees, his head in his hands.

CHAPTER 6

Mithrias's forehead nearly touched the sand. His splayed hands covered his face. Sudden, soundless, sporadic shudders convulsed through his torso.

At first, Topur assumed the king was injured. He scanned for an arrow, a wound, blood. The Romans!

He looked closer. Nothing. There was only a disconsolate king at his feet. Topur recoiled, helpless. "King Mithrias? What—what is wrong?" Afraid to breach decorum, Topur withdrew the hand he'd extended. "King Mithrias?"

The king gave no response. The silence was agonizing.

Through his hands, Mithrias finally spoke. "It will swallow me." For anguishing moments, that was all. His breath came in short bursts. The quaking rattled to a halt, replaced by stony stillness. When at last he moved, Mithrias's hands gripped his thighs, his head still bent toward the ground. It was the posture of a condemned man.

"I can't escape," Mithrias began. "I am losing command over my thoughts." He sat back upon his haunches, his gaze fixed and hollow. "There is this large, black space next to me...a void, empty, dark space. It hugs my side like a faithful cat. And though it doesn't demand my attention, I notice it again and again. Deep... Dark... Silent... Always there. An abyss of emptiness. It is my constant companion." His gaze moved to the sandy ground. "There it is." His obsidian eyes rose to meet Topur's. "The abyss—it's still there."

Never one to display strong emotion, Topur felt uneasy and inept if others exhibited theirs. For him, choking on his words while speaking of Najiir was an intense and uncharacteristic display. He bit his lower lip, glancing around anxiously, like a prisoner plotting an escape. "I am not gifted with knowing what to do with others' distress, but whatever it is, I am here to help you... if you think I could help?"

Mithrias's stern stare overwhelmed Topur. "This," he said, "this will consume me."

"What? What is it that torments you? Who is it? Please tell me."

"You mentioned a boat." Mithrias's voice was that of a beaten man. "My life stopped when a boat..." He swung his head as though shaking off water. "No, I can't—I shouldn't. Not yet." His eyes turned glassy. "Thank you, my friend, but I am being unfair. I...I will be fine."

"No—please!" said Topur. "You listened patiently to me. I wish to offer what you so freely offered to me."

Mithrias waved both hands. "You don't need to shoulder my burdens. Your focus must remain on this caravan. The time will come, my friend. If there is anyone on this journey who might understand my desolation, it is you. I know that now."

"Then please, go on," urged Topur.

"You found it difficult to resurrect the past, to recall events that brought you pain? I am no different. Maybe more afraid?" The king's face softened. "My condition frightens me. I fear that if I unburden myself and relive certain events, I'll return to the past and be unable to claw my way back. And you'll see, then, the abyss has won. I will have fallen into it. No, we will have our time together to talk of this." He sighed. "I assure you."

"I am only a merchant. I claim no special powers. You might find more comfort talking to your horse instead of me, but I promise you, I will listen. Why such pain for someone so undeserving?" Mithrias's chiseled features now appeared hollow in the amber firelight. "Is this about your son,

Salnassar?"

"Salnassar?" Mithrias said with a sneer. Uttering the name ushered a dramatic change in Mithrias's comportment. "Salnassar? No, it has little to do with him, though he presents his own sack of snakes for me. I assume you notice what an unpleasant person he is." He gnashed his teeth. "That malicious boy is the son of my second wife—a political arrangement. He is a rude, arrogant, insolent, selfish, pampered brute." Mithrias's voice turned gruff. "I realize it. Every goodness one can possess, Salnassar lacks—to the extreme. I brought him with me so I would have a kingdom to return to. He couldn't be trusted while I was away. I feared what he might do to undermine me and...and threaten the rest of my family. I prefer to travel without him, but it is better he is with me than scheming behind my back."

"I didn't know." Topur needed a moment to evaluate this revelation. "How could I? He has not said one pleasant word to me on this trip."

"And he won't. He'd speak to you if he wanted something from you. That is how Salnassar operates."

"But he should look up to you. You're his father. You're a king—a great king."

"I have little influence on the boy. At home, he spends his time either with his mother or among the soldiers. You see, Salnassar just turned sixteen and is already comparing himself to a young Alexander." Mithrias chortled. "A new Alexander. He is delusional. His only interests are in stories of fighting and killing. The boy does have ambition. That is painfully apparent. But it's ambition without talent. He is a bully and not terribly gifted at being one of those. He despises me."

"He stands alone, then."

"I was hoping to show the boy there are ways of relating to people—to the world—beyond conquering it, but he's paid no attention. He wants to experience 'military life' and stays in Regulus's shadow, believing he'll absorb what he needs to learn.

The boy commandeers my horse to keep up with Regulus and refuses to sleep in my tent at night, preferring to bed with the soldiers. And for now, that is fine with me. I can barely stand the sight of him. He is first in line for my throne." He cast a sharp glance toward Topur. "No. Not if he remains as he is. I'm sure you realize the implications."

"And that isn't the reason for the abyss?"

Mithrias's eyes narrowed to slits. "No. No, it is not."

"I can't make sense of this. You are beloved by everyone, yet have no influence on your son? It doesn't follow. I see he does cling to Regulus."

"Yes, Regulus. I owe that man an apology. He suffers from my neglect. As long as Regulus can speak about swords and horses and spears and of men killed and treasures taken, he will find Salnassar by his side. I can't boast of such things. I won't do it." He gazed absentmindedly at the camp below. "Have you been in battle, Topur?"

"God has spared me. No, King Mithrias; gratefully, I have not."

"I have led men into battle many times. I have seen men killed. I have killed them myself. Unlike Alexander, I take no pride in that. Other kings invite battle seeking glory. I am different, I guess. I have not shied away from it, but I have never found war to be glorious. Many find my attitude unusual, not befitting a king. Many more find it unforgivable. To Salnassar, it means I am weak. To him, my actions, my beliefs, are disgusting," Mithrias shrugged.

Topur pulled on his beard. "He is young. He has not tasted the bitterness of loss. Salnassar will come around. He has to. One cruel and belligerent empire on this earth is one too many—we surely don't need another. You are a kind king, a gracious and thoughtful king. The world needs more rulers like you, King Mithrias. Stand firm against your abyss."

"Look who comes toward us now." Three riders trotted uphill from camp atop the only horses in the caravan. Their silhouettes were unmistakable. Xaratuk was in the lead, followed by Regulus and, of course, Salnassar. "Your audience is coming to you tonight, Topur. We will discuss this important decision you say we need to make."

Topur squinted into the darkness. "I must talk to them, but I wish you and I had more time alone. We are unfinished here."

Mithrias squeezed Topur's shoulder. "We will talk, my friend. I know I can rely upon you. Thank you. But first, you need to tell the others what we've discussed. "

"Will King Xaratuk listen? I suspect he's not inclined to believe me. I must convince everyone there is peril before us."

"King Xaratuk is no stranger to peril. He'll face danger. My friend can be uncomfortably indifferent to danger. At times, he can appear reckless. King Xaratuk will take profound chances on behalf of his people. But he understands there is a difference between danger and destruction. He will not lead this mission to disaster. He believes this expedition has a great purpose. If he needs advice that will keep him—keep all of us— alive, then you must speak up. I'll support you."

The endorsement was welcome, but Topur's stomach remained in knots. "This is an awful gamble. All this risk, and in Judaea? Why go on? Sir, I know this region well. What you seek seems so unlikely. It simply doesn't exist."

"If there is anyone or anything possessing strength or power, King Xaratuk will find it. He is drawn to it." Mithrias stepped out of the fire's warmth. "Shoulder to shoulder, he stands with the powerful. He regards his proper place to be among them." Mithrias moved to prepare for the riders' dismount. "Ignore my petty complaints about him. The king is an honorable man. But he feels second to no one and is accustomed to achieving his goals. He'll find some way to bend this star, whatever it is—whoever it is—toward his purposes."

"So doubtful. Merely keeping all of us alive may mark his only success." Topur softened his tone. "And you? What is in this for you? You assume the same risks. What will be your reward?"

A bitter smile crossed Mithrias's face. He draped his arm over Topur's shoulder and left it there.

Well ahead of the others, Xaratuk guided his tramping horse to the men near the fire. "King Mithrias, why are you up here?" he asked, dismounting into the soft sand. "We are ready for our meal, and you are nowhere to be found." Reins in his hand, he prepared to remount.

"King Xaratuk," said Mithrias, standing firm. "Topur wishes to speak to us—vital concerns we must address—tonight. We must talk. Here."

Xaratuk slapped the reins in his palm. "Talk? Talk about what?"

Xaratuk's compact, stocky body was rarely at rest. An impatient tapping foot or clenching hands revealed his nervous compulsions. Flailing arms or pointing fingers accented most every word he spoke. If inclined, he could radiate a dazzling, infectious smile, his oversized white teeth emerging under a full but carefully managed mustache. That dark brown canopy drooped slightly at the corners of his mouth, then ran toward his ears—a large, furry line bisecting the top of his face from the cleanly shaved bottom.

He hastened toward the fire, ignoring Topur. "We need to talk? King Mithrias, it was little wonder that the ox cart kept getting stuck in the sand. It wasn't a broken wheel. It was an axle. Serious trouble. Difficult to repair in these conditions—especially when the cart is full. But it will be fixed. I suspected bringing my wheelwrights on this journey was a mistake, but after this, I am glad they are with us." Pacing, Xaratuk rubbed his hands together. "Though this is a large caravan, there is not one person too many. Everyone has a duty. Everyone has value. Very smart." He clapped his hands together and repeated, "Very smart."

He finally regarded Mithrias, eyes narrowing. "You don't look well, my friend. Is something wrong?"

Mithrias self-consciously drew the back of his hand across

his cheek. He tipped his head. "I am well enough, thank you. I am fine."

"Well, you look different to me. I hope you are telling the truth. I'll know soon enough if you aren't." He walked closer to Mithrias, studying him. "Soon enough."

Regulus rode up, spraying sand as his mount halted. He was clad in his everyday warfare uniform. A breastplate of fish scale armor was attached to a stiff leather backplate using leather straps adorned with large rivets depicting the sun. He wore spotlessly clean buff-colored pants. His pant legs were stuffed into leather boots that stopped mid-calf, giving the pants a ballooned effect at their base. Underneath the breastplate, a light tunic with black and brown sleeves completed his uniform. His hair was cut shorter than was the fashion of civilian kinsmen, and his beard, with the recent addition of gray, was kept neatly trimmed. Though he rarely smiled, he was unflinchingly courteous and polite to superiors while businesslike and efficient with subordinates. Whether riding, walking, sitting, or standing, Regulus kept a perpetually rigid posture—a product of his rigorous training and his endorsement of it. Regulus was entirely military and scrupulously looked and acted the part.

As he dismounted, Regulus swung his horse aside to avoid the uncontrolled arrival of Salnassar, whose bouncing elbows and shoulders exposed him to be far less than the horseman of his imagination. He nearly collided with Regulus's mount, forcing Regulus to grab the reins and bring Salnassar's horse to a halt. Instead of a proper dismount, Salnassar slid off the horse on his stomach. Momentarily off-balance, he quickly grabbed the reins back from Regulus, rejecting any implied need for help. Regulus could only project a controlled exasperation.

Salnassar had procured a pointed helmet from one of Xaratuk's infantrymen. The martial accent provided an absurd contrast with the rest of his flouncy, princely wardrobe. As soon as he found his footing, Salnassar began to strut, a helmeted pigeon convinced he was pure peacock.

Xaratuk walked back to his horse, grabbed the reins, then thrust them toward Salnassar. "Hold the horse."

Salnassar sneered. He made little effort to offer his hand, forcing Xaratuk to push the reins into a petulant palm. Salnassar turned his back to the king.

"Regulus's, too," barked Xaratuk.

"What?" snapped Salnassar.

"Regulus's, too. He has a horse." Without further word, Salnassar clumped to Regulus and grabbed the reins of his horse. He stomped away, jerking the reins. The horse reared, refusing to move. Salnassar's shoulders slumped. He seethed.

"Easy... boy," ordered Xaratuk. "If your mistreatment causes that horse to bolt into the darkness, you'll stay out in that desert until you bring him back." Xaratuk's threat was slow and deliberate. "Horses are more important than princes on this trip."

Salnassar glanced around the windswept sand. "And where am I supposed to tie them?"

"Tie them?" Xaratuk was openly condescending. "I don't believe you'll find a place to tie them. Not here." He paused, then strode to Salnassar, butting him with his chest. "Someone will have to hold them." With a withering stare, he added, "That someone is you... boy."

Salnassar turned, muttering through his clenched jaw. Xaratuk and Mithrias shook their heads.

Topur thought it wise to change the mood. "Your wagons have held together in these conditions better than I presumed they would, Your Excellency."

"What? Oh, yes." Xaratuk moved back toward the fire. "Those ox carts never gave us a problem until today."

"We rarely see ox carts out here in the desert, being so heavy," Topur said carefully. "They can be difficult in the sand, and the oxen are slow and need so many supplies of their own."

"Our trip has only recently involved this much sand."

Xaratuk kneeled, grabbing a fistful of the dry grains, letting them flow between his fingertips. "Those carts are efficient. We've found plenty of water and forage along the way. This desert makes travel more of a struggle. Still, I need them." Xaratuk walked to the kindling and pulled a stick from the depleted pile. The fire was too intense for him to get near. "I need them for the tents. Regulus needs them. And my advisors need a cart of their own for all those items they've brought—all those charts and scrolls and codices and whatever else. Those things will crumble, pounding on the sides of some camel. I needed something substantial. Yes, we're slow, especially through this sand, but we'll get there. We have come a long way, and it can't be much farther now."

"Those tent poles are quite heavy," said Topur. "No camel could pull them. I see it takes four men to manage just one."

Xaratuk eyed Topur. He threw his dry stick into the fire.

"Amazing wood, those tent poles," Xaratuk said. "The trees are from an area north of us. Regulus has been there. He told me about those trees. Tough and durable wood." Xaratuk smiled slyly. "Not one tent has folded into the wind, am I right?"

"You are right," Topur said. "The designs you have carved into them are quite attractive, too. Beautifully done."

"Aha, you noticed," said Xaratuk. "Those designs are at the behest of my advisors. Certain shapes are good omens for travel. Indeed, those poles are splendid. Nothing has fallen over yet, so those poles are well chosen, too."

Xaratuk scanned to his left, then to his right, nodding with approval. "If you say we have something to discuss, we shall do that, but we shall also dine here tonight, around this fire," he declared. "A suitable spot." He walked up to Topur, standing uncomfortably close. "I have the cooks preparing the rest of the pig. Knowing your restrictions, I had them butcher one of the sheep, too. We'll serve that as well." His self-satisfied smile acted as proof of his thoughtfulness, though Mithrias had made that suggestion earlier.

"You," Xaratuk growled, pointing to Salnassar, who stood brooding outside the fire's glow. "You head back to camp. Tell the others and tell them we shall take our food here tonight. Bring us some rugs."

Salnassar's face drained. "I am not some errand boy," he declared.

Xaratuk's back stiffened as his frame rose to its full potential. He marched until he could put his nose against Salnassar's, making it impossible for the prince to turn away.

"You're wearing the helmet of my army?" With a quick backhand, Xaratuk struck the headpiece off Salnassar's head. The helmet lodged, point first, into the sand. Salnassar shut his eyes. "In my army, there are no errands, boy. There are only orders." He locked upon Salnassar's eyes, waiting for them to reappear. "And those are yours."

"We're not asking you to bring all the rugs yourself," Mithrias interjected. "Get help."

Xaratuk's frown was a silent objection to Mithrias's input. "You relay my orders to any of my people down there, and you will see action. You tell them the meal, along with rugs, shall be brought up here. You'll see what people do when their king expresses his wishes. You'll see them obey—without question or hesitation. Pay attention to that, boy. Learn from them. Learn how to respond to the wishes of a king."

He grabbed Salnassar by the collar. "And don't forget this, boy." The words came with spit flecking Salnassar's cheek. "Your father is your king. I don't think you understand that." He removed his hand from Salnassar's collar with a shove. "Watch my people—and learn."

Salnassar wheeled about, grabbing his horse's reins while dropping those of the others. He clumsily mounted, refusing to look at anyone.

"One more thing, boy," shouted Xaratuk. "Tell Merkis and Khartir to come up here at once. Bring rugs for them as well. They must dine here with us tonight."

Salnassar urged his horse forward.

"Wait!" shouted Xaratuk once more. Salnassar stopped but did not look back. "Bring a rug for yourself."

Salnassar looked back, expressionless, and pointed his horse toward camp.

"So you are left with him," said Xaratuk, walking to Mithrias.

Mithrias froze.

Xaratuk put his hands on Mithrias's shoulders. "Unusual boy. You have had to endure so much, and his actions toward you are repugnant. We all see he shows you such undeserved contempt. It was time I said something. Putting on the helmet of my army..." Xaratuk raised a clenched fist. "That makes him mine." He chuckled. "I hope you don't object to my corrections."

Mithrias swallowed. "I welcome them and thank you. I admit I should be the one to correct him." He coughed, then added, "He has turned away from me in every respect."

"Respect," murmured Xaratuk. He turned to Regulus. "Those horses don't need to be tied up, do they?"

"The horses will not move from where they now stand unless ordered to, my king."

"I thought as much," said Xaratuk, exposing his oversized smile. "I thought as much."

Those remaining at the fire watched the petulant prince traipse down the long hill, showing no apparent sense of urgency. Xaratuk grunted while folding his arms across his chest. He wordlessly stared at the looming star, inhaling as if he might ingest the luminescence. His toothy grin reemerged.

"Magnificent!" He strode to Topur and put his arm around him for the first time. "Can there be any other reaction? Positively magnificent!"

"Yes, Your Excellency, magnificent," said Topur obligingly, though he was stunned by the show of familiarity. Xaratuk's self-assuredness oozed from every pore.

"Where do you suppose we are? I assume you know."

"Yes, I do know, King Xaratuk." Topur didn't elaborate, believing any frank assessment would snuff the king's buoyant mood.

"Well? Where, then? Where are we?" Xaratuk persisted, removing his arm from Topur's shoulder.

"We have now entered Judaea."

"Judaea, then. Judaea. I never supposed this star would bring us to Judaea." Xaratuk paused, blinking rapidly. "But that is fine. Among your people now? That must be of comfort to you."

Topur gave a respectful nod. "I suggest, sir, we discuss this. What you consider comfort for me may be quite the opposite for you. We invite calamity if we continue to follow the star in that direction." Topur wished his voice might produce a firmer tone of authority.

"Calamity? What are you saying?" Xaratuk scowled.

"The star pulls us to the south. I had hoped for a different direction." Pointing, Topur continued, "If we go straight to it, we could not avoid Jerusalem."

"Jerusalem? Ha!" Xaratuk slapped his thigh. "We are that close to Jerusalem?" His eyes brightened as they widened. His broad mustache rose like a slinking caterpillar. "We have come far! I have always wanted to see Jerusalem." He clapped his hands. "I have heard about the great Temple. Since we're this close, I would like to see it." Xaratuk's glee could not be suppressed. "Mithrias, think of this. It is said there is no more beautiful building in the entire world than the Temple built by King Herod. Considering your elegant city, that is a bold boast. I will judge for myself."

He turned to Topur, pointing his finger. "But you said something about calamity. What? Why? What could be wrong with going to Jerusalem?"

Topur's stomach rumbled. "The Temple there is beautiful, beyond my abilities to describe. But what is next to the Temple concerns you more."

"What are you saying?"

"It is called the Antonia Fortress. Herod built it, too."

"Antonia Fortress? Never heard of it."

"As beautiful and impressive as our Temple is, Antonia Fortress is the opposite. Bland but functional. It was built to serve as the barracks for the Roman garrison, housing no fewer than six hundred soldiers, double that if the city should become unruly."

"Oh, yes, the Romans. Quite right. I am in no hurry to see them."

"You, Your Excellency, must not see even one," said Topur. "If you enter Jerusalem, you will see Romans—and they will see you."

Xaratuk sucked his cheeks as if to bite them—another nervous habit.

"Though it would be far easier to stay on roads," Topur said, "any road we take will lead us directly into the city. The Romans wouldn't let an excursion of this size go unnoticed or unquestioned."

"I see." Xaratuk sounded genuinely disappointed. "I don't wish to get involved with any Romans—you are correct about that." He faced the star once more, hands behind his back. "Though I'd like to meet your King Herod and hear how he organized such an impressive achievement." Inspired by his own suggestion, he continued. "What if I could find some way to see King Herod—alone? I could become familiar with him while he showed me his Temple. I'd convince him I'm his ally, someone able to help free him from the Roman grip. Yes! This is my opportunity to go directly to King Herod, gain his goodwill, and together we can discover what lies underneath this star."

Topur struggled to conceal his exasperation. "Your plan, Your Excellency, is based upon unsupportable assumptions. Seeking King Herod's support will not protect you from falling into the clutches of the Romans. In fact, it is quite the opposite. You'll—"

"I'm concerned about the Romans," Xaratuk snapped. "Of course I am. I was raised to hate them. Friends and family told of what a brutal and vicious opponent they fought at Carrhae. The Romans are a relentlessly treacherous people, resolved to conquer anyone or anything they desire: Greece, Syria, Egypt, Anatolia, Carthage, Iberia—other places with names I can't remember. So who is next? Who will be the next victim of their covetous generals—or whatever they have now—an emperor?"

"Augustus. The Jews are familiar with the man."

"No Roman emperor will ever rule over my people," Xaratuk fumed. "I assure you. Two tigers cannot live in the same valley." He stabbed a finger at the chest of a non-existent listener. "I would make Hannibal seem like a friendly cousin compared to me."

Mithrias barely glanced toward Salnassar, who had returned empty-handed, evidence of his determination to remain removed from any servile tasks. Instead, Mithrias addressed Topur. "Your people worship at this Temple? The Romans allow this?"

"So long as a daily sacrifice is made to the emperor, yes," said Topur. "King Herod and the priests have made some arrangement, we presume."

"Arrangement? So Jews are able to live with the Romans and be—"

"Not with—under. Under the Romans."

"Yes, I see. What has it been like for you and your people?"

Topur was qualified—if reluctant—to speak on behalf of his people. Any answer was tricky; not all Jews had reacted to Roman subjugation in the same way. For Topur, the strategy was to ignore and be ignored, to aim for a grudging mutual tolerance. Not being a resident, he didn't have to endure the everyday humiliations and servitude borne by Jerusalem's residents. But he was well aware of their sufferings.

"What is it like to be a Jew underneath the foot of the Romans, you ask? I'll tell you a true story." Topur's chin quivered. "This was my friend. His father and grandfathers were from Jerusalem, as were the generations before them. He was a humble man of trade, not some soldier, and not a warrior pledged to take Roman lives or die trying. He was a shopkeeper, but he could easily have been a farmer, a teacher, a student, or perhaps a landowner who held a productive olive grove. These are the kinds of Jews Rome views as a grave threat.

"They came for him at night, but it could have been at any time. There's never any warning. Four soldiers, all with short swords, burst into the home. They put a rope around my friend's neck and wrists, then dragged him away without charge or comment. Too surprised, too stunned, he never thought to choose the better option, to fight there and then. Death would have been quicker, but perhaps his inaction saved a son or two who may have bravely but carelessly intervened.

"They threw him at the feet of the prefect, and they gave him what the Romans call a trial. They accused him of sedition, but they produced no proof or evidence. We're left with hollow speculation. Maybe he was too outspoken about his belief that it was improper for Jews to sacrifice to the emperor. Perhaps it was his refusal to trade in the blasphemous Roman coin. Maybe his complaints about being overtaxed had fallen upon jealous ears. He was guilty of nothing more than wanting to live in his homeland, the land he believed God himself had given to him, his family, and his people."

Xaratuk nervously bit his lower lip. The others remained still, silent. The desert wind complied, its gritty bluster now a motionless chill.

"The prefect castigated and berated him," Topur resumed, "reminding him that abiding by Jewish Law can be a threat to the emperor and Rome's most perfect order. For such outrages, the prefect condemned him to death. His stricken family was mortified. They pled on his behalf. They were ejected. A more zealous prefect would have ordered more crosses to be prepared. They dragged my friend from the court for immediate execution. His punishment couldn't be more torturous or more public. Romans show a shrewd purpose in being certain you die painfully, publicly, slowly, on a cross. His family was forced to watch. They insisted upon being present to fend off the crows that would peck at his eyes while he remained alive, to chase away the dogs gnawing at his bloody toes. But any tender-hearted aid only prolongs the agony. Roman soldiers nearby would taunt and laugh. Men assigned such grisly duty are plucked from the very worst. They flaunt their crass power and threaten to confront any challenge with brute violence." Topur could feel himself quaking underneath his robe.

"How can your people endure this?" said Xaratuk softly.

The servants with the rugs had arrived. Xaratuk ordered one rug to be placed near the fire, then sat upon its edge, staring ahead. "Your people are so... so...particular. You have rules and traditions about eating, working, worshiping, what you wear— so many concerns. You must answer to all those decrees and now answer to the Romans as well?" He turned, then motioned for Topur to be seated next to him. "How can you manage?"

Topur crossed his legs, then sat. He pulled at his beard. "We wait. We wait for some miracle from God to repel Imperial Rome. It will require one. In the meantime, provided we make sacrifices to Augustus at the Temple, the Romans allow us to be Jews." Topur shrugged. "Which is more than most of our previous conquerors were willing to do. We can have our Temple, a High Priest, and our sacrifices. For most, that is enough."

Topur felt empty, as if he could fold himself in half. He felt guilt and shame. A healthy merchant economy required stability, a goal he shared with the Romans. They built good roads, maintained effective security, encouraged and supported trade, and mercilessly punished any hints of banditry, all beneficial to the merchant. But to look away from his people's mistreatment, as he recognized he did, turned his stomach.

"It is as I told you, King Mithrias," said Xaratuk, rising to his feet. "It is just what Topur has said. These Romans do not think like the rest of us. They must not move beyond here to spread their filth and depravity. They must be stopped! And this journey shall help us do exactly that!"

He spread his arms magnanimously. "With all of you as my witnesses, I swear these Romans will not come closer." He turned to Topur. "What if this star—the person we'll meet—is just the miracle you Jews are looking for?"

CHAPTER 7

Topur shifted nervously upon the rug. He'd never considered the possibility of anyone powerful enough to expel Roman dominion. The prospect was enticing but amounted to nothing but another example of Xaratuk's wishful thinking. No matter who might arise, the Jews of Jerusalem, with their stones and clubs, were no match for Augustus's swords.

"Topur, where is your God in all this?" Stunned looks crossed the faces of those gathered. Such a remark was intrusive, impertinent. Xaratuk rose and began pacing, though the soft sand imposed limits.

"King Xaratuk," said Mithrias. "I don't—"

"No, it's fine." Topur looked directly up to Xaratuk, drawing back his shoulders. "It is a fair question." He rose. "You are not the first to ask it. We Jews have asked this same question over and over. Where is God, indeed?"

Xaratuk persisted. "I'm simply trying to better understand you and your people, Topur. With your magnificent Temple, the sacrifices offered, your priests praying, why isn't your God well-pleased? If you can't beat back these Romans with your God on your side, maybe there is little hope for me. This is what I'm trying to comprehend."

"No, no, I understand," Topur replied. "Where is our God? Why isn't he allowing us to repel our enemies? Might God require us to be more deserving of his blessings?" Topur cleared his clenched throat. "You need someone better than I who is versed in our scripture and our teachings and can give you the answer you deserve, King Xaratuk. I spend too much time in the company of donkeys and unscrupulous traders, and too little with priests and rabbis. My wife knows the Law and scripture far better than I do. Her family is rich with teachers and scribes. They included her while they vigorously debated such questions. Atarah and her brothers could offer you a well-supported answer. When we reach my home, we will ask this again."

Topur gazed about the horizon while he searched for the correct words. "I recollect them saying the current High Priest at the Temple is not worthy of sacrificing to our God—we've not had such a man for some time. There is unholy collusion. The High Priest's office is up for sale to the one most able to impress and placate the great King Herod. God won't listen to the prayers or note the sacrifices offered by those who bribe and conspire. So, the Romans remain among us as long as King Herod allows a fraud to be the man closest to God."

Xaratuk placed a finger over his mustached mouth. "Your answer seems rather shallow and unbelievable," he sneered. "Is the man who built you this beautiful Temple condemned because some High Priest pays him for the position? If you claim Romans fill Jerusalem's streets because your God sees Herod take a bribe here and there, then I'd say your God is overly sensitive. I've seen far worse."

"Neither the man who acts as High Priest, nor the man who appoints him, are worthy in the sight of God."

"What are you saying?"

"I'm saying Herod is not our king and therefore has no right to select the High Priest."

"Perhaps I'm no expert, but neither am I some fool. Should we enter Jerusalem, and were I to ask anyone to see the king, I'm certain they would take me to Herod's court. Am I wrong?"

"If you ask to be taken to the King of Judaea, you are right. If you ask to be taken to the King of the Jews, you will find a mixed response, or none at all. Herod considers himself King of the Jews, but he's not my king, and almost every Jew I know feels the same."

In exasperation, Xaratuk threw his hands up. "King Mithrias, what kind of simpleton have we picked to guide us? Are you listening to this?"

"Every word," said Mithrias calmly. "Please, Topur, continue."

"You consider Herod to be King of the Jews? Though he may act like it and believe he is so in his heart, he is not. He is King of Judaea, I concede, but that is by virtue of Roman consent.

"Rome had installed Herod as their choice to govern an unruly province they had recently re-conquered. Familiarity governed that decision. While still young, Herod had taken refuge in Rome to escape the turmoil in Jerusalem as Rome struggled to oust their Parthian enemies. He ingratiated himself with those in power and was rewarded with Roman citizenship. When leadership over chaotic Judaea again fell into dispute, Herod was dispatched to his homeland equipped with Rome's blessing and an army supplied by his benefactors. He fought his way back into Jerusalem, killing other Jews in the process and, with Roman approval, proclaimed himself the ruler over Judaea and his people. Without their support, he'd be nothing."

"Nothing?" His arms folded over his chest, Xaratuk looked at Topur with scorn. "Like so many, you lack the least ability to appreciate the benefits of effective leadership. Your Temple is something, is it not? Isn't King Herod the champion who finally built that Temple? Your people flock to it. They think it is something. Hasn't he reconstructed Jerusalem, lifting it from an insignificant jumble to become a flower amid the desert? Nothing, you say? He's an innovator with vision! I feel desperate to speak to such a man!"

Instead of convincing Xaratuk to turn back, Topur was inadvertently pushing him forward. He felt dreadfully inept. "No," he said through a grimace. "No. Falling into Herod's grasp is the same as surrendering to a Roman. If Herod finds you, he'll set you before his Roman friends at the first opportunity, then wait for the reward."

"He'd recognize my name. He'd know who sits before him. I will convince him I am a friend, an opportunity. I can point out the benefits of an alliance, how friendship with me is preferable to one with Rome."

Topur shook his head in frustration. "No, Your Excellency, no. What you have heard is a tiny slice of King Herod's story. The rest is not so complimentary. He is an unstable man. He is vicious and violent, even to—especially to—those closest to him. Please listen to me. He imagines stealth and treachery surround him, even when none can be found. You confront a man who ceaselessly fabricates conspiracy. Everyone is suspect."

Xaratuk looked away, dismissive. Salnassar moved closer.

"It would be ruinous to surprise this man." Topur stood even with Xaratuk, feeling he was failing to bolster his argument. "There is every reason to suppose he would view you and this mission as a threat. You have arrived at his borders unexpectedly. You are here without invitation and without warning. You bring thirty armed men to what—threaten the Romans? Threaten him? What is he to make of that? Are you confident you'll persuade him that such powerful kings as you are merely passing through—just following some star? What are the chances he'll believe you?"

"I hadn't thought of making contact in advance. Until tonight, I didn't realize Jerusalem was nearby. Of course I don't want to confront the Romans, but I still don't believe our small group poses the least threat in Herod's eyes." Xaratuk's expression was impassive. "You are speculating, Topur."

Fear of Herod was not speculation. "Any group with armed men will alarm Herod. And when alarmed, he'll look for support, and that support will come from one source—his Roman benefactors. It all comes back to them."

"You seem too harsh. Not King of the Jews? You've yet to tell me who is king if Herod is not. He works with the Romans because he has to. He has no alternative. But I could supply that alternative. I am not persuaded that Herod and I could not work out some arrangement. We are important visitors, announced or otherwise. Herod would respect that." Xaratuk turned to Mithrias. "Wouldn't Herod respect that, King Mithrias?"

Mithrias feigned a smile. "I am happy you asked, King Xaratuk. I presumed Topur joined this caravan to advise us about which things we should be wary of, or are a danger to us in this unfamiliar region. He is doing that, yet you maintain we should doubt him and should overrule his guidance. As for me, I would be interested in any opinions our chosen guide might share. If Topur says King Herod presents a danger, I believe him, and would welcome suggestions on what we must do."

"I'm not doubting him," Xaratuk growled. "Well, maybe I am. I wish Merkis and Khartir were here. They need to evaluate this, too." Xaratuk squinted toward camp. He turned to those gathered around the fire, then locked his gaze on Salnassar. "Salnassar, didn't you—"

"I told Merkis it was your order that he bring Khartir to the fire immediately," Salnassar interrupted. "Merkis said they would join us once he secured their materials—whatever they were reading."

Topur watched the silhouettes of two men walking uphill, followed by another figure leading three laden donkeys. "They are coming," he announced.

"Good. We'll see what they think." Xaratuk spun back toward Topur. "I am listening to you. But a man like Herod—in that position—will not be popular with everyone. I consider this from my point of view as one who rules over a kingdom. There is nothing more difficult, I assure you. Only a select few can manage, despite popular opinion believing otherwise. I judge a man by his actions and his accomplishments. Along those lines, King Herod achieves high marks."

The punishing wind had tempered to an afterthought. Merkis and Khartir stepped within the fire's glowing ring. Each wore a substantial hooded robe. Merkis's hood was up, protecting his tall, aging frame from the night's chill. His long, gray beard flowed over his frock and down his chest. He smiled politely, his raised hand offering his greetings to those assembled. The smell of woody, spicy incense followed him, which translated to the scent of wisdom for those acquainted with him.

Khartir was much younger than his mentor. His hood drawn back, he looked less imposing and exhibited fewer expressions of a lifetime dedicated to thoughtful investigation. His youthful face naturally spurned the idea of a fine beard like Merkis's. He kept his black, full hair short. His nose was too large, making his small mouth seem even smaller. His countenance was a peculiar combination of sober seriousness mixed with an urge to reveal something essential. If he spoke, his audience understood they were privileged. His intellect was quick, agile, and accurate; his understanding was deep and wide. Few took a second opportunity to challenge him.

Khartir raised a hand in unspoken greeting, then unraveled two rugs at the edge of the semi-circle forming around the fire. Najiir and his troop of donkeys arrived with their ponderous cargo of kindling. After unloading, he stoked the embers with fresh fuel. Flames rose. There was a moment of silence where those gathered welcomed the emerging heat.

"I hope we have not kept you waiting," said Merkis. "Sorting and packing our materials can take time, but it's an important duty." Looking at the horizon, he acknowledged the star. "We are so close now—very near. Our certainty grows. We will no longer require most of the documents we pored over earlier."

"We stowed most of them away for good," Khartir added. "I agree. We are close."

"Well, you're finally here," said Xaratuk, failing to mask his impatience. "I'm encouraged to hear we're close, but there are some issues we need to discuss. Merkis, do you know where we are?"

Merkis shifted to observe the star again, then looked back to his king. "Well, I presume we are in or near Judaea by this time, though I will defer my opinion to our capable guide, Topur." He extended a gracious smile. "Am I correct?"

"You are right!" Xaratuk, not Topur, answered. "And underneath that star, do you know what city is there?"

Merkis nodded. "Our assumption is Jerusalem."

"Precisely!" shouted Xaratuk, clapping his hands together. "Precisely! Brilliant!" He turned to Topur. "I told you these two were brilliant. You see how much they comprehend?" Xaratuk flashed a gloating, toothy smile.

"We are in Judaea," Merkis confirmed, shrugging off the accolades. He shifted his attention from the star to Topur. "This is the homeland of your people. We are quite fortunate that your culture is so disciplined about writing. We've collected a considerable amount. There is a great deal to consume. Your ancestors speak extensively about this region, why they are here, what they expect from each other, and even what they expect of the future. You have many prophets."

"True," Topur said. "We are a people with many opinions, not to mention many instructions."

Merkis chuckled. "These writings help us determine who— or what—is the focus of this star. We have put away those documents about the Egyptians, the Greeks, and the Assyrians. It was a surprise to realize the Jews and their writings would prove crucial to our mission. Now, we refer them exclusively."

"Merkis, might this star lead us into Jerusalem itself?" asked Xaratuk.

"It could. There, or nearby." He glanced at Khartir, who nodded his agreement.

"And so it becomes interesting, for Topur says we should avoid Jerusalem."

Merkis's expression froze; his head bobbed. He shifted his

gaze to Topur. "You say we should avoid Jerusalem?"

"I do."

"Khartir and I are best suited to identify the proper location and interpret what we find there," Merkis said. "But how to get there, or where we ought or ought not to go, I willingly cede those decisions to you. I believe I know, but I wish to hear from you why we should avoid Jerusalem."

"Because there are Romans there," Xaratuk blurted.

Merkis nodded. "Yes. Yes, I thought so. Romans."

"It is essential we avoid the Romans," said Khartir.

"Perhaps," said Xaratuk. "But Topur says King Herod isn't to be trusted, either. He thinks Herod will turn us over to the Romans."

Khartir attempted to respond, but Xaratuk wasn't finished. "I am still trying to understand why a king who has accomplished so much for his people is held in such contempt. He may be the Jews' greatest king ever, Topur, and I find it shocking that you speak ill of him." His hand punched his palm with each successive word. "What prevents you from paying him the honor he deserves?"

Topur's patience teetered. He had made no progress in the face of Xaratuk's stubborn resistance. Mithrias's claim that Xaratuk was inherently seduced by power was evident. Whether power was used for good or evil seemed of little consequence.

"Honor the man?" There was one more revelation Topur needed to reveal. "Herod isn't considered a Jew." He waited for the spark to hit the tinder.

"Not a Jew?" Xaratuk threw his arms into the air. "You mean to tell me... King Mithrias, help me. While Herod sits on a throne in Jerusalem, our guide claims he isn't a Jew."

"Mostly Arab, isn't he?"

Topur was stunned to hear such words. Who among this group of foreigners would appreciate this detail?

"Or, at minimum," Khartir continued, "half of him isn't

Jewish. Wasn't his mother Nabataean?"

"Yes. That is so," Topur stammered. "From Petra." He stared at the young magus. "She was not born a Jew, but how did you know this?"

"It is as Merkis said, your people are very willing to write things down. We have encountered a few writings addressing this. Most of them agree with you. Herod is not very Jewish." A tight smile crossed Khartir's face.

"Herod's father's family were only recent converts," Topur added. "His grandfather converted—forced to by the Hasmoneans. Herod is an Idumean but was raised as a Jew. There is no dispute about that, but his family is without the generations of background required to make decisions such as who should be High Priest."

"You deny him his authority because of a short pedigree?" Xaratuk barked.

"You think we are rash, King Xaratuk?" Topur snapped. "Are you willing to cede your kingdom over to some… Sarmatian?"

Xaratuk looked away, refusing to answer.

"Herod acts as if he is one of us," Topur continued, "but to most Jews, he is not, or is barely, Jewish. To an outsider, this may seem trivial. But he fought and killed Jews in his struggle to become our king. His motives and his background deserve inspection."

Xaratuk still refused to comment.

Topur resolved to speak calmly. "He is king because the Romans have said he is king. Without them, Herod would not be king of anybody or anyplace."

"Well, good for the Romans, then!" Xaratuk snarled. "They chose a man with the boldness to build you a Temple! Your appointed king restored Jerusalem to its greatest glory ever!"

Topur flexed his jaw. "The Temple is a bribe. It is there to impress the Romans and placate the Jews. It is beautiful, I grant you. But Herod did not build the Temple for the Jews to revere

God. He built it so that his Greek and Roman friends revere him. Without question, the Jews appreciate the Temple. We finally have what we have yearned for since Babylon. Herod is a compulsive builder. He has erected forts and ports, aqueducts, and theaters. But all these are clever tactics to—"

"Tactics!" Xaratuk stomped a foot into the sand. "Clever? It is more than clever! These are noble and ambitious undertakings, and he gives you a center of worship that will be admired for countless generations! You should feel indebted to him and worry less about what your wife and her family believe are proper bloodlines. It is actions, not breeding, that make the difference!"

"Then we shall discuss his actions, those beyond building the Temple. There is much to say there, too." Topur strained to control the quiver in his voice.

"Such as...?" Xaratuk said sarcastically. "I mean, beyond making Jerusalem a city now esteemed by the world."

"Murder. Murdering the High Priest, for example."

"Murdering a priest?" asked Xaratuk.

"His brother-in-law."

"Which was it? I am confused—a High Priest, or his brother-in-law?"

"One and the same." Topur found his calm voice and, with unusual elegance, told the story of a king tortured by his insecurities who met real and imagined threats with ruthless cruelty. At the behest of Cleopatra and Marc Antony, Herod's wife's brother, Aristobulus, was installed as the high priest. The young man, only nineteen, had charm, character, and the pedigree Herod lacked. He proved too popular. Even Rome was shocked when Herod had the boy drowned, but Herod beguiled and bribed his way back into good favor. Then, he installed his choice as high priest, who was now obliged to restore Herod's personal fortune. "Money, not Hebrew, is Herod's native language," said Topur.

"Distasteful, maybe, but hardly unprecedented, and hardly

an action worthy of your overarching condemnation."

"I am not finished. Regarding murder, there is much, much more to be said."

Xaratuk, bored, sank back upon the rug without saying a word.

"Herod's wife, Mariamne, never forgave him for having her brother drowned and hated him even more than she did when she was forced to marry him. She despised him. He executed her, too."

"Mariamne? I believe I know this story," Khartir interjected.

Topur extended his hand toward Khartir. "It may seem more genuine if your king hears this from you. If you could speak of this tragedy, please go on."

"I hope I tell it correctly," Khartir began. "Tell me if I stray." He leaned forward, his hands in motion, embellishing his words. "Mariamne was Herod's second wife, I believe." He looked at Topur, who nodded. "Yes, and Mariamne was an actual Jewish princess. Like her brother, she had the pedigree that Herod lacked. Some say Herod took Mariamne as his wife to solidify his standing as a Jewish ruler. But anyone fortunate enough to have looked upon Mariamne recognized she was also the most beautiful and desirable woman in the entire kingdom. Herod's lust for Mariamne was immediate and only grew, but she loathed her husband with equal intensity. She bore him children out of obligation to her people and a desire to keep her family in line for the throne. But she took every opportunity to belittle Herod and keep him as distant as possible.

"Being married to the loveliest woman in Judea, Herod assumed and imagined treachery. Anyone coming near Mariamne was suspect. He went mad with jealousy, concocting all manner of accusations against her and others. Those around Herod could convince him to ignore his exaggerations and imaginings for a while, but that couldn't last. He saw intrigue everywhere. Finally, in another fit of madness, he accused

Mariamne of adultery based upon false stories fed to him by his sister." Khartir looked to Topur. "Am I right about this so far?"

"Every word," Topur replied, smiling.

"Herod couldn't execute Mariamne solely at his whim—he had to procure Roman consent, so he arranged a trial and, of course, though completely innocent, she was found guilty. He ordered her execution. He murdered this beautiful Jewish princess—his wife—because he couldn't control his unfounded jealousy. His madness continued until the awful deed was done. That seemed to jolt him back to reality, but then he began drowning in remorse. He cried out for her day and night and has remained like this ever since. It is said he continuously wails for Mariamne—speaking to her as if she were there." He looked once more at Topur. "May I tell them about the honey?"

"I wish you would."

"It is said that after he claimed Mariamne's body, he had it preserved in a chamber of honey, placing her in a room inside the palace that only he could enter. He continues to visit that room at every chance. His regret has been boundless. Imagine being so racked by guilt that, to him, she is still alive. He's carrying on conversations with a murdered wife."

"All true. Every word," said Topur. "You tell the story well, sir."

Xaratuk heaved a sigh. "This is what you are reading so late into the night? Where do you find this, Khartir? It sounds like idle gossip to me. Great men have many things said about them—and any number of them can be untrue. There is a price attached to greatness. Perhaps she was an adulteress. It would hardly be the first time. And maybe it grieves Herod to distraction to punish her disloyalty so severely."

"Begging Your Excellency's pardon," Topur interjected, "but Mariamne's execution was due to a flaw in Herod's character, not hers. Mariamne is only the beginning. There are many more murders—especially those related by blood to Mariamne."

"More murders, you say?" Xaratuk sighed.

"Many. It is our good fortune we are not members of the family," said Topur, his hands clasped as if in prayer. "He killed another brother-in-law, Kostobar. He executed Mariamne's grandfather, then her mother, Alexandra."

Xaratuk's eyes widened, but he gave no other response.

"He murdered his eldest son, Antipater," Topur said, "and more recently had two more sons put to death, Alexander and Astribulus. Even Augustus, from his throne in Rome, recognized Herod was acting heinously. He ordered him to stop the carnage, but Herod ignored even the emperor. I hear Augustus refuses contact with Herod, making the man even more unstable."

Xaratuk rose, readjusted his clothing, and with renewed composure, sat again. "You make Herod out to be monstrous. Maybe it is so. I don't know. But who knows what evil lurks within families?" he added, his gaze moving to Salnassar. "I understand all too well that being from the same family doesn't exempt one from treachery. To assume my throne, I had to kill my uncle. Circumstances forced that action. After he murdered my older brother, the rightful heir, I assumed I would be next. I am trying to say that sometimes a king has opposition where he should least expect it, and yes, it can be from within one's own family."

"Though you sympathize with the man, you and Herod are not alike," Topur responded.

"I suppose I should take your words as a compliment."

"The man you wish to meet is imbalanced and unpredictable. He is unable to distinguish aid from threat. He sees betrayal and deception where it does not exist and imposes the highest penalties."

"He sounds like a beast to me," said Mithrias.

Salnassar delivered a muffled snort. Topur recoiled at the impertinence, though Mithrias appeared deaf to it.

"I understand you, Topur," Xaratuk said, "and I appreciate

your desire to inform us. I simply wish the others here might balance what you are saying with another point of view. Herod has had to make some unpopular appointments. He will never please everyone and should never try. You don't say the Romans object to his choices. The Jews must understand that the Romans will allow only certain things and certain people. As part of the empire, you must accept that. Herod has. He is doing what he must, and maybe what is best, for those who consent to live with the Romans."

Xaratuk stood, ready to issue a pronouncement. "The sole reason for this mission is to make certain I will avoid having to make the decisions and concessions Herod and his people must make daily. No Roman foot shall fall upon one stone in my kingdom. My people will never conform to this malicious culture." He turned to face Topur. "I feel for Herod—for his dilemma. I understand his struggle. Herod has been Jerusalem's king for a long time. What does that say? Perhaps he knows what is best, even if his people disagree. That is why he remains king. I offer that as something to think about." He sat down. "But yes, it bothers me he can appear reckless, duplicitous, and even—perhaps—cruel."

"I must protect you from him, King Xaratuk," said Topur.

Xaratuk shrugged. "Perhaps I shouldn't defend the man. You know more about him than I do. My own advisor knows more about him than I," he said, gesturing toward Khartir. "I may lack any personal basis to defend him, but I say again, ruling a kingdom is not a simple affair." He looked skyward. His teeth shone in the firelight. "This journey—these efforts—will reward me." He raised both hands. "That star will reveal that certain someone who will help me, help my kingdom, and my people!"

Merkis and Khartir exchanged a cautionary look. Their chests heaved, though they said nothing.

Xaratuk leaned in. "In my youth, I never heard of Jerusalem. No one spoke of it. Now, everyone has some familiarity with

Jerusalem. And why? Why now, and not before? I say it is because Herod accomplished something amazing, well beyond the capabilities of ordinary men. I wish I could understand how that was done and see it with my own eyes. The Romans were going to be in Jerusalem, with or without Herod. Fortunately for the Jews, I'd say, your king has found a way to mollify your conquerors. That is highly uncommon. You cannot argue with me on that. He has found a way to make Jerusalem flourish, even under Roman subjugation. Yet you tell me he is condemned for it."

Xaratuk stepped back from Topur, muttering, "I don't begin to understand."

CHAPTER 8

The meal relayed to the hillside fire was unusually robust, especially for travelers: pieces of bread soaked in olive oil and herbs, figs, dates, grapes, raisins, lentils, roasted grains, and, of course, savory meat. Xaratuk invited those who brought the rugs, the wine, and the food to dine with them. Never cut with water, the wine was eventually and thoroughly depleted. Every man ate their fill. Sated, the slaves and servants cleaned the area, thanked their king for his generosity, then stumbled back to camp.

Food only tormented Topur's agitated gut, though the wine soothed his anxious head.

"Merkis, Khartir!" Xaratuk hissed, moving his head to verify those departing to camp were beyond earshot. "What do you say now? We are almost there?"

Seated with their backs to the star, the advisors turned to it in unison. Merkis's voice, though weakened by age, was measured and authoritative. "This star's beam is closer than ever, its angle the sharpest. Every twilight, I worry it might not appear. But tonight, our star shines on, I am pleased to say."

"The star shines on, yes." Xaratuk's knuckles bleached, his anxious hands clenched. "Days. How many more days will it take us to reach this place?"

Merkis and Khartir looked at each other before Merkis spoke. "Two to four days, we estimate. How fast can our caravan can move?"

"Two days?" Xaratuk beamed. "Two days, you say?"

"That, or more, depending upon the recommended route," added Khartir. "We arrived at this fire amid the mention of the Romans. You insist we avoid Jerusalem?"

Topur yearned for a more appreciative audience than Xaratuk. The advisors remained mysterious men, but they were his last chance to convince this caravan to return home.

"Quite unfortunate." Merkis sighed. "I understand the need to avoid detection. I also understand my king's sentiments. It would be wonderful to see the Temple. To be this close, at my age, without seeing it for myself, is frustrating beyond measure. I hear it is magnificent."

"It is," said Topur. "You could also declare the Romans, with their shields and spears, to be impressive, too. For us, it is best to avoid both."

A sullen mask fell over Merkis. "Coming this far was not entirely unexpected, but Romans—to be challenged by Romans would likely have, shall we say, grim consequences."

"And there is no way to smuggle us through, maybe at night? It isn't your Passover or any other holy day. It might be relatively peaceful," said Khartir.

Topur stared at the young advisor. "Romans don't sleep."

"If only there were some way," said Khartir. "Perhaps, when we are ready to return home, a few might linger behind. We could investigate, make some inquiries, then initiate more proper arrangements. "

Xaratuk broke in. "Can you tell me exactly where you believe the star directs us? You say we are close, but can you be more definite? What if it is Jerusalem itself? What then? I have been patient thus far, but don't you have some idea?"

In unison, Merkis and Khartir replied, "Bethlehem."

Merkis spoke alone. "We agree it is Bethlehem, my king."

Topur stared at the ground, incredulous. "Bethlehem?" he muttered quietly. "Not what I expected."

"Never heard of it," Xaratuk rose, casting the remains of his wine into the fire. "Topur, what do you know of this city of Bethlehem?"

"Well," Topur began, "I have heard of Bethlehem, though to call it a city is out of proportion—"

"Maybe there is a fortress there, or it's an estate," offered Xaratuk, thinking out loud. He turned to his advisors. "Why do you say it is Bethlehem?"

Merkis stood as well. "As the star's position became more definitive, the many possibilities dwindled to only a few."

"And now we're in Judaea," said Mithrias, entering the discussion.

"Correct, Judaea." Merkis fingered his long, gray beard. "We predicted it to be Judaea, or nearby, about the time Topur joined us. It has become conclusive in the past few days. Our destination will be somewhere within Judaea's borders. Fortunately, we packed most of what we collected regarding Judea. We've purchased more texts along the way, even in your city, Topur. The Jews are uncommonly gifted writers. Our work would have been much harder with a less literate culture. More than a few times, we find mention of a new leader expected to emerge. That was notable. The star could be related to this figure predicted by the Jews. Sometimes the texts call him 'king,' or 'King of the Jews.'"

"A name?" asked Xaratuk. "Any mention of his name?"

"No," said Merkis. "Not that we've encountered. Other texts refer to a 'Messiah', though, and we believe this refers to an even more powerful man, an anointed one whose destiny, they say, is to shed the shackles of their oppressors."

Xaratuk's mouth fell open.

Merkis continued, "A few texts claim he will lead a new government and usher in a new era of peace. The Jews are a very prophetic people, and there are many accounts and prophecies to pour through, but one in particular... from some prophet...."

"Micah," interjected Khartir.

"Micah, that is right. You recall these things so much better than I do." He patted his clever protégé on the back. "Micah names Bethlehem specifically and says this is to be the birthplace of this great Jewish leader." Merkis shifted toward Topur. "So now I turn to you, Topur. I don't know where Bethlehem is. You do?"

Before Topur could answer, Xaratuk bawled a warrior's yell, vigorously pumping his fist into the air. "Perfect! This is perfect! A new king! I thought so! An ally against the Romans! One predicted by his own prophets to overthrow their oppressors! This is what we have been searching for, my friends! It's all fitting into place!" Xaratuk shook with excitement. "We must get there quickly. Very quickly! I will have much to say. Much to see. Much to discuss." He gathered himself and realized he'd interrupted. "Yes. Yes then, Topur, where is Bethlehem?" Xaratuk punched the sky one more time, his toothy face beaming.

"It is about a half-day journey out of Jerusalem... farther south." Turning from the star back to Merkis, Topur nodded. "This star, tonight, lines up with what you claim. Bethlehem is in exactly that direction."

"Of course it is!" shouted Xaratuk with boyish glee.

"Yes, good. Good," said Merkis. "Topur, I should ask what more can you tell us about Bethlehem?"

"Bethlehem? Well, let's see..." Topur massaged his temples. "There isn't much to say. It is not very—"

"Can you speak to its history, or who has lived there?" Merkis interrupted.

"Again, I wish I could speak more intelligently on such subjects. I believe Rachel is buried there on the edge of town." His words were drawn-out and uncertain. "Mother of our forefathers, she is known to every Jew. I have never been to Bethlehem. I've no reason to go there." He paused, "Oh, I almost forgot—and it is by far the most important thing: I believe King David's boyhood home was Bethlehem. He is from there."

Smiling, Khartir nodded. "We were hoping you would say something about that."

"Indeed," echoed Merkis. They glanced at each other, barely concealing their smug certainty.

Khartir continued. "The Jewish prophecies also confirm this new king will be from the House of David, and we expect the chances of that to be increased in a city which claims David as their own."

"Oh, this is so exciting!" Unable to stand still, Xaratuk strode toward Merkis and Khartir. "My advisors are rewarding me with their wisdom once again." He sounded as if he might burst. "You two—so smart! You continue to amaze me. I swore I would never make an important move without your wise counsel, and I maintain that still. This is why!" He patted both his advisors sharply on their shoulders. He turned to his captain, who had remained silent throughout the discussion. "Regulus, we are heading for Bethlehem!"

"Topur, you look as if something is wrong," said Mithrias. "Is there more we must understand about Bethlehem?"

Without responding, Topur stepped to the piles of kindling. He withdrew a stick, then strode to the lines he had etched in the sand. He beckoned the others.

"I'm surprised to hear Bethlehem is our destination, but if so, this route becomes even more practical." The men formed a circle around his sandy outline. Topur looked each man in the eye before speaking. "One final chance. I beg you to reconsider, but are all of you determined to continue?"

Xaratuk glared at him.

"Yes, so I'll proceed." Topur waved the stick over his drawing. "To reach Bethlehem while avoiding Herod and Jerusalem will require a detour through an extensive canyon. It will take us a half day to reach it. We'll meet an unsurmountable ridge that will force us to use this narrow canyon. I have taken this route four or five times before—though not recently. But I know what to expect."

"Canyons are to be avoided," said Regulus, scowling. "Why not go around? Why not avoid it and Jerusalem and take another route?"

"The canyon provides a direct route, useful for our purpose. The existing roads are well-placed because the wilderness ahead is far different. It is rocky and hilly, and the crevasses and ravines become more frequent and severe. But we must leave the roads if we are to avoid Roman scrutiny. Going around means six, seven, or maybe ten more days in the desert. There are no towns where we can buy provisions. Will the star continue to be patient?"

"Just get us to Bethlehem. Quickly. That is all I ask," said Xaratuk.

"I need to know more about this canyon. I can make plans if I can anticipate what I am facing," said Regulus.

All eyes remained upon Topur as he retraced his lines. "The canyon floor is narrow here and here," he said, pointing, "at the beginning and again at the end. The entrance has a width of about four oxcarts side-by-side—not much. The walls remain narrow and curve back and forth like an ancient river channel. Then, it gets much wider in the middle—a small valley. It stays wide, but near the end, it gets narrow again. Once out of the canyon, the land is flat, and I can get you to Bethlehem without taking roads and without passing through Jerusalem."

Regulus studied the lines as if looking at a map. "Much about this bothers me. How long will this take?"

"This group will need most of the day. A smaller, more maneuverable group could do it in half that time."

"And is there sufficient room to assemble again once we are through?"

"Plenty of room, and we'll find forage there, too. It is considerably different from the conditions here."

"I see," Regulus murmured, scratching his head. "I'm neglecting something. Once I realize it, I will find you." He turned to Xaratuk. "I will speak to my men about the need to be vigilant. Topur, should we expect Romans to be in or near this canyon?"

"No," said Topur, too quietly. "Little chance of that. Their absence is why I recommend this route." He deliberately withheld any mention of the reasons venturing inside those walls might be perilous. Yes, he'd been through there, and he swore never to return, but this was the only alternative. His stomach felt as though it might flip from his torso. The serenity of the wine was spent.

Xaratuk studied his captain's face, then looked away. "King Mithrias," he said, "if you have no objections, then I don't either. I only wish to get there. We'll go through this canyon. Our only objective is to reach Bethlehem swiftly."

Before Mithrias could utter a response, his son interrupted. "If you want to go through Jerusalem, do it! Do it and be proud! You are kings! You should behave like kings and not like frightened sheep! If I were a king and in front of a Roman, I'd demand to see his highest superior. I would like to see their reaction when they found out someone so magnificent had entered their land under their sleepy noses. You're a king!" he said, pointing at Xaratuk. "Herod is a king! He'll respect you! A great king would be welcome in any fine city and should march along the broadest avenues among the cheering crowds. He had better respect you! And the same for any Roman! They wouldn't dare harm you, or they'd have Carrhae to deal with all over again."

"Pardon me," snapped Mithrias through a furious sneer. "My son's mouth works independently of any reasoning." He shook his head, muttering, "Why am I left with... him?"

"Jews do not line the streets to cheer any foreigner in their midst—ever," said Topur. "You're more likely to get a stone to the head. And I hope, for the sake of the great King Xaratuk, we make no more mention of Carrhae. The Romans have long memories, and that is a very bitter one. So please, all of you, never speak of it."

Mithrias grabbed his son by the wrist, yanking him, then began dragging him to the camp below. "Wait," yelled Salnassar. "My horse!"

"It is not your horse, it is my horse, and you'll leave it alone." Mithrias continued jerking a recalcitrant son down to camp. Without looking back, he yelled, "I will prepare for our journey through the canyon."

"Sheep!" yelled Salnassar, clumsily failing to wrench his wrist from his father's grip as they stumbled down the sandy slope. "Sheep!"

CHAPTER 9

"It is settled, then." Xaratuk stood alongside his horse. Dropping the reins, he strode to Topur, not stopping until their noses almost touched. "With regrets, I'll agree to this adjustment *if* it is our quickest path to Bethlehem," he said. "Later, I will contact Herod properly, making my visit to Jerusalem official. I intend to meet the man. It would be on the condition that he would keep us away from the Romans, of course. It would be disappointing to be this close and not see your Temple."

"There is a crocodile in your path." Topur's slow delivery revealed his frustration.

"The world is awash with crocodiles. Jerusalem would hardly be my first."

"I say avoid Jerusalem—avoid Judaea—completely."

"Topur, I look at your face and see the lines on your forehead, by your eyes. You are a man who worries." Xaratuk pointed to either side of his own face. "Look at me. What do you see? Do I look like I worry?" He strutted to his horse. "And I'm not worried now."

Reins in hand, Xaratuk readied to mount but halted. "I'll be blunt with you. Yes, I urged you to come, but recruiting you was not my idea. I didn't see the point. We had no problems following the star, and I wasn't expecting any. They were insistent," he said, pointing to Merkis and Khartir. "They were adamant we not go unguided past your city. As you see, their advice is sound. They told me your name and said I must persuade you to be our guide. So, if that is what they wished, I would accomplish it. You're with us, but now you think you can give the orders—tell me what to do. I don't mind being guided, Topur." His eyes were slits. He stomped back, poking Topur in the chest. "But I'll not take orders—from you—or anyone."

"Your Excellency," was all Topur could muster.

Regulus, already atop his mount, turned. "I still can't think of what I must ask you about that canyon. It will come." The riders trotted back to camp, Mithrias's mare in tow.

Merkis and Khartir remained, waiting until their king was beyond earshot. Together, the magi approached. Merkis placed his hand on Topur's arm. "We need you, Topur. King Xaratuk tells it plainly. It was we who insisted upon a guide. By the time we reached your city, we had presumed Judaea was our destination. If we were correct, that could only mean Romans, and that meant trouble."

"I confess we did not expect the strength and numbers you mention," Khartir said. "I didn't realize they saturated Jerusalem and had placed themselves in a fortress."

"We needed someone to temper our king's—I fear saying it aloud, but I must—reckless enthusiasm," Merkis said. "You know what dangers await, dangers he is too willing to ignore."

"We knew this moment would arrive." Khartir shared a deep look of apprehension with Merkis. "It had to. Until tonight, you had mentioned nothing, and we feared you were not concerned our group might encounter the Romans. Thankfully, that wasn't so. We need you, especially if Jerusalem stands between us and our destination. We need someone with the knowledge and the contacts to help conceal us. You are that proper person."

"Couldn't you have warned him about Jerusalem—and the Romans? He follows your every word."

"I hope I can rely upon your discretion," said Khartir. For the first time, his voice lacked certainty. "What I am about to say, I cannot take back."

"Of course," said Topur. "Of course."

"When our king claims he follows our advice," Khartir began, straining, "he is not accurate." His next words were carefully chosen. "The king is a complicated man requiring special treatment. Through experience, we've realized he responds far better to suggestions than arguments. Even better, he is most receptive if he adopts another's suggestion, believing it is his own. It sounds disloyal, but we spend considerable effort anticipating or manipulating his proposals. All too often, it is necessary to counter his impulses."

Merkis chuckled. "He won't admit it, but he agrees with us only when it suits him."

"He follows his own counsel, despite anything he might say about us," added Khartir.

"We believed our voices alone were insufficient to convince our king he must avoid any Roman contact," said Merkis. "We needed a strong local authority—you—to confirm that. I'm so relieved you chose tonight to come forward."

"We were prepared to broach the subject tonight if you hadn't," said Khartir.

Merkis faced the star. "Truthfully, I never imagined we'd be called this far. Judaea is well beyond what I expected. Our suspicions turned toward Bethlehem some time ago. I'm sure we made you anxious by withholding any mention of our destination. Delay was crucial. We had to prevent our king from forming any alternate plan, taking us exactly where we ought not to go. I mistakenly overlooked any consideration of King Herod as a threat. I dearly wish I could see your beautiful Temple, too. But Khartir and I admit you are correct. The Temple and King Herod, though tantalizing, are far too dangerous. Standing firm in your insistence upon avoiding them is crucial."

"But you suggested meeting King Herod after seeing Bethlehem. I must warn you, even that—"

"We plant the seed," interrupted Khartir.

"Then poison its roots on our schedule, not in reaction to his whims," added Merkis. "We make the suggestion, then use every opportunity to crush it. Watch as we approach our king with reasons to avoid meeting King Herod."

"It has already started. I took up your account of Mariamne's tragedy to begin to sow misgivings about King Herod. It was a potent beginning."

These were genuinely mysterious men. They were practically confessing their disloyalty, though claiming to act in their king's best interests. They had accurately predicted the dangers ahead and involved him in their defensive strategy. Was Xaratuk correct? Were their insights uncommonly superior? Might there be something in Bethlehem after all?

"I had hoped to persuade all of you to turn back. I have failed miserably. Though I can haggle with anyone over the price of a rug, I am unconvincing when predicting catastrophe."

"It was not a matter of persuasion," said Merkis. "We are unshakable in our belief that the star will reveal something that may change the future of mankind. The most eloquent argument had no chance of success. But there are threats, and your perceptive evaluation has earned our confidence. With your courageous help, I'm certain we shall arrive at Bethlehem." With a polite bow, he turned but halted. "Topur, may I ask you something?"

"Of course, sir. Anything."

"From camp, I thought I saw you alone with King Mithrias."

"Yes. I was quite honored. He is a considerate man."

"He is," said Merkis, nodding. "I hope you don't suspect I am prying, but will you share with us anything he mentioned? We are extremely worried about him."

"Worried?" Topur hesitated, wondering if any bonds of confidence were threatened, though Mithrias had offered only the slightest glimpse of his agony. "You may be justified. He does seem troubled." Though uncertain he should, Topur continued.

"He said he felt unable to control his thoughts, that an emptiness plagued him. He would not tell me anything more."

"The man has suffered. You are entitled to be aware of that," said Merkis.

"You know what troubles him? I thought it might have something to do with his son, but he denies that."

"It is his son," said Khartir. His small mouth drew tight. "But not Salnassar. It's his first son, Deioces. Prince Deioces drowned while on a diplomatic mission with a delegation of the palace staff, a mission King Mithrias had advocated and planned."

"A magnificent young man," Merkis added.

Khartir nodded. "King Mithrias had such hopes for him. Deioces was, with justification, respected and adored by all. He was a rare assemblage of character and kindness—much like his father. If possible, even more so. King Mithrias was wise to note such ability and was determined to share this with the world. If any single person might improve the lives of his people, Deioces was the one. He embodied the most revered qualities mere mortals can display."

"When the news of Deioces's death reached King Mithrias...you can only imagine." Khartir looked to the ground.

Topur's hands quivered, his chest deflated. "Poor, poor man."

"The world lost a decent and promising young man," said Khartir, "and King Mithrias lost his world."

"King Mithrias's first wife, Queen Doria, the boy's mother—" said Merkis.

"Stunningly beautiful," said Khartir.

"As wondrous as Mariamne, I suspect. But unlike Mariamne, Queen Doria was exceedingly kind and in love with her husband. I had several opportunities to be in her company. She, too, was universally adored, and for good reason. You could almost touch the love and admiration between King Mithrias and his queen. It was that palpable."

"But she was so overcome by Deioces' death," said Khartir.

"She blamed her husband, claimed he shouldn't have sent someone so young on such a dangerous trip. I doubt she meant it, but her grief was so overwhelming." In synchrony, the men shook their heads in disbelief, looking dejectedly at the sand below. "Killed herself," Merkis whispered.

For a moment, Topur couldn't speak. "She what?"

"Yes," said Merkis softly. "It happened after King Mithrias had joined our expedition. I don't believe he ever suspected she was capable. And now, King Mithrias is convinced he caused the deaths of the two people he loved most."

"He can't go home," said Khartir. "He has little interest in this star, Topur. He has no premonition, no grand expectation, unlike our king. King Mithrias joined this journey to escape his sorrow, but that is not happening. His sorrow remains, stalking him step for step."

"I'm uncertain he'll ever return to his kingdom," Merkis added. "And worse, I fear he will never find a corner of the world where he'll be free from his torment."

"The abyss," Topur murmured.

"Abyss?" said Merkis.

"Yes," answered Topur. "He called it an abyss. His constant companion—no more details than that. But my chest ached as he described his anguish. How devastating to understand the reasons."

"King Mithrias describes his darkness well," said Merkis. "We wanted you to know, Topur, because the man is struggling. He does his utmost to conceal it. To my knowledge, he has kept news of his wife's suicide quiet. I don't believe Prince Salnassar is aware. Only King Xaratuk knows, and in confidence, he informed us. All our information is secondhand. It is doubtful that King Mithrias would confide in us. He is a wonderful king and a splendid man. If you win his confidence, it may be an immeasurable help to him and this journey."

Topur's thoughts reeled, a dreadful mixture of astonishment and grief. "How?" he croaked. "How can he endure? How can he find the will? How can he...?"

Merkis pulled at his long beard. "Greatness takes many forms, and it isn't always backed by an army. But we see signs he is succumbing—one foot over that abyss."

Khartir clapped his hands. "We've left you with much to consider, Topur, but we should return to camp. There is much to discuss now that we understand our route."

"Thank you for your time, Topur," said Merkis. "We are so grateful you consented to join our trip." He squeezed Topur's drooping shoulders.

Topur watched until the magi were only silhouettes. Rising from the nearby rug where he'd remained seated, Najiir trotted to Topur.

"Will you need more wood?" he asked.

Topur looked at the remaining piles. "No. This is enough."

"Poor King Mithrias. I should return the donkeys to camp."

"Don't stay out too late," Topur mumbled. "Tomorrow will be important."

Topur felt battered. His gaze softened as he looked upon Najiir. That boy was the closest thing he would ever have to a son, and his heart was breaking with the revelation that Mithrias had lost his.

"It is much colder tonight. Your blankets are waiting when you come back." He rummaged through some of their belongings and produced a woven cape. He tossed the cloak to Najiir. "This will help cut the chill."

"Thank you."

"I didn't expect any of this," said Topur, barely audible. "Both kings are such vulnerable men."

"I'll come back after I return the donkeys." Najiir grabbed the halter of the first. The others followed, untethered, in a line.

"Sure," Topur responded. Alone, he kneeled on the ground, then lay on his back. The soft sand formed to the arc of his spine. He stared at the thousands of tiny lights shimmering, densely packed into a clear, onyx sky. He felt small, insignificant, and very much alone and ached for the comfort of his wife.

"Atarah," he said, "what am I bound to? In two days, I could be in Bethlehem before Micah's king, or will I be at the feet of a Roman judge, condemned to the salt mines?" He felt his chest deflate, stifling his urge to breathe. His head was fuzzy, dizzy, awash in a potent mix of dread, fear, and sorrow mixed with abundant wine.

"Dear God, what are you doing? Why bring us here—bring ME here? Why can't you let me go—be far from these men—so I might live? Let them chase their star, find their champion." He blinked back tears. "There is no champion, is there? No mighty warrior bathed in starlight. Not in Judaea. Not anywhere." His thoughts turned to Mithrias, and though it seemed his heart was already flattened, it sank even more. "That poor, poor man. He deserves none of this."

He wiped his cheek. "Neither do I. God, is this your will? Is it? This? Because it is not mine."

He rose to prepare his customary prayers, but offered them more fervently and earnestly than usual. He removed his traveling clothes, then moved into the empty tent, adjusting the blankets. His gaze flowed past the tent's open front, over the barren slope, past the smoldering embers, then beyond the camp. The star remained, its beam so low on the horizon that it cast a thin, shimmering line upon the sandy earth.

An illuminated directive.

CHAPTER 10

T he ascending sun brought encouraging hints of warmth. In the burgeoning light, atop a dune east of the camp, King Mithrias faced his homeland. A long white robe with two black vertical stripes hung elegantly from his perfect posture, accented by a brilliant red cap. His appearance was reverential, pure, with no kneeling, no genuflections, no outstretched arms, no praying hands. He was a man, alone, standing at peaceful attention.

Tears seeped from the edges of Mithrias's closed eyes, running down his smooth cheeks. Each tear retraced a single pathway over his short beard down to his chin where, one after another, like clear, hot wax, they dripped to the avaricious sand below.

The ancient grains at Mithrias's feet were eager to receive moisture in any form. Even strings of salty tears dripping steadily, rhythmically, were greedily accepted. For centuries, these ancient grains had been far more familiar with tears than with raindrops. In the centuries to come, that would not change.

His lungs ached, compressed by dread. Mithrias trembled. Surrounding him was a black ring of nothingness. A phantom snake of ebony coiled, beckoning him, daring him to take the slightest step and plummet into an emptiness where gravity no longer held, where being no longer mattered, and rescue was hopeless.

***

Topur had stuffed his meager pack. He should have been happy with a partial victory. His proposal to retreat was rebuffed, but Merkis had convinced him elevating that prospect to a viable choice was absurd. The detour through the canyon was accepted, though, in Topur's opinion, their chances of evading Herod and the Romans rose from nonexistent to unlikely.

The effects of the previous evening's wine made hoisting the bundle onto his back more onerous. He stopped three times to catch his breath before reaching the camp. Those in the caravan ate on the run, as the typical morning meal would not be served today. Once packed, soldiers busied themselves sharpening, stringing, or sheathing the weapon of their choice. The crews assigned to dismantle the tents worked at peak efficiency. Only the ornate tent poles remained to be lowered and placed on the ox carts. Shepherds approached Topur, respectfully requesting he point them in the direction to begin their march since they were usually the slowest group, having to herd the unpredictable movements of unburdened pack animals and meals on the hoof.

A buoyant Xaratuk sat astride his unusually nervous horse. Unable and unwilling to suppress his toothy smile, Xaratuk noticed Topur. "What a wonderful day! And what good progress we are already making! Just think of it, Topur. Bethlehem! Mere days away!"

"Indeed, it is exciting," said a more subdued Topur. "Sir, have you seen my boy, Najiir? He did not come back to our tent last evening, and I can't seem to locate him."

"Your boy? No, I have not seen him," said Xaratuk distractedly. "And I have not seen King Mithrias yet. Have you?"

Topur pointed east of camp. "I saw him earlier, taking in the sunrise."

"Good. You've seen him. We must discuss what we'll need to consider once we get to Bethlehem. Success is mostly due to correct preparation, Topur, and we must prepare ourselves for this!" Xaratuk wheeled his horse in Mithrias's direction.

Soon, the caravan was ready, though Najiir was still absent. Xaratuk was impatient to begin. The missing boy could easily find the group's tracks. He ordered the caravan forward. Reluctantly, Topur started the morning's march alone again.

Moments later, Topur felt an unexpected touch on his elbow. He spun about, expecting Najiir—but it was Mithrias.

"Prepare yourself for a long day, Topur," Mithrias said, raising his eyebrows. "I believe I have placed us in some jeopardy with King Xaratuk. He is quite angry with me because he seeks my help to concoct some strategy—for what, he can't say. Such pretension leaves me numb. I wish to walk with you today. He'll revive."

The prospect of Mithrias's company buoyed Topur, but his tongue held fast. The previous evening's revelations from Merkis and Khartir rattled within. Should he say something? Anything? Drop a hint? He didn't wish to probe or pry. He merely wanted to help, but Mithrias might take offense and never confide in him again. For Topur, offering consolation had always felt awkward. They walked in silence, but for only a short distance. Overruling his better judgment, Topur stopped. Unable to look at Mithrias, his words were muffled and brief. "I know. I know about your son, Deioces, and his mother."

Mithrias halted. His balled fist struck his forehead. "Merkis, I presume?"

"Only because he and Khartir are deeply concerned about you, not to gossip. They believe I can be of help. I hope they are right."

They trudged in silence, then Mithrias cleared his throat. "I wasn't certain they knew. Well, they saved me the torture of reliving it. I should be grateful. I'll tell you this, my new friend, and then it will be some time before I can speak of it again. I had an intelligent, faithful, beautiful wife and an abundantly promising son." His voice trailed to a whisper. "How I miss them."

They took twenty paces before Mithrias would speak again. "And how I miss living in a world I understand. I find that frightening. There was a clear path for me, Topur. I understood what to expect and what was expected of me. Now, it's as if I have stumbled into a dark cave. I can't see forward, and I dare not look back, but it doesn't matter. It's black—everything is black. Any step I take is blind. Step after step, and toward what end?" Mithrias pounded a fist into his chest. "Nothing. Makes. Sense. No more talk of this. You know, now. You understand what torments me."

The only sound was the crunch of feet on the sand.

"You are mistaken to believe you are alone in that cave, sir. It may be too dark to see, but others are with you. If you'll realize that—"

"For the very first time, I feel that." Mithrias stopped and placed his hands on Topur's shoulders. He tipped his head. "Thank you. Thank you."

And they spoke no more that day about Mithrias's abyss.

Instead, from that point on, Mithrias peppered Topur with question after question about Judaea, Jerusalem, the Jews, the Romans, King Herod, and the Temple. It was as if Mithrias could become two distinctly different persons. Topur found he was doing most of the talking. If he tried to reverse roles, Mithrias quickly responded with more questions of his own. The conversation was so spirited that Topur could not query Najiir when he finally joined them, to ask him why he had been so late, nearly ruining the caravan's early departure.

CHAPTER 11

Regulus stood, hands on hips, assessing the ridge. Though hesitant, Topur stepped closer. The opportunity to discuss the details of the canyon with Regulus had never materialized. Presumably, Regulus would ask for them now. Topur found that likelihood distressing.

"Impressive," Regulus murmured. "Impressive and unusual. I have been to many places but have seen nothing like this. It's an enormous jumble of rock cast into the middle of... nothing. From here, this ridge appears much taller than I imagined." Regulus squinted, then raised a fisted hand. "That's it!" he shouted. "I realize now what I wanted to ask you. The tops of the canyon walls, what are they like? From here, they look flat."

"They're flat. Quite flat."

"Oh, no. Is there some means to reach the top?"

"Many have tried, but I've never heard of any success."

"I don't like it. Enemies can position themselves above us and command our movements. We are exceedingly vulnerable." He glowered. "This canyon renders us nearly helpless. I am concerned you're pursuing this. Tell me, have you ever been attacked in there, Topur?"

Topur inhaled deeply to smother any trembling. "Me?" This was not the moment to be completely forthcoming. "No." That wasn't true. He refrained from mentioning the ten or fifteen stories of attacks others had described.

Regulus's stern visage turned grave. "I don't like this. I'm going to recommend we not go through." He turned to a group of soldiers nearby. "Get some rope, then find me some way to the top."

The soldiers sprinted back to the supplies.

"Anyone could effortlessly kill all of us from there." Regulus's articulation felt like knife points. "And pick over our corpses at their leisure." He frowned. "I never concede the high ground. My outlook has changed. I will inform King Xaratuk." Regulus mounted his horse and dashed away.

Regulus passed Mithrias, who was approaching on foot. "I believe I have tamed King Xaratuk somewhat," he shouted as he drew near.

Mithrias stood with Topur assessing the towering rock wall. "Point out the entrance into the canyon for me. I see no trail leading into it."

Topur directed Mithrias's gaze to a dark slit among the many cracks just to the right of the center. "You'll rarely find tracks to it. Few go in, and these winds sweep away any trails almost instantly."

Regulus and Xaratuk rode up at a fast gallop, leaving the caravan behind. Neither dismounted. "Our guide tells me the tops of the canyon walls are flat," Regulus grunted. "This concerns me. We are decidedly more vulnerable should anyone be based there—Roman or otherwise."

Xaratuk considered the topography ahead. "Have you heard of attacks, Topur?"

"Attacks?" Topur tried to look at Xaratuk, but the sun was directly behind the king's head. "There's always talk...rumors. They describe any encounter as more of an annoyance than a threat." That wasn't true, either. Those weren't rumors, they were fact, and some stories were alarming.

"Could Romans be up there?" Xaratuk shouted through the stiff wind.

"Not likely. They don't venture this far from Jerusalem if

they don't have to." Topur's heart raced. He sensed their suspicion. The canyon may present danger, but his failure to emphasize that was not duplicity. Even if he'd been more forthcoming about the threats, there was no other option. They had to go through this canyon.

"I don't like it," said Regulus. "We will be stretched and too vulnerable, not knowing who or what may be ahead of us—or over us. I can't command my men when I can't see them." His horse danced impatiently underneath him. "Topur, there must be some other way."

"Regulus, let's go," Xaratuk said. "Let's get on with it. We're here, we're ready, and we have the men in place to protect us. There's been no hint of adversity on the entire trip, and there is no need to run from it now. If this is the quickest way to Bethlehem, we are going to take it."

"Very well, sir. I shall prepare the men."

"I'll walk with Topur," Mithrias interjected. "I am of little use to anyone on my horse. Leave Salnassar on him and use him as you see fit."

Startled, Regulus looked to Xaratuk. Xaratuk merely shrugged. "Very well."

"You, my king," Regulus said, "will be protected at the rear. My men will disperse throughout, and I will move wherever I'm needed." He waited for some sign of approval. Xaratuk took only a moment. With lips pressed together under his enormous mustache, he nodded his consent.

"We will organize the group out here," Regulus stated. "It is too tight to maneuver inside." He looked again at the ridge top. "There is much not to like about this." He pulled on the reins and directed his horse to the rear.

The caravan began the day trudging through loose sand. As it progressed, the ground beneath changed to light sand over rock. Now, it was mostly rock, easier and faster to walk upon. Topur watched as Regulus and Xaratuk galloped back and forth on crusted earth, assembling the members. The king barked his orders, and his subjects raced to comply. After organizing the assembly, Xaratuk ran his horse to the front, then turned around and shouted his commands. "Come forward as I call you."

Four soldiers would be the first to enter the canyon with their bows and arrows, the front line of attack or defense. Behind them was Topur, alongside Mithrias and Najiir, then four more soldiers. Hastily armed servants, cooks, and craftsmen followed. Then came the shepherds and the livestock. Controlling these animals would be a significant challenge. Next came six more soldiers to assist with driving the livestock forward and preventing strays. The long array of pack animals and cargo were next, and behind them were their attending slaves and servants. Six more soldiers, including those who were unsuccessful in finding any pathway to the clifftop, defended them to their rear. The ox carts were last, kept apart from the other cargo at Xaratuk's request. Trailing at the back were Khartir, Merkis, and Salnassar. The remaining soldiers safeguarded the tail, brandishing bows and arrows, or swords and spears. This arrangement would provide close protection for the most important members and afford general protection throughout the line.

Regulus evaluated the assembled formation. "No. I don't like this. We should be tighter—more compact. We must remain as close as possible." He turned to Topur. "Is there a way we can bunch together? Will the canyon permit it?"

"Not until we pass halfway. The entrance is narrow, no more than ten to fifteen paces across. Later, it will broaden into a valley over two hundred paces across. Beyond that, the canyon narrows once again until we reach the end."

"I didn't realize our front would be so separated from our rear. The thinner we become, the more vulnerable." Regulus scanned the long line. "It will be imperative," he said, his voice amplifying, "that each of you watches those in front and those behind. I will instruct each member never to lose sight of those around him. That will help." He stared directly at Topur. "Those in the lead must not become separated. Stay in contact with those behind you."

"I will make certain of it, Regulus. You have a sound plan."

"We'll need luck. I detest relying upon luck." Regulus galloped off to attend to those at the back of the formation.

Mithrias stepped next to Topur. "Ah, Topur. This will be fine. I am happy Regulus consented for me to continue enjoying your company." His early morning torment, alone on the dune, was invisible. "What are our chances of getting through the day unmolested?"

"Quite good. I feel good about this. I do." It was as if a nest of worms wriggled in his stomach, contradicting his optimism. They resumed their slow walk. "Regulus has implemented an excellent plan. And look," he said, pointing to the eight soldiers before them checking each other's equipment, "who would be so brave—or so foolish—as to mount an attack with these men around us? We are well prepared."

Xaratuk dashed up, his horse spraying loose sand at their feet. "We are almost assembled and ready. Regulus has told you not to lose sight of those behind you, correct?" He waited for nods of confirmation. "Don't get too far ahead. Salnassar will be a messenger from front to rear. If we need to communicate with you, he'll do it."

"I don't expect we will have much to report," said Mithrias.

Xaratuk squinted down the long line and waved to Regulus, positioned near the end. Regulus waved back.

"That is his signal to begin, Topur. Archers!" Xaratuk shouted to the soldiers standing just in front. "Begin a slow march. When you reach the mouth of the canyon, look to my command to enter. Be alert for signs of trouble. Never lose sight of those you see now behind you."

The archers, standing at attention, bowed to their king. He saluted in return and urged his horse down the long line.

Mithrias and Topur fell into their assigned places and

stepped forward. Soon, the expedition stood before the unmistakable mouth of the canyon. The impermeable formations rose dramatically from the desert floor. The cliffs were stacks of squashed, pocked, dull-magenta rock arranged haphazardly. Layers formed, heaping up to a flattened top, their misshapen edges refusing to align. The scabrous walls were stark and impenetrable, indifferent to the needs of living things. Stones and boulders littered the interior path like banished castaways. Narrow and gloomy, only the noontime sun would fleetingly warm the canyon floor.

Dread surged inside Topur as he stepped toward the canyon's passageway. He felt as if he were about to witness something frightful, to be the first upon a corpse. He pulled the rope around his robe tighter and reached for his dagger once more.

Mithrias removed his red hat. "No need to offer a target."

Topur laughed nervously. "Your dagger? Is it with you? I don't see it."

Mithrias reached underneath the front of his robe. He pulled out a gleaming silver blade. His hand covered the golden hilt. "My father's. If you knew him, you'd appreciate how it has proven useful."

As instructed, they awaited the king's signal before entering the canyon. In time, Xaratuk motioned them forward. Topur drew in a deep, sober breath. He met Mithrias's gaze and shrugged.

Mithrias put a gentle hand on Topur's back. "We should go."

The forward archers, now within the canyon walls, crept forward. Each soldier grasped one arrow, poised for nocking. The canyon's shadows enveloped them as they inched, their eyes adjusting to the dim light. Topur, Mithrias, and Najiir followed.

The ground at the entrance had changed yet again. Throughout the morning, the trekkers became accustomed to the ease of the harder, rockier surface. But just before the canyon, persistent desert winds heaped loose sand into bothersome pools and miniature dunes. Solid footing was elusive.

Upon reaching the canyon's shadow, Topur's right foot buckled, accompanied by a loud pop. He cursed, howling in pain. Najiir sprang to his aid. He slid one of Topur's arms over his shoulder and guided him, hopping, to a large boulder. Groaning, Topur sat, his eyes sealed shut.

"Your foot. What is it—broken?" asked Najiir.

"No, I don't think so." Topur wheezed. "I think—I think I only twisted my ankle." The initial sharp pain was now a throbbing ache. "Badly, however. I see it swelling."

Mithrias moved to them. "Can you walk?"

"I think so. This happens every so often. My ankle will hurt for a while, and then it will be as if it never happened. I think so. I need a moment, though."

"I will get a staff from a shepherd," Najiir suggested.

"That will help," said Topur.

Najiir ran, shouting for the shepherds. Eager to help, they offered many options. Staff in hand, he sprinted back. He found Topur still seated, laughing with Mithrias. Neither man seemed to consider this incident a severe setback.

"This should do well, Najiir. Very nice." Topur stood. His ankle protested, but he was familiar with this weakness. The staff would help, and the worst pain would become merely a nuisance. He took tender, tenuous steps in the shifting sand. Najiir remained at his elbow. They hobbled their way into the shadows of the canyon walls.

Following their captain's instructions, the archers had waited, but forward movement prompted them to resume their stealthy steps into the sinuous gloom, meandering like cautious cats. Intermittently, they would follow their orders, each man glancing behind to ensure their appointed followers remained in view. Topur noted the now-familiar camp servants, followed by more soldiers. The twisting corridor made it impossible to see anyone beyond them.

Once in the canyon, all went mute. Eyes widened while throats tightened. The only sounds were footsteps over crunching sand. Topur felt like an apprehensive tomb robber plundering a gritty crypt. He dared himself to look up. It had never occurred to him to fear an attack from above. Regulus was right: they were vulnerable. The cautious archers provided only tepid reassurance.

Such vigilance made progress feel interminable. When most of the day seemed to have been spent, the canyon's choking twists and turns finally ceased, and patches of sunshine broke ahead. Upon reaching the expanded canyon walls, the archers separated. Enormous gray boulders littered the crusty valley floor. Slim caves lined the walls like wrinkles on an aged face. One archer wordlessly motioned for the group to continue forward.

At the back of the procession, there was frustration. The loose, shifting ground that had twisted Topur's ankle had subdued two ox carts piled with their cargo. The unmerciful sand refused to release its sunken prisoners even when the soldiers nearby shouldered their weapons to help free the laden carts. Human power, combined with ox power, made no impact. Xaratuk called out for Regulus, who heard the plea but struggled to pass astride his mount through the narrow corridor. "Get more help!" Xaratuk ordered. "We need ropes and more people back here. These carts are hopelessly stuck."

Regulus found Salnassar. "Get to the front and tell them to stop," he commanded. "Do you understand? They must be halted!" Salnassar nodded, then turned his horse into the canyon. Regulus shouted, "And send me more men to help pull these carts!"

Salnassar saluted, then pushed and threaded his way through the canyon, shouting demands to let him pass. He shoved his way through the burdened beasts and met the first set of soldiers. "The ox carts are stuck!" he cried. "King Xaratuk orders you to move to the rear to assist him. Now!" Six soldiers sprinted, dodging through the animals in a race to the rear. Salnassar pressed ahead toward the next group, screaming his orders. Six more soldiers raced back. Some servants rushed with them toward the rear.

Some, but not all.

Others kept moving, urging and prodding the nervous livestock forward. Through the tangle of men and beasts, Salnassar kicked his horse ahead, determined to reach the front.

The warmth of the desert sunshine spread like warm oil upon Topur's forehead. He felt renewed and relieved. The soldiers in front walked in crooked lines, creeping forward from one potential hiding spot to another, arrows at the ready. Topur looked behind. More soldiers had entered the valley, fanning out, much like their brethren. Behind them, a few servants, relishing the sunshine, emerged. Satisfied, Topur moved ahead. He realized his ankle was not as troublesome. A good omen, he figured. Still, he limped. He and Mithrias renewed their conversation in hushed tones.

"I didn't like those narrow spaces. Too much like a tomb," said Mithrias.

"Enjoy this. It won't last. It narrows again, but not for long."

"And your foot? You are better?"

"Much better. I think I will make it after all, and Merkis won't have to rearrange his trunks to find room for me on his cart."

Both stifled a laugh. Topur allowed himself to feel more confident about their security. His plan was working. After this, Xaratuk might be more inclined to listen to him and might consent to a plan that wouldn't kill them all. The sun's warmth revitalized him. Topur silently gave thanks for Mithrias's genial companionship. This was the closest he'd felt to believing this journey might have a positive outcome.

Mithrias resumed their earlier discussion, especially

intrigued by King Herod's apparent willingness to be supported by the Romans. Neither man abided by the directive to take periodic note of the others. When the valley's end loomed, Topur was startled by their neglect. He stopped in mid-sentence, turning to look behind. There were no more archers. The shepherds were there, doing their utmost to keep the donkeys, sheep, goats, and a solitary pig in some order. Servants marched two-by-two in a line, talking, obviously comfortable with their present circumstances.

Topur blinked. Something was wrong. There was a gap. About one-half of the caravan was in the valley, but most everyone should have arrived by now.

"King Mithrias…" he said, his voice trailing. "King Mithrias, have we gotten too far ahead? Shouldn't there be more? Maybe we should—"

An enormous wheel of dense, flaming brush tumbled from the canyon's flat top at the far entrance to the valley. It smashed onto the canyon floor, bursting into fiery chunks. Another followed. The inflamed bundles held fast as they tumbled, giant wheels of fire that erupted upon impact. Another plummeted. Showered with a downpour of sparks, the people and animals closest to the growing inferno raced forward. A soldier shot an arrow at the canyon rim, but no culprit, no target, emerged. One more bail was heaved, more fuel for a wall of flame now choking the valley entrance.

The caravan had been split in two.

CHAPTER 12

"**I**'ll be back!" Najiir yelled as he bolted toward the chaos. A rider, clinging to his horse's neck, blasted through the burgeoning flames, the last caravan member able to enter the valley.

The fiery bundles sired alarm and panic. Frightened animals stomped over terrified trekkers as they bumped and bashed into each other, scattering from the blaze. The soldiers deployed haphazardly, straining to get a view of the enemy, cursing and shouting while attempting to establish some defensive response.

Silent bandits scampered unobserved into the valley floor. They pounced upon the forward archers, their backs exposed, their attention fixated on the malevolent fire. It was Mithrias who let out the initial sound of alarm.

"Bandits! They're here! Bandits!"

Shaggy men swarmed over the first victims. For one archer, Mithrias's warning was too late. Already, an assailant was pulling him backward off his feet, a cord around his neck.

The attackers were a ragged bunch, most dressed in animal skins. They were thin, dirty, bearded, and desperate. Most brandished knives. Topur pawed fruitlessly for his dagger. A hairy man pounced in front of him, knife in hand. Topur's immediate defense was to swing the staff he'd converted to a crutch. The bandit jumped back—air. Topur swung again. He struck the bandit's shoulder, but the blow was feeble. This staff was an impotent offensive weapon.

The proximity of the assailants rendered bows and arrows useless. Those being attacked resorted to knives in hand-to-hand combat. Several bandits broke off, running toward those trekkers closer to the fire, while even more bandits emerged into the valley. Topur screamed, "Bandits! Attack!"

A lone bandit pounced in front of Mithrias. The attacker clutched a long knife in one hand while waving a pathetically short chain in the other. Mithrias lunged to his left as if to attack, then sprang away to his right. The bandit wobbled. Immediately, Mithrias's knife blade pierced his lower back. The robber fell forward, thrusting his hands outward, releasing his knife. Grimacing, he lay unmoving but alive. Mithrias bent down, grabbed the blade, and stuffed it inside his robe.

Topur's attacker was filthy, dressed in sheepskins, with a matted lion's mane of hair. His large buck teeth broke through his unkempt beard. His intense eyes were too open, too wide, making him look crazed and dangerous. He moved confidently, tossing his knife from hand to hand, laughing, making stabbing motions at Topur's belly. Topur wished to switch to his dagger, but the staff required both hands. He swung. Air.

The battles continued, punctuated by an occasional shriek of pain, a groan, a shouted instruction, or a plea for help. Every man was matched, each fighting for his own life. Topur's attacker rushed him again, a quick knife swipe through the air, then a retreat. He stared into Topur's eyes. Topur kept the blade within sight. The bandit could weave around all he wished, but his torso defined his limits. Topur advanced and swung his staff once more. *Whoosh.*

Mithrias's knife had found the stomach of another robber, leaving him curled and lifeless on the valley floor. Beside the raider was Xaratuk's archer, the first man to be attacked. His eyes were open, vacant, his hands still clutching the cord around his neck. Mithrias's gaze shot to the fire, hoping to glimpse Salnassar. He spotted the purple tunic. Salnassar had stumbled off his horse and was wrestling an attacker. Some deep parental instinct erupted, compelling Mithrias to come to his son's rescue.

Free from imminent attack, Mithrias reached for the bow from the fallen archer. He grabbed three arrows from the quiver. He ran fifteen swift paces to get within range. Salnassar was still locking arms, grappling with his foe, upholding a stalemate. Mithrias halted, nocking the arrow onto the bowstring. He stood, feet perpendicular to the target, glancing to each side to evaluate any threats. None. He moved the bow up, pulling back the bowstring. He sighted his target and raised the arrow to it. He was breathing too hard, too quickly. He couldn't fix his aim and drew a deep, calming breath. "Hold him off as long as you can, Salnassar." He aimed. The sides of the fighters were exposed, limiting the shot. Then, they pivoted, revealing the attacker's entire back. Mithrias relaxed the fingers of his string hand. The arrow flew. Simultaneously, the fighters turned again. Mithrias froze as the arrow sped beyond any control toward his son. He breathed a sigh of relief as it zipped silently, impotently, past the fighters.

Salnassar saw the arrow pass. His assailant did not. Retracing the arrow's path, Salnassar recognized his father already aiming another arrow in his direction. He struggled to maneuver his attacker. The wait wasn't long. Once he had the bandit positioned, Salnassar looked up. The arrow was already on its way.

The bandit cringed, then screamed. The arrow pierced his back, going through his spine, below the ribs. He reached behind but fell immediately to the sand, his legs no longer responsive. Salnassar stared dumbfounded as the man, still screaming, wriggled his shoulders, trying to find some way to remove the arrow. Salnassar grabbed his knife. He hesitated, checking for anyone nearby. There was only his father, now running toward him. Acting only on impulse, Salnassar bent down and ran his blade under the fallen robber's ear, through his bearded throat, then to the other ear. There were no sounds of protest, only the coughing and gurgling of a dying man as his warm, thick blood poured onto Salnassar's hands.

Staggering backward on tentative, shaky legs, Salnassar murmured, "So this is what it's like." He dropped his bloody knife to the ground and ran with no more sense of purpose than the sheep he nearly stumbled over.

The brassy blare of trumpets, in unison with ram horns, blared from the canyon rim. Shaken, some skirmishers broke from their combat. The trumpet chorus sounded again. Topur's attacker remained oblivious while continuing to poke at Topur, trying to unfold some weakness.

The trumpets sounded a third time, followed by a verbal command. A clear voice shouted, "In the name of the Great King Herod, King of Judaea, all fighting shall cease!" The order came again in another tongue, then another, until it had been issued in four separate languages. For the bandits, despite their confusion, this was their last opportunity. The skirmishing began anew.

Topur's robber had one strategy: thrust and retreat, attempting to throw Topur off-balance. Had either man been able to look to the canyon's rim, he would have seen a ribbon of soldiers standing flush to the wall's top edge as far as the valley stretched. The trumpets sounded once more. The commands were shouted again. The fighting continued.

From above, there came the sound of a man screaming, pleading. Shrieks imploring for mercy reverberated through the canyon, bringing the fighting to a halt. Attention was drawn to the canyon's flat rim. Along the precipice stood four burly soldiers facing each other from four corners. Each soldier held a limb of a shabby, begrimed, squealing man, begging them for his life. His flailing and wriggling did not loosen the grip of his tormentors. An order was shouted. The four soldiers began to swing their victim back and forth. Once. Twice. With every rocking, the bandit's pleas rose in pitch: "No! NOOO! NOOOOO!"

At the end of the third swing, they released the bedraggled vagabond. The man plummeted, grasping and clawing. The thud of impact on the canyon floor silenced his screaming. His torso heaped unnaturally upon his head and shoulders. Most skirmishers from both sides ceased their struggle. The soldiers at the canyon rim were serious.

The trumpets heralded a shorter order. "Drop your weapons and cease all movement." Knives, short swords, daggers, chains, and spears made metallic clanks as they hit the rocky sand.

One threadbare fighter used this distraction to thrust his knife toward Topur, who had just enough time to use his staff to deflect the strike. The attacker now grabbed the rod. They struggled, each trying to knock the other off-balance.

"Stop!" pleaded Topur. "They told us to stop!"

The bandit continued to wrestle. Topur fought to maintain a stalemate.

"They want us to stop—so stop!" Topur ordered. "Leave me!" The attacker gripped the staff, using his leverage to move Topur to his right. Topur felt the snap in his injured ankle. His leg gave way. He released the staff, shuffling to regain his balance. The attacker rushed, finally able to place his blade on Topur's chest, aiming for the heart. Topur tried to push away, but the blade had pierced Topur's garments and found skin. Topur felt the point upon his sternum. It stiffened his defenses, but his weakened ankle abandoned him. The blade sliced through his skin as it moved across his chest.

Then it stopped.

A high-pitched *thwiiiingggg* was followed by a sharp thump, sounding like a fist pounding into a piece of meat. The attacker's body stiffened. Nose-to-nose with Topur, the man's eyes grew wide, his eyebrows arched, and his mouth formed a taut circle. He screamed into Topur's face. The arrow's fletching was visible above the attacker's shoulder blade.

Topur fell limp, his weight pressing upon the bandit,

foolishly relying on his attacker for support. The bandit made one last thrust, moving the blade farther across Topur's chest, running it over his ribs, then coming free above his hip. Topur howled. The bandit freed himself from Topur's grip and turned, looking accusingly in the direction of the shot. Topur wobbled, clutching his side.

He heard the *vvvviiiiimmm* of another arrow. *Thwak.* It hit the attacker at the base of his neck. He let out a gurgle and fell to his knees. The arrow in his neck held firm, forcing the slumping body to fall to the side. Topur found the strength to stagger away.

The blast of the trumpets came again. "Drop your weapons and cease all movement!"

Najiir had scrambled back, holding Topur as he screamed in pain, struggling to keep them both upright.

"Master!" he screamed. "Master, you are hurt!" Topur fell to his knees, bringing the boy with him. Najiir clambered to Topur's back, his bloody arms supporting Topur's shoulders, trying to prevent him from dropping to the sand. Topur shrieked. Najiir released him. Together, they fell forward, face first, into the sand. Najiir heard the arrow cross inches above his head, then lodge into the sand just behind them.

The call went out, "Drop your arms and cease all movement." This time, all movement ceased—entirely.

The commands of the horns and trumpets were replaced by the entreaties of the wounded. Those unharmed from both sides waited for what would come next. Soldiers from the canyon rim repelled down craggy walls. The fires at the valley's entrance ebbed.

Najiir bent closer to Topur, who remained face down in the sand. Blood oozed past Topur's garments, pooling on gritty sand. Crying, Najiir stroked his master's head. "Don't die! Don't die!" he wailed. "Kings!" he called. "You must live!" Louder. "Kings! Here! Help us! Kings! Help us, please!"

Unable to lift his head, through lips flecked with grit, Topur called to Najiir. Najiir bent down, his nose beside Topur's, flush with the sand. Topur gave his instruction: "Tell them to say nothing," he said. "Tell the kings... to say nothing... Herod won't...." His world went dark.

CHAPTER 13

They were on their way to Jerusalem.

Bandits and trekkers were herded into one undistinguished mass. Rough and impatient soldiers culled criminal from star chaser. The robbers from the canyon floor, and their supporters on the canyon rim, were chained together at sword point to begin the slow, forced march. Heads bowed, they uttered no sounds of protest. Six were already dead. Two others, including Mithrias's original attacker, were wounded. Herod's soldiers executed them on the spot. The dead were left to rot on the valley floor as a sacrifice to the repugnant whims of nature, to be consumed by the wild and uncivilized and be defecated three days hence. Their sun-bleached bones would serve as a silent testimony of their unworthiness, a last rite of disrespect, the pinnacle of indignities.

The bandits who survived may have wished they had not. Four women and seven children were among the mix of those taken captive. Their fate, probably slavery, would be deemed more lenient than what lay in store for their adult male counterparts. Like bandits found there or elsewhere, those men would be bound over to the Roman authorities.

Banditry had been on the rise. The Temple was nearly finished, creating a surge of insolvent and unemployed workers and their dependent families. In concert with the High Priest and his cronies, Romans seized prized land for themselves, displacing entire families, if not entire neighborhoods. The numbers of those with no home and no prospects had swelled uncontrollably. Those reduced to robbery were no longer a motley collection of a few irredeemable outcasts. The avocation had evolved. Bands had become more numerous, more organized, better led, and more adept.

In response, the Romans became more intolerant. Banditry was deemed a scurrilous affront to good order. This was a capital offense. Those caught could expect to be crucified, a punishment—despite its frequent implementation—even the Romans believed broke the barrier of decency. They saved such grim treatment for slaves and the most despised criminals, providing a clear and harsh lesson for the native population should they consider challenging Rome's most perfect order. Perhaps understanding this kept Topur's attacker on his obsessive offensive.

The fires at the valley entrance were smothered, and the ox carts righted. The divided caravan was unified once again, now escorted by an armed detachment of King Herod of Judaea's army. Their new destination was the palace of King Herod the Great.

"I am quite distressed there was no prior announcement about your visit to my country." Herod's tone was stern, denouncing. His stare was both accusing and suspicious. With only slightly greater gentility, he added, "I could have prepared a much better reception, one worthy of such noble guests." A bony finger emanated from his sleeve, directing them to three tall, stately chairs nearby. "Please be seated so that I may talk with you."

Herod took the short, uncertain steps of an aged man as he shuffled behind, flanked by an attendant at either elbow. His watery eyes were yellowed and dull and sat upon large puffy bags of dark skin. The remnants of earlier meals stained his royal robes. His long, mostly gray beard harbored crumbs, seeds, and other indistigushables.

Groaning, Herod slumped into the middle chair. His aides stood behind on either side, at silent attention. He motioned for his guests to be seated.

Herod turned to Xaratuk, blinking his moist, red-rimmed eyes. His breath smelled like day-old fish. "'Xaratuk: King of a Hundred Cities,' they say. I must tell you this: Even I am a bit awestruck to be in the company of one as powerful as yourself."

Xaratuk managed a nod.

"It comes as a complete surprise that I would find someone like you here in Judaea." Herod patted Xaratuk's knee, as a grandfather might do to his grandson. It was disrespectful to touch a king without invitation, though Xaratuk's instinctive flinch went gratefully unnoticed.

Herod's faint, insincere smile reappeared. He turned to Mithrias. "And you, King Mithrias. Your beautiful capital gave birth to the word 'paradise.' Your people have a long and glorious history that you take great care to honor and protect. And now here you are, both of you, with me." He paused, artfully concealing any genuine feeling.

"But no prior word of your arrival. I find you, instead, amid those awful bandits. They could have finished you. They are awful men, desperate men, animals, really, the way they live. I send my men out there every few months, and we find another troop of brutes every time. By next week, those wretches will be replaced by others just like them." He looked from one king to the other. "I should have been informed. I could have taken such delight in welcoming you in a way befitting your exalted status, but you sneak in and look at what happens—attacked by outlaws. Not fitting."

"We are eternally in your debt, Great King," said Mithrias.

"Yes," added Xaratuk, speaking like a man unaccustomed to subservience. "We are...grateful."

"A thousand thanks," offered Mithrias. "We are humbled when we see the glory and grandeur of this most Holy City. I had heard of its beauty, and in my opinion, those words were insufficient." Convincingly, he added, "Its majesty is without equal. I should know. As you say, my capital is also beautiful, but this is splendor. Mere words cannot express its overwhelming appeal."

Xaratuk followed. "Yes, I may have many cities in my realm, but none can compare. Jerusalem has become a jewel."

"You are both so kind to say these things," said Herod, his wry smile revealing a jumble of yellowed teeth. "If I fail to make myself clear, I will say it once more: I am genuinely happy to have your company here today. But you have seen so little of my city. I hope you can stay as my guests much longer. The Roman governor would wish to see you, too, but he has traveled to Antioch on business. He isn't planning to be in Jerusalem for some time. Knowing it was you, he might—"

"At this point in our journey, it is best we skip any visit with the governor," Xaratuk interrupted. "In fact, we would prefer no Roman be aware of our presence here. We desire to remain anonymous to the Romans and be on our way as quickly as possible."

"Oh," responded Herod, clearly surprised. "No mention to the Romans? I see." He shifted forward. "You make this sound so secretive, so furtive. Though we have our differences, my Roman friends have supported me, and they assume they can also count on me to support them. My guests, we must understand each other. Is your presence here a challenge?"

"No, nothing whatsoever of that," Xaratuk stammered. "Though—"

"Nothing. Nothing remotely like that," Mithrias added, stifling Xaratuk's maneuver.

Herod paused, collecting his thoughts. His diction was soft but stern. "It is important for you to be truthful with me—both of you. I have sacrificed much to achieve what you see in my city. To accomplish great things, I have made friends whom others in Jerusalem view as enemies. It's good to have friends, my fellow kings. It's good to have friends."

"Yes, King Herod, it is good to have friends," said Xaratuk. "However, those I count among my friends are not those Rome would count among theirs. It is simply this...as you know, Rome has clashed with kingdoms friendly to mine. No one should have to explain their allegiances or past actions—not at this time. That is not our purpose here. We prefer to go on, as tiny and insubstantial as we are, posing no threat to you or the Romans."

"Well, it may already be too late." Herod turned to his assistants. "Have we mentioned this incident to the Roman authorities?"

The aide to Herod's right answered, "Yes, prisoners were taken to Fortress Antonia for questioning and deliberation."

"I see," said Herod. "And was any mention made of our guests?"

"There was not, Great King. Since we could not confirm their identities, we did not say. The Roman guards were content to take charge of the prisoners we brought."

"And the rest of the caravan? Where is it?"

"Under our escort, we assembled the rest outside the city walls. They are camped on the southwest side, where many visitors to our city stay."

"Did any of the Roman Guard ask about them?"

"No, my king. To them, our guests are merely travelers, like many others who come to our city."

Herod turned back to his guests. "Well, it seems we've protected this secret so far, though I think you overestimate the vengeful inclinations of my Roman associates." There was an agonizing pause. "But I will not press you to change your minds. Before I grant this, though, I require you to answer two things. First, tell me about whom I have in my palace so that I may feel more comfortable. Tell me the identity of the wounded man brought to us. Who is he? Is he a king, too? My soldiers report someone yelling 'king' around this man. Is there another king with me?"

"No," snapped Xaratuk. "He's—"

"He is no king, Your Excellency," Mithrias broke in. "He is a trader, a merchant we invited to help translate. He acts as a guide, too. We hoped he could help us avoid the circumstances that befell us. He is a recent associate, nothing more, and I cannot explain why anyone would confuse him as a king."

"My soldiers tell me he is a Jew." Herod's voice was devoid of friendliness.

Mithrias bit his cheek. His mind raced, calculating the consequences of harboring a Jewish man mistaken for a king in their midst. His arms strained. Hesitatingly, he spoke again. "That is true, but again, he's no king."

"Is he from around here?" asked Herod.

"No, we found him much farther north," said Mithrias.

"A guide?" Herod hissed. "He must not be from here because nearly everyone knows to avoid that wretched canyon. A worthwhile guide would never have sent you through it. Well, he is being cared for, whoever he is, in the palace ward I reserve for the sick and injured. I personally arranged that. I saw him. A terrible wound. Those bandits were Jews. Jews attacking other Jews. There is too much of that." Herod shook his head. "Not a king. Why the confusion? Why do my men report others calling him king?"

Mithrias burped out a nervous laugh while Xaratuk inhaled sharply, equally confused.

"In all the turmoil," Mithrias began, "I am sure many things were said—some of which were misunderstood. I was standing near the man, and perhaps comments were directed at me. It was a very tense moment."

"I was wondering what Jew was being called a king." Herod launched a piscine belch without remorse. "He has the absolute best of care, in any case. Once he improves, I will have a long talk with him." Herod turned to Xaratuk. "As for the second thing—"

"Dear King Herod," Xaratuk interrupted. "We will forever be in your debt for coming to our assistance. Though we were prepared for such an event, those bandits had us at a momentary disadvantage. Your troops' arrival hastened and secured the defeat of our attackers. And beyond that, I add my appreciation for your tolerance and hospitality. I am honest enough to concede you could choose to do otherwise. Again, I offer you my gratitude from one king to another. I must impress upon you that our presence in your kingdom was unexpected, even to us. We do not imply any challenge to either your dominion or that of the Romans. Had we been unchallenged, you would not have witnessed any consequences of our footprints on your land."

"How well-spoken, King Xaratuk." Herod struggled to get to his feet. "It is words—honest words—which bond me to men. I am sure to like you better. Our kingdoms will enjoy the fruits of our warming friendship. But, I must clear my mind about this. I wish to address the second item. What brought you to, or as you are saying, through my Jerusalem? Why have you come to my kingdom?"

Najiir had dutifully reported Topur's admonishment to both kings: they were not to disclose the true purpose of their trek to Herod. But they had to say something. Adherence to Topur's directive would only invite more suspicion.

Xaratuk began to stammer, but Mithrias interrupted. "If I may, kind King. We never intended to be in Jerusalem. Are you interested in the long explanation?"

"I'll take any explanation." Herod sat. "Go on."

"Recently, I endured a great tragedy within my family, having lost my eldest son, the heir to my kingdom, in a shipwreck. I admit I was utterly devastated. I needed to be away from the darkness that stalked me, so I thought it best to travel, to be removed from my gloomy palace. I left to visit my friend, King Xaratuk. When I arrived, I found him preoccupied and excited about an unusual celestial event. There was this unexpected and persistent star in the heavens every night. I had seen it, but it meant little to me. King Xaratuk's close advisors, men who are deeply knowledgeable about such events, suggested—no, more accurately, demanded—he explore this. It is a harbinger of great importance, they declared.

"When I came upon King Xaratuk, he was nearly finished with his preparations. He suggested I come with them." Mithrias's eyes locked upon Herod. "This is important: none of us knew where we were headed. Not even the advisors. We would follow the star's light wherever it took us. It might guide us to Damascus, or Tyre, or Sidon, or even Crete—we did not know. But if it emerges again tonight, the star's light will shine down near Jerusalem. And that, Your Excellency, is why you find us here, with you, today."

Herod patted Mithrias's hand with his frail fingers. He chuckled. "A star! You are challenging the high esteem I had for you both." His watery gaze moved to Xaratuk. "This is true? That is the most unusual story I have ever heard. A man of your position chasing nothing more than a star."

"It is true," said Xaratuk. "All King Mithrias tells you is true. He left out one detail. Once underway, a messenger came to tell us his grieving wife, a noble woman whom he loved dearly, in her anguish, had killed herself after he departed his palace."

Herod stiffened. He turned back to Mithrias, again patting his hand. "My dear, dear man, I feel your pain. This is a sad, sad journey for you, King Mithrias. I, too, have known great love only to have lost it. I grieve to this day."

His face lost all expression, as if consumed by a trance. After an unusually long pause, Xaratuk spoke, "King Herod?"

Herod's composure was tenuous. "I am sorry." He shook his head. "So, what are you expecting to find, my new friends? Perhaps I've seen a bright star. I assume it is the one of which you speak. I see many stars, though."

"We're not entirely certain," responded Mithrias. "That is why we brought two advisors from King Xaratuk's court. They are very learned and very thoughtful. To them, we will leave the task of determining the meaning." He leaned toward Herod, speaking softly. "It has eased my mind to be absorbed in something beyond my grief. Involvement in this trek has been an enormous undertaking and a helpful distraction. That effort is even more rewarding now that we unexpectedly encountered Jerusalem and are the objects of your most gracious hospitality."

Herod scanned Mithrias with a critical eye, followed by a tiny smile. "I am happy that you are finding comfort. Building the Temple helped distract me from my grief." He simultaneously patted both men on the knee. "I am most happy you are here. I will not say a word of this to the Romans."

He stood. "I would like to continue our discussions. You have much more to tell me. You will stay with me in the palace. I will have your rooms prepared. Change out of your traveling clothes in the room next door. You are free to go throughout the palace." Any hint of warmth was absent. "We will dine tonight. You will be my guests."

CHAPTER 14

"I don't understand why our guide was so insistent," said Xaratuk.

"Insistent?" murmured Mithrias without further comment. His focus was elsewhere. He stood with Xaratuk atop the highest level of the Phasael Tower, the tallest of the three ornate towers at the north end of Herod's elaborate palace. The massive three-tiered structure provided the ideal location for viewing the entirety of the holiest city in the empire while distancing the kings from any Roman soldier. Through the crenellations, the kings were free to admire the architecture of a city actively, anxiously merging centuries of religious fervor and tradition with the technology and tastes of a new but foreign influence.

"I'm sorry," Mithrias finally mumbled, still captivated by the view. "Insistent? About not revealing the details of our journey?"

"Oh, that too, I suppose," said Xaratuk. "I was wondering why he was so insistent we avoid Jerusalem. The Romans—I understand that. But with little effort, we have found a way around them. Why would it be so unfortunate to meet Herod? The king is old, disheveled maybe, but he hardly seems the unpredictable madman our guide described."

Xaratuk inched closer along the tower wall, brushing alongside Mithrias. Mithrias gave no response, his eyes, wide as plates, fixed upon the complex wonder of Jerusalem at dusk. "I should have hated to miss this," Xaratuk whispered.

The two men stood for minutes, admiring Herod's many ambitious projects: the three-story theater to the southeast, the Greek-influenced amphitheater, and a Roman-inspired hippodrome near the city's center. The aqueduct and the massive, hulking Antonia Fortress lurked in functional contrast. "It is beautiful," said Mithrias.

Also magnificent was the immense palace Herod built for himself, wherein they stood, pampered, and, they hoped, protected. Both kings were accustomed to luxury, but this was splendor. Three-story, tiered atria housing spacious apartments anchored the opposite ends, attached by a courtyard paved with large gray and white tiles set in dazzling geometric patterns. Water fountains, thoughtfully dispersed, provided bubbly, immoderate refreshment in defiance of the arid climate's natural decree. As they followed their escort, the kings strolled through vine-covered arches, around flower gardens, and past potted palm trees providing cool comfort.

During their climb up the interior of the Phasael Tower, the kings had fallen to clandestine peering, snooping inside the lavish living quarters lining the main stairway. Upon reaching the tower's upper platform, they observed the nearby Hippicus Tower and the Mariamne Tower. With its three tiers of Greek columns gracefully stacked one atop the other, the Mariamne Tower was the loveliest. In the tower named for the wife he so passionately loved—and murdered—Herod spent most of his time while residing in Jerusalem.

"And you agree with me, then?" Xaratuk's question broke another long silence. "It would have been unpardonable to have bypassed this."

Mithrias refused to give a direct answer. "Our current circumstance is better than we deserve. Were it the Romans who found us in that canyon..." His voice trailed. His focus on the Temple overwhelmed him. "Undeniable grandeur. Enormous and bold, yet inviting. The Jews have transformed a solid mountain of pure snow into their Temple."

"The Temple is far larger than I had imagined," Xaratuk said. "I assumed it was small—attractive but unsubstantial, a decorative affair, available for rituals and holidays. But this is utterly enormous. Those within the courtyards are rendered tiny, even insignificant."

"Those doors," Mithrias said, noting the gigantic entry to the Holy of Holies. "So heavy. Surely, no one man can open them by himself. And those columns—have the Greeks made any taller than these? The awesome, pure white of the walls—I am overwhelmed."

"It is a remarkable achievement. What a show! The gold band along the top must be as tall as I! It fits like a crown. The setting sun makes it shimmer—like liquid."

Xaratuk looked over at the blunt, unimaginative Antonia Fortress, then back to the Temple. "I think Herod is bragging. This Temple boasts of its grandeur. It knows it is supreme. Herod is saying, 'This elegant Temple is ours.'" He pointed to the Fortress. "'You Romans can have that.'" He chuckled.

The setting sun's rays reflected upon the resolute marble of the Temple. Fickle hues of pale yellow, deep orange, or livid pink flickered across the otherwise serene white Temple walls. Though twilight approached, hundreds of people milled restlessly, most within the vast Court of the Gentiles.

The sacrificial altars were tirelessly aflame, sending urgent, pious entreaties in the guise of acrid smoke upward into the holy ether. The smell of the roasted flesh of sheep, goats, birds, and other creatures mixed with the stench of burned hair, blood, hide, and feathers. Even at this distance, the din of the beseechers, combined with the cries of outraged animals, composed an unsettling score.

To the north, beyond the city walls, barely visible, twenty Roman soldiers tended to large wooden crosses. Neither king sought to mention them.

"Jews are serious about their worship. That is obvious,"

said Mithrias.

"But why here, Mithrias? I mean, there is no ocean, no river, no prosperous land nearby. It is not a particularly defensible location. Why all this glory here?"

"It is a city built upon beliefs, Xaratuk—firm beliefs, absolute beliefs that go beyond economy, or warfare, or productivity. The beliefs are about the traditional and the eternal, about who they are, and who God is. And the Jews believe God is here, within those strong, beautiful white walls. It is a city that exists to show the devotion of a people to their God, and I don't believe there is another like it anywhere."

"It sounds as if you have been talking to that merchant," said Xaratuk. "You seem to know something about these people. They remain peculiar to me. They have strange ideas. All those codes and laws and rituals. And one God—their God—who dwells here? Yes, quite strange."

In the waning light, the Temple looked softer and more resplendent. "The sacrifices," said Mithrias. "So many. Constant appeals to a God, inside a temple, in their city. They have made him approachable, but can he truly be there?"

"I am much more comfortable with my advisors. They tell me all I need to know about the gods."

"All this beauty, and for what? What do all these people pray for—what do they wish?" said Mithrias, turning solemn. He moved to the very edge of the wall, arms outstretched. "Do they pray for their own needs, their own happiness? Are they seeking comfort or atoning for some guilt? Do they pray for their family, their country, or their people? What do they see or hear in return?" Mithrias's tone turned bitter. "The Romans swarm like rats throughout their city. Such a beautiful Temple, but nothing lives there." He pounded the tower wall. "Nothing! No one!"

"Mithrias!" Xaratuk stepped to the wall, placing his hand on Mithrias's back. "This isn't like you. Why are you so bothered? They're Jews. They're different. You're not one of them. What matter is it to you if the Jews believe their God is in that Temple?"

"Because no god lives, Xaratuk—no god—not anywhere. Since Deioces was taken, I've come to understand that." Mithrias moved to a corner of the tower amid the concealing shadows provided by diminishing daylight. "We did everything our priests asked of us. We prayed. We fasted. We sacrificed. We prayed again. That boat was worthy. The crew was seasoned. Doria blamed me, but I couldn't summon a murderous storm! Xaratuk, if there is a God, he is fickle. He is fickle and hard-hearted, undeserving of this tribute." Devoid of expression, Mithrias stared at the city. "Look at those Romans filling their streets. I don't see how our hosts can explain it differently. Either I am right, or their God is weak and has dominion over far less than they credit him." He folded his arms in a protective cross. "What do you pray for, Xaratuk?"

Xaratuk's face turned coy. He shook his head. "I don't pray. You know that. Oh, I pray when my people expect me to—at certain times of the year or during those festivals that demand it. I must show them I am reverent. I waste little time with this. These subjects are for Merkis." In a softer tone, he added, "I realize I haven't let you speak more about your son. I should have seen it still troubles you deeply. How strange that you arrive in this city built upon belief, yet you say you have lost yours. There is something here. As you said, being in Jerusalem compels one to dwell upon the eternal. It is what stirs the minds of people here. With that Temple so dominant, so commanding, so powerful, no one can go through the day without such thoughts."

In a half-hearted chuckle, he added, "I guess I have always been more focused on being able to handle what the gods throw at me, not at convincing them what to throw." Xaratuk waited to see if Mithrias was listening. "Still, I don't like seeing a man lose faith."

His quivering chin stifled Mithrias's attempt to smile.

Xaratuk continued. "Merkis and Khartir tell me the sky is just another parchment, but the gods write upon it themselves—or a single God, if you prefer, like our Jewish hosts. They say the stars and the moon can be read—if you understand the language." He looked away from Mithrias, up into the glimmering firmament. "But there is no teacher available to help them translate the heavens, is there? Still, my advisors do their best. They've always, always helped me, Mithrias. I have not waged a campaign, sealed a treaty, initiated an expedition, or picked a wife without first consulting and heeding their advice. Any big question or consideration I face, I seek to include them, and to this very day, they have not once let me down." A staccato effect emphasized the last few words. "Maybe they will help you as well. I hope so."

"I wonder." Mithrias closed his sad eyes. After a deep breath, he straightened. "They should be here. Merkis and Khartir should join us at dinner. I am sure they would find the man most interesting."

"We think alike," said Xaratuk. "I will ask Herod myself."

"So, the heavens can speak?" Mithrias sighed. "One just needs to interpret the message?"

"Something like that, yes," replied Xaratuk.

"I wish them luck because I see no purpose in any of this," said Mithrias, his voice quaking.

"Mithrias, your condition alarms me. You seem lost. I had hoped my company would provide a distraction, but, frankly, I've run out of things to say."

It had never occurred to Mithrias that Xaratuk's incessant talking might have been an attempt to soothe. "You are a good friend. My grief is burying me. I...I failed to recognize your concern. I don't want anyone to feel this, to feel as I do now. At times, it's as though I am drowning with my son. I used to meet life and its challenges with skill and confidence. All that is gone."

"Mithrias," Xaratuk said softly.

"I'm powerless to overcome it. I'm consumed with doubt.

How can I presume to lead others?" He slumped. "It seems the world was not created to conform to my happiness. Perhaps that is what I must accept."

Mithrias fell against the portico wall, propping himself against it. "No. No. That isn't correct. It's far, far more. The deaths of my wife and son affect so many. My entire country has been damaged, Xaratuk. The future—our future—was irredeemably harmed. So I ask God—any God! — what lesson am I to learn from that? There is none!" Mithrias stared at the Temple, anger flashing in his eyes. "Merkis and Khartir will find no message in the heavens for me."

CHAPTER 15

"**I**'m not dead."

Miriam dropped the linen strips she'd been folding. Behind her, the man lay motionless on the raised platform that spanned one side of her dimly lit, windowless room. Startled, she turned to her new patient.

"So, you can speak," she said, concealing her amazement. His return to consciousness came sooner than she'd predicted. She addressed him in Aramaic, following his lead. Picking up the fallen strips, she placed them next to an unfolded bundle on the nearby table. She resumed folding, pinching the linen, reconstructing a finished stack.

"What did you say?" she asked him.

Pain thinned Topur's voice. "I am not dead yet." He shifted slightly. A punishing spasm snapped through his torso like a burning whip. His shoulders fell back. His damp head throbbed. "I smell...the myrrh." He struggled to form his words. They came out slowly. "That is for the dead...and I am not dead yet."

"You can thank me for that. You were close to it when they brought you to me." Miriam swapped the moistened cloth on Topur's forehead with a fresh one. "I have arranged for death to visit you some other time." She gently peeled the bandaging she had dressed upon Topur's wound to peer underneath. "You are seriously hurt and need my help. That is a dreadful wound."

Topur tried to shift his weight, ushering in another burst of pain. "Oh, how it hurts! I am no warrior." He fell back. "I am not meant to endure these things."

"Don't get up. When you want to move, I will help you. Without me, you will suffer more."

Topur couldn't muster the will to open his eyes. "You are most kind." Feebly, he adjusted the damp cloth on his forehead. "Where am I, dear woman? Please tell me."

"You, Your Excellency, are in the palace of King Herod of Judaea."

Topur's eyes shot open.

Miriam continued. "And you are in one of my healing rooms within that palace. I am Miriam, and I have been healing the sick and injured for twenty-three years." She returned to her folding. "It is your good fortune they brought you to me rather than some priest who would only sacrifice a luckless lamb or two on your behalf. Whether it be a king like you or a peasant—no matter, I give the care required."

"Pleased...to meet you, Miriam," Topur sputtered, "but king? I am no king."

There was little Topur could do to assess his situation. If this was the palace, he could trust no one, not even someone who claimed to be saving his life. Miriam was likely just another of Herod's spies. If she was attached to the palace staff for as long as she declared, the conclusion was obvious.

"Well, I was told you might be. Some of Herod's soldiers thought so," Miriam said. "And there are others with you who seem particularly important. Our king has the entire palace staff scurrying. He doesn't do that for ordinary visitors. People are making inquiries of you, including King Herod."

Topur's slackened mind strove to comprehend his predicament. Everything pointed to the worst scenario possible. He had been filleted like a fish, rendering him helpless, fixed upon a stone slab in Jerusalem with Herod's eyes and interests upon him. What would Herod want from him? What could he say? And what were the kings saying? Was all the commotion a prelude to surrendering the kings? Would he die before or after their execution?

"As for the myrrh," Merriam continued, "that came from your belongings. A young boy helped bring your things. He said he's your servant."

"What?" Topur struggled to comprehend. "Oh. A boy? That would be Najiir. He is my...servant, yes. Is he here?"

"Oh my, no. King Herod allows only his staff to attend to his guests. Your boy is probably with the rest of your caravan outside the city walls. Everything of yours is in the next room. I used some of your myrrh for the salve on your wound." Miriam gently placed another pillow underneath Topur's neck. Her touch felt like warm, smooth glass as her hands moved about Topur's bare arms and shoulders. "I would have asked your permission to use it, but you were not very talkative at the time."

Through his scowl, Topur focused on her for the first time. She was Jewish. He could tell that, even in the dim light. A plain scarf covered her head. Her dark hair, falling past her shoulders, revealed small streaks of gray. Her hands were thin, but her face was soft with few wrinkles. "You lost a great deal of blood," she went on. "That's stopped now. Your myrrh will help the healing."

She moved back to the table, attending to the columns of linens and bandages. "That, and I am very zealous about keeping things clean. No Temple priest is stricter about cleanliness than I am. Clean water, clean linens, and clean wrappings. I washed you before putting on your bandage. You will heal sooner this way. You'll see." Again, she replaced the cool cloth on his forehead. "There is no more blood soaking through your dressings. Any stain is from the salve."

Topur was content to believe her. "The others in my group, they are here, too?"

"Some of them, yes," Miriam confirmed. "My friends inside the palace tell me they have seen two other kings with Herod. Does that sound right? King Herod has prepared rooms for them and will host a dinner in their honor tonight. He is lavishing attention upon your friends as if they were senators. Are you sure you are not a king? You must be important, but you're a Jew."

"You can tell?"

"I can."

Topur wanted to chuckle, but the pain was too great. Miriam went on. "I hear bandits did this to you."

"You seem to know a great deal."

"I know everything that happens around here, Your Excellency." Miriam's tone turned serious. "I have contacts. We talk. I need not say more, just that I have trusted friends throughout the palace and Jerusalem." She stood before him once more. A thin, reassuring smile replaced her previously somber expression. Her dark eyes softened. "Your bandit sliced you open, but not deeply. I don't see that he got to your liver, or kidneys, or lungs. That is good."

Topur wondered how this person, a woman, could converse about lungs and livers. "He was aiming for my heart. He would have reached it had an arrow not sunk into his back."

"God's will," said Miriam.

"God's will," Topur affirmed. "I am so tired."

"You need to rest. I will wake you to change your dressings. You won't like me very much for it, but I must keep you clean."

Her slave, a skinny young Bithynian boy, had returned, knocking first. Stepping barely into the room, he asked Miriam if she needed more supplies.

"More linens, Kauib—the new ones," she replied. "And more water, but make sure they have boiled it first. And bring me more pillows. Here, take these. Burn them." She handed Kauib one pillow and some soiled wrappings. "Wash your hands after you burn those," she added. Kauib grasped the items between protesting fingertips, holding them at arm's length. He sped away.

Several quiet minutes passed. Topur's torment kept him

restless.

"Do you need me to move you?" she asked.

"I don't think so," Topur responded. "I ache." He tried moving his legs. "I want to fall asleep. I can't. My head keeps buzzing."

Miriam stepped to the corner of the room and poured from a pitcher into a small cup. "Here, then. This wine helps with sleep." She helped Topur raise his head.

Doubt about her and doubt about this drink mingled with his agony. Reluctantly, he sipped.

"Best to drink it all," Miriam said. After two more sips, he emptied the cup. Miriam gently laid him back and adjusted the pillows. Topur closed his eyes and delicately shuffled into a new position.

"You're not a king, then?" asked Miriam.

Topur sensed he was being quizzed. "No, not a king."

"A trader, then? A merchant?"

Topur remained quiet. Though this woman was helpful, this questioning assured him she was a spy for the palace.

Miriam pressed on. "But that can't be. Your group has almost nothing to trade. Robes, blankets, some rugs; a few precious stones; some glass; a bit of frankincense. Oh, and several trunks of manuscripts. How odd." She paused. "Not enough to build a trading caravan, it seems to me."

Any rest would be elusive so long as Topur assumed his healer was also his interrogator. He hurt. He just wanted to fall asleep.

"You're here for the star, aren't you?"

It was as if a ram's horn blared next to his ear. Topur's eyes snapped open. He was, despite the wine, very much awake. No more doubt; she was a spy.

"Star? I don't know what you are talking about."

"Oh, don't be so protective, Your Excellency. Like I say, word of this has reached only a select few of us."

"Again, I am no king. I have told you that. And I know

nothing about any star."

"Well, why would others call you that if you're not a king? What else should I call you? How should I know who you are? Maybe you will tell me?"

"I will be out of your way as soon as I am able, but in the meantime, there is not much more to tell," he said, certain this woman would try to procure any evidence she could to condemn him, even using spiked wine to loosen his tongue.

Miriam placed a stool next to him, then sat. "Your name is Topur."

The hair on his neck stiffened. "Are you some kind of sorceress or a very persistent spy?"

"Neither sorceress nor spy," she said. "Just a woman with good hearing and well-placed friends."

"Well, if you are not a spy, please keep this to yourself. I beg you."

"The chance to keep this to myself has gone, Topur. Others already know your identity. Some soldiers among those sent out to help also told me you and your party are following the star."

"Sent...sent out to help? What do you mean? They knew of us?"

"Yes, evidently. Someone in your group must have alerted Herod's men before you walked into the canyon. Our king has spies everywhere, Topur. Word reached someone that your caravan was headed to that canyon. It's nothing but trouble out there lately. So sad, but times are so desperate. Fortunately for you, King Herod's men were nearby."

"Then Herod intends to hold us? We are his prisoners?"

"No. He's done nothing to make me suspect that. I wouldn't worry too much about our king. Herod doesn't need to know everything."

This struck Topur as a curious thing to say.

Miriam rose, stepping to the active stone hearth at the end of the room. A small, steaming pot dangling from a tripod frame hovered above a compact fire. She let the used cup fall into the hot water. "Herod is not a well man. He doesn't make good decisions."

"When did you first notice that?" said Topur. "That particular problem has plagued him most of his life."

"Since our dear Mariamne..." Miriam halted. "Never mind. You seem worried. I can keep you concealed. After twenty-three years in the palace, I can tell friend from enemy." She returned to Topur's side. "By the time you arrived here, several soldiers already knew your group was following the star, but they've kept it a secret from those who don't need to know. If King Herod hears the star is the basis of your journey, your friends will have told him so."

"This is awful. It wasn't supposed to be this way at all." Topur worked to catch each breath. "I had tried to avoid Herod's notice completely. I had convinced the others it was better to remain unknown and unseen."

"It's evident you were trying to avoid Jerusalem. You lost that gamble." Miriam put her hand within Topur's. "Herod is extremely impressed by the fame and power of those kings. He must want more information, specifically what brought them to Judaea. Otherwise, all of you would be just as dead as those bandits left in the canyon. Somehow, he was convinced your group is not a threat—not yet." She stood up and walked back to the hearth. "Your kings must sustain that impression. Your group isn't set up to look like traders. Herod can tell that. To claim they are following a star might make this sound like a pleasure trip. Probably, that is better. I hope they can explain all those soldiers."

"Oh yes, soldiers!" Topur squeezed the bridge of his nose. "Have the Romans seen them? Has the prefect been alerted?"

"The Romans? Why, no, I don't believe so. There's been some strain lately. Neither Herod nor the Romans seek the other out. Unless your kings alarm him, it isn't likely that Herod will want to share the attention. For now, he'll prefer to keep your friends to himself."

"No Romans," Topur muttered. "Please, God, no Romans."

Miriam looked quizzically at him. Kauib returned with the supplies Miriam had requested. She examined the stack of linens. "Are you sure they boiled the water first, Kauib?"

"Yes, I told the cooks you'd be angry if they were not truthful. They don't like to see you angry."

"You did well. You are a good boy." She touched his cheek, though he moved slightly to avoid it. "Don't be so fearful. We have spoken about this. Thank you. Check back with me later." Then, in a whisper, she added, "Is someone posted outside the room?"

"No. No one at all until the Greek rooms," Kauib whispered back. "You are welcome, and I will be back later." Kauib smiled. Miriam patted his cheek again and sent the boy on his way.

Topur cautiously asked, "Are we being watched?"

"No, I can assure you we are not."

"I wish I shared your confidence."

"No one chooses to come back to these last few rooms of mine."

"What? Why?"

"These are the leper rooms. I treat them here. The last ones were here in this room about three weeks ago, and I—"

"Lepers?" Topur struggled to get up but fell back in pain.

"No need to panic. You are fine." She patted Topur's hand. "I knew I could help them. They were in the early stages. I have helped maybe a hundred in my lifetime already. I can't cure them—no one can—but I can prevent it from getting worse."

Topur was not convinced.

"Because I treat lepers," she continued. "No one in the palace will come back here. They are too afraid. I like that. Only Kauib, bless his heart, will come within forty paces of this room. Normally, Herod gets a spy within range of any visitor, but no one has the nerve to come to these rooms."

"Quite understandable!" said Topur with what vigor he

could muster.

"I tell you, Topur, it is all right. You need not worry. I purify myself and my rooms every day—more than once—and not with chants and charms. Since I was a young girl, I have healed all manner of injury and sickness—including lepers—and I am none the worse. If God wills I should become a leper, then it shall be, but I give him no cause." She tiptoed to the vase and brought a filled cup back to Topur. This time, he gulped the contents dry. "I thought you'd be more relaxed by now."

"I am terribly wounded, being held by King Herod, and receiving treatment in a room that housed lepers. Yes, I find it hard to relax."

"We are in the safest, most private room in the entire palace. That should put your mind at ease."

Topur snorted. "Just like my wife—instructing me on what I ought to think." His eyelids drooped. "And you know what, Miriam? Almost always, she is right."

"She sounds like a very smart woman." Miriam replaced the damp cloth on Topur's head and helped him lie back. "Maybe someday you'll introduce us."

Topur's head fell to one side. Finally, he was asleep.

"And I need to keep you alive for more reasons than that," she whispered over his still body. "At last. That family needs your help."

CHAPTER 16

Kauib steered Najiir along polished floors, through stony back hallways, and past cavernous, silent dining halls. He'd crafted their surreptitious route from his extensive knowledge of the palace and its bowels, a familiarity only an overlooked young slave could cultivate. Though much longer, this erratic path shielded them from any unwanted attention.

They'd met after palace guards caught Najiir attempting to sneak inside. He was unceremoniously dumped at the refuse pit where Kauib routinely took Miriam's spent bandages to be burned. Eager to connect with anyone from the palace, Najiir used his passable Latin, the language Kauib was most comfortable with, to endear himself to Miriam's young aide. They bonded over their shared circumstance: both young and both slaves. Najiir had stumbled upon the only person who could take him directly to Topur.

Kauib smuggled Najiir just short of the hallway leading to Miriam's rooms. He stopped, then peered around the edge, checking for guards. As expected, there were none. He signaled Najiir to follow as he crept up the torch-lit corridor to the final four doors. He brought his finger to his lips. They had already agreed that Najiir would not knock or request entrance. Miriam demanded no interference or interruptions during her healing. Kauib pointed to the last door. Najiir stepped in front of it, touching it gently, almost fondly.

"Thank you so very much, Kauib," he whispered. "I am

forever in your debt. You are a genuine friend."

"It is nothing. My Miss already knows about you. If she opens the door and finds you, she may allow you to see your master. But please, don't knock." Kauib looked up the hall once more, ensuring they were still alone. "Be sure to use the hallway on the left—as we talked about. It leads to the garbage pile. Yes, it is smelly, but no one goes there who doesn't have to, and it is never guarded. It's best to leave the palace from there. You must not get caught."

"And if they should catch me, I will swear I got here on my own."

"I believe you."

Najiir had pestered Kauib for any information about Topur but was unsatisfied with the lack of details. Kauib could only say the man inside was alive and heavily bandaged.

"I smell myrrh, don't I?" Najiir's nose tested the air. "That can't be good!" He began wringing his hands. "Oh, this has all gone so wrong. Until we went into the canyon, everything was fine. Now, I may never see my master again."

"I wouldn't worry about the myrrh. My Miss uses it for many things—not only to perfume the dead." Kauib looked nervously down the hall. "I must leave. They'll be looking for me soon. Good luck with your trip to Bethlehem."

"To where? To what?" Najiir turned back, hooking a finger around Kauib's arm, preventing him from leaving.

"Bethlehem?" said Kauib. "Isn't that where your caravan is going?"

"I think...so. The kings and their men discussed it before we reached the canyon. I have been so worried about my master that I forgot about Bethlehem. That name does sound familiar."

"Yes, Bethlehem. It isn't far."

"How did you find out we were headed there?"

"Everyone knows. It is where that star shines down. That is the place you are searching for, correct?"

"Yes?" answered Najiir tentatively. He hoped he wasn't

saying too much—again. He felt a pang of distrust. But Kauib had brought him to this doorway at great personal risk. "You know, I mean, you are certain the star shines on Bethlehem?"

"Oh, yes, I have been there—three times. Many from the palace sneak over to it when they are able." Kauib shot another glance down the hallway.

"You went? What did you see? What does the star shine upon?"

"It shines upon a poor house with a poor man, and a poor woman, and a poor baby."

It took Najiir a moment to absorb this. "And nothing more? Isn't there more than that, something more to tell?"

"No, not really," said Kauib. "There is nothing more to see." He stepped closer so he could speak even more softly. "Though I feel different when I'm there. It affects me. I can't explain it. Some say there has been healing taking place there. I told that to my Miss, and she took me there once. We didn't see any signs of healing, but my Miss said she felt better after being there, too."

"Did you talk to anyone?"

"No. There are so many other people around such a little house. Besides, I am too afraid. I am just a slave boy, after all." He stepped back. "I really must go now. I am already late."

"Thank you again, my friend." Najiir released his hold on Kauib's arm. "Just one more thing. How do I get to Bethlehem?"

Kauib gave the directions. Najiir watched him trot down the hallway, giving a wave before disappearing. Pressing his ear to the rough cedar door, Najiir listened. There was only silence from the other side, no conversation, no cries of distress.

Najiir backed away. His legs weakened, and he slumped to the floor. He sat cross-legged, head in hands, his wavy hair spilling over his fingers. His thoughts began to spin.

He was solely to blame for everything—everything—that had transpired. After the campfire meeting, he'd taken the donkeys back to the main camp. He and two others set out to investigate the glow from distant campfires. They met a small band of young men claiming to be merchants heading home to Jerusalem. The men were friendly and asked many questions. Najiir boasted his caravan would not be going to Jerusalem because royals—he mentioned King Xaratuk and King Mithrias by name—were among his group. He echoed Topur's assertion that persons of their stature were safer if they avoided the attention of both the Romans and Herod. He succumbed to bragging and impulsively divulged sensitive information to strangers who, he now realized, were spies for King Herod.

But, had Herod's men not arrived, wouldn't his master be dead?

It was all too confusing. What if Topur were to die? Najiir's mind refused to consider the possibilities. Life since his rescue had been easy. With Topur's family, he could come and go—without question, without responsibility—and be assured of comfort and acceptance upon return. One could barely consider him a slave. All of this was because Topur had shown mercy and compassion to a boy he'd never known.

On hands and knees, Najiir edged over to the door again. He pressed his ear to the door. Again, silence. "He can't die...he just can't die," he whispered. Hunched, he slunk away, his back to the rough wall. Head in hands once more, moist tears collected in his palms, then dripped to his wrists. He was not one to cry, yet the tears flowed unchecked. He tried to swallow. Then it came. Uncontrolled, it swelled from his feet, through his legs, then into his belly, and finally to his chest. He had never sobbed but couldn't restrain a heart-stopping bellow from bursting from his throat. He quaked. He realized he must not be heard, but here was the next one, involuntarily gushing forth, already releasing from his tightened gut. He shoved his sleeve into his mouth, gulping a large swath of fabric, then bit down. Falling to his side, he lay curled on the stone floor. The agonizing cry was stifled. Two more, then a third spasm of unfiltered sorrow hung within the linen plug. His curved body twitched with each convulsion.

The sobs stopped as suddenly as they began. He lay still, panting, sweating, unable to find the will to move. Finally, he sat up. Removing his sleeve from his mouth, he used it to dab at his eyes and ran it under his nose. The tears continued.

Inside Miriam's room, it was eerily quiet. The laced wine had Topur in a stupor, making it difficult for Miriam to clean and dress him. She thought she heard someone crying outside her door, but tending to her woozy, wobbly patient prevented her from checking. When Topur was finally on his back, resting comfortably, she placed the soiled bandages in the basket and tiptoed to the door. Opening it, she furtively glanced up the hallway, then across the hall, then to her feet.

No one was there.

CHAPTER 17

There was no play at the theater, no race at the Hippodrome. Apart from the throng at the Temple, Jerusalem was tranquil. Glimmers of golden lamplight escaped through the open windows of the Inner City's homes. The rare glow of a moving Roman soldier's torch punctuated the otherwise pervasive dominion of darkness.

Mithrias remained brooding atop the Phasael Tower's uppermost platform. Xaratuk was content to ogle the breadth and depth of Herod's accomplishments.

"I understand!" Mithrias blurted. He straightened, and his eyes grew wide. "I understand!"

"What? Understand what, Mithrias?" said Xaratuk. "The star? You understand something about the star?"

"No, no," said Mithrias. "No, no. Give me one moment." He moved to the wall, his arms gesturing over the crenellations. "I understand what Topur has been trying to explain."

"What are you talking about?" Xaratuk protested.

Mithrias patted Xaratuk on the chest, then directed him to look upon the city. "It's there, before us." He took Xaratuk's elbow, turning him away from the Temple fires. "I understand what Topur was telling us about Herod. And I am even more frightened than before."

"I don't begin to grasp what you are trying to tell me," Xaratuk said.

"You believe the star is attached to someone mighty,

someone incredibly strong and important."

"I do."

"And that he might be the one to help contain the Romans."

"Drive them into the sea forever."

"And Herod would welcome the opportunity to join you."

"Of course. And I don't see why he is blind to the opportunity that awaits him on his own doorstep. If I could just—"

"Look," Mithrias said, pointing into the city. "Look to the theater. What do you see?"

"Mithrias, it's dark. There's no one there. How am I supposed to tell you what I see?"

"Exactly. It's dark. No one is there. We both understand theaters can be open day or night. We've seen performances that use the night as their backdrop. But now, there's no sign of activity, no indication any play will open—day or night." Mithrias nodded in another direction. "And there is the Hippodrome. It, too, is dark."

"It's night, Mithrias. They may perform plays at night, but no one races chariots in the dark. This is ridiculous."

"We saw the Hippodrome in the daylight on our way into the city. No one was there—no colors, no banners, no signs of preparation for a race. We see no suggestion that any citizen of Jerusalem has the least interest in patronizing that Hippodrome."

"Coincidence. I'm certain King Herod has found sufficient use for both the theater and the Hippodrome."

"He may. But not with the Jews. Not with his people. Those beautiful buildings sit empty because Jews have little concern with plays and chariot races. Jerusalem was built, we said, upon tradition and beliefs, not entertainment and sport. We see where the interests of Herod's people are," said Mithrias, pointing to the Temple, "and where they are not."

Xaratuk's face turned sour. He shook his head dismissively. "I tell you, it is merely a coincidence. I'd wager that seven out of ten days, you would see lines of people waiting to use those buildings."

"All right, but who will those people be? Roman visitors, Roman soldiers, Greeks, foreigners, but hardly a Jew among them. They are at the Temple, resentful that their king should go to such lengths to make foreigners—invaders—feel so comfortable in their city."

"It is a virtue to show hospitality."

"To conquerors? Remember, Topur referred to a bribe. That Temple is a bribe to offset Herod's effusive accommodation. It is a distraction to counter gestures of overblown appeasement. Apart from the Temple, Herod's buildings stand as testaments to interests that have nothing to do with being Jewish."

"Don't put your trust in a common merchant, Mithrias. His viewpoint is inescapably narrow."

"Is it? Consider this: Topur said King Herod's qualifications to be King of the Jews are shaky. With Roman help, Herod became the most powerful Jew in the empire. Remove that support, and what is he? Would he still be king? Well, would he? And to whom, then, is he beholden? Unlike you, Herod may not be looking to the sky for intervention. Any change—any disruption—to what he has taken such great pains to establish may be extremely threatening."

Uncharacteristically, Xaratuk considered Mithrias's comments, but frowned and shook his head. "No. Herod can be defended for making concessions to the Romans. Look at the position he is in. Every single day of his life, Herod must face the very situation I fear more than anything. He has a vicious conqueror saturating his streets, imposing their will over his land—upon his people. He can't defeat them on his own, and he knows that. Listen to me. I have yet to meet one man, one king, one ruler who would prefer subjugation over self-determination. No, if Herod could successfully remove these Romans and rule Judaea independently, he'd take up arms the very next day. No man who calls himself king could think otherwise." Xaratuk jabbed at Mithrias's chest. "I mean to know this man better. Whatever that star reveals will be invaluable, especially to Herod."

Mithrias's shoulders slumped. "Please, tread lightly. Please. I believe Topur's words offer a legitimate warning."

Xaratuk huffed. "I'm beginning to think your friend Topur is a bit of an idiot, myself."

What else was there to say? Xaratuk declared it was time to prepare for dinner. Wordlessly, the kings descended through the tower stairway and arrived at the polished walkway of the courtyard. Behind them, two figures scampered down from their hideout in the crawlspace at the top of the tower, then darted to the opposite side of the palace. Their destination: the bedchamber of King Herod.

CHAPTER 18

Miriam placed her soothing hand on Topur's shoulder. "I must change your dressings again. I know you don't like this, but it must be done." Miriam stepped to the table to gather more clean dressings, then stood at Topur's bedside. "Raise onto your elbows the best you can."

"No new patients?" Topur groaned, blinking his eyes. Miriam's brow wrinkled. "No lepers with us?"

Miriam smiled. "Tending to you fills all my time."

Gritting his teeth, Topur managed to lean on one elbow. "How long?"

"What?"

"How long before I can leave?" He grimaced and shrunk back. Pain tore through his torso. Miriam lugged him into a sitting position and started to unwrap the bandaging. She placed the used strips in a basket at her feet while looking at Topur's face, gauging his distress as she continued to peel layer after layer.

"This part may hurt. It is the closest to your skin."

The bandaging reluctantly separated from the sticky salve coating his wound. He winced. Miriam dabbed the dressing with warm water and pulled.

"You're as tough as last week's mutton," she said.

Topur could only muster a soft chuckle. "Then I am a better actor than I thought."

When he opened his eyes, Topur, for the first time, could

look about the room. The hearth was still lit. On either side were tall, five-tiered shelves. Dark clay pots were carefully arranged, packed tightly but uniformly upon each rack. Each pot had its own lid and a dangling spoon tied to the neck. Before the hearth was a table stacked with linens and bandages to one side. There was ample room remaining on it to do the work of grinding and measuring and mixing. Across from him were longer shelves supporting larger clay jars and decanters. To one side was a small cot, neatly made. At its head was a tiny table with a lit oil lamp. The room was simple, organized, efficient, and clean.

"There. All the old bandaging is off, and the bleeding still looks to be stopped." Miriam examined the long wound from collarbone to hip, gently tracing it, her hand hovering slightly above his skin. "This salve I made is helping, and your fever is gone. You are making good progress but have a long road ahead. Now, I must make sure you stay clean." Miriam used her purified water to dab at the red crescent cleft across the front of Topur's torso. "I can see that would hurt," she muttered, then stood back. "Still, I have you past the point of greatest danger. You should survive." She used clean bandaging to wash the wound. Each dab stung, but the pain was less than Topur had expected. Once done, Miriam began to apply the new dressing on Topur, starting near his shoulder. "Hold this end for me," she said. Topur held the bandaging to his collarbone, above the point where the wound began.

"How long, then? You didn't say," he said.

"You tell me. I see the pain in your face. You are far from well, Topur." She continued to wind more bandaging around Topur's torso.

"Still, how long?"

"A week? Two?" Miriam stepped back, nearly finished. "Even then, you'll be in pain when you move. You can't walk. I don't see how you'll travel."

Topur grunted. Miriam provided exceptional comfort. Remaining in the palace with this woman would be the most satisfying choice. Why not stay? Bethlehem was not far away. Surely the kings could find it—if Herod allowed them to proceed.

Though some doubt lingered, Topur surmised Miriam was not a spy. But he had questions. Why did she presume he must be kept hidden? How long could she keep him apart from Herod and the other staff, even in these leper rooms? Might healing turn to holding? And why was she taking such profound risks on his behalf?

"No, it must be sooner—much sooner," Topur said.

"What is your hurry?" Miriam asked. "You'd leave too soon and erase all this good I am doing for you?"

"It is best for both of us if I leave as quickly as possible." Topur felt ungrateful. "You must understand that I appreciate all you have done and continue to do for me. But staying here with you is risky—and not just for me." He grasped Miriam's wrist. "I don't want to put either of us in unnecessary danger."

"Lie down." Miriam placed her arms around him so delicately it was as though bird wings helped him recline. Miriam was meticulous but also tantalizingly tender. Topur's eyes rolled backward, eyelids barely meeting, as his skin received her feathery touch. He wished for her warm, soft hands to be upon him for any reason.

Miriam bent to the basket of used bandages, lifted it, and stepped to the door. She called out for Kauib. Within seconds, he arrived at her doorstep. "Take these," she said, handing him the basket. "They must be burned. Understand?"

"Yes, Miss," responded Kauib. "They shall."

Miriam whispered, "Have they posted anyone nearby?"

"No, Miss. No one."

"Down the hall—anyone there?"

"No, Miss. Just me. I wait there and listen for you. No one is with me."

"Good boy. Tell Rachel to prepare a treat for you. You are a good helper. Tell her I said so."

"Thank you, Miss! I will have these burned. Thank you!" Smiling, Kauib turned and left the room.

"And wash your hands!" she yelled after him.

Miriam returned to Topur. His eyes were closed. "You are no danger to me."

"No?"

"I already know your group is headed to Bethlehem."

Topur's muscles locked. His eyes fixed upon Miriam. "Who? Who is telling you these things?" The depth of Miriam's understanding was confusing—confusing and alarming. "Dear woman, you seem to know more about me—about us—than I can comprehend. Is it my boy, Najiir? Has he been talking?"

"I haven't met Najiir, but Kauib has spoken to him." Miriam moved from the bed and began cutting the cloth on the table into strips of new bandaging. "But Najiir wasn't the one who spoke of Bethlehem. He doesn't have to. I know you are following the star, and I also know the star shines over Bethlehem."

Topur slapped his forehead. "How—how—how do you know this? How many others know this?" He managed to prop himself up on his elbows. Bethlehem? Miriam's news was astonishing, but equally shocking was the realization that Merkis and Khartir were, once again, correct. A star? Shining? On Bethlehem? In truth, he had not believed them.

"How many...? It's hardly a secret. You can't help but notice it."

"You're certain of this?" Topur stammered.

"Of course."

"Then I feel so foolish! I should have known—we all should! We aren't special. Everyone can see this light? Why not?"

"Yes, everyone can see this light, but few pay it much attention. It shines over such a humble village and an even more humble house—hardly worth another thought. Most people are not curious. I am curious, though, so I went. I took Kauib with me."

"Miriam, you've been there?"

"Yes," Miriam said, shrugging. "Nothing impressive. I'm still unsure what it is we are supposed to see. That light is about a baby—a boy. Of that, I'm sure. His parents are quite poor, though. I felt the strangest feelings while I was there. Kauib did, too."

"A boy, you say. In Bethlehem. That's it?"

"That's it. A child."

"And you're sure the star's light is shining right there. No mistaking that."

"No mistake. That is definitely where the star is shining."

Stories of unexpected healing had reached Miriam. Curious, she gathered Kauib, and together they investigated the tiny house and those within. She told Topur of the star, its light, of shepherds and visions, of a considerate but anxious father, and a doting mother. She repeated the impressions of those visitors who professed to sense grace and goodwill. But other rumors, many of them grandiose and magnified, were emerging. Should those rumors fall upon the wrong ears, they could be dangerous, even lethal, to those within that humble shelter and anyone deemed to be associated.

"If you know all this, doesn't everyone?" Topur scowled in pain, barely able to continue. "Herod must know," he groaned. "The priests must know. If everyone knows—?" Topur was in too much pain to continue.

"Easy." She coaxed him onto his back. "No, not everyone knows. Not the old king, and maybe not the Temple Priests or most of the Sadducees. The Sanhedrin doesn't know—or care. They're consumed by their pomp and their money. They're so eager to impress the Romans. Stars go ignored. They surely wouldn't bother with this. None of us speak a word of it to Herod or his little web of spies. We have all sworn to be silent."

"This is shocking. Sworn to silence? A baby? What could people say about a baby that would alarm Herod?"

"It never takes much. You realize that." She patted Topur's hand. Her voice was hushed. "It began with the shepherds, but now many others call this baby a savior."

"A...a savior?" Feebly, he tried to sit up.

"Don't. You must lie back."

"What do you suppose they mean by that? Save us—save whom?"

"Save us, the Jews, from the Romans, I suspect. Many around here would like that, but Herod wouldn't. The Romans would have something to say. Some visitors go even further. Some have called him 'King of the Jews'.'"

Topur shook his head. "Oh, not that."

"It's my understanding that King Herod believes the position is filled."

"King of the Jews—dangerous talk. Why are people saying such things?"

"Scripture, Topur. People cite scripture."

"My wife Atarah knows scripture. I don't—not as well as I should, anyway. Two men in our group, advisors, say they have pored over our scriptures during their journey here. They exposed how little I know, but they agree with you. 'Micah's king,' they said. But 'King of the Jews'—that's a death sentence if ever I have heard one."

"That is not where it stops." Miriam rose and stepped to the door. She opened it, poked her head through, then closed it. "Some believe he is the Messiah." Miriam returned to Topur's bedside, eyebrows raised. "A few within this palace passionately believe that. They think he is sent by God to change everything—absolutely everything. They call him the 'Chosen One'. I see the fervor in their eyes. I hear the zeal in their whispers. That frightens me. I agree we need change. I don't like the Romans here, but what army of revolution could the Jews muster out of tiny Bethlehem? David fought a single giant. Our sticks and stones are no match for legions of Roman swords and spears. I see only trouble. Besides, Herod loves the Romans, and as long as he is king, we'll see Romans in our streets. Still..."

"Picking fights with the Romans. Another sure death sentence," Topur murmured.

"And the stories become even more grand. Some say this baby has arrived to save not only the Jews, but all mankind."

"Preposterous!" Topur chided. "Is Bethlehem's well poisoned? You won't find scripture for that! These assertions are delusional!"

"It makes 'King of the Jews' sound like an inferior title." Miriam snickered.

"And you say Herod knows nothing of this?"

Miriam lifted a tiny stool and brought it to Topur's bedside. She sat, her face close to his, and began speaking in a whisper. "I know I have been asking you for information about your journey, information you didn't wish to share. You thought I shouldn't know your plans or figured I was a spy for Herod. That was smart—smart, but incorrect." She took his hand, placing it in both of hers. She absorbed his gaze, collecting his full attention. "Topur, I am telling you now things you cannot share. I feel I can trust you."

"Of course you can trust me," he said, puzzled.

"This goes with you to the grave, you understand."

"All right, I understand."

"Herod is a sick man. We keep Herod sick. The cooks and I—and other servants. Together, we make sure Herod is never well and will never be completely well."

Topur shuddered. "All right. That should go to the grave. I do understand now."

"He is a madman," Miriam said. "He has been for a long time—maybe his whole life. You recognize that. You comprehend what he is capable of. You tried to slip your kings past him and around Jerusalem. That is why I assume I can trust you." Her voice was barely audible. "We can temper Herod if he is weak and infirm. This has worked, more or less, for a while now."

"For a while now? What are you doing?"

"Some of us came together after Herod had Mariamne executed. We couldn't kill him—we believe in our commandments—so we tried to devise a way to restrain his bouts of madness. It took us a while to develop an association so tight that it did not mistakenly include one or more of his spies. We finally succeeded, though I lost a few close friends who allowed me, and the others, to live by keeping their mouths shut. We thought we had him restrained at one point and stopped interfering, but he grew mad again. Two of his sons paid with their lives. We renewed our efforts and still try our best to control him. But it's difficult and doesn't always work. He is a deeply suspicious man, and if he has the slightest inclination that he is threatened, he unleashes his evil against the lives of those in question. Only the Romans can equal our ability to blunt his worst impulses. Between the cooks, his bedchamber servants, some soldiers, and me, we use food and drink and my medicine to keep him in check."

"I cannot believe you have not been exposed!"

Miriam looked at Topur with pleading eyes. "I am trusting you with so much. You must not share this with anyone."

"Such courage—all of you! I would continually fear guards coming to my door, announcing they'd discovered me. How do you find a moment of peace?"

"When you see what he is capable of doing and being, you find your courage. Old Herod has slowed even without our help. It is easier to keep secrets from him because he isn't interested in Jerusalem's activity anymore. If it doesn't have to do with pleasing the Romans, or showing off the Temple, or resting at his villa, he's generally indifferent. There's an entire world operating unseen under Herod's nose—and with God's help, that is how we'll keep it. He still has spies planted everywhere, but we know who they are. They'll likely observe your friends tonight at dinner—and afterward. As of this moment, Herod is unaware of Bethlehem, and he'll remain unaware as long as we can keep that information from him." She released his hand and stood. "What more do those men, those advisors, say?"

"What they understand comes only from what they've read. There was no mention of a baby, no word of a tiny home. Miriam, tell me, what do you suppose is happening in Bethlehem?"

"I can't say. The child's parents, Joseph and Mary, seem so kind." A warm smile crossed Miriam's face. "He is a gentle man and far more composed than I expected. Mary is young but could not be a more attentive mother. But it is said she hears voices. They say she claims to have heard the voice of God speaking to her, which makes me uneasy. Charlatans roam our streets, also claiming they hear the voice of God. I have tended to a few. They may hear voices, Topur, but it isn't God's voice they hear. It's best to avoid them. Those around Jerusalem shouting they are the Messiah do not die of old age."

Miriam rose to pour two cups of wine and returned to Topur's bedside. "A new king. A savior for the Jews." She sighed. "There is no peace here in Jerusalem. Perhaps we do need to heal our souls. Perhaps we do need someone to show us how to be God's Chosen People again. I hope to be living when this child becomes a man. Ask me then. Until such time, who is to say?" She patted Topur's hand.

"Herod must never know."

"I agree," Miriam said. "But I fear it may already be too late."

CHAPTER 19

"**I** believe Herod intends to impress us," Mithrias whispered to Xaratuk as they entered the dining hall through two thick cedar doors. It wasn't the most prominent dining hall available. The kings had walked past several larger ones. But this room was more intimate. What it lacked in size was compensated by majesty.

"He has succeeded." Xaratuk chuckled.

An imposing U-shaped dining table, adorned with a shiny silk cover of purple and gold, anchored the room. A seven-candled gold menorah, taller than any man present, was centered between the table's wings. Bronze oil lamps rested on carved ivory posts. Commanding the room was the statue of a nude athlete positioned to launch his discus into the city. Servants intent upon completing their duties swished in and out of the room through copper-trimmed doors.

But the most impressive feature was the covered balcony at the room's far end. Supported by six polished, green marble columns, it was open to the elements, incorporating the city into the breathtaking view. The room felt expansive, able to float beyond the palace walls. Any sense of restriction was convincingly eliminated.

Herod had extended his dinner invitation to include the advisors, Regulus, and Salnassar. The retinue, already present, had congregated at the open end, left to marvel at Jerusalem's astonishing grandeur burgeoning through barren scrub.

The guests had dressed in their finest civilian clothing, careful to sidestep any overtly imperial or military suggestion. Even Regulus had abandoned the bronze breastplate for a less threatening cloak. While admiring Herod's achievements, they informed the kings of the baffling Roman indifference to their presence.

Herod entered the room unannounced with one of his remaining sons, Archelaus. Herod's long robe was a brilliant blue. A yellow sash, with its border of inlaid purple stitching, crossed the middle of his chest from his shoulders to his narrow waist. Brass balls dangled along the length of his sleeves. Within his impressive royal finery, Herod remained frail and disheveled. His servants had cleaned him, combed him, and he no longer reeked of old fish. But the skin surrounding his watery eyes maintained the same sallow color. Large, plum-colored bruises spotted each forearm. His long, bushy eyebrows remained distinctly and stubbornly removed from the ravages of age. They were dark black, a contrast to the gray hair and beard. Gold rings that once may have fit were an oversized adornment on every thin finger, accentuating the skeletal look of his blue-veined hands. Despite his bent and mottled frame, he projected an imperial air. He remained steadfast and assured, still comfortable being the center of attention.

The guests abandoned the balcony to greet Herod and his son. Behind them, unnoticed, a solitary figure crept onto the open terrace, successfully employing the walls, pillars, and shadows to remain undetected.

Herod stopped, then greeted his guests with a serious invocation. Every man paused and, one by one, bowed to his host. Acknowledging his son, who was also wearing royal colors of deep blue and gold, Herod said, "I will have our guests make their introductions."

Archelaus scanned the group with indifferent eyes to convey that this dinner was, for him, an ordeal.

Herod continued. "Two of my Temple Priests will join us in

due order, but I thought we might first enjoy some brief time apart from their company. We have much to share that doesn't concern them." He placed both hands upon Xaratuk's arm. "Let's begin here, Archelaus, with the Great King Xaratuk."

Xaratuk stiffened. Archelaus managed to raise one eyebrow, but his expression soon retreated to impatience as Xaratuk presented his captain of the guard and his two advisors. After each introduction, Herod said, "I am so pleased to have you with us tonight," but Archelaus said nothing, offering only a slight nod.

The introductions of Mithrias and Salnassar bored Archelaus. Upon finishing, Herod bid his guests to be seated around the large table. Mithrias, true to his diplomatic nature, told Herod and his son how moved he was by Jerusalem's allure—especially, but not limited to, the Temple. He mentioned that he and King Xaratuk found time to observe the city's beauty and watch its citizens. "The reality exceeds the renown, King Herod. It is something rarely achieved. What a tribute this city is to you, to your glory, and the glory of Jerusalem. Your people must revere you."

A sharp look crossed Herod's face, then mellowed. "Oh, my people have feelings for me." He chuckled. "And reverence is one I deserve, though it is rarely evident. Isn't that true, son?"

"Regrettable and, for me, unimaginable—but yes, true," said Archelaus. "But you are dearly loved and admired by those who count, Father, and by your family. The rest, I would say, are insignificant."

"Well, I should not say insignificant," said Herod. "It's simply that there are many opinions amongst us—some with greater merit than others."

The guests had found their seats. Pointing to the chair next to him, Herod took Mithrias's elbow. "Sit. You see, we Jews are an irascible bunch. We agree on practically nothing and are eager to fight and quarrel among ourselves. Groups here within Jerusalem compete for dominance and authority—the final word—and the ability to impose it upon the others. The Sadducees see things their way, but the Pharisees maintain they are wrong. I have an entire district within the city walls—the Essenes—who claim both others are wrong. Each faction claims to be the true interpreter of God and his will, and they'll heap scorn upon those who oppose them."

Grabbing Xaratuk's arm, Herod directed him to the chair on his other side. "King Xaratuk, my people should look to me, only me, to be their leader, but they don't. I am their king, but they believe the High Priest should tell them what God wishes." One of his bushy eyebrows inched up his forehead. "I know what God wishes. And I know what Rome wishes, too." A stick-thin finger wagged. "If only my people appreciated how infrequently they match." Herod was clearly wobbling. "I can talk about these things before the priests get here. I can speak more freely. They are so apt to misinterpret me. I have to include them—but later."

Xaratuk followed Mithrias's lead. "You have accomplished so much, King Herod. The Temple, the Hippodrome, the theater, the forts, the ports, the aqueducts...all done at your command and under your watchful eye, as well as the critical eye of the Romans. It is nothing less than amazing, an outstanding accomplishment! How is it your people could not revere you? You didn't build this for the Romans. What you built is there for your own people."

"Humbly, I accept your kind and gracious words, King Xaratuk," said Herod. "You state things well, and I appreciate your wise assessment of my predicament." Herod's voice softened. "I think I could grow comfortable calling you my friend."

"As I could you," replied Xaratuk, touching Herod on the shoulder.

"My accomplishments are ignored, and my authority to rule is constantly questioned. What more can I do?" Herod sighed, fingering the brass balls of his sleeve. "I can't change the past. I can't change who I am. They contend my heritage is not deep enough, not pure enough, to be their king. Being raised a Jew doesn't begin to be sufficient." As Herod spoke, his words for the first time were seasoned with sadness. "I am Jewish in constitution and comportment, yet I still fail their purity qualifications—as if failing to pick the correct father and grandfather is more important than building a temple and following the Law." He shook his head. He stared vacantly ahead. "They can think what they want, those dogs. I have found that there is no changing the minds of most people. But while they bicker and quarrel over family purity, I get things done. You just said it, King Mithrias." As he swung to look back at Mithrias, he nearly toppled. "Glory!"

Herod's footing stabilized. He blinked and regained his place. "In this sense, I follow my Roman friends. Say what you will about them, this one thing is true, they get things done! They accomplish great works, my friends. They build cities, they sail ships, they win wars. As for the Jews—they argue. How Solomon got his Temple built, I cannot fathom. My friends, I am accused of being a mixed-race Jew." Finally, he sat down, a signal for the others to sit. "So what? Maybe I am. If I am, then the better part of me—that which isn't Jewish—that part is doing glorious things. I am not content to merely argue and debate, gentlemen."

"If that isn't obvious to your people, it is obvious to me and to every person who visits this city," said Xaratuk.

"In the end..." Herod sighed. "The arguments and criticisms of the priests and of this group and that group will all die away. But my Temple will live on." A skeletal finger pointed at each guest in succession. "And so, then, will I. This is what I like about the Romans. They accomplish things, things that will last." A wry smile crossed Herod's face. "Granted, they can make it look dirty while doing it. I am not blind. I know, better than anyone here, what they are like, these Romans." Herod looked about the room. He pounded the table, startling all the guests. "But in the end, it is accomplished, and it lives on and on."

Herod did not wait for comment. "I built a temple larger than Solomon's. I built it, and not only do my people flock to it, by the thousands—every day!—but so do citizens of any country you can name." He looked directly at Xaratuk. In a teasing tone, he said, "Name a country, King Xaratuk. Name any country."

"I believe you, Your Excellency," replied Xaratuk, edging away. "I could name any country, and someone from there has traveled here to see your Temple."

"Any country," cooed Herod. His shaky arm swept out. "My farmers have markets. My shops thrive. My merchants see traders. My inns are full." His hand rested back on the table. "And is all this because my priests slit the throats of oxen? No! King Xaratuk, it's me! It's me!" Herod thumped his feeble chest. "There may be those who withhold it from me now, but glory, and all the glory, shall be mine—and mine alone!" Herod stood and peered up to his heaven. "My Temple will stand for a thousand generations, and the nine-hundred-and-ninety-ninth will still speak my name. They will all say, 'This is the work of Herod the Great. He built this for us, and we worship him for it.'"

He looked back at Xaratuk, his voice faltering. "I am right, am I not, King Xaratuk?"

Xaratuk smoothed his mustache. "You are, dear king. You are precisely correct. Action means far more than petty criticism, and glory is a powerful motivation to incite that action. A king's legacy is to be of enduring influence, to be the object of admiration, to leave a lasting, unique impression on the country and its citizens." His brow arched as he turned to Herod. "And on our enemies?"

Pleased, Herod nodded his assent.

Xaratuk resumed. "Yes, perhaps it is for glory we choose to rule—and the willingness to use the means necessary to continue that rule."

Xaratuk took this opportunity to begin his list of

accomplishments, as though proof of fame and glory was now some contest.

Mithrias's smile departed for the evening. He slunk into his chair, his head upon his hand. He tried to ignore the same drone of self-congratulation he had already spent weeks enduring.

While the kings formed a pact of mutual admiration, Mithrias felt a wedge of detachment separating him from the others. Grief had altered him. Former friends and allies held fast to opinions he now doubted or could no longer share. And he had feelings: new, strong, different feelings the others could not possibly understand, for he was unsure why he held them himself.

To his everlasting dismay, Mithrias found himself speaking. Perhaps it was out of frustration, having anxiously remained mute while the two kings shamelessly flattered each other. Or, it could have been a deep desire to remind the others that perhaps they were less than the perfect rulers they were projecting. Words formed within his mouth and escaped past his lips like doves released from their cage. He had no control and could not predict where they might lead.

"Glory? Is this glory you speak of always honorable?" Mithrias began. "Is something grand and marvelous the only and inevitable result of one's quest for glory? Can the pursuit of glory have tragic consequences, too? To me, the evil seems evenly matched to the good. Granting one man glory, while another is smeared in disgrace, is sometimes nothing more than who bloodied his sword first."

To a man, the audience looked upon Mithrias as if he had burst out in pustules. Chairs scraped on the marble floor in nervous readjustment. Throats cleared. Mithrias wished to reclaim his words, but his mouth kept moving because, even if unpopular, he was saying what he believed to be true.

"I have questioned many things lately. Decisions I made— for which I am responsible—resulted in the deaths of those closest to me. I have struggled with that. I now appreciate how my decisions can affect others around me—from a general to a sandal maker—in ways I had not considered nor predicted. What if something I willed made another feel as I do now? What right have I? What right do any of us have?" He looked up with trepidation to see reactions ranging from grim discomfort to undiluted derision. "Not everything we do, even with good intentions, turns out worthy of glory. I realize what I say may make me appear weak, but—"

"Weak! You are weak!"

Salnassar claimed exclusive use of the floor. He stood from the table. Enlarged veins in his neck nourished his flushed face. Pointing at his father, he said, "Here we go again. We have heard this countless times: You had a favorite son. He died. You're sad. What is left to understand?"

Mithrias glared. "I am sorry you mistake consideration and devotion for another as a sign of weakness. For your brother, feeling these things made him stronger."

"Our people need a king!" Salnassar pounded the table. "Not some overwrought old fool. I am sure this sandal maker wishes you to behave as his king—his leader—not like some weepy neighbor. A proper king would make sure his sandal makers can live and thrive and not end up the slave of some empire their ruler didn't have the stomach, or might, to face."

Salnassar's words echoed in the speechless room.

"Your son has a point, King Mithrias," Xaratuk volunteered, clearly amused.

Salnassar thumped back into his chair. A tentative grin formed.

"You want to be benevolent, King Mithrias—fine," Xaratuk continued. "That is in your nature. But that benevolence must be backed by the power—the dominion—to enforce it. You have the power—for now. You must continually defend it. If necessary, you must fight for it, and others must do that fighting, and dying, on your behalf." He nodded to Salnassar. "Listen to your son. There is your never-ending struggle. It is about one who has the power to rule the kingdom as he deems fit against those who want to establish a different order under their rules. If you are interested in your people's well-being, consider this: Only when you are at your strongest can you provide them with their best chance. Abandoning or neglecting your power will place them in the greatest peril. I should think you'd appreciate that the weak and the innocent need protection, but only the strong can offer it."

"It seems you may have another promising son, King Mithrias," said Herod.

"It is a side of him I've neglected to see," Mithrias managed. A buzz droned in his skull. He felt as if an iron wedge was thrust into his forehead. Grimacing, he adjusted his chair backward, looking below. The abyss was at his feet, so vast, so close. The legs of his chair seemed precariously perched above it. The infernal buzzing now formed words: "Let go. Sszzzo much easier. Sszzzo much easier. Why rezzzsist?" He felt trapped, immobile, as though rolled inside a wet, heavy carpet.

Why not, he wondered. Why struggle? What matters? Mithrias squeezed his eyes, wrongly supposing it would silence the voice drumming through his head.

The voice became more profound, more distinct. "You do not belong here. Go to the place where they know you. No one understands you here."

The voice was correct; this was no longer his world and would never be. The most powerful men in the room were concerned only with their selfish interests and some unquenchable impulse to dominate the thoughts and lives of others. People weren't important. They were merely instruments, tools. They were backs, arms, and hands to hold spears, irascible sources of revenue. What mattered to the men at the table were statues, palaces, hippodromes, and temples— stony edifices whose life-spans reliably outlasted the humans who built them. Bricks were more valued than babies. Fathers were no more than logs fed to the fires of war. Body count, not morality, was the one thing distinguishing glorious victor from infamous loser. When found to obstruct glory's path, entire populations lost homes or lives to war or legalized covetousness. Glory, underwritten by war, unsustainable taxes, slave labor, and an industrious but impoverished populace, pillaged the inhabitants, sparked riots, inflamed hatred, and forced formerly productive subjects to become displaced beggars.

"It is no longer your world. Go to the place where they know you." The voice became more insistent. Mithrias felt dizzy, separated from himself, outside his own body. He saw his head from above, chin pressed into his chest, brooding, the others in animated talk around him. This wasn't his world. Deioces was not like these men. He was full of love and admiration and respect—for people, not stones. He gave his heart, his intellect, and even his back so freely, so capably, and everyone he met was made better for it. Mithrias understood his son was the rarest of men, one who could only raise himself by first raising others, never imagining it could be otherwise. It was humbling to witness such natural, innate, unfettered goodness. And the world—this world—would never see it. This is not your world. Indeed, this is a world where men like Herod thrive, where Salnassar—the brute!—is considered wise.

The abyss had grown claws.

"If not you, who?"

Mithrias shook. His heart pumped. His torso rattled. *Doria? It was Doria! Unmistakable! It was her voice! Intoxicating! Doria? How sublime to hear that voice again!* His swooning head felt weightless; his body could float. It was like falling back into a thousand pillows. His ears strained. *Where was she?*

"Doria?" he gasped.

"If not you, then who?" repeated Xaratuk. "Mithrias, look at me. Are you ill?"

Mithrias's delusion collapsed, sounding in his head like a shelf of thin crystalline glass crashing upon a stone floor. He needed time to reassemble himself. He groped for words. "I am...what, King Xaratuk? What? What did you ask?"

Flustered and impatient, Xaratuk repeated himself. "To protect your countrymen, the people you claim to love—if not you, then who?"

"Oh, yes. I'm sorry," Mithrias stammered. "I guess, that is, it startled me...to realize...I have not given my son the credit he is due." Mithrias could only flounder his way back to the present. "I was momentarily at a loss for words." His gaze found Salnassar. For perhaps the first time in years, he looked upon his son without disdain. Salnassar never turned his head to see it.

"But as I say, King Mithrias, if not you, then who?" said Xaratuk, insisting the discussion move ahead. "You are the one best suited to protect your countrymen, correct?"

"Protect them...sure," he mumbled. "But what of your glory? Protect my sandal makers—what glory is there in that?" His words were halting, separated, like stepping stones in a stream. "It's mortality. Glory has us believing that acquiring it will make us immortal."

"And what, I ask you, is wrong with that?" asked Herod.

"Nothing. Perhaps nothing," said Mithrias, feigning a smile. "Though you say a thousand generations from now, your people will still praise you, but you'll never know, will you? You will be, after all, dead. It's merely a feeling that comforts you now."

"There is glory, King Mithrias," snapped Herod. "It's there. Great men are remembered. Great deeds are recorded. King David and King Solomon are glorified. I've made sure my name will be added to that list."

"I do not say we don't revere our ancestors. But for you, as it is for us all, once you breathe your last, there is no means of knowing whether your memorial will last for two generations or two hundred."

"I make sure because I do things," Herod reproved. "Who will future generations remember: the man who built this

Temple, or those who stood in my way?"

"As long as there are eyes to see it, your Temple will reflect your name, good King. I simply wish glory was appreciated and pursued in other ways with equal fervor. That's all."

"Then you think the Temple is a bad thing?" said Herod.

"No," Mithrias said, pursing his lips. "No, I have to tell you it is my honest opinion that your Temple is one of the loveliest structures I have seen in my life. Without reservation, I believe it to be an incredible and remarkable accomplishment." He looked directly at Herod. "I also sincerely believe you have done a great service for your people, Your Excellency." Through a frustrated sigh, Mithrias added, "I apologize to you. My company has been far inferior to the hospitality you've shown me. I regret any distress I have caused you. You have not deserved it. My head is somewhere else tonight."

"Five hundred years," came a voice next to Mithrias. It was Archelaus. "For five hundred years, our people lived with Zerubbabel's inferior structure in this city. For five hundred years, we could do no better. My father comes along, and in ten years, you see what we have today." His voice became very condescending. "That is what a man with glory on his mind can do—a man who comes along once in five hundred years. I don't know or care about this talk of immortality and such nonsense. Maybe it isn't the man who seeks glory. Maybe it is glory that seeks the deserving man. If anything, it is glory that is immortal and searches eternally for the proper mortal vessel that will allow it to flourish."

Herod beamed, then chuckled. He looked approvingly at his son. "Thank you, my son. You continue to show progress." A look, equal part grimace and smile, crossed his face. "I may change my will again soon."

Servants noisily burst through both side doors simultaneously. One side brought golden platters containing nuts, dates, raisins, pomegranates, and figs. From the other side came servants carrying cups while others brought decanters of wine. As the wine was poured, the guests lunged at the opportunity to consume their first gulps. The refreshments arrived at the most fortuitous time.

CHAPTER 20

Parting the large cedar doors, two bejeweled servants declared the arrival of the High Priest and his assistant. Each held a long, gilded staff to one side. On cue, King Herod and his guests rose to attention. The official introduction was shouted: "Honored Guests. From the sacred Temple of Jerusalem, Keeper of the Holy of Holies, His Most Excellent High Priest, Joazar." In unison, the servants pounded their heavy scepters three times, then separated, standing rigidly to the side.

A pasty, bearded man shuffled into the room, his stooped posture cloaked inside a long white robe covered by a dark blue sleeveless tunic. A cumbersome, gem-studded breastplate hung from his neck. His ornate wardrobe may have fit at an earlier time, but his bony frame was now insufficient support for such a ceremonial costume. As the High Priest moved, bells at the tunic's hem jingled. Atop his head sat a tall white turban spun from glistening thread. The headpiece helped augment the height that the High Priest naturally lacked. Beneath that, an enormous shaggy rug of gray beard began that spread until it reached Joazar's breastbone. The kinky mass of hair showed signs of earnest but futile attempts at order. A sullen frown dominated Joazar's face.

Once through the doors, the High Priest spoke. "May I introduce my segan, Eleazar? He serves me in all my Temple duties and oversees the other Temple priests. He is my invaluable assistant."

Eleazar emerged into the doorway with the enthusiasm of a cat being dragged on a leash. He was younger, also short, but plump, dressed in a simple but stunningly unblemished white, long-sleeved robe. A single scarlet sash with gold lining at its borders belted Eleazar around his ample middle. His head was covered by a plain white turban with a scarlet base that perfectly matched his sash. The frown on his face mirrored that of the High Priest.

"Well, King Herod, at your request, we are here," Joazar grumbled. He forced himself to glance at the assembled guests, but Eleazar seemed content to gaze blankly four paces ahead to the floor, his eyes blinking too slowly, as though that action was an effort.

Herod beckoned them. "Come in, come in. Meet our guests!" Snorting softly, yet conspicuously, Eleazar allowed his High Priest to jingle forward first. Both folded their arms about their middles and had yet to acknowledge anyone other than Herod.

The side doors burst open before the introductions could start. A troop of servants poured through. Besides those bringing food, there were musicians, servers, and cooks. They rushed past the honored guests, intent on performing their prescribed duties. The ruckus annoyed the new arrivals. They clearly wanted their exhibition of indifference to linger.

Herod appeared impervious to his priests' haughty show, having endured such treatment numerous times. He began the introductions.

Joazar scuffed his way to Xaratuk. He tilted his head forward while Xaratuk returned the same. "King Xaratuk? I am quite aware of you and your kingdom. I did not realize it was you who was a guest of our King Herod tonight. I was only told we would meet 'important men from the east'. Please pardon me. It is an honor."

"It is my honor as well, Your Holiness," replied Xaratuk,

exhibiting uncharacteristic magnanimity. Joazar extinguished his look of contempt. He turned to his unmoved companion. "Eleazar, surely you have heard of King Xaratuk."

"I have, Your Holiness. Everyone is familiar with the great King Xaratuk." Eleazar's abnormally slow blinking continued. "It never occurred to me I would have the opportunity to meet such a great man. You have traveled a great distance." The delivery of Eleazar's message was too flat, making it sound insincere.

"Yes," replied Xaratuk, smiling. "We have come a great distance. Seeing your lovely city has made it worth the effort."

"Yes. I suppose it would," said Eleazar. Xaratuk's smile vanished.

"We do have a city worthy of being home to God," said Joazar as he stroked his long beard. "But I am curious, King Xaratuk. Why were we not advised of your visit? I might suppose that entirely different arrangements would have been made to welcome one such as you."

"Yes," Herod said. "More about that later. Our next guest is King Mithrias."

When they stood before Mithrias, only Joazar would claim to recognize his name. Eleazar would not even feign familiarity. At the line's end, Joazar turned back to the guests. "I will admit I had other intentions for this evening's activities. But now, I am glad the late invitation was extended. Being with guests of such eminence is an honor. Our meeting will have value for all."

At Herod's instruction, the group was reseated along the table's U-shaped arrangement. Herod positioned himself with his son front and center between Xaratuk and Mithrias. Seated on the left were Regulus, Salnassar, and the magi. To the right sat Joazar and Eleazar, effectively splitting the room into opposing sides. Smiling servants presented volleys of fruit, meat, olives, wine, more meat, sweets, and more wine. Six servants always remained within the room, replacing dinnerware and refilling plates and goblets. A quartet of spirited musicians played spirited melodies in the background.

The conversation became livelier as the men shared common experiences and travels. Eleazar refused to be drawn in, doing little to conceal his resentment. Mithrias also remained silent, futilely listening for Doria's voice. He picked at his food, fearful that talk of the star would soon dominate the conversation. He deliberated on a means to suggest a reasonable alternative. Looking up, he met a sharp, rebuking glance from Xaratuk. He felt obliged to enter the conversation when Joazar edged the discussion in a perilous direction.

"Why have you come this far? Is it only to see Jerusalem? I will prepare a tour to show you as much as possible of our Temple. Or are you bound for somewhere else?"

Mithrias's chest tightened. Too many details had already been revealed. The priests might be important men to the Jews, but they commanded a temple, not an army. They were not entitled to any accounting or explanation. Mithrias assumed he could placate them with some concoction about being on a long, exploratory journey looking to expand trade, something too dull to generate too many follow-up questions. Then he'd change the subject. He hoped Herod would follow his lead.

"We have come here because of the star," Xaratuk said with blunt efficiency. "We're following that bright star that shines just beyond Jerusalem. It was noticeable, even as far away as my kingdom—and has been for months now."

Mithrias sat in open-mouthed shock. With no hint of restraint, defying Topur's instructions, Xaratuk exposed their mission to the priests. Herod already knew. Now the priests knew. Who would be next, the Romans?

Joazar suppressed a laugh. "A star, you say?" He absentmindedly adjusted his tunic. "That seems to me to be a rather fanciful notion. I don't see what importance can be traced to a bright star, but you are people of different beliefs than ours. I understand that." He managed a thin, condescending smile. "I hope you are not too disappointed if your journey should not produce satisfactory results."

Herod interrupted, pointing a bony finger at his High Priest. "You have seen this star? Have you noticed it, too?"

"Well, Your Highness, I have noticed a bright star—yes."

"And does it mean anything? What are people saying?" Herod's thin frame trembled.

"It has created a minor stir among a tiny number of your subjects," Joazar answered. "But any mention is almost exclusive to ignorant peasants and those most prone to superstition."

Merkis leaned to Khartir and whispered, "Ignorant peasants? We are ignorant peasants? Interesting."

Khartir stiffened, flashing a slight nod to his mentor.

"But I can assure you," Joazar continued, "that this star means nothing."

"It is a shame to see such esteemed guests travel so far only to return to their homeland with so little accomplished," said Eleazar, offering his first smug smile of the evening.

Merkis shifted in his chair. "Excuse me, but surely you have seen this star," he began in his usual measured tone. No one had communicated Topur's edict of silence to him.

"We have," said Eleazar, folding his arms upon his chest.

"Then you realize it is dominant. It is remarkably brighter than any other star. It appears nearer to us—larger than any other. It remains in a fixed position. It has the characteristics not only of a star, but a beacon. And there is no record of it in the celestial arrangement prior to its sudden appearance. There is no history of this particular star in your books and teachings. Am I correct in all of this?"

The priests shrugged, saying nothing.

Merkis's tone intensified. "Have you no curiosity about such an event? It's at your doorstep. Aren't you compelled to find out what it means, what impact it could have?"

Joazar spoke first. "Perhaps events like this stir imagination in your homeland. We Jews, at least the learned among us, do not look to the heavens to notify us of what is important or what is to come. Our ancestors and our prophets have done that work for us already. God has spoken to and through them. He has given us words—not stars—and we must concentrate on those teachings and their meanings. If a star is particularly bright, it is because God has willed it so. It is pleasing to him. Nothing more. If God has willed it, we shall see it. It adds to the beauty of the firmament." He turned to Herod. "It is most assuredly not a sign."

"We Jews are God's chosen people," Eleazar declared. "At the risk of sounding condescending, God has spoken to us, the Jews, directly. He has spoken to our forefathers and has told us, through the prophets, all we need to know. He does not need to resort to tricks, signs, or symbols to express his meaning or intentions. We have his words, not some star or moon, and those words have been written. And now, it remains our duty to obey the Word and not concern ourselves over some imagined, undecipherable code projected amid the night sky."

Herod quaked. "I'm not sure I have seen this star. I don't understand what all this fuss is about." He glowered at his priests. His voice boomed to fill the far corners of the room. "I expect to be informed of what my people are noticing—no matter how trivial you may consider it!" His eyes remained fixed on his two priests. "I am still their king—yours, too!"

Khartir entered the fray. "From our calculations, the star's beam falls a day's walk from Jerusalem. From what we figure, it would shine down in the exact area your scriptures predict your own king shall arise." Concentrating on the priests, Khartir failed to notice Mithrias's wide-eyed warning.

"Our scriptures, you say?" challenged Joazar. "How would you know anything about our scriptures?"

Khartir sat forward, elbows on the table. "It's as you say. Your people have written these things down. It's there. If we could find it..."

Merkis's hand fell upon Khartir's knee, squeezing it. "We're not ignorant," Khartir muttered, pleading with his mentor. "This isn't about superstition. It's their words—"

"Quite true," whispered Merkis in return. "But step lightly."

"This isn't some guessing game," Khartir resumed. "So far, it all adds up. Your own scriptures point to Bethlehem." He pointed past the menorah, past the musicians, past the stony Greek Olympian, past the green marble columns, and past the flickering Temple altars. "Go. Go to the end of the room. Look from there. Look where this star is shining."

Mithrias hung his head. Everything was now out in the open. This was bound to inflame Herod's suspicious nature. Mithrias began to pant. He could only blame himself for not personally instructing the advisors to limit what they reveal. From where he sat, he could say nothing to stop Khartir, though admittedly, he was proud of the defense the young magus had mustered.

Herod leaned across the table, pointing at Khartir. "Before, what you said, 'King'. What are you saying about some king?" He didn't wait for a response. "Is there someone claiming to be king out there?" He scowled at his priests. "What is he saying?"

"Yes, we are all interested in what you presume to know." Joazar smirked.

All eyes fell upon Khartir. "We left our homeland not knowing where the star might lead," Khartir began. "We brought with us the writings of many regions, many cultures which could be the one surrounding our destination. The closer we came, the more we concentrated on Judaea and the writings of the Jews. As we encountered nearby cities or other travelers, we would ask about materials we could examine or buy. We spent our nights studying Jewish texts to become more familiar with what you believe this star may signify."

Mithrias lay his head in his hands. "We will be in shackles by the time this is done," he mumbled.

"You recall your prophet, Micah, correct?" Khartir looked to the priests for confirmation, but neither would offer a hint of recognition. "Yes, Micah prophesied a ruler of Israel would come from the town of Bethlehem. Isn't Bethlehem close to Jerusalem? Might the star shine there? We believe Bethlehem will reveal the information we are seeking."

Joazar shifted in his chair. The arched eyebrows of contempt returned, carved into the countenances of both priests.

"I am sorry." Khartir folded his hands. "My remarks may have unintentionally aroused some anger. I merely wish to justify and illustrate the basis of our journey and why we are with you tonight, merely passing through your city." He then took one last swipe. "I simply assumed this was common knowledge among—"

"It is," Joazar interrupted. "Is this all? You appear to be very learned men about affairs outside your own domain, or so you would have us believe."

Khartir looked to Merkis for permission to continue. Surprisingly, Merkis gave it.

"Of course there's more," replied Khartir. "Surely, you wouldn't think we'd stop with just one assertion. We looked for confirmation. Even a peasant knows to do that."

Xaratuk's chortle burst out, though he quickly extinguished his smile.

"Isaiah," said Khartir, then sat back.

"What about Isaiah?" growled Joazar.

"Your prophet Isaiah said there would be a sign and one born of a virgin, who would be a king to deliver the Jews—but deliver them exactly from what he does not define. According to your prophet Isaiah, your God uses signs to communicate with his people. It is there. Isaiah says this."

Herod pounded the table, startling all those in the room to attention. The musicians stopped playing. Without cue or permission, they scrambled to gather their instruments and dashed to the closest exit. Herod looked about the room, glaring at each face, never uttering a word. Moments passed. Finally, his gaze rolled to Khartir, offering him a vacant smile. "Go on, please. I didn't mean to interrupt you."

Khartir's pace quickened. "And there was Jeremiah. He mentions a king from the House of David, and according to your writings, Bethlehem is—"

Merkis tugged lightly at Khartir's sleeve. "Enough for now."

Every guest looked vacantly to any available space not occupied by the perplexed face of another. Khartir had made his point. He had proven that this journey's goal remained intact. Something rare and wonderful demanded an investigation, even if the local pundits claimed otherwise.

Xaratuk was the only smiling person in the room.

Joazar broke the silence. "Clearly, our guests inflate their wisdom by choosing some unfiltered anecdotes from our writings, naively culling words to misrepresent our prophets. I'll admit I'm impressed with the attempt—especially from those who live so far away and are otherwise unacquainted with our people."

"We have studied the ways and beliefs of many peoples," said Merkis. "The more we can know—from any source—the better we can understand, and the better we can be of service to our king."

Herod pushed back from the table, then stood, pointing to the advisors. "They sound genuine to me!" He scowled at his priests. "What service are you to your king, my loyal priests?" he roared. "What do you know about Bethlehem being the birthplace of some King of the Jews?" He held up a fist. "I am king, am I not? And I have never been to Bethlehem!"

He lowered his arm, then staggered from his seat, using the backs of the other chairs for support. He shuffled slowly, clumsily, until he stood between his priests. Bending over, he put a painful grip on their respective shoulders, his head between theirs. "But I haven't been there because no one told me I should consider it." His gaze repeatedly switched from one priest to the other. "No one thinks it is important for me to know things like stars, or signs, or someone in my own country claiming to be King of the Jews. No one tells me there is scripture prophesying this new king." Both priests stared fixedly at the opposite wall. Herod's heavy hands raked over their shoulders as he lumbered back to his chair. "Are they right? Are there such prophecies?"

Joazar stood. He coughed, clearing his throat. "My King, please be seated. Your guests are deliberately trying to upset you, and for no reason." Herod flopped into his chair. "Strictly speaking, you could find these comments in our scriptures, yes. No one is trying to conceal these words from you, Your Excellency. They have been there for hundreds of years, but they simply do not apply in this instance. No. The context, my king, does not support the scriptures nor any claim that this is a crucial event. This star is not a sign, not at this time, and not at this place." He turned back to the advisors. "No king has stepped foot in that backwater hamlet for centuries. And there is no king there now."

"Your Excellency, if I may," began Eleazar. "Talk such as this from your 'honored guests,' or among anyone else spreading it, is just gossip—unworthy of your attention. It serves only to excite and distract."

"But you say others are talking about this. Under my very nose, people are talking about this...king?"

"It is the most inane gossip," restated Eleazar. "Talk like this is ignorant and unwarranted, King Herod. As you know, I can go outside the walls of Jerusalem on any given day, and by the afternoon, I can produce for you five men all claiming to be the next King of the Jews, or maybe, even more gloriously, our Messiah." Eleazar let his assertion sink in. "The times are, well, somewhat tense, what with the Romans in our midst and all that implies. Threats are everywhere—some from within, some from beyond. You are well aware of that." Eleazar got no more reaction from Herod than his hardened stare. "People are only too willing to be encouraged by those who assure them of their deliverance. If I were to place at your feet every scoundrel who calls himself 'Messiah', you would never have had the time to build your great Temple."

Eleazar rose, moving deliberately toward his king. He placed a light hand upon Herod's shoulder, then kneeled to keep his face even with Herod's. He chose a comforting tone. "It is for your own well-being that we keep news like this from you. You said earlier you haven't felt well, so what good comes from throwing some addled madman at your feet who claims to be your successor? Or why bother you with talk about some insignificant star which has placed itself 'miraculously' in the heavens, which only the superstitious and ignorant believe would be our deliverance?" Raising his hand, he pointed at the magi, condemning them. "What do they imply, Your Highness? Deliverance? Deliverance, I ask, from what—from whom?"

Eleazar stood, one hand still resting upon Herod's shoulder, the other stabbing the air. "Do these men imply your people wish deliverance…from you? These foreigners are in our city, in your palace, eating from your table, seeking someone who claims to be our new king? Are they offering you wisdom, or is this artifice? How despicably bold! They upset you with hearsay, with malevolent insinuations, with abject lies—even after you provide such gracious treatment and generosity. Have they come here to stoke rebellion among the sadly mistaken, disloyal boors who claim this star will be their deliverance—from you?"

Herod swung around to Mithrias, casting a confrontational and contemptuous scowl. Mithrias felt his breath catch. He did not look away. Herod's withering gaze shifted to Xaratuk. Each took the measure of the other. The room was as silent as a day-old corpse.

"No one believes that," Herod finally blurted. His attention returned to the priests.

Mithrias exhaled.

"If anything, those people are looking for deliverance from

the Romans, not me," said Herod.

"Well, the Romans then," said Eleazar. "The Romans can be the occasional nuisance, if I may speak frankly, my king. But Jerusalem has never been this rich. We have never had more citizens. We have never had more visitors, more commerce. We are now the most important city in the region—greater than Damascus. The Romans allow me, without reservation, to assist the High Priest in making sacrifices to God. We may observe the Sabbath." He pressed his knuckles into the table. "If for no other reason, my dear king, there is no Messiah in Bethlehem because we do not need one."

"The servants," said Herod, all but ignoring Eleazar. "Are the servants in my palace talking about this? Right under my nose?"

"Servants talk of many things," replied Joazar. "Things unworthy of royal attention."

Herod coughed. It was a coarse, hacking, choking cough. Attendants rushed to Herod's aid, allowing him to disgorge greenish phlegm into a large napkin. After a long, disturbing minute, Herod sat back in his chair, panting.

"Servants talk, indeed they do," added Eleazar. "It is only idle talk. It does not dominate their discussions. You have many concerns and worries, and this need not be one."

Glaring at his priests, Herod asked, "Have you gone to see this for yourselves?"

"No. Emphatically no," said Joazar. "No one has gone to Bethlehem," he repeated. "No one of importance should consider it. It is trivial and beneath our consideration." Turning to the advisors, he added, "And I feel compelled to say I think it is very ungracious that your guests should conjure such outrageous tales and cause their generous host such unwarranted duress."

Herod maintained a stony countenance, though tears rolled down his cheeks, the lingering evidence of his coughing spell. He looked lost in thought. Suddenly he shouted, "Find out if anyone has gone there and bring them to me. Bring. Them. To. Me!"

Xaratuk rose from his chair, turned to Herod, and assumed a slight bow. "Perhaps we can be of value to you, King Herod. You have indeed been a most gracious host, and we never intended to cause you any distress." His eyes flitted to his advisors, then to the priests. "With your blessing, we will go on to this town of Bethlehem tomorrow. We will see if there is anything to report. My advisors will learn what they can. You have been such a gracious host. I look upon your city and see all you have done for your people. I sincerely admire you, King Herod, and you deserve much better. It would be an honor for me to serve as your envoy, collect the information you need, and make our report, if you should welcome our return."

Herod looked up at Xaratuk, expressionless. He nodded and rose stiffly, steadying himself with a hand on Xaratuk's shoulder. "You see, all of you? It takes a stranger from a distant land to comprehend my desires. My own people, King Xaratuk, do not understand me. Do you see what I put up with? Please go. Find out if this star shines on Bethlehem and what it could mean. Maybe God chooses the next king instead of me. I should like to know. I will make sure you have a restful night to prepare you for your journey." He heaved a sigh and patted Xaratuk's hand. "Thank you."

CHAPTER 21

The kings, sensing an obligation, accepted Herod's offer to spend the night in the palace. It was Regulus who suggested that he and the others politely decline. The atmosphere in the palace remained charged; staying might incite more confrontation.

Xaratuk pulled his captain aside to reinforce his directive to pay particular attention to the tents and center poles. The plan was to meet at the west gate tomorrow mid-morning, where an elite contingent would begin the momentous final leg to Bethlehem. The rest of the caravan would remain behind. This timing would assure their arrival at dusk when the star's beacon should be brightest.

Regulus and the rest were escorted to their camp by a detachment of palace guards. No Roman thought to investigate.

The kings lingered near the table, reviewing the earlier events. "I never intended to upset our host," Xaratuk said. Mithrias's shoulders drooped. He looked weak and defeated. Xaratuk moved in for better inspection. "But I understand why my advisors were provocative. I'm glad they said what they did." He placed his hand on Mithrias's arm. "But you. I couldn't follow you. It seemed you went out of your way to minimize the man. You probably soured his mood."

"I did. I feel responsible. Something came over me. I can't explain it."

Xaratuk snickered. "That priest—the one with the red sash. What a condescending, arrogant little man. I'm glad my advisors put him in his place. Those priests underestimated us."

"In sum, our group has provoked King Herod."

"Probably so." Xaratuk chuckled again.

"I am quite worried. I fear we may have incited more danger when I recall what Topur told us about the man."

Xaratuk shook his head. "I think I have him appeased."

"Your men showed one thing," Mithrias added. "They knew more about Hebrew prophecy after just a few weeks than Herod has gained over a lifetime. Topur may be right. Herod is not as Jewish as he might believe."

"I think you're unfair, Mithrias, and I know our useless guide is." Xaratuk took Mithrias's elbow and started toward the balcony. A slim figure used the shadows to conceal a retreat from behind the farthest pillar, trailing away into the inky darkness. Mithrias noticed, but said nothing.

Xaratuk continued talking as they stepped to the balcony's edge to observe the elegance of Jerusalem at night. "I maintain Herod is misunderstood. The Jews are not strong enough to stand against the Romans, and Herod is almost alone in understanding that. He is able to work, if not flourish, within that constraint—even if his subjects can't, or won't." He tugged on Mithrias's sleeve. "And he is building a city that captures the attention—I daresay admiration—of the very people who rule over him. He has won Rome's approval, and that is no minor accomplishment! At the same time, he has converted this city into a religious shrine for his own people." He pointed to the Temple. "If that Temple were not present, Jerusalem would be a marginal destination at best. If the Jews value their religion so much, hasn't Herod been the one to enhance it?" He made a sour face. "I can't explain it. His people should fall in line to wash his feet." He placed a finger on Mithrias's chest. "And what if he didn't know the obscure rantings of some loose-tongued prophet from hundreds of years ago?"

"He killed his sons, Xaratuk."

Xaratuk turned away. "Yes, yes. And I killed my uncle. Sometimes events force hard choices. I was not wrong about having done what I had to do. Why should I not presume the same for Herod? I don't know."

"And his wife," Mithrias added, "and his stepmother, and his brothers-in-law—"

"I get your point," Xaratuk said. "He has been an excellent host to us. He has honored our wish to be kept apart from the Romans."

"Let's hope that continues, and we are not within some trap waiting to be sprung."

Xaratuk looked down at his feet, shaking his head. "Mithrias, the man sent his army out to save our lives! Are you not at least grateful?"

"You are right about that. We do owe him."

"We do. We do. And I hope we can repay his hospitality. My offer to Herod is genuine." Mithrias sensed Xaratuk becoming unreservedly enamored with their host. Their conversation lagged. Xaratuk seemed lost in thought. Mithrias was content to let his own thoughts wander. Finally, in a soft voice, Xaratuk spoke. "All this is more confusing to me today than when we started this journey. It is exciting but strange to ponder what this star will reveal."

Away from the city, sitting low in the sky, the star shone brightly.

"How can anyone not see that?" said Xaratuk. "Or see it and not be moved? How strange Herod didn't know about it and, until tonight, didn't much care."

"He cares now, my friend. He cares now."

Beckoned by a servant, they left the fresh air. They followed him from the dining room down a stairway, then onto an arcade that spanned the length of the palace.

In the courtyards, groves of groomed Syrian cypress trees stood in dark silhouettes. Gurgling water splashed in the fountains. Astonishingly realistic statues throughout the grounds reflected Herod's taste for Greek nudes and the human form. Decorative pots as tall as a man's chest were placed with precise regularity along the colonnade walls. Their sheer size was impressive. Each pot was topped with a small palm tree. Roman arches blended artfully with Greek columns. The palace's design and decor displayed Herod's interests in art, leisure, wealth, and modernity. The kings were not inclined to rush through such elegant beauty.

Most rooms adjoining the walkway had long linen drapes separating them from the arcade. Other, more infrequent rooms had wooden doors. At one of those, the servant stopped, opened the heavy door, and informed Xaratuk that this would be his quarters for the evening.

The room was enormous, with a mosaic floor depicting a hunting party chasing a lion. The ceiling was tall with thick-hewn beams. Inside was a massive bed upon a raised stone platform. Long tables piled with fruit bowls and wine decanters lined the far wall. Oil lamps provided a warm, luminous glow. Four enormous pots with palm trees added lively elegance to the room. But the room was occupied.

Four people were already inside. Two were women, young, attractive, their heads uncovered, clad only in sheer garments. They had just finished preparing the bed. The two young men were seated with musical instruments at the far end of the room. One woman spoke, batting her lovely eyes. "We are here to keep you entertained, Your Highness, with whatever may amuse you." She bowed her head.

Xaratuk smiled at Mithrias with a wide-eyed look of satisfaction. "I am to be amused, it seems. With that, I bid you good night." His grin was effusive. "Do not sleep too late. But no need to rise too early, either. I am sure you understand what I mean." He drew nose-to-nose with Mithrias and whispered, "Mithrias, one more thing. Merkis and Khartir mentioned it earlier—what is this about a Messiah? What is this word?"

Mithrias whispered back, "I do not know, my friend. Topur and I never spoke about it. It did seem to make Herod and his priests visibly upset."

"I must find out what this Messiah is. Before we get to Bethlehem, I will ask Merkis and Khartir. I must be thoroughly prepared." Xaratuk patted Mithrias's chest. "Well, I am off to be 'amused', as they say. I love this city."

"I trust you will have a fitful rest." Mithrias gave Xaratuk a mock salute as he left the room. The door clicked shut behind him. A woman giggled. He smiled.

Mithrias continued with the same servant strolling through the courtyard's gardens to the arcade's twin on the opposite side. The servant stopped before another wooden door. "Your room, sir." The servant pressed the latch. As the door opened, he stepped back. With his usual courtesy, Mithrias thanked him.

After months of trekking, the attack, and the lingering effects of an anxious dinner, Mithrias felt spent. He had no interest in the indulgences offered to Xaratuk. Rest, indoors, alone on a comfortable bed, was far preferable.

Mithrias slunk into the doorway, eyes cast to the floor. He heard voices. He raised his face. Again, there were two men and two women, waiting. The men held musical instruments. One woman was arranging flowers. She was young, almost too young, petite, with smooth, flawless skin and an innocent expression. She welcomed in a high, sweet voice, "We are here to make you comfortable, Your Excellency. Please tell us what we might do. We can begin with some music."

The door closed behind Mithrias, nudging him into the room. The men began to play, one on a lyre, the other on a small drum. The young girl sang, her voice uncommonly strong. It was a strange song to Mithrias's ears, a song whose language he did not understand. The notes seemed to jump haphazardly. Though he didn't care for the melody, the musicians performed well.

Her back to the doorway, the other woman stood at the far

side of the room before a long table, pouring wine from a tall decanter into two cups. Her hair was dark, though not black. It was wavy and uncovered, falling just beyond her shoulders. She wore a sheer sleeveless dress that clung to her curvaceous form. Light scarves of purple, red, green, and yellow were attached to a thin belt low across her flat waist, making the see-through nature of her sheer dress more mysterious. This was no girl. She was a stunning young woman in full blossom. She turned to Mithrias with a cup of wine in each hand. "Something to soothe you?" she offered.

Mithrias studied her face. Her sinuous hair was pulled back and tucked behind each ear. Her dark eyebrows arched to a muted peak above the eyes, then tapered to her temples. Her eyes were large and of a rare color—an umber hue transmuting to earthy green. They were clear, penetrating, but not demanding. Her long, slim nose was gracefully set upon two beautifully proportionate lips accented with a red shine.

Mithrias was a king. He had seen scores upon scores of beautiful women. Because of his own appearance, they often sought him out. But this beauty, standing in front of him, was profoundly rare. To his eye, she was entirely without flaw. She was no majestic beauty, elegant only from afar. Hers was a beauty that drew one heedlessly closer, sparking the impulse to possess and never stop looking. Even her collarbones below her slim neck aroused him. Alerted by his rapid breathing, he realized he had done nothing but stare at her from the moment he entered the room. He was unaccustomed to being the one stammering for something to say.

Words stumbled from Mithrias's mouth. "Yes, I will have—whatever you have there."

She walked toward him. "My name is Rizpah."

Mithrias felt like a rustic boy. He reached for the cup in her hand. "I am Mithrias—"

"I know who you are. The entire palace knows who you are, Your Excellency. The entire palace wishes they were the ones here to greet you." Her voice was low and breathy, yet friendly and relaxed. Mithrias could feel he was already flushed, standing before someone so beautiful. He struggled to remain composed.

"Your doorway would be choked with admirers if those in the palace had their way," she said. Her eyes continued to command his. "But I am the fortunate one who will attend to your wishes tonight." Her gaze moved to the cups. "Here, you will like this. It is warm and very soothing." Rizpah's eyes closed slowly, seductively, then opened again. "And I do mean it when I say I am the fortunate one."

"I thank you, Rizpah." Mithrias fought to gain back some small measure of control. Experience had taught him that being tactfully truthful, rather than coy, was an effective way to diffuse an uncomfortable situation. "Rizpah," he began, "before you say another word, I must tell you I find you one of the most attractive women I have had the privilege of meeting. Your beauty is so complete and so rare. I don't know what compels me to say that, but if I don't, my thoughts will linger there, wishing to be expressed and might embarrass me later. So, I say it now. I am awestruck by this vision before me."

"I am the one who is embarrassed now, Your Excellency. I am grateful for your kind and generous words." For the first time, she revealed her smile and one small dimple on her right cheek. She returned to the wine decanters and put her cup down. "You have my undivided attention for the entire evening."

Being transfixed, Mithrias had neglected to notice the music. The tempo had changed. The young girl sang without words to the music. One man had switched from a lyre to a flute, while the other struck a drum that produced varying tones and timbres. The tune was upbeat. As Rizpah now showed with her undulating hips, it was music for dancing.

Rizpah swayed to a luxuriously padded chair near the wall, then placed it in the middle of the room. She returned to

Mithrias and gently took his arm. Her arousing pull gave him goosebumps. He hoped they wouldn't show. The hair on the back of his neck rose. He was grateful for her touch. He craved it. She led him to the chair, then placed both hands on his shoulders, encouraging him to sit.

The drummer beat a rhythm Mithrias felt in his chest. The flute's notes trilled fluidly while the young singer provided pleasing support. Mithrias realized it was best to sit; his arousal made its impertinent presence known. He hadn't felt this way for months—maybe years. Rizpah moved seductively around him. At times, she bent to brush her breasts upon his shoulder or head. As if splashed by a wave of cold water, Mithrias felt every part of his body tingle. He yearned for the next time her body would touch his. He forced himself to look directly ahead, feeling that if he followed her with his eyes, he would lose all composure and ravage her in front of the others. She was that irresistible.

Rizpah tossed her hair, letting it touch Mithrias's shoulders. She moved in front of him, collecting his eyes. A purple scarf fluttered from her inner thigh, snaking a sinuous path to the floor. She looked for a reaction. Mithrias closed his eyes, only to open them at precisely the spot upon her body Rizpah had intended. She dropped to her knees and grabbed his thighs, pulling them apart. Her hands crept up, and she thrust her head forward, throwing her hair into his lap, exposing her bare neck. Slowly, her hair and hands retreated, melting Mithrias into the chair. Rizpah rose and began a series of spins and rotations around the chair. On each side, Mithrias received a tantalizing nip on his earlobe, leaving him with a sensation of lightning scorching a hot path through him. Muscles tensed with anticipation, he sat awkwardly, earnestly hoping she would never stop.

Around the chair, Rizpah spun, lingering at his ear. She threw her hair forward, hiding her face from the others, and spoke a single word.

"No," she said. But it was not in Greek. It sounded as if she uttered the word in Mithrias's native tongue. But the word was too short. He wasn't sure. Rizpah danced to the other side, pressing her breasts to the back of Mithrias's neck. Again, she thrust her hair forward, her lips upon his ear. He treasured the lightness of her hair upon his head, her hot breath steaming his neck.

"Talking," she whispered. This time it was clear; she was speaking in his native language. He put the two words together. No talking. Puzzled, he looked at her for clarification. Rizpah stared intently into Mithrias's eyes. Mithrias moved his head to follow her wherever she went, hoping to glean some clue. Not only was she lovely to watch, but hearing words in his own tongue enhanced his arousal.

With successive revolutions around the chair, Mithrias received the message, one hushed word at a time: "Only... speak... Greek... when... musicians... are here... after... that... no... more." Once she conveyed that message, her dancing became even more erotic.

Rizpah stopped rotating around the chair and stood directly in front of Mithrias. She swayed and curled as she removed one sheer scarf, then another, then another, revealing more and more of the thinly covered skin beneath. One hand massaged and caressed her breasts, then the other inched slowly down to her inner thigh, loosening one more veil. She continued until only two remained.

Her rotations around the chair began anew, and with that, a new message: "Eyes," she said, "under... the... trees... see... us." Mithrias understood the words but not the meaning. He failed to conceal his confusion. Rizpah glanced at the potted palms placed around the room. Mithrias tried to examine the pots unobtrusively. He discerned small holes in the decorative paint, just wide enough for a pair of eyes.

Rizpah was losing Mithrias's focus. She stopped the dancing and began caressing him from behind, working her hands rhythmically underneath his tunic while pulling her way up his chest and over his shoulders. The music intensified, coming to a peak. Rizpah moved in front of Mithrias, fell to her knees, and put both hands into Mithrias's crotch. She grabbed the only thing there meant for gripping. Her eyes met his, and she slowly drew her lower lip up Mithrias's leg. The music paused. Rizpah rose, put an arm around Mithrias, then sat in his lap. Her chest, inches from Mithrias's nose, heaved.

"Did you like that dance, Your Excellency?" Her skin glistened. Some hair, moistened by her exertions, lined her forehead in thin strands.

Mithrias answered, as instructed, in Greek, "I liked it very much, very much indeed. But there were parts I may have missed, so if you would do it all over again—"

"You are a charming man. Handsome *and* funny." Rizpah kissed Mithrias on his lips, then rose from his lap. Mithrias longed to keep her in place, to return her kiss. But he released her. They continued with small talk in Greek while Rizpah regained her breath. The musicians talked amongst themselves.

Rizpah stepped to the back of the room to retrieve her wine and downed it in a gulp. She turned to the musicians, speaking in Aramaic. "Out! I want you all to go—now!" The musicians were dumbstruck; none could muster one word in response. But once they recovered from the shock, their objections took flight.

"No, no, Rizpah, you know that isn't how it goes!" said the flute player. The others immediately joined him, all talking at once.

"King Herod won't like it! He doesn't like you working alone," said the drummer.

"I will get in trouble for this! Don't get me into trouble, Rizpah," said the young girl.

"We were told to remain here all night," the flute player added.

Rizpah strode to the door, opened it, then returned to the

musicians, yanking them to their feet. She forced the instruments into their hands and pushed them toward the entrance.

"Here, don't forget this." She picked up a lyre and tossed it toward the door.

"Rizpah, King Herod will surely hear of this. You know he is already angry," said one.

Rizpah gave one more push on the musicians' backs. "I am with his friend. Our king knows I will be useful. Now go. Get some sleep for a change. You'll thank me sometime." With that, she maneuvered them and the wriggling girl out the door and locked it behind them.

Since they conducted the entire fracas in Aramaic, Mithrias understood none of it.

"We don't need to use Greek anymore," Rizpah said in Mithrias's language. She retrieved his cup and moved to the table. She returned with two cups, giving both to Mithrias, then kneeled to gather the scarves shed earlier. "I won't need these again tonight, will I?" she asked.

Mithrias wondered how to respond. "I would suppose... not?" He hoped that was the correct response. She glided a single scarf across Mithrias's upper thigh, then teasingly drew it away. She laid the scarves on the bed and slipped into a thin robe, which she left open. Her firm, upturned breasts pressed against the sheer fabric.

She caught him looking and smiled. "We are not done for the evening, great king, unless you wish it so. And I don't think you'll wish that. Not tonight."

Mithrias, summoning all his willpower, shifted focus. "The others—why did you send them away?"

Rizpah took her wine from Mithrias, drank, then poured more. "Did you want them to stay...with us?" she responded playfully.

"No, I'd prefer they leave, but will you answer this? Were they spies?"

"Spies?" said Rizpah coyly. Her face turned away from his. "Of course they were spies. All of us inside the palace are to work for our king all day. Or all night." She returned and rested a hand on his shoulder. "That makes me a spy as well."

Mithrias's head jerked back. "You are a spy, then?"

"Of course," she said. "But I sent those musicians away because, for tonight, I am off duty. I am not Herod's agent tonight." She took a finger and propped it firmly underneath Mithrias's chin. "I am here for you, and only for you. Your words and your feelings are mine and mine alone. You are safe with me." Her blunt truthfulness, if that was what it was, left him unbalanced. He scanned her for more cues. The only thing his senses could interpret was confirmation that Rizpah was perhaps the most strikingly beautiful woman he had ever seen. They would not offer an opinion as to her trustworthiness.

Rizpah moved her hand from Mithrias's chin, then stood behind him. She placed her fingertips on his forehead and rubbed lightly. "Tonight, I want to make you the happiest you have ever been. I suppose I have some competition to account for." She scratched her fingernails through Mithrias's thick, dark hair, then continued to massage his temples. "You are a handsome, handsome man, King Mithrias."

"You are well on the way to achieving your goal already, but you remain a mystery to me." Her touch both soothed and electrified him. He wanted her to keep touching him—it didn't matter where or how. "Who are you? How do you know my language? Where do you come from? Why are you here in Jerusalem—and in the palace? How did you know my—"

"Shhhh, so many questions. I am trying to relax you, and your brain has a fever!"

She moved in front of him. Her robe fell to the floor. She raised one arm high. With the other, she traced the length of her raised arm from the wrist, down the elbow, to the shoulder and then crept her hand across from one breast to the next, her hips gently swaying. "We don't have to talk." She looked at Mithrias, expecting him to reach for her. He didn't. She lowered her arm, bemused that this dependable titillation had, for the first time, failed. "Or, I can tell you some things about myself, if that is what you wish."

"I don't wish to be this intimate with...a stranger," Mithrias said. "And I feel I should be more than a stranger to you. I can't say why—not yet—but I don't want tonight to be my only night with you."

Rizpah's eyebrows raised. "The future is hard to predict," she said. "I don't want us to be strangers, either, and since I already know much about you, I guess I can offer more about me, though it isn't much to tell."

"Where are you from? How do you come to speak my language?"

Rizpah bent for her robe, then wrapped it securely around her.

"Is it all right if I sit here?" she said, then sat on his lap. "I will be most comfortable here." She was remarkably light. It was as if only the robe had been placed upon him.

"Of course," Mithrias responded. Rizpah placed a firm kiss upon him, her lips slightly parted. It was a hard yet gentle, lingering kiss. Mithrias closed his eyes. The only destiny for this kiss was to end too soon, and it did.

"I am honest with you when I say I remember little of my childhood—not my house, not my village, not even my family." Her expression became vacant. "I remember being hungry. I have to assume that I was born and raised, for a time, in or near your kingdom. Our language is the one I first knew. I haven't heard it spoken in so long. It is like listening to a mother's lullaby, familiar and comfortable. I am surprised I remember so much of it. We don't get visitors from your country through here, so I never get the chance to speak it."

"You remember it very well. You had to be no more than a child when you left the country."

"Yes, but as I said, I remember so little of my youth. I was still a child when I arrived in Jerusalem. I wasn't with my parents—I haven't any recollection of them. I remember being given to a priest and his family, and then, within a month or two, I was here at the palace." She rose, poured another cup of wine, and then returned to Mithrias's lap. "Here, have more wine."

"I will if you guarantee this is not some potion that will make me sleep instead."

"You will be awake, alert, and aroused for the duration."

Mithrias took a sip. Then Rizpah took Mithrias's cup and drank from it.

"I drink what you drink."

"So you have been at the palace since you were a child?"

"Yes. I remember almost everything that has happened to me since my arrival here. I was maybe five or six years old. For several years, I helped keep the bedrooms clean and ready for visitors or did some work in the kitchen. One day, a guest attacked me. A guard was able to intervene, but it came to the attention of Herod, and ever since then, I have been under his, shall we say, 'watchful eye'."

"You were brought here as a slave, then?"

"And that is what I remain, good King. A slave in the court of Herod the Great."

"Might you be King Herod's mistress?"

Rizpah's face, for the first time, turned serious. She avoided his eyes while her delicate jaw tightened.

"I guess you could say that. It is that, and more." She looked down. "I am in an unusual situation—mostly of my own making, I suppose. As much as possible, I try to control things. I really should talk less and be here for you instead." She used a finger to pull Mithrias's chin up and met his lips with another kiss. This time, Mithrias cut it abruptly.

"I want to know more; I will be happier knowing more."

"Very well."

Rizpah curled an arm around Mithrias's neck. "Herod has always been rather obsessed with me. I wasn't in the palace when he had Mariamne killed. That was before my time. But I am told I remind him of her. He was intensely jealous of anyone who paid attention to her, and he is much the same with me. Though he has several wives and other mistresses, he wants me for himself—not that he can do much about that. He is very sick and quite unable to perform. It has been that way for many years now. Still, he likes to see me and talk to me and have me dance before him. He still enjoys that."

"Any man with a heartbeat would feel the same. I can appreciate Herod's desire to keep such loveliness to himself."

"You are most kind to say so, but if you want the truth, there is more."

"Go on."

"He keeps me for himself but sets me aside for rare, special assignments. If there is someone he wants to impress, or information he is urgently looking to gather, he uses my talents to extract secrets from the visitor. I am the one he picks for special guests." She rose and doused the light in two oil lamps. "I can usually manipulate the situation enough to maintain a shred of dignity."

"What are you saying?"

"Herod uses me, but only sparingly. And then, I usually end up with men who are more used to luxury than physical exertion." She looked Mithrias up and down. "Most men I meet in the palace I find revolting, at best. Not at all like you. I ought to be more grateful. Herod obsesses over me, so he's largely unwilling to utilize me in the manner I have been trained." Her look was cynical. "I have a great deal of free time."

Mithrias reached to tuck a strand of moistened hair behind Rizpah's ear. "You said others are watching us. Will they report you? Can they understand us?"

Rizpah smiled. "Understand us? No. You can be certain of that. Maybe you've seen men like these before? They are small and will never grow taller, but they are sharp and shrewd. They squeeze into those pots and stay there for hours. Herod keeps them very secret. Almost all the workers in this palace are completely unaware of their existence. I know every one of them, however. Each one owes his very life to Herod. If they were forced to live on their own, they'd be called demons or be killed or banished." Rizpah laughed dryly. "They owe much to Herod, but he also owes much to them. They are extremely good at what they do."

"How are you able to know them when so many of the others don't?"

"As I said, I have a great deal of free time. Herod gives me blanket permission to visit any room in the palace whenever I wish. All these men are housed in a secret, locked room near the guest dining hall. They are never without an exclusive, armed escort. They use only the secret corridors. They remain invisible. And, though most of the little men are fiercely loyal to Herod and remain indifferent to me, there are four or five I can count on—the type who will keep and share secrets with me. I may put on a little show of mine just for them, to keep the friendship fresh, if you will."

"Even if they can't understand us, I still feel rather uncomfortable with them here—watching."

"There is nothing I can do about that. I hope they will not inhibit you too much." Rizpah's eyes fluttered as she returned to the chair, retaking his lap. "All of them have been in these situations countless times. It is one of Herod's most successful ploys. I'm unsure of Herod's reaction should he find out none of them could understand our conversation, but I plan to explain that. It shouldn't place us in any danger."

Rizpah resumed a playful look and lightly traced Mithrias's chin with her finger. "You will forget all about them. I'll make sure of that. Besides, notice how I had the pots placed so that none of them can look toward the bed. They cannot watch us."

Mithrias could not suppress a smile.

"Some of them have been very loyal to me. One informed me of your presence in Jerusalem and that you would be at dinner. He told me where you are from. He knew I would be interested. He did not comment on how handsome you are. I was happy to find that out for myself." She gave Mithrias another brief kiss. "I arranged to watch you from the balcony at your dinner. You were so serious."

"That was you? I saw someone—"

She put a finger to his lips, then kissed him hard, finishing with a flick of her tongue. "I decided then that it would be me who entertained you in this room tonight—me, and no one else." She stepped back, allowing Mithrias to observe her entire face. "I had to be here. I wanted it to be me who spends the night here with you." She directed his arm to her shoulders and pulled him closer. He responded with a warm grasp. "I am what I am, King Mithrias. There is no point in pretending otherwise. But I am not pretending to want to be here with you. One night is not enough, but it may be all I will ever have."

Mithrias was used to compliments. He'd received an ocean of them. Few were heartfelt. But he believed this woman. He studied her downcast gaze. Her slumped shoulders made her appear sad and vulnerable. With a finger, he lifted her chin. Her eyebrows rose, and her eyes opened wide, as if expecting pain. Wordlessly, Mithrias moved them both from the chair. Standing, he took her wrists, pulling her close, placing her hands behind his waist. With one hand, he guided her head to his shoulder and held it in place. His other hand found the middle of her back. He held her.

"At dinner, I heard what you said about the sandal maker," she whispered. "I heard you say common people had as much right to happiness as kings. I hear so many things at this palace, but no one has said anything like that. Those who come through here only speak of themselves and how much they should be adored." She fingered the hem of Mithrias's tunic. "You make me feel that someone like you might care for someone like me." She halted. "Oh, I'm so sorry. That is going beyond what I have promised you."

Mithrias backed up, his hands upon Rizpah's shoulders. "Rizpah, you have kindled feelings within me I haven't felt for so long. I didn't think I would feel them again—ever. But you shake me, Rizpah, right through to the floor. This is much too quick, but you fascinate me. I find this...amazing."

Rizpah stepped back into Mithrias's embrace and clenched him. She felt the quickened pace of his heart. "My looks will fade. Herod hasn't much time left, and I don't know if I will be willed to one of his sons or be sent out to the street. But I don't want to talk about it now. Tonight is ours. I will make it your most beautiful memory."

She did as she promised. And in her time with Mithrias, Rizpah came to understand that she had forever been a target: for men's eyes and men's hands, for their desire, for their sense of privilege, and their carnal pleasure. She had been a target for their selfishness and possessiveness. She had known desire solely as being an object. Never once had any man shown the slightest concern for her beyond her ability to please him. As beautiful as she was, she had been treated as a mute statue made of seductive flesh.

But this patient, quiet, beautiful man possessed hands that cared, caressed, and relieved. His gentle words were supportive, inquisitive, and attentive. Desire, for the first time, was lit within. She could not consume enough of him. He could not touch her in enough places. He could not hold her close enough. Now, everything she wished for surrounded only him.

Rizpah had always been painfully aware that love was absent from her life. This arousal, this new longing—was this part of love?

He had asked about her tears, and for the first time since they began talking, she lied. She told him it was because of the things she regretted about the past. But in truth, it was her fear of the future. She knew that after this evening, her future would be equally stark, equally bleak, and equally unfulfilling as her life had been up to this point. Once this man left, there was nothing to anticipate with any sense of joy.

She offered Mithrias a most meaningful, most tender, and most beautiful memory. And what she received in return was her own most exquisite memory—an expression of caring previously denied for her entire existence—one that now would have to last a lifetime.

As for Mithrias, during his evening of unexpected bliss, the abyss that had shadowed his every move for the entire journey had edged far away. For a few brief hours, he did not feel its empty haunting. For a few short hours, he was the man he had once been, cradled in the joy of being alive.

CHAPTER 22

Miriam had dozed, confident the timidity and superstitious fears of others concealed her and her wounded patient. So, the insistent rapping on her door came as a shock. Her first thought was for Topur. He lay motionless. More quick knocks. Through the door, she heard Kauib's urgent whisper.

"Please, Miss! Please!"

"Oh. You." Miriam rolled from her cot. She straightened her robe and placed the nearest scarf on her head. "Kauib, I am coming." Barefoot, she shuffled to the door and opened it. Before her stood Kauib, wriggling his tangled hands. "What is it? Are you all right?"

"Miss, yes, but—" His hands continued to writhe before his chest. "But your man's companion—his boy—he is being held. He was caught trying to sneak into the palace."

Miriam gasped. "You did the right thing, Kauib. I will see to this."

"He was not trying to hurt anyone or steal anything," Kauib rushed to add. "He only wants to see his master—that's all. He wants to know if he will live."

"I know the boy is harmless, Kauib. But he must not be taken to the captain of the guards—he must not."

Miriam returned to her cot to choose a different head covering, one for public appearance. Her mourning shawl was closest. She wrapped her head and shoulders with it. "I must speak to the guards myself. I will convince them this boy is no threat. Then I will make it clear to your friend that my patient must not be disturbed."

Topur roused. "Who is there? I hear a boy. Is that Najiir? By all means, let him in." He gingerly rubbed his eyes.

"It isn't Najiir, and you stay down. You rest. You are not ready for visitors."

"Not Najiir?" Barely moving his legs, Topur tried to sit up. A shock of pain smothered that notion.

Miriam turned to her patient. "Quit moving, or you'll break the seal, and we'll have your blood all over." She stepped to Kauib, placing her hands on both shoulders. "Kauib, which guard found Najiir? Is it anyone we know?"

"It is Bartholomew," said Kauib.

"Oh, Bartholomew. That's good. Is anyone else there?"

"Not so far, I think."

"If it is only Bartholomew, run to him. Tell him I said the boy may come to my room. Bartholomew shouldn't be a problem, and I can stay here. If he has questions, he can come here with Najiir. Otherwise, you bring your friend directly to me. But don't let anyone see you. Now go. Be quick."

Kauib sped away.

Miriam rubbed her forehead. "Oh, this could be terrible. Najiir is determined to reach you. Pray that it is only Bartholomew. Lucky, lucky, lucky." She closed the door. "I'll let you speak to Najiir, but only once. It is too soon for visitors. After you see he is well, you must rest."

"I must be ready to travel with the others," Topur rasped.

"Look at you! You can't even sit up on your own. If you can't sit, you can't walk. If you can't walk, you can't travel. You can make arrangements to meet your kings later."

"I can't come this far," said Topur through clenched teeth. "I can't come this far and not witness the end. Besides—"

"If you leave now, you won't reach the end." Miriam inspected her handiwork. "I have done a marvelous job of patching you, but you are far from healed."

There was a soft knock on the door, and it opened with a long squeak.

"Is that you, Kauib?"

Kauib's head peered around the door. "Bartholomew says he trusts you, but you must arrange a meal for him with Rachel. He said he would talk with you later."

Miriam's shoulders slumped with relief.

From behind the door, Najiir's head appeared. He looked directly at Miriam. "Your mourning shawl! Miss, he's not dead, is he?" Najiir burst past his friend to the bedside of Topur. He fell to his knees, holding Topur's dangling hand. The tears began. "My master, my dearest, dearest master."

"Oh, Najiir. Don't bury me just yet. Stand up—let me see you!" Topur's free hand groped for any part of Najiir it could find. "Miriam requires that I remain among the living." He tousled Najiir's hair. "This makes me so happy—so happy! Stand by me. Stand up, my boy. I need to see you." He used his good arm to pull Najiir closer, then kissed him on the head. "I have been so worried."

"And I have been so worried about you," said Najiir between sniffs.

"Thanks to Miriam here, I will live. She accepts nothing less from her patients." Looking straight at her, he added, "She is a remarkable woman. Had they brought me here in pieces, she would have fit them together again. I am in the best of hands, so no more worrying."

Topur had felt so helpless imagining Najiir out in Jerusalem by himself, wandering too far, saying too much, being too curious. But Najiir was now in front of him, and Topur found it infinitely easier to breathe.

"Where are you staying? Who is taking care of you?" Topur asked.

"We have made camp just outside the city walls. The expedition rests there. They seem comfortable. Everyone is there except for the kings. They stayed in the palace."

A hiss escaped through Topur's clenched teeth. "So, the kings are with Herod in the palace?" Topur's hands tightened. He stared sharply at Najiir.

"Of course they are here," said Miriam. "Where else would such esteemed men be? Herod will want to know why they are in Judaea and show his respect." Under her breath, she added, "And he'll want to keep them where he can see them."

Eyes closed, Topur rubbed his forehead. "The kings might speak too freely, and Herod's imagination is too unstable. Najiir, do the kings seem free to come and go? Can you tell?"

"I haven't seen them," Najiir replied. "I did hear King Herod had dinner with them last night. The others were there, too—Regulus and the advisors."

Topur pinched the bridge of his nose.

"This morning, I overheard a few guards and servants talking," Najiir continued. "No one mentioned much about the kings. There was much more talk about some priests."

Miriam raised her head.

"Well, I admit I expected worse," said Topur. "What about the Romans?"

"I see them," said Najiir, "but not as many as I thought I might. It is easy to move around the city without them noticing me. Outside the city gates, there are few, if any."

"That is good. Thank God. One small piece of good news."

"Now that I think about it," Najiir said, "I didn't see a single one on my way to Bethlehem."

Topur drew his hand back from his brow. "What?" Stymied for words, he absorbed Najiir's revelation. "You? *You* have been to Bethlehem, Najiir? Why? How?"

"Kauib said he'd been there. Some others mentioned it, so I decided I—"

"Of course." Topur grimaced. "There is nothing about this journey I have predicted correctly—nothing. And so it goes. The first person from our caravan to reach Bethlehem was not a king, not the magi. It was *you*."

"Yes, when Kauib mentioned he had been there, it reminded me of the advisors and what they said, so I thought I should investigate. I didn't want to leave you, but it isn't far. I can run all the way."

"Tell me—tell me what you found," said Topur.

Clasping her folded linens, Miriam stepped closer.

"It is where the star's light ends. You can see that from far away. The star shines upon Bethlehem, but the light is upon a small house, almost like a...a hut. Inside is a poor family. They keep their home very tidy, but they have so little."

"No palace, then?"

"No. No palace, no soldiers, no Romans, either. It's all so... simple. If a star didn't shine down upon it, no one would think to notice."

"Aha!" Miriam interjected, placing the bandages at the foot of Topur's bed. "Isn't that what I told you? As I said, it is a humble place with humble people. There's no lavish new city. Bethlehem is as it has always been."

"Nothing more?" Topur said. "This is so unbelievable, the light upon one spot, one small house? No. There must be more to it. A star—this light—has no more purpose than that? What is happening over there? Is this a family of sorcerers, some magicians?"

Najiir shuffled his feet. "I don't believe so, Master. There weren't many people when I arrived—about ten. But that doesn't count the shepherds outside guarding the house. There are many of them. They make sure unknown visitors understand some rules. No one gets inside the home without their permission. So I talked to them. After a while, they allowed me inside."

"No! You spoke with those people? What did you say? What did they say?"

"The father's name is Joseph." Najiir sat on the edge of the bed. "He seemed so tired. I introduced myself, and he seemed pleased to meet me. I don't know why." Najiir bit his lower lip.

"I asked if I might help—were there any chores that needed attention? He took me to a small cave behind the house. It held a few animals. I offered to feed them so he could return to the house, but he stayed with me. We talked. I think he enjoyed a moment away from the house. He told me neither he nor his wife know what the next day will bring. He hasn't worked since the baby was born. If not for others' generosity, they would have little to eat or wear and no place to live. His wife's name is Mary. She was very quiet while I was there. Their child made no sound. He was asleep, I guess. I told Joseph about us—that we would be coming to Bethlehem." Najiir hesitated, looking at his feet. His words were tentative. "I told them who would be visiting. I told him the names of our kings." He cringed, ready to be admonished. He wasn't, so he continued. "Joseph seemed impressed. I hope I wasn't wrong to tell him."

Topur thought for a moment. "I hope so, too."

"Topur," Miriam began, "many have been to Bethlehem. I've been to Bethlehem, and so has Najiir. Not one of us can say with authority what is there. No one is certain, but there are many, many rumors and so much talk. Will your kings be able to discover something the others have not?"

"Yes, rumors," said Topur. "Najiir, did the visitors tell you what they think?"

"I overheard some others. They agree that the star's light proves the baby is a king. And one man, one shepherd, kept calling him 'Savior'."

"It's just as you said." Topur stared in disbelief at Miriam. "A baby whom people claim is a king."

"The shepherds have their own stories," said Najiir. "Fantastic and amazing stories. They claim they are changed. They are completely devoted to the baby." Najiir paused, his voice softening. "Even I felt something, but I can't say what or why. I am eager to go back."

Miriam rose from Topur's bedside. "When was the last time you had something to eat, Najiir? You must be hungry."

"I don't think I have eaten since the canyon," he answered.

Miriam looked at the door. "Kauib, are you still here?"

Kauib stepped from behind the open door.

"Go to the kitchen and tell them to give you some food for Najiir. Wait. Get food for all of us. Get something for yourself, too."

Kauib dashed away. Topur tried to swing his legs to sit at the edge of his bed. Miriam put both arms around him to assist him. "Don't open that wound," she admonished. Topur grunted.

Najiir stood. "Master, I am afraid. What will the others think?"

"Yes, Najiir. What will they think?"

"Afraid?" asked Miriam. "Why? Which others? What are you two saying? The kings? If they don't find what they expected, won't they shrug their shoulders and go home?"

Under his beard, Topur's jaw waggled. "Probably." He didn't mean that. This was likely to be a great shock. It was a great shock to him. "Xaratuk expects a warrior. He'll find a peasant's baby. This might be a great disappointment."

"Perhaps we should inform them?" asked Najiir.

"I think not." Topur questioned his conclusion. "You are right to be concerned. The star will reveal what it will, no matter what we presumed. We must adjust, but for now, we remain quiet. I'm even more certain I must go to Bethlehem with the others."

Miriam shook her head. "You're not ready. Wait until you improve. Your friends would welcome the chance to spend a few more nights, or weeks, in this palace. Najiir, you agree with me, don't you?"

Najiir looked down at his feet and shrugged.

"What?" Miriam said. "You can't tell him he should stay here and heal?"

"It's just that—"

"Just what?" asked Topur.

"It's just that I stopped by our camp on the way back to the palace. Regulus was there. He was busy—very busy—but I was able to speak to him. I didn't tell him I had been to Bethlehem. I wanted to tell you first. He said the kings had ordered him to prepare to leave for Bethlehem—this morning."

Topur's head throbbed. "So soon? No."

"They want to arrive at dusk," Najiir said. "The star should be at its brightest. If you must remain here, don't worry. Regulus said they would return to Jerusalem. King Xaratuk promised King Herod he would come back with a full report."

"Xaratuk promised what?" Topur rubbed his fist against his forehead.

"Return?" mumbled Miriam. "Oh, I don't think—"

"Then I assume they have told Herod everything." Topur inhaled but was cut short by the pain. He scowled at Najiir. "Najiir, did you tell the kings they were to say... nothing?"

"I did," Najiir pleaded. "I told them both—before we were out of the canyon."

"Weren't you emphatic? It was crucial—"

"Don't bully the boy," Miriam said. "I'm sure he did everything he could. Kings don't take orders from merchants— or their young slaves." She put a consoling arm around Najiir. "Besides, it was an order your kings couldn't hope to follow. If Herod wants you to talk, you'd better talk."

"But if Herod has heard any suggestion that the child might be some kind of king—"

Topur stopped. His mind raced. He tried to think as Herod would, and when he did, he saw the gaping maw of a trap. He could imagine Xaratuk being enamored with Jerusalem and with Herod. A man like Herod would exploit that. He'd let the kings travel on to Bethlehem, let them make their inquiries, do their investigation. He'd encourage their return while he remained behind, arranging the resources needed to expose these kings and their subversion. These were foreign men, potential enemies of Rome, trying to sneak into Judaea, traveling for months to establish contact with some usurper to the Jewish throne. He'd caught them without lifting a finger. Upon their return, he'd expose the kings' treachery and execute all those involved. If there were complaints from Rome, Augustus could be placated. Herod had successfully performed that farce countless times.

"Herod," Topur declared, "will wish to kill the very thing the kings intend to see."

"That must not happen," said Miriam, "I agree. But you are not ready. Your wound will break open. You'll bleed—perhaps to death. There will be no one to tend to you."

"I must go. Please help make me ready."

"I can keep you hidden a few more days. We can delay them. Even a few more days would help."

Topur stared at Miriam. "It's a trap. Without me, these kings will fall into it without so much as flinching. And it is more than the kings. The whole expedition—every one of us including me—will meet the same terrible fate. Herod will eliminate us soon after he finishes with that family in the tiny house in Bethlehem."

"You are simply not ready," said Miriam, carefully enunciating each word. She backed away from the bed. "You can't walk. You can't use a crutch. A cane won't be enough. You can't lean on little Najiir here for the entire trip." Frowning, she began to loosen Topur's bandaging. "I'll do what I can."

Topur was pleased to find he could tolerate Miriam's exertions with less discomfort, though the occasional sting reminded him of his dire condition. He earnestly wished to remain in this room with this woman, receiving the comfort and care only she could provide. Her goodness toward him was extraordinary. But he knew that once out this door, he would never return to the palace of the Great King Herod or to Miriam's soothing hands.

Kauib appeared with food from the kitchen. Najiir helped himself to the ample selection of bread, fruit, nuts, olives, and garlic-scented lamb. Topur had no appetite.

"You'll need clothing," Miriam said. "The garments you came in with were ruined, and I had them burned. Kauib, get two robes from the room over the Great Hall. Do you know the room I am talking about?"

"Yes, I think so," said Kauib.

"Bring some tunics, too. They'll never be missed." She kneeled before Kauib and whispered, "But don't let anyone see you go inside. You know how to do that. Once you have everything, come directly to me. Stay clear of the palms. Fold the robes so you can walk quickly with them." She stood up. "Now go."

Again, Kauib was out the door.

Miriam returned her attention to Topur. She removed his bandages and examined the wound. Topur couldn't bring himself to look. It was clear from her proud expression that Miriam judged her work as nothing short of inspired. Her hands traced lightly over the torn flesh and muscle. "You are improving. Last night, you couldn't sit like this—not on your own." She reached for the new bandages. "Help me with these."

As she worked on wrapping the wound in fresh bandages, she looked into his eyes. "You can't walk," she said.

Topur felt her warm breath upon his face. He nodded. Miriam was right.

"You'll need a cart or something," she said.

"I suppose."

Miriam sighed. "I'll get you a cart."

"I thought I might use one from the camp."

"I will not have you sitting in some animal's feed wagon. There is a cart we use to move guests who have trouble walking. You can have that. You'll need your own donkey, though."

"I can arrange for that. You are most kind to me."

"If the situation were reversed, I would behave just as you are." She finished wrapping the wound and straightened up. "That doesn't make it right."

"It's tighter this time," said Topur.

"It has to be. You'll be moving around more, and it has to last three times as long." Miriam withdrew a satchel from under Topur's bed, intending to fill it with extra bandaging, but her nervous hands dropped the folded stack. "Topur?"

"Yes?"

"Those kings. Should I be worried?"

"Perhaps?" he said. "Who is that in Bethlehem, Miriam? King Xaratuk expects an ally, a prince, or a champion strong enough to help him thwart the empire. The chilling part comes when you hear him boast about how he plans to convince Herod to join him."

"There is no one like that there." Miriam's tone grew anxious. "And Herod won't be persuaded to turn on the Romans. Topur, this is too much for one man, let alone a wounded man from the back of a cart."

"I see no other option."

Miriam collected the bandages from the floor. "Couldn't you convince those kings to return home without this visit? You've heard about Bethlehem, and it's not what they'd assumed. Tell them they were wrong—accept it and go home. Or explain the danger of trying to turn Herod against Rome, then leave here; leave Judaea as swiftly as you can—for good."

Miriam's frankness startled Topur. "You have a clear grasp of what we face." He touched Miriam's cheek. "You have a clear grasp of most everything, but there is no hope they'll abandon their quest. I've already lost that debate. Instead, I'll try to convince my companions to be patient and understanding. King Xaratuk's advisors are thoughtful. They'll help. I am more worried the kings will insist on returning to the palace. Herod has a way of persuading people."

Bearing neatly folded garments, Kauib stepped into the room. In his arms were the lustrous robes of royalty, snow-white, made of silk and cotton, stitched with golden thread, and trimmed with an accent of purple. Miriam had asked Kauib to plunder a room that belonged to a prince—a murdered son of

Herod.

"I cannot wear these," Topur snorted. "Thank you, lad, but these robes will be missed, and if I am caught wearing one, I will pay a heavy price."

"Don't worry about that," Miriam said. "I have a cloak to cover you as you leave the city. After that, no one will care." Miriam turned to Kauib and gathered the robes. "Good boy. You chose well."

She moved to Topur, clutching one robe at the shoulders. "Do you think you can stand?"

Gingerly, he stretched one foot to the floor. He delicately stepped upon it. A searing blast of pain swept upward to his neck. Immediately he withdrew the weight. Miriam put the robe down on the bed.

"Just as I thought," said Miriam.

Topur knew where this was headed. "Let's try this again."

Topur stretched a foot to the floor once more. Miriam tucked under his arm, away from his wound, for support. He leaned heavily on her shoulders, suppressing a mutinous voice. The other foot came down. He was off the bed. His pain prevented him from standing without stooping. There was no hope of moving forward without someone under his arm.

"You can't walk, can you?" said Miriam.

"No. Najiir?"

Najiir hurried to Topur's side while Miriam attended to the robe. She moved between Topur and the bed, positioning the robe on Topur's shoulders. With tender care, she grabbed the wrist closest to Topur's wound, then bunched an arm of the robe. Expecting severe pain, Topur grimaced. Patiently, Miriam worked the sleeve up his arm and over his shoulder.

"In case it needs repeating, I am eternally grateful, Miriam."

"I shouldn't allow you to go." She pulled the sleeve up Topur's arm, finally reaching his shoulder. "Can you reach the other arm behind you?"

Topur reached back as far as possible. "I wouldn't leave

such commendable care unless I had to. Who wouldn't wish to stay?"

Miriam returned Topur's thin smile with one of her own. "You're still an old fool."

The other sleeve was easier. Topur labored to stand erect. Najiir resumed his position under one arm. Miriam pulled the two sides of the robe together. She looped a matching purple belt delicately around his middle. "You'll rightly be called 'king' now." Tenderly, she patted his shoulders, then tipped her head, bowing to him.

He coughed. The robe felt light as gossamer on his frame.

"Sit," Miriam ordered. "I will get a pack for the other things—your bandages, my salve, this other robe, and tunics. The cloak and blanket I give you must cover you until you are well past the city." She left the room.

As soon as he was certain Miriam was out of range, Topur nodded at Najiir. "We are not returning. Do you understand that? No one is coming back here, not under any circumstance. Herod is on to us." Topur lifted an arm. "Help me try to walk around the room."

Najiir placed himself under Topur's good arm, and together they shuffled in small, cautious steps.

"We are, all of us, going to Bethlehem—the kings, the caravan, the animals. But right now, I need you to tell Regulus to break camp. Pack up. Tell him the order comes from Xaratuk if you have to. Xaratuk will fight me on this because he thinks we are coming back, but we must be ready to move."

Najiir nodded.

Topur gripped the boy's shoulder. "Najiir, you must be especially convincing. I will take care of the kings. But you must make your appeal to Regulus and the others. Get them working as quickly as possible, and quietly, too. If we have avoided the scrutiny of the Romans so far, we surely don't want it now."

Topur realized this minimal exertion exhausted him. "This hurts. Help me."

Delicately, Najiir assisted Topur back to the bed.

"I can cope from here," Topur said. "Now go."

CHAPTER 23

"How? How can I do this?" mumbled Mithrias. Rizpah cradled her head against Mithrias's neck as they lay entwined. "What I would give to take you to Bethlehem with me." He kissed her soft hair. It smelled of calamus and cinnamon. He drew back to look upon her loveliness. "The Greeks tell a story where the most beautiful woman in the entire world, someone just like you, was stolen away by a visiting prince. Things went badly."

Rizpah let out a small, unconvincing chuckle.

"A cautionary tale," Mithrias added.

Rizpah remained silent.

"Herod will have to adjust to your departure. He'll simply have to."

"Yes. He'll have to," purred Rizpah.

"Rizpah." Mithrias's tone turned serious. "During this journey, I questioned whether I wished to be a king. I was about to conclude that I did not. But had I not been a king, I would not have come here. I would not have found you or known this time with you. I may never be able to explain why being with you has touched my very core. Perhaps later, I might find the words. I realize that being a king has brought me to this moment, and I won't question my circumstances anymore."

Rizpah's eyes began to fill. She felt incapable of movement. This experience had no precedence, no familiarity. Her life's circumstances required detachment. She had never cared about the comings or goings of any individual—not one, not ever. Last night crossed a line. She allowed this man to raze the stoic walls she had so diligently erected for protection. From this rubble, he would rise, and he would leave—leave this room, leave the palace, leave Jerusalem, and leave her. The fortress surrounding her heart had been shattered, and she would be the sole casualty.

Desire. Future. Hope. Rizpah had considered them meaningless indulgences. Overnight, they became potent and personal and potentially devastating. Passion was lit, but everything she now desired had so little likelihood of fulfillment. Herod would never release her. He'd never cede her to another man. It was madness to believe otherwise. But madness or not, she determined she would devote her considerable energy to making this seemingly hopeless dream come true. The alternative was too bleak to consider.

Tentatively, she began in a chiding tone. "I should be angry with you."

Mithrias's frame stiffened.

"King Mithrias, I will never know happiness unless I am with you."

She pressed her entire body onto his. "Do you believe that is fair to me?" She tried hard to smile but remained too close to tears to make it convincing. "This is so new—all these feelings tangled with someone else."

"Feelings are dangerous," Mithrias whispered. "I will not mislead you. But unlike you, I have experienced happiness. I had it, then lost it. Feelings. Before last night, I would have advised you to ignore them and run from them as fast as possible. But you, Rizpah." Mithrias gently raised her head. "You have shown me the truth behind all our lives, that living becomes worthwhile when you accept the risks that come when you care for another. I owe you. I vow to you, I will find a way to be together."

"I want to believe you. But, as I say, the future is so

uncertain. Herod is not an easy man."

She kissed him with a passion designed to ensure his return or, barring that, nourish them both for a lifetime. Their lips finally parted.

"I always knew what to do," she murmured. "Now, I know nothing. I have many matters to consider before you return." She struggled to rise from the bed, putting on her robe. "But I have so many wonderful things to think about—because of you." She moved to the tables, but the thought of food was unappealing. She needed a distraction. If she allowed herself to look at him, she would disintegrate into a thousand downy feathers drifting to the floor.

In silence, Mithrias dressed, then stood by the door. "Please, come here," he said.

Reluctantly, she stepped toward him. He drew her in and held her closely.

"I don't know what it is like to love someone," she said. "It has never happened." She placed his head between her hands. "But this feeling seems like what I expected it to be." She began to quiver. "But what of it? You are a great king—you must leave."

"Rizpah…Rizpah," said Mithrias. "Please. I will return for you. I will be back. Don't doubt your feelings. I feel them as well. After Bethlehem, I will make my appeal to Herod until I am successful. We will be together."

Tears spilled from Rizpah's eyes. "Can such a thing ever be?" she whispered.

"Rizpah, if you should need to reach me, include this word, and I'll know it is you." He whispered in her ear. "Do you understand? Whisper the word to me."

She whispered it back. Mithrias kissed her salty tears and held her in place. "I am returning for you." He kissed one hand, then the other. "We are meant to be together." Unable to say more, he left.

The iron clang of the lock sounded of finality: dream over.

Rizpah's sobs saturated the room. Any movement came with clumsy, irrepressible shaking, preventing her from gathering any belongings. She carelessly dressed, powerless to think about anything but escaping this room, this palace, and her dreadful future. He wouldn't come back. He couldn't. Her head bent, she wept into her robe as she pulled the door shut behind her. Three sets of eyes watched her depart.

CHAPTER 24

Perplexed and dazed, Mithrias walked through the courtyard. He blinked away tears, trying to muster some minimal comportment. Potted palms lined the colonnade. Were these among the spying outposts, as Rizpah claimed? Passing one pot, he bumped it with his thigh. Herod was a shrewd man.

Down the corridor, women were giggling. Mithrias stepped toward their voices. The door to Xaratuk's room was already open. Xaratuk filled the entryway, clad in a martial breastplate and the crisp blue tunic of a soldier. A short sword dangled from his side. He was dressed to meet royalty.

The women were at either elbow, kissing him, playfully touching him, primping his regal wardrobe. Xaratuk was smiling and teasing back. Two male musicians, their hair askew, with sallow complexions and bloodshot eyes, staggered out of the room, bid their brief farewells, then stumbled on their way. The women kissed Xaratuk on the cheek, and he took turns kissing them both on the lips. Now he was laughing, too. When he saw Mithrias approach, he told his companions to hush, but squeezed them to his side. "Ah, mighty King Mithrias, I trust you had a good rest."

"Yes. And you?"

"Yes, but how can I call it rest?" He grinned at both women in succession. "Hmmm? I will be back tomorrow sometime—perhaps the next day," he told them. "And I shall ask specifically for you two. I am sure King Herod will consent after the report

I give him." He clutched handfuls of posterior flesh and said, "Tell whoever arranges this that we must share the same room when I return so that I may look forward to it!" While one kissed Xaratuk's cheek, the other slowly dragged a hand across Xaratuk's chest. They turned, giggling, and scurried down the arcade.

"I love resting," said Xaratuk. "And those two made me love resting more than I thought I could."

Mithrias whispered, "I hope you followed Topur's advice last night and kept silent about your true intentions regarding the star."

Xaratuk motioned Mithrias inside. The room revealed every sign of a reckless affair: overturned cups, blankets bunched in disarray, tipped lamps, toppled chairs, and clothing dangling from the fronds of the potted palm trees. "Why?" Xaratuk laughed. "Why are you concerned? My men laid it all out at dinner. They knew more about Jewish texts than those priests bargained for. They showed them! Herod sees we are serious and legitimate partners." Xaratuk gathered some of his remaining belongings, including a long cloak. "Funny, even those girls claimed the king isn't much of a Jew. What Jew would send girls to entertain a visitor as they entertained me? I salute whatever allows Herod to keep his visitors so satisfied. Oh, what a night!"

Grabbing his arm, Mithrias hauled Xaratuk outside the room, as far from any potted palm as possible. In an urgent whisper, he said, "Did you mention anything about forming some alliance with Herod against the Romans?"

Xaratuk pulled his arm away. "Oh, I don't know what I did or didn't say. It was a long night, and we spoke of many things. So what of it, Mithrias? They are just a couple of court entertainers and can do us no harm. They adore me—they said so. If I showed the least interest, they would abandon Herod to come live with me. Those girls wouldn't compromise me even if I did say something."

"They're spies, Xaratuk."

Xaratuk's eyes widened. "No," he began. "Stop with that talk. Those girls are not spies. They're merely courtesans. Who would take their word on anything?"

"Well, if Herod won't take their word, he'll believe the others in your room."

"Those two lousy musicians? We got them drunk immediately, and they stayed blind drunk until we woke them. They didn't hear a thing, and they can't say a thing—I assure you."

"It wasn't the musicians," said Mithrias. "It was the potted palms."

After Mithrias explained the clever outposts, the two kings began their unescorted walk to the palace gates. Palm pots lined the colonnade. Mithrias felt exposed. The probing eyes of others—many others—were upon them. He insisted any conversation be whispered since eyes were always matched with ears. Xaratuk struggled to control his volume. He rejected any assertion that Herod had hidden spies inside his room. "Tiny men?" Xaratuk scoffed. "You're too gullible."

Mithrias slowed their pace. "Eye slits," he said, "in the lion's paw." Xaratuk studied the decorated pot while scuffing ahead. "In the back. A crack," Mithrias mumbled. "The entry." Pretending to be lost in absentminded conversation, Mithrias bumped into the next pot, giving it a glancing nudge. Both kings heard the shuffling as the diminutive spy within tried to reestablish himself.

Xaratuk fell silent. Mithrias knew he was wrestling within, trying to remember what was said, what was not said, while judging the consequences of any wine-embellished pronouncements. Without further conversation, they arrived at the palace gate, where they had agreed to meet Regulus.

Regulus was prompt and ready. Salnassar, on Mithrias's horse, had also ridden to the gate. He gave his father a tentative greeting—the first he'd extended on the entire trip.

From beyond the gate, Najiir ran toward them, pulling a two-wheeled cart. Mithrias saw the boy and dashed to meet him.

"Najiir! I am so happy to see you!" Mithrias grabbed Najiir's shoulders, evaluating the boy. "You seem well, but..." He stopped short. "Topur—have you heard anything?"

"I have seen him, King Mithrias. Good morning to you." Najiir looked over Mithrias's shoulder. "Good morning to you, King Xaratuk." Xaratuk gave a dismissive wave, never looking at the boy. "He is alive but terribly hurt." Najiir dropped the cart handles.

"Oh, at least he is alive!" Mithrias lunged forward and hugged Najiir, who fell clumsily into Mithrias's embrace. "I was terrified that would not be the case. But why the cart? Is it for him?"

"Yes. I have permission to take this," Najiir replied.

"Can he be ready to resume traveling?" he asked. "This quickly?"

"He has been under the care of a woman in the palace named Miriam, and she believes he is not. She says my master shouldn't move, but he insists he must go with all of you." He reached behind, adjusting some blankets already in the cart. "When I left, Miriam was preparing him. He should be here shortly."

"Why doesn't he stay here until he improves? He has done so well to get us this far, and look—we are fine. We'll return after visiting Bethlehem. I'll assure him of that. He shouldn't go. It's much too early."

Najiir looked about to see who might be listening. His voice diminished to a tentative hush. "I must tell you that my master says we will not be returning to the palace after Bethlehem. He is determined we all must leave Jerusalem and never come back."

Mithrias stopped breathing. Why? Why would Topur insist on this? Any failure to return meant he would not collect Rizpah, a thought too dreadful to consider. "Najiir, why would Topur say that?"

"I don't think he trusts King Herod."

"Yes, yes." Mithrias stroked his short beard. "But I can report King Herod has treated us very well, and we have yet to encounter a single Roman soldier. Topur's opinions might be exaggerated, or maybe King Herod has changed?"

"He ordered me to tell Regulus to break camp."

"Break camp?" Mithrias quickly spotted Regulus, who stood at stiff attention in conversation with Xaratuk. "And did you?"

"Yes, I told him, but I don't think he listened to me."

Najiir smiled. He had followed Topur's instructions, but Regulus wasn't about to obey the orders of a slave boy. That didn't matter. As Regulus left camp to meet King Xaratuk, Najiir moved within the caravan among the servants, slaves, soldiers, and shepherds he'd spent weeks cultivating as friends. When he told them they must prepare to move at once, they obeyed his directive as if their king had commanded it himself.

Four stretcher-bearers brought Topur down to the palace gate. Reclined, Topur used a large pillow to prop his head, allowing him to view his carriers' progress. Another servant walked behind, carrying a large bag packed by Miriam. He also held a jar of the salve she had been applying to his wound. Miriam assured Topur that these particular servants would not be too inquisitive about him, the bag, or the others he was meeting.

Mithrias greeted him effusively, but Xaratuk paid no attention. With the servants' help, Mithrias and Najiir arranged comfortable seating. Once adjusted, Topur addressed the kings. "Tell me what you think Herod knows."

Xaratuk remained unresponsive. Mithrias hesitated, but answered. "I should admit, Topur, that King Herod is aware of our intentions. He wants answers. Much was discussed at dinner, including Bethlehem."

Topur glared at Xaratuk, but Xaratuk refused to be drawn in.

"This could ruin everything," said Topur. "We must break camp at once and leave immediately if we stand any chance of finding the one you intended to meet—should we find anyone at all."

Ignited and indignant, Xaratuk took seven long strides, positioning himself in front of Topur. He glowered, thrusting a denouncing finger into the air. "No! There is no reason to break camp. I forbid it! We are expected back at the palace after we are done in Bethlehem. My people stay—stay exactly where they are." His voice lowered to a growl. "And frankly, Topur, I'm through with your 'advice'."

Emphatically, Topur continued. "And once underway, no one returns to Jerusalem. When we finish in Bethlehem, we leave Judaea immediately, and it will not be through Jerusalem." He stared defiantly back at Xaratuk. "Give. The. Order."

Xaratuk squeezed the cart's top rail. "I have made a promise to King Herod!" He shoved the cart, stepped away, then wheeled back to Topur. "If you wish to leave, I suggest you do so. You're worthless to me. You have been wrong—dead wrong—about everything! We followed the star without incident before you. But you—you drag us through a canyon everyone else knows to avoid. You claim a visit to Jerusalem will seal our doom, yet we stand here unharmed! You say King Herod is a vicious madman, but he has been nothing but gracious. You tell us we'll fall into the hands of the Romans, but we have yet to see anything but the backs of a paltry few."

Topur looked askance. The words were hard to hear.

Xaratuk went on. "You are wrong about everything! Maybe your wife has poisoned you with her petty objections. I've made a promise to your king, and I'll keep it because most of all— most of all—he has been courteous and hospitable to me!"

Topur did not allow himself to flinch. "You underestimate the man. You underestimate his friends. People who make that mistake don't live long."

"You! You are the one making all the mistakes!" Xaratuk roared. "We are King Herod's guests. We haven't been dumped in some jail. No, no jail. He honors us with an extravagant dinner. Yes, we told him about the star. We confronted his priests—"

"You spoke to his priests? Now they know, too? After I advised you to say nothing? Do you not understand Herod already may have sent his men up there to destroy whatever it is you are looking for, if the priests haven't beaten him to it? If either senses the least threat—"

"Topur, it is best you remain here." Xaratuk's voice became condescending. "You have suffered. That injury must cause a great deal of pain and distress. You'll wait here. Don't you agree, King Mithrias?"

Mithrias did not respond.

"Our small group will go on," Xaratuk continued. "We shall find something truly amazing, and we'll share that with King Herod. Though you despise him, King Herod seems to have arranged some capable care for you. I thought there was every chance you would not leave this city alive. But here you are, mended, made strong enough to contradict my wishes. Tell me, Topur, how do you square that?"

Topur took in a long breath. "Because, unlike you, Xaratuk, I am a nobody." Topur knew that omitting the king's title would not go unnoticed. "I am not worth his time or attention, so I am spared through neglect. If he could have identified me and my reasons for being in Jerusalem, he would not have allowed me to live through the night."

Topur turned to Mithrias, hoping his appeal would land on more receptive ears. "I was pulled from my home because you thought it best to have a guide with local knowledge. You felt I was the best man for the job. You were right. I am. I know this land and its people because my life has been lived here. You have been here two days and a night and are convinced you have the better perspective. What you have seen has been carefully planned. It is not the reality of this city or this man. You know what he wishes you to know—nothing more. I am telling you to break camp and move now, or everything you journeyed for will be lost."

Xaratuk's eyes narrowed. His nose was high in the air. "We will do no such thing. What we shall do is separate from you here—this instant. We no longer require your services, peddler. You may have a horse for that cart, and that is all. We are going to Bethlehem. You are going home. I terminate our association with you."

He looked to Salnassar. "Get off that horse, boy. Regulus, tie that horse to that cart and send that man away."

A woman's voice called out from the palace.

CHAPTER 25

M iriam hurried toward the kings, carrying a sack containing the remainder of Topur's myrrh. Out of breath, she reached the cart where Topur was seated. "I must talk to you. It is urgent." She beckoned him close. "Two priests dined with Herod and your friends last night."

"I heard."

Miriam raised her voice. "I don't know if your companions realize it was Joazar and Eleazar they were speaking to and how high those men rank in the Temple priesthood."

"Joazar and Eleazar—both?" said Topur. "That made it a noteworthy occasion indeed. I am surprised they found time in their busy schedules." He turned to the kings. "This is Miriam, my healer. You should understand those priests you met are, after King Herod, the most important and influential men in Jerusalem, and they—"

"They sit in jail!" Miriam interrupted. "Now! This morning!"

Their mouths agape, every man surrounding Topur fixated upon his healer. "Neither has been seen since last night," she continued. "They're being held. They never left the palace after that dinner."

"What?" spurted Topur. He stared at the kings and their wide-eyed faces. "What did you say last night? What did they say?"

Since neither king would utter one word, Miriam answered instead. "It seems King Herod is convinced his priests have withheld information from him, and his guests made that quite clear. He senses betrayal." She turned to Topur. "It's terrible. It's like Mariamne all over again. No amount of convincing or arguing or evidence has any effect. He'd have executed them, but failing to advise the Romans would infuriate them. His own people would rise up and revolt! At least he's not that mad— yet." Taking a handful of his beard, she pulled Topur's face toward hers. "Leave here—leave Jerusalem now! And don't even think of returning! If he thinks all of you are part of—"

"This is an outrageous assumption!" Xaratuk stomped to the cart, waving his arm. "You have no proof of what you are saying. You're merely pandering to some palace rumor. Those priests are fine and will be seen in public soon. Even if they are not, proposing they are in danger is spreading irresponsible gossip."

Miriam placed a hand on her hip, glaring at Xaratuk through a cross frown. "It isn't gossip," she spat. "I learned this from one of the men sent to collect those priests. Not gossip. Information. I expect a man of your stature to understand the difference." She wheeled about, turning her back on him.

"Topur," she said, tears in her eyes. "I hate to say this because I was still thinking of ways to convince you to stay, but you must go." She reluctantly placed the sack of myrrh in his cart. "If he finds you, he'll kill you."

Xaratuk stomped on the ground, shaking his fist at Miriam. "Insolent servant! I am personally going back into the palace to quash your vicious impudence and offer King Herod a brief and friendly farewell. King Mithrias, come with me." Xaratuk huffed and began his march.

"I will be with you in a moment," said Mithrias. With Xaratuk beyond earshot, Mithrias slid over to Regulus. "Break camp, Regulus," he whispered. "Gather all our things and be ready to move—everything and everybody—quickly."

"But..." Regulus's face conveyed confusion and apprehension. "Begging your pardon, King Mithrias, but those are not my king's orders."

"I will make it right with your king. You must prepare our caravan while I persuade him. Be quick." Regulus did not move. "Please—it may be the crucial difference we'll need. If Herod is this mad at his own priests, it could easily be us in chains next to them. Look, if she's wrong, and it is nothing, all our efforts will merely be an inconvenience to us—busy work. We break camp every day. But if she is right, and we haven't moved, it might spell disaster for every single member of our journey— including your stubborn king. Think about that."

Regulus gave a grudging nod. He turned his horse toward the camp. Salnassar mustered a muffled complaint, recognizing he'd have to walk back.

"Everything I had hoped to avoid has instead happened," said Topur. Miriam tucked his blanket more tightly to conceal the royal robe underneath. "Perhaps my wife is right. I need to be a better Jew."

"So you're a bad Jew? I wish I had known this earlier. Maybe I should not have worked so hard to make you better."

"Miriam, you joke, but it seems God has opposed me and has placed me, this entire expedition, and now—even you—in such peril. Xaratuk wishes to banish me from the caravan."

"He's a buffoon. He doesn't mean it. And what he says doesn't matter—not to you. You've delivered those kings. They no longer need you, but that family does. It is more important than ever that you continue. I realize that now." Her eyes welled as she touched his cheek. "You go to Bethlehem, dear man. There is something—someone—extraordinary up there, and he needs your attention and protection. I fear your kings as much as I do Herod. Only you and Najiir understand this. You must go there, and you have to hurry."

"Were it not for you, I would be a dead man with no family nearby to bury me. You have allowed me to continue." He winced. There had been no pain during the arguing, but it was back.

"You can't return here," Miriam said. "I had forgotten your myrrh. It's here. There's a great deal left. It works well in that salve."

"You are an angel of mercy, Miriam. Atarah told me I had to make this journey because it was God's will. Despite all that has happened, your tender attention proves that God is not done with me yet." He took her hand. "May He protect you from the madman's wrath," his voice cracked, "because I cannot."

"Oh, I still have some influence," Miriam replied. She squeezed his hand. "I can arrange it so our king will not think of Bethlehem for a while. I can make him... less adventurous."

Topur looked about, confirming there were no listening ears. "I'm not certain I understand what you mean, but I am proof you accomplish what you set out to do. If you need to contact me, mention this word, and this word only, to anyone related to this caravan, and it will reach me at once. I will know it is you and find you as quickly as possible."

He drew her closer and whispered in her ear. She nodded, then gave him a long kiss on his cheek. Topur took both her hands in his and kissed them. He looked into her eyes. Bowing his head, he said, "May God watch over you and keep you now and forever. You have saved me, Miriam. You have saved me."

CHAPTER 26

Xaratuk ranted while he and Mithrias followed their palace guard. Mithrias tuned out the harangue; he was consumed with devising a plan to collect Rizpah.

Upon reaching the cedar doors of Herod's bedchamber, the guard knocked and announced the visitors. Moments passed. The kings strained to hear an indecipherable, muffled shout of acknowledgment. Blunt noises emanated from the room. Then, a crash and the unmistakable sound of a fallen platter rolling on the stone floor. Inside, urgent but stifled voices argued, ordered, and protested. Outside, the kings waited. More items crashed, followed by frequent indistinct exclamations. Xaratuk stroked his mustache. He looked at Mithrias.

"They know we are here, correct?"

Mithrias shrugged, looking to the guard for confirmation. The guard withheld comment, his attention riveted to the doors. More voices. More shuffling. Finally, there was the clanking of the latches. The doors swung outward.

King Herod, turban askew, was propped in the doorway. A servant was at either elbow, each doing his utmost to maintain a man who could not stand on his own. Underneath his tilted turban, a dark, sticky substance coated Herod's hair and beard, leaving them matted and stringy. His yellowed eyes, though rarely open, alternated between expressions of horror or sleepy disinterest. His robe was untied, revealing stains and spatter on his undergarments. Some splotches looked like food, some like vomit, and some like blood. One was unmistakable: a blotch of urine confirmed by its stench. The two visiting kings glanced at each other. Xaratuk was about to speak, but Herod interrupted.

"Are you on your way, then..." A loud belch escaped, smelling like sour feet. "Bethlehem? Excuse me." His eyes rolled back before they closed. "I am not feeling well." He stumbled forward, only to be caught by his attendants. He struggled to keep his head from rolling. "They told me to stay in bed," Herod slurred. "I told them I must see my friends."

Shoulders back, head held high, Xaratuk surged to stiff attention. "Yes, dear King Herod, we are your friends, and yes, we are proceeding to Bethlehem." Herod's chin remained pinned to his chest. "We depart soon, but we wanted to express our gratitude for a splendid evening. Your nobility is only exceeded by your hospitality. We look forward to extending our friendship and proving our worthiness with our report."

Xaratuk waited for a response to his pledge of allegiance, but none came. "Are you all right, sir?" he asked, reluctantly placing his hand on Herod's shoulder.

Herod's head rolled back. His eyes opened wide, though briefly. His head drooped toward his chest again. "Old age has made early mornings my enemy." He gave a faint and insincere smile.

"Old age is not for cowards," said Xaratuk, removing his hand. His astonished reaction to the condition of the man before him went unrecognized.

"Yes." Herod fell into another stupor, then stiffened as if startled. His servants' rigid arms struggled to keep him standing. Squinting, he looked, for the first time, directly at Xaratuk. "What about your friend—the one that was hurt? Is he still here in my palace?"

"He is better, thanks to the care you have given to him. He is well enough to insist upon making the journey with us and is already outside the palace making his preparations to depart, though I think—"

"Hmmmmph," Herod grunted. "I told my staff he was to stay where he was." His words were drenched in anger. His turban tottered as he turned to the servant at one elbow. "But it doesn't matter what King Herod wishes, does it?" He turned to the servant at the other elbow. "Hmm? I have no one who obeys me around here. I can't get my priests to tell me what they know, and now I can't keep some wounded intruder locked up." Herod pivoted, swerving on his anchored feet, forcing his handlers to tighten their grips. "For his well-being, of course. Travel—not good."

Precariously balanced, Herod cleared his throat and attempted to convey an air of dignity. It wasn't convincing. Another foul belch erupted. "And Xaratuk," he added, trying to point a finger, "you send a messenger to me here, at the palace, ahead of your arrival this time. I'll have the chance to prepare for you properly." Herod could not hold his head up any longer. His turban fell to the floor.

"Yesss. I shall do that, King Herod. You shall hear from me," said Xaratuk.

"That is, if I can get anyone around here to listen to me!" Herod snorted. "Mariamne, my dear Mariamne! No one listens to me anymore! You must help me! I am all alone here!" With this mention of the dead wife, one servant offered the kings an apology, then stated Herod needed his rest. The servants turned their king away from the door and struggled mightily to walk him back. The king, stumbling, continued to wail, sobbing for Mariamne.

Mithrias shut his eyes. His hand stroked his forehead. "Now can you appreciate what Topur is trying to convey?"

Xaratuk, his mouth open, eyes blinking, remained still. "Rather alarming."

Without thought, Xaratuk brushed his chest as if doing so would dislodge the collected scree of Herod's inexplicable paroxysm. Politely, he ordered their guard to direct them back to the palace gate. As they walked, he whispered, "Well,

Mithrias, what do you think? Should we break camp?"

"We have already done so, great king. We have already done so."

CHAPTER 27

Camp had been dismantled. By the time Mithrias and Xaratuk reached Jerusalem's outer wall, most of the caravan had lumbered away, supplied with Najiir's directions. Mithrias held fast to Xaratuk's side as Regulus approached. The loyal captain walked stiffly toward the harsh rebuke that awaited but was met by Xaratuk's silence instead. His sole communication to Regulus demanded he surrender his horse to Mithrias, an unmistakable reprimand.

It took little time to catch the main group. Once in the lead, Xaratuk ordered Mithrias to remain with him at the head of the procession. It was no request. With Jerusalem well behind and beyond the view of any Roman, Xaratuk halted. He removed any garment that concealed his royal stature. He ordered his soldiers to shed their cloaks and reveal themselves in ceremonial battle regalia. The new king awaiting them in Bethlehem would witness the full splendor of the great King Xaratuk and this mission. Initial impressions were critically important.

With every forward step, Mithrias was besieged by Xaratuk's endless monologue of complaints and criticisms. Kings must be obeyed, Xaratuk asserted, not second-guessed. His rants fell hard upon Topur. He fumed that some petty merchant would dare to place himself in charge. Topur's clumsy attempt to maneuver himself into a position of authority meant he was no longer welcome. Bristling, Xaratuk suggested that

Herod should have been the one accompanying him to Bethlehem had he not been in such a compromised condition. Mithrias wondered if his own association with Xaratuk was now in peril.

"Can it be that peddler is correct?" Xaratuk muttered. "The man at dinner and the man who met us at his chamber door were complete opposites. How can that be the same man? And that reference to keeping Topur locked up. Locked up? Khartir's story of Herod's dead wife was verified. How could such a man convince a city to build a temple? Why would the Romans support a lunatic? Did he jail those arrogant priests?"

Mithrias could no longer tolerate bearing sole witness to Xaratuk's burgeoning anxiety. Politely, he told Xaratuk he wished to check on those at the tail of the procession. Xaratuk shrugged. Breathing a sigh of relief, Mithrias broke away and directed his horse to the rear. He soon came upon Regulus, looking solemn and chastened. Mithrias dismounted and returned the horse to its proper owner. Regulus reached for the reins, then pulled back.

"This is not my horse," said Mithrias. "Captain, you have probably saved your king's life." Shrugging, Regulus took the reins. He cordially thanked the king but, reins in hand, continued walking.

Mithrias continued past the marchers moving in the opposite direction. At the back of the caravan, Najiir guided Mithrias's horse tied to the cart carrying Topur. Packed within pillows, facing the rear, Topur sat with eyes closed. Mithrias greeted Najiir, who gave a friendly wave in return. The king pulled even with the cart and walked alongside.

"Topur, are you resting?" Mithrias asked.

Topur eyes blinked. "Yes, though at times it's difficult."

"Are you hurting?"

"Very sore. But I expected worse."

Mithrias patted Topur's good shoulder. "I am so relieved you are with us, my friend," he said. "Riding with King Xaratuk brings its own pain. I wince with every new declaration from that man." Quietly, he added, "He has worn my patience to its very end. I have never been around one so satisfied with all he does and thinks. Maybe there is room for me in this cart?"

Topur snickered. "Tell me, what is he saying now?"

"Topur, it was just as you said," Mithrias began. "When we bid Herod farewell, he met us at his chamber door. It was obvious he wasn't expecting visitors. You should have seen the man...."

Topur listened with rapt attention to Mithrias's depiction of the bedraggled king, then to his summation of the debate between the advisors and the priests.

As dusk loomed, Najiir, privy to the entire conversation, stopped the horse and turned to Topur. "It's not much farther. Would it be all right with you if I went before the group? I want to go to the house to let Joseph and Mary know we are near."

Topur nodded. Mithrias stepped ahead to be the horse's new guide. Najiir sprinted away.

Mithrias pulled the horse to an abrupt stop. He circled back to Topur. "Topur, what was that? What did Najiir say? Who are Joseph and Mary? Has he already been to Bethlehem?"

Topur nodded again.

"What a remarkable boy." A faint smile registered upon Mithrias's face, then disappeared. "What did he find? He mentioned a house?"

Topur gave a final nod. "That's it—a house. And not a very impressive one at that."

"No palace?"

"No. And maybe not a king—though there is considerable dispute about that."

Mithrias tilted his head. "A house? Oh no. This will not go over well—not at all. I must get to the front and be ready to handle Xaratuk. How long have you known?"

"Not long—and what I know isn't much. What Najiir found

was confirmed by Miriam. Their stories match up perfectly. The star shines upon something none of us had imagined."

"Miriam has seen this, too?"

"Yes."

"No fortress? No palace?"

"No."

"He's going to explode." Mithrias pulled on the horse, grabbing its bridle, urging it forward at a trot. He was oblivious to Topur's shrieks as the cart bumped and jerked its way up the line.

Reliably, the star appeared, illuminating Bethlehem in the distance. Its long, silvery-white light formed a glowing beam that left everything around it in a contrasting eerie hue of dark sapphire. Clouds obscured the star for moments, but the beam was low, its intensity strong. For every person in the caravan, the excitement, the apprehension, the anticipation was at a crescendo. It was apparent: at long last, they were here.

Mithrias's run had pulled him even with Xaratuk, who had stopped the procession to converse with a lone traveler—the only one they'd encountered emerging from Bethlehem. Xaratuk had asked the man if they were on the correct road.

"Yes," the traveler replied. "This is it. This is the one." Mithrias, out of breath, stood beside Xaratuk, listening. Topur could hear the conversation but remained relegated to the cart. The traveler continued. "Bethlehem isn't far now—it is just ahead. You'll walk right to it."

Xaratuk turned to Regulus. "This is where we make camp. See to it we operate from here. I will not have everyone going into the city and spark confusion. I'll choose which of us will go ahead. We must not arouse suspicion or undue inspection, Romans or otherwise." Xaratuk clapped his hands together. "This is it, my friends!" He looked at the traveler. "What other roads are there into Bethlehem?"

"None, this is the only one. There are footpaths and animal paths, but this is the only thing you would call a road."

Xaratuk's eyes narrowed. "Very well," he drawled. His excited expression shifted toward confusion. "And once in the city, will we recognize the palace? Is it obvious? Are there guards? Any Romans? How many?"

The traveler raised his hands to quell the questions. He smiled, allowing a light laugh. "Guards? Romans? In that village?" He shook his head as if admonishing a child. "Are we speaking about the same Bethlehem? There are no guards in Bethlehem, I assure you. And as for Romans, they don't bother with it at all. There probably hasn't been a Roman there for years, not that I am an expert. I spend little time there. No reason to stop and not much to do. Besides Rachel's tomb, it is only the homes of the few people with farms or stock in the area. Oh, and if by 'palace' you mean the inn there in Bethlehem...well, it's no palace." He chuckled. "It's just a place to lay one's head down for the night. The innkeeper seems pleasant."

"Why are you laughing?" asked Xaratuk. "Why are these questions amusing? We're talking about the star, the light. There is something significant there. Isn't this star shining on a palace? A fortress, perhaps?"

"Oh, the light," said the traveler, speaking more somberly. "The star. Such commotion over a poor family." His eyes reflected surprise while his shoulders broadcast indifference. "That star shines down on a tiny home. Inside, it's a poor mother and father and their baby boy, they say." The traveler moved his gaze from Xaratuk to the star, then to the tiny town. "Still, it might be worth your time. Usually, a few people line up outside the doorway, waiting to get in. You'll likely find no room at the inn because that star's light has attracted the curious from all over. Steady business for such a small town. But I've only walked by. Mind you, there are shepherds outside—some of them have knives. They'll inquire as to who you are and question your purpose. They're very thorough, I hear."

"Shepherds?" croaked Xaratuk.

"But you have come at a good time," the traveler resumed. "Some excitement, finally. Strange things are going on inside that house. That's what brings all the visitors. Astonishing things, some say, and that star guides people straight to that door. I try not to get too caught up in all the talk and speculation. Good way to get yourself on the wrong side of the High Priest." The traveler looked over Xaratuk's shoulder. "Well, if there's nothing else, I should be going. It's never wise to be on this road alone after dark."

"Wait, wait!" Xaratuk reached out for the man's arm. "This isn't at all what I expected." He turned. "Regulus! Fetch Merkis and Khartir and bring them to me at once." Regulus mounted his horse and headed to the back of the procession. Frowning, Xaratuk turned back to the traveler.

"Sir, I really must go," said the traveler, "and there's little more to tell. You'll see for yourself. If it is a palace you are looking for, try Jerusalem or Damascus. I am told the palace in Jerusalem is as fine as any in Rome itself. I can't enter, but I can tell you it is lavish, even from the outside." He cinched his belt, gathered his belongings, and slung them across his shoulder. "But as for Bethlehem, there is no palace in Bethlehem. May God grant you safe travels."

"You as well," said Xaratuk absentmindedly as he patted the traveler on the shoulder.

The caravan began to assemble. Clouds continued to intermittently obscure the star's impact. An air of excitement and anticipation penetrated throughout. Xaratuk paced, awaiting his advisors. Though the interim was brief, the impatient king rebuked his men for their delay. His harsh words did not diminish their smiles.

"Have you heard about Bethlehem yet?" Xaratuk's jaw jutted forward. "Have you heard anything about this hamlet we are about to descend upon?"

Merkis and Khartir were dressed in the most befitting attire for this occasion. Each wore a dark green robe with a scarlet sash about the middle and a bright yellow turban. A shining cut stone reflected the star's light in the center of each turban, just above the eyebrows. The wise men looked their part.

Impatient and testy, Xaratuk drowned out Merkis's response. "It's little more than a gathering station for shepherds," he said. "There is nothing to the town. It has nothing—one small inn and a few houses, that's all! No palace, no temple, no army, no armory—nothing. And apparently, my new ally is some infant whose parents are nothing more than peasants. No king. No prince. Maybe no one at all!" He scowled at them. "All this way for...for...for this!"

"Most Excellent King, please do not judge this too quickly or too harshly." Merkis's voice remained calm. "We have not yet seen what is at the end of this star. I urge you to keep an open mind."

"An open mind—about a child in a mud hut?"

"The star will lead where it will lead—that is out of our control," said Merkis. "You, my king, may have envisioned a palace and an army. But in all this time, I beg you to recall that we neither confirmed nor denied the impressions you suggested. Predicting who or what sits at the end of this light is beyond our abilities, but advising you to get to it, no matter where it stood or what it might be, is still the soundest advice we've ever given. I am certain of that. And look, we are nearly there."

Khartir nodded in silent agreement.

Xaratuk shook his head. "What a day this has been, what a loathsome day! No one listens to me. My wishes mean nothing. I command my caravan to stay in Jerusalem, but we scurry away at the whim of a peddler. Now, after months of searching, my effort is to be rewarded by a brief visit with a dirt farmer's family? This is the culmination of Jewish prophecy? The writings in the night sky lead me to this? Months and months we've struggled, and now I wait to see if these pissant shepherds will allow me to visit some peasant child?" He pointed an accusing finger at his advisors. "This had better not be, you two. This had better not be!"

CHAPTER 28

Every member of the expedition witnessed Xaratuk's petulant outburst. He discharged his anxious energy as he always did, confronting, criticizing, and stomping about while barking commands. Nothing could be done that he judged to be acceptable. The caravan's mood recalibrated. In moments, it had swung from gleeful anticipation to sour doubt. What would become of the expedition should Xaratuk's expectations implode? Every man, from Regulus to the animal handlers, reexamined their own predictions. So much effort had been spent, and so much risk assumed. For this journey to culminate in an unrewarding conclusion was beyond contemplation—until now.

Mithrias and Topur stayed far apart from Xaratuk's ring of acrimony. "At least he's prepared for some disappointment," Mithrias said. "I admit I'm disappointed, too. He is acting rashly, but he may be right. It appears that Bethlehem has little to offer."

Topur rummaged for the elusive comfortable position. "Najiir tells me this is worth investigating. Miriam agrees. Those who visit that home leave it claiming they are changed. How? Why? Rumors swirl. Predictions fly. Why would we ignore this? Two priests sit in chains because they chose to remain oblivious. And look at this light! It alone deserves our attention! No matter what visions and expectations we have concocted, we must see for ourselves." Topur closed his eyes.

"But a commoner's child? Think of it, Topur. A mere peasant boy? Parents of no particular consequence? It seems so improbable to me, too."

"Parents of no particular consequence...yet." Topur placed his finger firmly on Mithrias's chest. "They may surprise us."

The pain had paled Topur's face.

"Are you sure you should go on?" Mithrias asked. "You don't look well, my friend. I promise to return for you if there is someone—something—you shouldn't miss."

"Oh, no. I must go. I must." Topur groaned. "If nothing else, someone ought to contradict our quarrelsome king." He managed a strained smile. "Merkis is right. We all had ideas about what we would see. I did. I was certain the advisors were mistaken about a star shining on one spot and, even if so, not on impoverished little Bethlehem. I was wrong. It seems I've been wrong about many things—what else?" He paused. "I must be there."

"As you wish." Mithrias rearranged the pillows surrounding Topur, helping to restore some comfort. "What is taking Najiir so long? He should be back here to help you."

"Joseph and Mary are the parents. They will remember him from his visit last night. He wants to prepare them for us. He is likely talking to the shepherds outside the house, convincing them we are friendly. King Xaratuk has chosen to look rather imperial, even intimidating. I hope that doesn't become a disadvantage."

"I should say the same about you," said Mithrias, smiling. "I see that purple collar sticking out above your blanket." During the travel up to Bethlehem, Topur's blanket had descended. Much of his chest and shoulders revealed the regal robe. "What is it you have on? Maybe Xaratuk isn't the only one overdressed for the occasion."

"Oh, I had forgotten. My clothes were ruined. I needed something. Miriam gathered these robes." Topur looked down at the delicate embroidery stitched in royal purple. "The original owner was a prince. I objected, but the only orders Miriam follows are her own. So here I am, covered by the robe of one of Herod's murdered sons. It sends chills down my back to think of it."

Mithrias stepped back. "I think you look magnificent. It now covers the shoulders of a man who deserves to be a king. Let me take that blanket from you." Topur protested but offered little more than verbal resistance. Mithrias gathered the blanket and began to fold it. "That is a fine, fine garment for you." His teeth shone like pearls in the evening light. "I am compelled to call you King Topur. It seems fitting."

"Hush," snapped Topur, barely containing a grin.

"Are you coming?" Xaratuk barked from a distance. Mithrias looked up, then moved before the cart, grabbing the horse's bridle. They began the last small leg of the journey that would take them into Bethlehem.

Clouds continued to dapple the usually clear desert sky, but their swift movement never completely veiled the silver beam. The objective was impossible to mistake. It was reasonable to have expected the light to illuminate a large area, perhaps the entire town. But the star's glittering column penetrated through the mottled darkness to touch the earth, touch Bethlehem, and touch one house.

The ramshackle stone and mortar dwelling, built at the far edge of the village, was an unremarkable pale, two-story structure with the usual flat roof. Light from oil lamps spilled through two window openings. A wooden door marked the sole entrance. The dwelling could scarcely accommodate more than the family currently calling it home.

The traveler they'd met earlier described the town well. It was small. Diminutive stone houses nestled tightly together in rows. Bethlehem's streets were narrow and not particularly straight. Moving in toward the village meant climbing a modest hill. The higher the home on that embankment, the more comfortable—though still modest—it appeared. Unlike most neighbors, the house bathed in light was not attached to any other. Behind it was a small stable, more aptly called a cave. Remarkably plain, the dwelling was the very opposite of a palace.

Vigilant shepherds were present and in force. They could not be considered an army, but each man carried some weapon: a knife, a dagger, a short sword, a club. A few were stationed along the road as it led to the village. Others were positioned on the rooftops of nearby houses. Some were in the branches of the infrequent trees nearby, but the greatest concentration remained near the house.

Xaratuk and Mithrias led the group that approached tiny Bethlehem. Regulus, Merkis, and Khartir were only steps behind. Finally, caustic Salnassar, visibly opposed to the duty, guided the cart pulling Topur.

Topur strained to turn around, trying to look forward and bear witness to their approach. Tracing the star's light absorbed him. It was so remarkably defined. To him, it seemed—but it couldn't be—that the origin of the light might not be from the star but from the home, as though the light went *to* the star, not *from* it. Reluctantly, he dismissed the notion. It was too taxing to turn and twist for further scrutiny. Confused, he looked away.

Two of Regulus's soldiers completed the entourage.

The procession moved slowly and was soon among the outermost shepherds stationed along the road. The shepherds said nothing but made ominous efforts to display their weapons. Some patted their daggers. One pretended to be sharpening his short sword. As the kings drew closer, the density of shepherds grew. Those on rooftops walked to the edges, standing with arms crossed.

Visitors exited the house: two, then three more. In supplication and reverence, those departing bowed back toward the open door. Finally, Najiir emerged. He, too, stepped backward, bowing, then turned to see his fellow travelers approaching. He muttered something through the doorway, then addressed two of the four shepherds guarding the entrance. He took up his characteristic trot toward the kings.

Merkis halted, dropping to his knees. Repeatedly he said, "Please, I beg. Open my eyes so I may see. Open my ears so I may hear. Open my mind so I may understand." Khartir kneeled, too, his arms outstretched, breaking into a chant. Both men remained kneeling, eyes closed, preparing themselves, encouraging their skills to be commensurate to the magnitude of this experience.

Khartir finished his chants with a final request. "Do not allow me to leave ignorant. Permit me to grasp what you are trying to show." His eyes opened. He stood, mouth agape, staring at a house steeped in glowing, silver light. His gaze drifted to the star while his head swayed. "Such a place." Merkis, on his knees, murmured his same chant again and again.

Xaratuk spotted Najiir trotting toward them. "Why is that boy coming out of there?" he snarled. "That's Topur's boy! Is this some trick? That peddler intends to swindle me!"

Mithrias shot back, "I don't follow you. Are you suggesting Topur can fix the light in the heavens to shine down where he chooses?" He stood back from Xaratuk and murmured, "Sometimes you utterly surprise me. Why would you say such a thing?"

Xaratuk strutted, pacing back and forth, swearing. His breathing was rapid and short. He slapped his sweating forehead with one hand, then pushed Mithrias out of his way. "So that peddler can't control the light, but he can plant his impostors in that house, and maybe I've caught him at it. This cannot be the place. I don't care where that light shines, this is a mistake." Veins bulged along the sides of his neck.

Najiir tried to slip past, but Xaratuk grabbed him at his chest, easily pulling him off his feet. "I didn't come this far to have you set up some sham act. I don't know what you think you are presenting here. This cannot be the spot I have traveled for months to discover at considerable expense." He sought to throw the boy to the ground, but Najiir was too nimble, remaining on his feet, inflaming Xaratuk even more.

"It is the place. It is exactly the place you have wished to see," replied Najiir calmly.

With an elbow, Xaratuk shoved Najiir and stomped toward the house. "Get out of my way. You are just some idiot slave! The slave of a swindler, at that! You are both frauds and impostors!"

Mithrias approached Najiir. Smiling, he placed his hands on Najiir's shoulders. "Good boy, Najiir. I should not have been so surprised to hear you had already been here—not at all." Najiir returned the smile. "Are we expected?" Mithrias asked. "And those men standing guard? Are they friendly?"

"They'll be friendly to us if we are friendly to them," answered Najiir. "You must understand they believe they alone protect a special gift from God. They are determined to defend that family—and they don't care if the threat is a king or a fox—they'll uphold the family with their lives."

"I had better deflect King Xaratuk. You get Topur out of the cart and bring him to me. I will need his help."

Najiir ran while Mithrias sprinted to catch Xaratuk. Reaching him, Mithrias grabbed Xaratuk by the wrist, holding him in place. Xaratuk's withering glare was fearsome.

"Let's wait for the others so we go through introductions only once," said Mithrias between quick breaths. "You'll want your advisors here, and you can't be certain those inside understand Greek. Just wait a moment."

Xaratuk swore. "Wait? I'll wait for no one. I will expose these charlatans for what they are!"

"Wait for the others!"

Merkis and Khartir drew closer. Regulus helped Najiir extract Topur from the cart. It was a slow process, but to everyone's surprise, Topur struggled forward on tentative, shaky legs. He clutched his midsection, keeping Miriam's bandaging in place. Najiir placed himself at Topur's elbow. Regulus walked behind, a hand on either shoulder. Progress was wobbly and slow.

Xaratuk stormed toward them. He stopped only inches from Topur's face. Topur couldn't stand erect. Pain dictated that he stoop. Straining, he returned Xaratuk's stony stare eye-to-eye.

"This is treachery," Xaratuk said, "and you are its leader, you snake. You bring me here, after all we've been through, after all I have done for you, and you bring me to this barn...this pit...this hovel...and try to persuade me this is the place we've been searching for? You fox! You viper!" He turned, eyes ablaze, spittle forming at the sides of his mouth, and pointed to Najiir. "And you get your slave boy to prepare your actors, telling them what to say and how to behave, so it looks convincing. You intend to trick us—cheat us! I see your accomplices in the trees and rooftops. I'll have Regulus clean them up and feed them all to the dogs—"

"King Xaratuk!" shouted Mithrias.

Topur drew a breath. "I am weary of defending myself and my motives to you. I nearly paid with my life bringing you here. If you see that as a conspiracy against you..." Topur shook his head and looked to the star. "You asked me to bring you to the place the star shines upon. I have done that. What you wished to accomplish once you arrived here is none of my affair. So, whatever you intend to do, I suggest you get on with it."

"Yes, let's get on with it, indeed." Mithrias stepped forward. With Najir's help, he moved Topur toward the door. Without acknowledging their king, Merkis and Khartir followed.

Xaratuk intercepted his advisors, pushing his hands into their chests. "You cannot possibly believe this is the star's conclusion!" Xaratuk stomped his feet. "This is sorcery. These are lies!" he yelled, sweeping his arm toward the house. "This is treachery!"

Khartir began to withdraw, but Merkis held firm, halting his young companion even as Xaratuk's stomping renewed. Xaratuk waved his arms and then stopped, grabbing Merkis by the chest. The frail Merkis lost his footing, nearly falling into Xaratuk.

"I will have you horsewhipped—now!" Xaratuk screamed. He turned to Khartir. "Then YOU!" Xaratuk pushed Merkis away. "Then you again!" he hollered. "Regulus! Where is my whip?"

Two of the shepherds placed in the trees dropped to the ground.

Mithrias grabbed Xaratuk by both shoulders. "Xaratuk! Compose yourself! You are a king, not some madman!" He released the king with a shove. "You are every bit as frightening as Herod was this morning! This is beneath you! Stop!"

Merkis dabbed at Xaratuk's spittle that dotted his robe. He took Khartir's arm. Composed, they stepped past their king toward the house.

Xaratuk's voice quaked. "This is insubordination, Mithrias. Insubordination! I have never tolerated it, and I will not do so tonight—of all nights. My advisors have thoroughly failed me, they've failed my kingdom, and they'll answer for it. I assure you of that." With a menacing finger, he pointed at Mithrias. "And so will anyone else caught up in their spell."

"Your advisors have not been insubordinate." Mithrias's calm voice quelled the tirade. "There is no spell, no magic. Merkis and Khartir have proven their wisdom and insight. They have earned your respect. Let them examine this mystery because it may transcend all others." He smiled while raising his hand toward the star. "No such light had ever appeared in the night sky, but here it is." Mithrias drew a deep breath, then put his hands on Xaratuk's shoulders. "And here you are—finally. So the light doesn't rest upon a palace or a fortress. At least it doesn't shine upon some Roman villa. The star didn't guide you to an enemy. Your advisors have faithfully brought you to the doorstep of the place you were seeking. In your disappointment, you judge before you know anything about what is here." He squeezed Xaratuk's shoulders. "That, my friend, is wrong."

Xaratuk's rigid stance softened, and his brow rose.

Mithrias continued. "Before we determine Bethlehem offers no benefit for you or your kingdom, we owe it to all we have sacrificed, to all we have endured, and to all those who have come with us to examine this properly. A good king would do that for his people. You are that good king. You must do this."

Xaratuk heaved a sigh. He nodded with a vacant, begrudging stare. Without moving, he hollered, "Merkis! Khartir!" The advisors arrested their progress toward the house. Xaratuk walked to them and, looking down at his feet, said, "I shouldn't have said those things. And I have no intention of harming either of you." A hissing, deflating moan poured out. "I am unhappy, but it isn't your fault. I shouldn't have spoken like that."

"My king," Merkis spoke evenly, "we must speak to these people. We understand too little of what lies within. This setting is a shock to me, as well. I will be frank and admit that this challenges my expectations, too. But we must go on. We must know more."

"Proceed," said Xaratuk.

The next steps took them from the road to a worn path leading to the house. At least twenty men stood on either side. Four men, their daggers drawn, stood in the doorway, blocking immediate entry.

Watching the kings' approach, one man spoke. "Whom do we have the pleasure of meeting tonight?" It was a mocking tone, and it was not in Greek. "Why does that one appear in armor? Watch him. He's dressed for a fight." Some incidental laughing emanated from the double line. "Be prepared, everyone," he shouted.

The scant light through the windows faintly illuminated the kings as they approached. Najiir scampered to place himself in the lead.

"Amram, it is me, Najiir," he said in a firm voice, speaking the local Aramaic. Najiir raised his right hand. He offered a greeting he had heard others use upon approaching the threshold. "May the peace of God be with you always." His hand swept behind. "These are the kings I spoke of."

Xaratuk looked at Najiir in disbelief. "Who elevated that slave boy to be my spokesman?" he growled. Mithrias raised a finger to his lips, imploring his friend to be silent. Xaratuk's jaw thrust out.

Xaratuk pulled even with Najiir. He had a withering stare ready for anyone who dared look upon him. Najiir began his introduction. "This man is King Xaratuk, King of Kings and Ruler of a Hundred Cities." Xaratuk, though not understanding Najiir's words, stiffened his spine, acknowledging no one in particular. Najiir continued with a glowing introduction of Mithrias. Believing Najiir had finished, Mithrias tipped his head toward the shepherds. Najiir's introduction of Topur was likewise inflated, and the shepherds paid respectful attention. Topur mustered a passive wave of his hand.

The four shepherds bowed as if on cue. Xaratuk, startled, stepped back.

"These are the kings and their advisors who have been called to this place by the star," Najiir continued. "Their journey has taken them many months, but they are finally here. The family has been expecting such an arrival." The shepherds parted before the door, heads bowed in submission. "I assure you, these men are here to honor the child."

As the kings stepped toward the house, the shepherd, Amram, snagged Najiir's arm, halting any progress. "One of them seems quite agitated," he said. "At a minimum, we insist he remove his short sword before entering."

Najiir looked to Topur.

"This will be delicate," said Topur.

"What are you people saying?" Xaratuk cut in. "Speak so we can all understand. What is going on? Let us go in."

Topur felt a wet trickle moving haphazardly from his torso down his leg. One droplet, followed quickly by others, seeped past his bandages. He leaned upon Mithrias even more. "King Xaratuk," he wheezed, "I will speak plainly because I can only remain standing for a little while longer. I must get inside. We are trying to get you the permission needed to enter. It seems your little outburst has shocked these men. They think you are too unsettled. They are reluctant to have you enter the home with a weapon. As a precautionary measure, they want you to surrender your sword before entering the house. You'll get it back when you leave. Under the circumstances, their wish seems fair."

Xaratuk folded his arms across his chest. "If they think they'll keep my sword, they are mistaken. It will never leave my side. No one touches the king's sword. Anyone who lays a hand upon it, or me, will die with it in their chest. Is that clear?"

"Very well," said Topur, "I understand you and will say that under no circumstances will you relinquish your sword." He turned to Amram but first added, "We'll see how far that gets us through the door."

"I will have Regulus remove the door if I must, and with it, any insignificant shepherd who tries to stop us," Xaratuk spat back.

"Master?" said Najiir urgently.

"Before you tell them anything," interjected Mithrias, "tell them I will take full responsibility for ensuring King Xaratuk's sword remains in its sheath. I guarantee the safety of everyone within."

Topur relayed Mithrias's assurance to the shepherds. That started a debate that grew clamorous and insistent. Topur, eyes shut, thought to say more, but as his eyelids opened, he looked to his feet and the shiny pool of blood collecting on the sandy ground below his ankle. Amram touched Topur on the shoulder, whispered to him, then broke off and went inside the house. No one moved. Topur could barely raise his head.

"That shepherd's name is Amram." He could not speak above a hoarse whisper. "He supervises the others out here.

Inside is another man named Simon. He is the leader of all the shepherds. Amram is not inclined, but we can go inside if Simon approves. It is up to him."

Xaratuk looked with disdain at the downcast head of Topur. "No. It is not up to some shepherd." Xaratuk patted his sword. "Regulus, step up here," he ordered.

"Regulus, stay where you are!" Mithrias countered. "No one moves! We don't need to get this excited—"

"Stay out of this, Mithrias," Xaratuk warned.

Topur was undone. His voice would not support the sharpness of his words. "We have come all this way—we are at the conclusion of this quest—and you're willing to abandon it over whether you can keep your sword. You can stay out here, dance back to Jerusalem, run home, for all I care. Stomp on the ground all you like and see what difference you'll make. I have no sword. Mithrias, with your help, I would like to go inside. Najiir, you come, too."

"I will be glad to assist," said Mithrias. Seeing the blood at Topur's foot, Mithrias moved forward. "You're going inside. Now!"

The door creaked. Amram emerged through the doorway. "The family wishes to invite you inside. Some of us will remain with you while you visit," he added, looking directly at Xaratuk. Xaratuk offered a grunt of indignation, then patted his sword.

"I could have ordered Regulus to set fire to the whole town," he muttered under his breath.

Amram made the announcement. "You have noble guests arriving from the east."

CHAPTER 29

Najiir walked through the short doorway, hands folded, head bowed. He stood aside, then beckoned the others. One-by-one, they entered. The compact, stone-walled room could accommodate a small family but not eight new arrivals. Low ceilings intensified feelings of confinement. Seeing the room's limitations, Regulus offered to remain posted outside the door. He motioned to Salnassar to do the same.

The air was dense and sticky from overuse. The floors were dirt, trampled shiny from decades of use. One small, doorless room adjoined. It provided a bedroom but little privacy. A short, makeshift ladder rose to a tiny loft at the room's far end.

The furnishings were sparse. A blackened kettle hung from a tripod above smoldering sticks at the meager, raised hearth. Faint traces of burning kindling mixed with the smell of cooking lentils, accented by whiffs of garlic and cumin. To the side, small bowls were neatly stacked on the stone surface. Three stools, solid but without flourish, hid under a long table, the room's largest item. One lit oil lamp lay upon it. A modest cot rested on end in the corner, an accommodation made for the improvised security detail.

A man and woman sat on stools near the hearth. The woman held a baby wrapped inside a beige blanket, a small wooden cradle at her feet. Two men, both dressed in animal skins, stood in opposite corners.

Mithrias, guiding Topur, was the last to enter the house. As they came through, the woman gasped. She placed the baby in the cradle and rushed from her stool. "You are hurt!" she said in Aramaic. "Simon, please get a blanket—and some pillows. Caleb, lower the cot. Our guest must lie down." The men scrambled to follow her requests.

"Thank you, dear woman. You are most gracious," said Topur through his grimace. "I wish I could tell you not to go to any trouble for me, but I fear you must."

Simon quickly returned. Caleb lay the cot on the floor, facing it into the room. With the help of Simon and Mithrias, Topur eased onto the cot, his back propped upon tattered cushions arranged against the wall. Finally off his feet, he sighed, clutching his side.

Topur looked at his hosts. "This is so much better." He winced. "Again, I do thank you." Najiir kneeled at Topur's side as Mary tucked the blankets. She placed her diminutive hand on Topur's forehead.

"You are terribly injured," she remarked.

Xaratuk turned to Mithrias. "What is he doing here? Why is he staying?" he said, pointing at Najiir. Before Mithrias could answer, Najiir spoke.

"Mary and Joseph rarely speak Greek. I understand both Aramaic and Greek, as well as some of your language, King Xaratuk. I thought I could help."

The seated man, Joseph, rose. "I would like Najiir to stay," he said in halting Greek. "I find him to be of great benefit. He knows some things about us and can help me better understand all of you. I would like him to remain."

Xaratuk looked suspiciously at Najiir, then at Joseph. "My captain of the guard leaves while he stays?" he mumbled, then shrugged. "More confirmation my wishes mean nothing. Fine. Do as you wish." He stared through Najiir. "You two seem to know each other, yet we have just arrived. What should I make of that?"

"Najiir came earlier to inform us of your arrival," said

Joseph. "He is right. I do not speak Greek well. I apologize for that." His back straightened, and his head rose. "I am Joseph of Nazareth. This is my wife, Mary." The travelers' ears strained, adjusting to Joseph's accent.

Mary continued to minister to Topur. "We are especially honored, dear kings," she said in her own labored Greek. "You have traveled so far." She examined the royal robes wrapped about Topur. "You are such noble, influential men. You have suffered much to be here." She placed a soft hand over Topur's.

Mary's touch was intensely gentle and comforting. Topur studied her. She appeared younger than he had imagined, conveying freshness and vigor. A blue headscarf covered her head but allowed her rich black hair, parted in the middle, to show upon her forehead. Her nose was long and angular, fixed between close, dark eyes. Lips, still naturally soft and red, lined her mouth. Her face was smooth, absent of any lines depicting worry and weariness. Topur sensed a warm beauty, a loveliness enhanced by genuine kindness. His eyes followed her as she tiptoed back to her stool, pulling the baby from the crib and placing him in her lap.

As she sat, Mary saw Topur looking at her. She smiled at him. "I wish I could do more. If there is anything, please tell me." Topur could only nod.

"I would like to introduce our friends, Simon and Caleb," said Joseph, pointing to the corners of the room. "They have been with us since...since the beginning. They are a comfort, and we feel more at peace with them nearby. Simon is originally from Jerusalem." Simon nodded. "Caleb's family has lived here, tending to their farm, for generations." Caleb meekly acknowledged the group.

Joseph offered the stools around the table, though everyone politely declined, preferring to remain standing. There was an awkward pause, then Merkis broke the silence. "We are so honored to meet you and your wife, Joseph. Let me state our purpose. I'll begin with the obvious. Your house has a...has a...a star's bright light upon it. We have come all this way to find out why."

Joseph smiled. "The light is impossible to ignore, and our lives are surely changing because of it. You may count on our cooperation."

"That is the first of our many questions," Merkis continued. "We don't wish to annoy or offend you or let our curiosity appear intrusive, but this is such an extraordinary event. So much to ask. Please be patient with us."

"And you with us," Joseph responded. "I'm not sure anything we say will have value." He placed a hand on Mary's shoulder. "Please realize that this experience is new to us. We seek answers to our own questions. Prior to this, our lives did not invite such inspection."

Joseph's Greek was better than he had led them to believe.

He continued. "I am aware others, separated from our experiences, might not understand or believe us. Our explanations rely heavily upon trust and faith. What has happened might sound incredible or absurd, but please realize what seems implausible to you may be just as implausible to us."

Khartir bowed to Mary and Joseph. "You are leading us on a fascinating adventure. With your permission, may I begin with this question? Have you determined why this star shines upon this house and only this house?"

"Any explanation we may offer is lacking," said Joseph. "We haven't been here long. I know there was no such light in Bethlehem until after this child was born, so it must have everything to do with him. But I fall short of answering your question. I'm not sure I can."

"Might the light be a sign?" asked Khartir. "We come from a people who study the stars and the skies. This star is unique and exceptional. There is no precedent. Might it signify something profoundly special? What might that be?"

Joseph peered at Mary and met her eyes looking at his.

They shuffled in silent agitation. Finally, he spoke. "We agree with you. It is a sign, and you wish to know what meaning is attached to this sign." Joseph looked to Najiir. "Help me if my Greek goes badly. Words of explanation are insufficient in my own tongue. It will be even harder for me in Greek."

Najiir, eyes wide with attention, nodded.

Joseph resumed. "We feel—no, we believe in our hearts— that God has sent this child to witness what is happening here on earth and to be a part of it. He has a message. But beyond that...beyond that..." Joseph looked down, then his gaze once again went to Mary. She looked anxiously back at him. "Beyond that, it is just too early to say. I understand my answer is meager. I can tell you what I believe. I can tell you some of what Mary believes, and you must hear her speak because she experiences things I do not, or cannot."

Joseph searched for the correct words. "The light means something. This child means something. Everyone knows that much. I think the star foretells something beautiful, helpful, even..." He looked to Najiir, falling back to Aramaic. "Righteous," Najiir translated. "But others find their own meaning, or meanings." Joseph frowned. His look of doubt was superseded by one of deep concern. "There are already so many expectations of him, of us. At times, I feel overwhelmed and inadequate. But this is our duty. We must see this child gets the opportunity to tell us—himself—why he is special."

"Others see this light and are curious," said Khartir.

"Oh yes. People arrive continuously, day and night. We see neighbors, people from other villages, people from Jerusalem, and people from far, far away—like you."

"And what do you tell them?"

Joseph looked away. "We speak little," he said. "What could we say? For now, it is better to remain quiet. When the child can speak for himself, we will know more."

Khartir paused, looking down at the cradle. "What is the child's name?"

"We have named him Jesus."

"Jesus. I see. Is that a grandfather's suggestion or another family name?" asked Khartir. Unable to resist the impulse, he kneeled before the cradle. He extended a finger toward the child. "Welcome to Bethlehem, Jesus. Welcome to this world. I think many, besides your parents, are happy you are here." The infant grasped Khartir's finger. Khartir smiled. The baby smiled back.

"He likes you," said Mary.

"The idea of naming him Jesus did not come from family." Joseph became slow and selective with his words. "Mary had direction—words spoken only to her—about this."

"You've heard voices?" Khartir withdrew his finger. He stood up, looking at Mary. "Interesting."

Merkis stepped forward, gently putting his hand on Joseph's elbow. "Perhaps we should refrain from going to the heart of the matter so quickly. That will give us time to gain comfort with one another and to prepare our thoughts and questions and allow you to gain confidence with your answers."

He turned to his companion. "I don't mean to overshadow you, Khartir, because you allude to the essence of our visit. But we have many questions, and perhaps it is best to wrestle with the harder ones later."

"As always, you are so right," said Khartir. "I was just so excited."

"Sir," said Joseph, "none of this is new to us. Our visitors ask such questions daily. We ask these same things, within ourselves, even more frequently." Joseph's hand rested on Mary's shoulder.

"Can we begin here? How long have you lived in Bethlehem?" asked Merkis.

"Only since the baby was born."

"Oh?" said Merkis. "I had imagined you both to be lifelong residents. I was wrong. I realize I hold many expectations that are being challenged." He cleared his aging throat and smiled. "I find that delightful."

"We came here following the census decree," Joseph said, "and had arrived in Bethlehem when, that same night, the baby was born. It was the culmination of a difficult time for us. Mary endured so much."

"She did?" Merkis responded. "I'm quite surprised. You had her travel—in her condition? How far had you come?"

"We are from Nazareth, in Galilee," said Joseph. "We came back to Bethlehem because my family was originally from here. I was born here. But soon after, my father found work in Sepphoris and moved the family there. Once on my own, I moved to a nearby town, Nazareth, where I met Mary. We were married there. When the census decree was issued, the timing was right to return to Bethlehem. It offered an excuse to leave Nazareth because things there were becoming...difficult."

"Difficult?" asked Merkis. "Difficult? Why?"

Joseph sighed. "This isn't easy to speak of. Mary and I know the truth, but many people—most people—won't listen to our explanations, and they condemn us. Reluctantly, we must accept that. What we require others to acknowledge is too difficult, even unbelievable. It is far easier to be apart and away than to stay, continually offering explanations everyone eventually rejects. It hurts." Joseph drew in a long breath. "Mary began hearing voices. A voice told her of a birth, through her, of a child favored by God. It was the beginning of a complicated time that has continued to this day."

Joseph paused. He examined the reactions of those in the room. His gaze dropped to his feet. "The timing of our marriage came into question. People, even our own families, had suspicions and doubts about me, and more so, about Mary." His head moved slowly, side-to-side, in a disbelieving shake. "Mary deserved none of that. God chose her for this, and she received only scorn from those around us." His eyes fixated on the far wall. "It was best for us to move on, even in her condition." His jaw moved forward, and the waggle of disbelief continued. "The census just gave us reasonable justification for our departure."

Joseph sat on the stool next to Mary. "So we are here in Bethlehem. It is such a small town. Many others were already in the village for the census as well. For a while, it was a busy place—busy for Bethlehem. When the baby arrived, there was nowhere to stay, but soon after, this house opened, and we've remained here ever since." He nodded toward Simon. "Our new friends made certain we are comfortable."

Khartir spoke again. "Those in Bethlehem appear very accepting of you and Mary and your new circumstances, Joseph. If you are originally from here, have you any family that remains?"

"No, not any, to my knowledge."

"I'm surprised. None? But your lineage begins here. Do you know your lineage? Are you able to trace your ancestry?"

Joseph had a ready answer. "I didn't expect foreign men to be interested, but my father was well-rehearsed about our family's ancestry. He could name every generation and boasted he could follow it back to King David. He was immensely proud of that."

"And you? You are not proud of it, too? Isn't King David's name significant in your people's history?"

"Oh, I am proud of it, indeed. But I soon realized that his descendants are numerous and scattered to the winds. We are a multitude. To claim King David as an ancestor is an honor but brings no special privilege. We are not in line to be High Priest," he said, smiling. "It doesn't even help me find work."

"But you are from the House of David."

"As I understand it, I am."

Merkis and Khartir looked at one another, barely concealing their smug smiles.

Khartir continued. "Mary, you and Joseph agree your son is special, but why? Aren't all children gifts from God? What is it? Have you noticed something decidedly different or unusual?"

"If you mean can the child walk, or talk, or fly about the

room? No," Mary replied. "Maybe that isn't the answer you are looking for."

"We simply wish to know what you know," said Khartir.

"So far, he is a normal child. As my husband says, we must wait. Time will reveal why he is special."

"The star has drawn many visitors," said Joseph. "Not one arrived hoping to see tricks, or magic, or sorcery. The people coming through our door are those familiar with pain, or sorrow, or loss, or disillusionment. Life has carved an emptiness within them."

Mithrias edged forward. An earthquake would not have divided his attention.

"Those who visit here take with them an understanding they did not have before," Joseph continued. "They find new and different meanings within their hearts. They tell us this is so. And I believe them, for I have seen it, though I can't explain it. A mere child, and already such influence." His hand passed to his chin. "With God's help, Mary and I will provide. We will encourage this child to grow. Later, we will all witness what makes him special."

Merkis allowed time for Joseph's words to settle. Then he kneeled next to Mary. "These voices you hear, Mary, how do they seem to you? Are they like a voice in your head, or is it as we speak now?"

"I know the difference between listening to my own thoughts and hearing another's voice," she said curtly. "These thoughts are not my thoughts—the words are not my words. I can't summon it. It isn't a conversation. When I hear the voice, I can't ignore it. It is clear to me I hear another."

"I understand." Merkis rose, nervously pulling at his beard. "Mary, I do not wish to offend. I sense I distress you. I apologize. My sole purpose is to understand more precisely what you experience." Merkis raised his hand to his brow, frowning. "I must be honest with you—we must be honest with each other. In fact, you are not the first person I have met who claims to hear a voice. Khartir and I have encountered others who claim to hear things, claim they talk to some divine being. I can assure you that they do not. But they want to convince any audience they do. You may have met such people yourself. We want to keep you, your message—this message—separate from them. We feel a responsibility to conclude you and your husband are being genuine."

Topur opened his eyes for the first time. He saw Mary's jaw clench, a visible prelude to her withdrawal from the conversation. *Please, Merkis, don't turn this into an inquisition. She says we must wait. Don't accuse her.* To Topur, Mary didn't look defiant. She appeared rankled, tired of the endless questions, the doubts, the challenges, the speculations, the predictions. *Poor woman. The family confessed they were uncertain. Can't we do what they ask? Can't we wait?*

Merkis, alarmed by Mary's stoic gaze, tried to reassure her. "Mary, again, I mean no offense, but—"

"Mary isn't the only one who has heard a voice." A new voice spoke, but in perfectly accented, if not formal, Greek.

CHAPTER 30

"**W**hat? What is this? Someone else has heard voices?" Merkis searched for the speaker. Simon, the shepherd leaning in the corner, stood upright, his hand propped on his dagger.

"I said, Mary isn't the only one who has heard a voice." Simon's eloquent elocution was in stark contrast to his animal skins, the lowly garb of the menial shepherd. "Others of us have heard and seen things as well."

"Once more for me. Just who are you?" It was Xaratuk.

"Simon. I am Simon."

"So, Simon hears voices, too." Even in Greek, Xaratuk's sarcasm percolated. "What luck. We travel for months to arrive at a hovel crammed with people who hear voices."

Merkis provided a polite and necessary contrast. "Simon, it is a privilege to hear your story. Tell us more. Is the voice you hear the same as Mary's?"

"It isn't the same voice. At least, I don't think so. But it's not only me. Others heard voices, too. Those men outside—the ones beyond that door, in the trees, on the rooftops—all of us heard a voice." Simon sought confirmation, and Caleb nodded his agreement. "All of us here with this family heard and saw the announcement of Jesus' birth."

"You—a pack of shepherds—were told of this birth?" Xaratuk mocked Simon's words. He looked at the baby in Mary's lap. "Did bells go off? Did flags unfurl before you?"

Simon frowned. "If you would like to hear my story, I will continue. If you would rather force your fantasies upon my experiences, proceed with your ignorant embellishments. "

"Please, Simon, please go on," said Merkis.

"Understand, this isn't just my version. We all saw the same thing. Ask any of us to describe what we saw, and we'll tell you the same thing."

"You are speaking of your fellow shepherds?"

"Yes. We were out, at night, in the valleys outside the village, like any other night, tending to our flocks."

"A normal night? There were no other indications, no warnings or other signs?"

"No, certainly not. It was late, and that night was particularly dark—no moon. Some say they had been asleep, but I was not. Without warning, out of nowhere, the sky filled with an enormous light." Simon flung his arms wide, palms outstretched. "It did not leave a trail like a shooting star. It suddenly appeared—whoosh! The light took up half the sky. It was so bright that I had to hide my eyes. I looked at the others beside me. All were wide awake—everyone—bathed in brilliant light. It was fearsome. We didn't know what to think or what to do. We had no weapons. Where could we run? Run from what? We all sat captivated, unable to move."

"It was like some giant star above you?" asked Khartir.

"No, not exactly," said Simon. "It was more of an opening— a rip in the night sky, and behind it, a bright room—the brightest you can imagine, like an entrance to somewhere beyond our imagination."

"All of you who saw this were together?" asked Mithrias.

"No, making this even more strange. But those who saw it were outside the village in the fields. No one in town claims to have witnessed this." Caleb's head bobbed in confirmation. "We were in small groups of two, four, five, scattered about four different valleys outside the village."

"And how many shepherds in all?" asked Mithrias.

"Forty. Exactly forty," replied Simon. "And I can summon every one of them with a loud whistle if you wish." Simon folded his arms, his hand finally coming off his dagger. "All of us have been remarkably changed. This has brought us together. We need to remain with Jesus and support Mary and Joseph."

"Forty," murmured Merkis. "That is a large group to achieve consensus on a sighting. I've heard of more, but rarely. And you were in small, separate groups, not together in a single place?" Simon nodded. "Simon, if I may, go back to the voice. What was said to you? Were the words exactly the same for everyone?"

"They were the same, the same for us all. Caleb, you recall it better than I." Caleb stepped forward, but Simon continued, "First, the voice told us not to be afraid. It was too late for that, wasn't it, Caleb?" The two shepherds smiled at each other. Caleb spoke for the first time in the same heavily accented Greek as Joseph.

"It began, 'Unto you, born this day, in the city of David, a savior.'" Caleb's eyes grew wide. His arms and hands, moving like a dancer's, traced arcs in the stagnant air as he spoke of light, of trembling, and a booming voice, louder, more distinct than any ever delivered. The voice instructed the shepherds to go to Bethlehem and search for a child. They would recognize this child because he would be a newborn baby, wrapped in swaddling clothes, lying in a manger.

Fingers splayed, arms raised, he said, "Imagine. A savior. Born in lowly Bethlehem. In a barn. In a box."

Caleb's voice rose. "Then the light, which had been brilliant white, turned into dancing, spinning colors, and as they twisted, they grew even larger. The one voice became many—a choir— men, women, children, the loudest collection of voices I have ever heard. 'All praise be to God!' they shouted in unison. 'Glory to God in the highest, and on earth peace and goodwill'." He stopped, panting. "Their sweet song rang in my ears."

The room was silent. No one moved.

"Then, just as quickly as it came, it vanished," whispered Simon. "The sky was black once more."

"I was afraid," said Caleb. "But I wasn't afraid."

"It enthralled us," said Simon. "We had to act. We secured our sheep, then ran back to town. We came upon the only lamps burning in the village, light coming from the caves behind the inn." Simon's voice softened. He nodded toward Mary. "And there we found Mary and Joseph...and a newborn baby in a manger."

Caleb continued his story. "Simon and I were the first to arrive. We didn't realize others had seen this as well. But now, from outside Bethlehem, all these men came running—shepherds, all of them. Some we knew well, and others were almost strangers. They were excited. They'd also seen the same vision and heard the same words. At first, there were five, then ten, then twenty. It finally grew to forty of us surrounding the inn the rest of the night."

"Their arrival was beyond anything I could comprehend," said Joseph, "and nothing has been the same since."

"We are all changed people," offered Simon.

"A savior," Xaratuk mocked. "Born in a barn. Flanked by a legion of mundane herders. Most impressive."

"You may think us mundane and lowly if you like," snapped Simon. "You seem quick to judge and certain of your conclusions. I was a citizen of Jerusalem, as was my family for generations. My father owned a prosperous farm, as did his father and his father's father. He had land and wealth. I was schooled in Antioch. Hardly mundane."

Simon folded his arms, moving from the corner to confront Xaratuk eye-to-eye. "But Judaea had years of drought. It devastated our land and our herds. My father fell behind on his taxes—taxes Herod had increased to support his Temple. Those taxes, plus those the Romans took, eliminated my family's wealth. The High Priest, whom the Law says cannot own land, nonetheless offered to buy my father's farm for a fraction of what it was worth. My father would not sell, so Herod and the Sanhedrin let the Romans confiscate it from us. The shock of losing land that had been in his family for generations killed my father. They threw the rest of us into the street. Today, the High Priest runs our land, raising animals he sells for sacrifices at the Temple. Thanks to Herod and the Romans, he gets richer and richer, and we are left to beggary. My oldest brother was so outraged that he joined with some radicals trying to create support for overthrowing the Romans and their Jewish collaborators. He was caught and executed without a trial. I have two other brothers who have taken up with bandits, I'm told. I don't know what has become of my two sisters.

"I left Jerusalem because I heard the Romans had told Herod I, too, was a radical. If I am caught, they will execute me just like my brother. That Temple is stained with the blood of my family—and not only mine. Hundreds, maybe thousands of us, have had to flee to the hills. If 'mundane' means mistreated and hunted down like a jackal, then I would be mundane. But I understand Greek as well as you. I can read, translate, cipher, and write. I am reduced to wearing animal skins to cover me, but I am the equal of any man here."

"So you speak well, but that doesn't mean you have something worthwhile to say," said Xaratuk.

"None of us expected to see what we saw that night. Whether given to shepherd or sage, the announcement was made. We were told to meet a savior, which we did. Like you, we wish to understand more."

Simon turned away from Xaratuk, stepping to the crib. "A savior," he said. "No mistaking that. Jerusalem surely needs one. He will lead us—in time. He will make Jerusalem ours once again." Simon returned to his corner, resuming his scrutiny of Xaratuk, placing his hand upon his dagger. "And, I might add, this child—still in a crib—has already surpassed you and your influence. No bright light announced your arrival on earth, King."

"Did Antioch teach insolence as well?"

"Joseph told me to expect the skeptics. He and Mary were met by skeptics even before the child was born. There will always be those who will not wish to understand. But I was called here. My brethren shepherds were called here. And we faithfully remain."

"Each of us makes himself available," added Caleb.

"But this light, this voice in the valleys—it was gone? Just like that?" said Khartir, snapping his fingers. "Nothing more?"

"Like that," said Caleb, snapping his fingers as well. "Nothing more."

"And who do you suppose it was?" asked Khartir.

"I never saw a figure within the light," said Simon. "It hurt my eyes. It was brighter than the midday sun against the black backdrop of deep night. Others claim they saw a silhouette within the light, a body, maybe, or a face. I didn't. But we all heard the voice." Simon's hand went to his chin. "And there is one more thing. I had an overwhelming feeling of peace and joy when the light disappeared. My life has been a struggle lately, so I was sure to notice."

"And the others? No more voices, no more announcements, no more visions since?" pressed Khartir.

"That was the one and only," said Simon. Caleb nodded.

Khartir turned his attention to Mary. "You didn't see or hear what the shepherds experienced?"

Mary shifted her weight on the stool and patted the baby's blanket. "No. I was minding other things."

"Yes, yes, of course," said Khartir. "That was thoughtless of me. I apologize." He looked at Joseph. "And you? Did you witness any announcement?"

"No. I was distracted, too, tending to Mary, trying to secure better lodging for us. I saw nothing. The voice Mary hears, and the vision shown to the shepherds, are not granted to me. You asked Mary if she understood the difference between listening to her thoughts and hearing voices, and I would say I am privy only to my own voice. God may grant me His help in making good decisions, but I am not told what to do—unlike the others."

Turning to Mary, Khartir said, "I do wish to ask you more about the voices you hear."

Wearily, Mary looked toward Joseph. She adjusted the baby upon her lap. "Not many voices—just one."

"Just one voice—always the single, same voice."

Mary nodded. "One voice."

The sound of metal upon metal clanged. Xaratuk's short sword clanked against his armor as he paced in the few short steps available. He threw his arms up in the air. "Honestly, Khartir? A woman? The words of a woman?"

Merkis rushed to intervene. "It is unquestionably vital to hear what these people have to say. Joseph relates what he has experienced. The shepherds can give their accounts. However, it is Mary who has the greatest involvement and, thereby, the greatest insight. We are obliged to listen to her."

Xaratuk grunted.

"Mary," Khartir said, clearing his throat, "we dined with King Herod and some invited priests last evening in Jerusalem, and they said—"

"Out! Out now!" ordered Simon. "Every one of you, leave! Now! Mary, stand back!" Simon and Caleb leaped from their posts, daggers drawn.

"Wait!" Joseph blurted. "Wait! I don't understand. You've come from King Herod?" He looked anxiously down at Mary, who looked back with equal alarm. She brought the baby closer to her chest. "Yes. Simon's right. We should stop. You should leave."

"If I may, Joseph." Merkis raised his hands in supplication. "If I may, by explanation, reassure you. We are not an emissary of King Herod."

Mithrias glared at Xaratuk. His sharp look warned the king to curb any thought of contradiction.

"We have been months on this journey," Merkis pled, "and

we never intended to meet King Herod before we arrived in Bethlehem. Indeed, on our way to you, to this house, it was our guide's intention we avoid Jerusalem altogether." He made a sweeping motion with his hand toward Topur.

Having listened to the discussions with his chin on his chest, Topur raised it. "That is true," he said in Aramaic. "As their guide, I thought it best to use a route that would avoid Jerusalem and, thereby, King Herod. I paid a price for that suggestion."

"That is why you are injured?" Joseph asked. "It was Herod's men?"

"Could we keep this in Greek, please?" snapped Xaratuk.

Topur stared with cold indifference at Xaratuk, continuing the discussion in Aramaic.

"No, it wasn't Herod's men," said Topur. "It is a long story, Joseph. When we have time, I will explain. Truthfully, some of Herod's soldiers were nearby, and they helped us." His gaze moved to Simon. "It grieves me to tell you this—it was bandits, Simon. You said your brothers took up with some bandits. I hope he was not part of that group. I am sure those not killed outright have been nailed to Roman crosses."

Simon bit his lip. His eyes welled.

"Joseph, I did all I could to have these kings avoid Herod," Topur said, "but in the end, I failed. These men were only inadvertently Herod's dinner guests." Topur looked over to Merkis. "Please continue, sir," he said, returning to Greek.

Merkis cocked his head, unsure of what had transpired. Stammering, he began again, explaining the canyon, the rescue, and the dinner as unintended guests. "We were asked, understandably, to justify ourselves and our presence in Judaea, and we answered in earnest. Our only desire has been to arrive here. We are not agents of men. We are agents for understanding."

"But he knows about us, then?" asked Joseph.

Merkis continued his plea. "Herod knows we follow the

star, Joseph. He knows this is the culmination of our journey. What details he understands about you or your child is uncertain. At our dinner, he appeared to know little. He and his priests had been rather disinterested."

Simon stepped before Joseph. "Joseph, I told you it was simply a matter of time. There have been too many visitors here, and we can't stop them from talking. This has grown beyond our ability to control. If Herod has any realization of what is here, we must be prepared for the worst."

Merkis listened helplessly to the two men discussing in Aramaic. He looked to Topur. "Topur, tell them of our goodwill and good intentions. Mary," he implored. "Look at this man. Look at his injuries. He has paid dearly for our wish to be here with you. No one from the palace is with us. These men can search our camp. And...and...we brought our entire caravan with us. They are assembled at the bottom of the hill outside town. We left no one waiting in Jerusalem."

That was what Topur had waited to hear. Nothing could be more satisfying. He raised his eyebrows in smug satisfaction. His directive was vindicated—though not in the way he had expected.

Consumed by spite, Xaratuk rolled his eyes.

"Herod has many spies," answered Joseph. "We can never tell—"

"Simon, sir, if you please," Najiir interrupted. Speaking in Aramaic, he addressed Simon, but made sure Joseph and Mary could hear. He recounted the names of servants and slaves within Herod's palace, known supporters of Mary and Joseph— names he'd learned from Kauib and even Bartholomew— names he was confident Simon would recognize. These people had visited this house many times and had guarded its secrets. Najiir asserted these same people had been essential in seeing no harm came to the visiting kings and helped ensure the caravan would be allowed to leave Jerusalem unharmed to proceed to Bethlehem.

Joseph looked into Merkis's stricken face. His gaze moved to Mary, but her concentration was still on the baby in her arms. Why did such momentous decisions come with such meager clarity and so little direction? In vain, he listened for a voice.

"Simon?" said Joseph. Simon moved to Joseph's side, maintaining his cold scrutiny of the others. "What do you say?"

"My first thought was to throw them out immediately."

"And now?"

"Najiir makes me reconsider. Joseph, either these men are genuine and trustworthy, or are the perfect spies. Either way, you'll lose nothing if you toss them out. It would give us time to make preparations concerning Herod."

Joseph tapped his forehead. "Oh, Simon. There must be some reason for this visit." He looked intently at Najiir. "I have to trust someone...something."

"You trust us, Joseph," said Simon, "Herod changes everything, but—"

"Greek!" Xaratuk growled through clenched teeth. "Talking in code. Poor actors. Poor performances. What kind of fool do you take me for?" He glared at his advisors. "And why are you so taken with them?"

Joseph touched Simon's arm. "Simon, Caleb, we must temper our apprehensions. Allow these men to remain." Switching to Greek, he looked upon Mary and added, "Gentlemen, if you have more questions, we will do our best to answer them."

Merkis heaved a sigh. "Oh, thank you. Thank you."

CHAPTER 31

They could stay.

Topur prayed his own silent thanks to God. Withdrawal from the house was beyond consideration. He wasn't sure he could stand. Walking was impossible—not again—not so soon. The discharge from his wound persisted. The bandaging felt soaked and heavy. Most important, though, was this mystery, one he had never expected to witness. Since their arrival, it had only become increasingly complex, even unfathomable.

He wanted more. He needed to know more. There was so much to absorb: the shepherds, the visions, voices, a baby! And to propose that from these meager circumstances, the King of the Jews would arise? Incredible! So much more to know! Reaching for Najiir's sleeve, he gave it a feeble tug.

"Well done, boy. Well done."

Najiir looked back and smiled.

Khartir kneeled before the cradle. "Mary, Joseph, thank you. Our sole purpose is to understand more about you—about him." His head bent to the child. "About all this." He rose. "You've been patient and tolerant while total strangers ask uncomfortable questions. We would never bring harm upon you—ever. I hope you believe that." He looked for acceptance. "Please believe that."

Mary's nod was more of a shrug. Khartir continued. "At our dinner, we heard claims that there are many in and around

Jerusalem who say they hear God or speak to God."

Mary's face was expressionless.

"Our hosts implied they are routinely dismissed, considered false prophets at best, madmen at worst. Mary, what you experience must be different. If we understood what you have heard, it might reveal clues that hint at the meaning behind your child's life."

"Clues? You'll get no clues," Xaratuk shouted.

Khartir scowled at his irreverent king. "Mary," he said, ignoring the interference, "though you rarely hear this voice, what do you recall?"

Xaratuk snarled, clumping away from his young advisor.

"The first time was in Nazareth." Mary looked apprehensively up to Joseph.

"It's all right," he said. "Don't alter what was said for ears that might not understand. The words were what they were."

"The voice told me I was to be the mother of a great person," Mary began. "I thought I was possessed. The voice calmed me and told me not to be afraid. God had found favor within me. There was to be a child, this child, and he would be the Son of the Most High and would sit upon the Throne of David to rule over a kingdom that would last for all times."

Simon and Caleb dropped to their knees and bowed their heads. Mary acknowledged the gesture and went on. "The voice explained how this would come to pass. I was shaking but could say I would be honored to be a servant of my God."

Merkis waited. "And that was all?"

"And I was told to name the child Jesus."

"Jesus," Merkis repeated. "You say you spoke back?"

"Yes. Only once. I was so frightened. Me? I had yet to be a mother. I was not yet a wife! Why me? I felt unworthy, so I said so."

"Had it been me," Merkis said, "I would have been frightened beyond description. It must have been bewildering. You didn't make any requests? Maybe ask for clarification?"

"No, no," Mary said, then quickly added, "Yes. I mean, yes. I did ask for something. I asked for patience, strength, and guidance."

"Were you answered?"

"In words?" Mary hesitated. "No. Though perhaps my request was answered. I can speak before strangers about unusual and difficult subjects that surpass my comprehension. I have been given the courage to appear before great kings." She looked directly at Xaratuk. "You are right—I am a peasant. Yet before me stand men, rich men, powerful men, wise men such as you. Hasn't my request been answered?"

Mouth open, speechless, Khartir moved away from the cradle.

"Indeed, it has," Merkis smiled. "Mary, has this voice given you instructions to pass on—orders to relay? Are you being commanded in any way?"

"No. This would be easier if there were commands. As it is, I am asked to understand things that can seem beyond my abilities."

"Mary, do you tell others what you've heard?" Khartir asked. Caleb and Simon rose to their feet. "Surely everyone would be interested in a voice—God's voice?—speaking to you."

"No, I only speak to my husband." She looked with tender appreciation at the man who now placed both his hands on her shoulders. "He has been faithful to me beyond my ability to comprehend." She grasped one of his hands in hers.

"Mary is not looking for an audience," said Simon. "She never has. She does what God asks, quietly, without bragging or bluster. We respect her for that. It makes her even more beloved."

Khartir paused, silently nodding to the shepherd. His eyes narrowed, returning to Mary. "The voice you hear is that of a man?"

"Yes," said Mary. Then she hesitated. "That is…" A look of

confusion swept across her face. "It does seem..." She halted in mid-sentence, looking to Joseph for a hint of guidance. His eyes widened. They had already encountered enough disapproval and disbelief without suggesting that the voice she heard, perhaps God's own, was not thoroughly male. Mary looked blankly ahead and softly murmured, "Comforting."

She did not look up to see Khartir's small smile.

Mary continued, "The voice I hear is calming, reassuring." She moved upon her stool. Her countenance turned severe. She lowered the baby into the cradle beside her, tucking in the blankets. She grasped her hands and sat erect. "It is as though I am blind, then find a hand offered to me. I cannot see what is before me, before us. I have not been told what awaits. But I find reassurance. I can manage. I can cope. I can move through the dark to the next destination. I have not been asked to endure this alone."

"Mary," said Mithrias in a breathless whisper. "You sense this? A hand extended to you within the darkness?"

"How touching," Xaratuk snapped. "We have a woman who hears voices that console her. The world is not amazed. Listen to me! We've found no reason a star should identify this house—and we won't. You can't honestly believe this! A baby? What can some baby tell us? Nothing! We know nothing more than we did while we sat in Jerusalem!"

Mithrias was vexed. "Of course this child can't speak," he said. "That makes Mary's experiences even more important. Listen to her. Consider what Joseph says, what Simon has told us. We must contemplate it all."

"Correct, King Mithrias," said Merkis. "And we've only begun. Mary, you say he is to be a king? Who will be his subjects?"

"There's nothing to add. I'm sorry. I was told this child will sit upon the throne of David and over a kingdom which will last for all time." She looked at Simon. "I know what Simon believes. He believes this can only mean Jesus is King of the Jews."

"Our Messiah!" shouted Simon. Caleb grinned.

"A king? And no more specifics?" said Khartir. Once more, he fell to both knees before the crib. His face was pained. "This is so daunting. There is no guidance about where you should go and whom you should meet? Who should educate this child for such an important position? How will he grow? What will he learn? Or is everything already within, like the seed from which a mighty cedar unfolds?" He stood up, the gaze of his close brown eyes affixed upon Mary and Joseph. "Who? Who shall raise this child to be the king your God claims he will be?"

"Apparently..." Joseph swallowed. "Us."

"But, Joseph—"

"And I cannot tell you why it is us. There is little in either of our lives to suggest we, and only we, are especially worthy of such responsibility. Why not a mighty king, you're thinking. Or a priest? Or some rich family?" Joseph moved next to Khartir, who was still absorbed with the infant. "The responsibility does seem overwhelming, but what am I to say? 'No, thank you, I'd rather not'...to God? I'll not say no to this woman. Ever. I'll not say no to this child. And I'll not say no to God. Maybe someday, He'll reveal the reasons behind choosing us, but in the meantime, this awesome responsibility is ours, and we are proud and willing to accept what comes."

Khartir rose from the baby's cradle to stand by Joseph. "What...what will become of you, this family? What can all this mean?"

Joseph put a hand on Khartir's shoulder. "This is no Greek play at the theater in Jerusalem. There is no script. We are unsure of the right things to say. The other actors are unfamiliar to us. We can't predict the next act. We surely don't know how the play will end. Triumph or tragedy?" He looked at the baby, swallowing hard. "Triumph, I trust."

Joseph moved his hands to Mary's shoulders. "We understand this: We have accepted a grave responsibility. And lacking the direction we crave, we must then trust. We must place our trust in the One who gave us this responsibility and feel secure He has chosen wisely."

"May God bless Joseph and Mary," Simon whispered.

"Plainly spoken," said Merkis, "you genuinely believe you have been called to perform a sacred service."

Topur blinked. The room had changed. The air suddenly felt chill, full, pure. His lungs filled. The hearth's flame grew, then flickered. Perplexed expressions covered every face in the room. There was an awkward silence.

Mary's gaze turned to the baby. Her face contorted. She bent toward the cradle. Barely perceptible, she uttered a single word. "Love."

Merkis kneeled in front of her. "Mary, is it the voice?"

"Love," Mary repeated. "Show love to the child, so as a man, he will show love to the world." Mary did not blink.

"Now there is a useful message!" stormed Xaratuk. "Love! There's your savior! Put your arm around a Roman and give him a hug!" Xaratuk began pacing and waving his arms. "No need for that dagger there—whatever your name is," he declared, looking at Simon. "Is that what your child-king will do to liberate you Jews from the Romans? Put an arm around your enemy's neck and tell him you love him? That will surely bring down an empire! That will protect you from your enemies! Invite them over to dance and make merry with your women, too!"

He paced until he stood directly before Merkis. He thrust a finger before the face of his advisor. "This is preposterous! Preposterous, I tell you! A king? From here? From this?"

"You suggest it can't be," said Merkis calmly. "I suggest it can."

Xaratuk snorted. He slid to stand in front of Khartir. "Here is some peasant woman, the wife of an out-of-work laborer, claiming their dismal circumstances are due to a voice. This is pure myth, and you're falling for it. King of what? By virtue of whose army? And you think they are not trying to sell you something? They take you for fools! There is no kingdom here. No army. No power. No influence. There is a baby. I say we leave, and I mean now!"

There came a knock at the door.

CHAPTER 32

"I regret this interruption." Regulus's martial figure filled the doorway. "I believe something crucial has happened, and I wish to advise my king."

"Yes, yes, Regulus," Xaratuk growled, still breathless from his tirade. "What is it?"

"The star, sir. It is gone."

"The star is gone," Xaratuk repeated apathetically. He dabbed at his sweaty brow. "I'm not sure why I need to know that, but thank you. We're done here, so prepare the others for departure. We leave soon."

"Wait!" hollered Merkis, rushing to the door. "What do you mean, gone?"

"It is absent from the sky, sir. It no longer illuminates the house. It has vanished."

"Vanished?" Khartir stepped behind Merkis. "You're certain it isn't behind some clouds? Has it merely settled below the horizon earlier than usual?"

"The star is no longer in the night sky, sir," replied Regulus. "It was there one moment, not the next, as if a lone candle was snuffed. The change was abrupt and quite noticeable to those of us outside. Even some of those inside their houses came out to investigate. I expected someone to come out of this house. Wishing not to be premature, I ordered Prince Salnassar to count to five hundred before I might approach you."

Regulus stepped back, allowing Khartir to rush outside into

the darkness that engulfed the village. "No sign of it!" Khartir shouted.

The heavens appeared as they ought: orderly, predictable, recognizable. Khartir studied the assembled neighbors as they milled about, pointing, talking, and scratching their heads. "Trying to make sense of the insensible, just like us," he mused.

Khartir returned to the crowded house. He stood before Xaratuk, who rocked back and forth on impatient heels. "Sir, it is gone."

Ignoring him, Xaratuk turned to Regulus. "That should be all. Order your men to make us ready, but don't you go far." Regulus saluted and departed.

Topur felt Najiir's hand on his shoulder. Merkis held his hand over his mouth, shaking his head in disbelief. Mithrias closed his eyes, blocking any input. Khartir stared, mouth open, at the hearth. Xaratuk showed no sign of contemplation as he gathered his cloak. After an agonizingly long pause, Merkis broke the silence.

"My friends," he began, directing all eyes to him. "Listen to me. He that was summoned, he whose presence our star demanded, is here, in this house, within this room."

Joseph smiled.

No one breathed except for Xaratuk; his indifference was expressed in his blank expression.

The hair on the back of Topur's neck tingled, temporarily distracting him from the pain and the accumulating moisture within his bandages. His thoughts swirled. He felt unnerved. Among them was the one this star, this cosmic aberration, had invited. The very heavens had been altered for this person. But who? Why? Himself? No. Joseph was right. This was God's play. Not only were Joseph and Mary not given a script for their parts—none of them were.

"Mercy."

Every face turned to Mary. "Show mercy to the child so that he may show mercy to the world."

"Oh, here we go." Xaratuk's palm slapped his forehead. "Let the murderer of your wife and sons go free. And don't forget to hug him before he leaves! I can't believe we are still here."

Khartir reached into his robe to retrieve a piece of charcoal, then began writing upon a small piece of folded manuscript.

"Hush!" Merkis scolded. "We must listen!" Xaratuk stepped back, alarmed to be chastened in such a manner. He advanced toward his advisor, ready to admonish him, but Merkis, studying Mary, brushed him back.

"Comfort," said Mary, staring at the cradle. "Offer comfort to the child so that he may be of comfort to those in need."

Xaratuk stamped the ground. His tantrum went unnoticed. The others locked their undivided attention upon Mary. But her next words were in Aramaic.

"Charity," she said. "Show charity to the child so that he may show charity to the world."

Xaratuk, displeased, looked for Najiir. Without prompting, Najiir translated. Xaratuk rolled his eyes.

Once more, Mary spoke. "Forgiveness. Practice forgiveness so that he may show others how to forgive."

Najiir translated.

"Aren't you just about done?" Xaratuk yelled at Mary.

"Be still, Xaratuk!" Topur yelled from his bed. "Let Mary speak! You keep saying you've heard nothing, but she is talking, and the words are abundantly clear!"

"The baby!" fumed Xaratuk, pointing down to the cradle. "It is words from this future King of the Jews I am interested in—from his mouth. And I will never hear them, will I?"

"Compassion," said Mary, still in Aramaic. "Show compassion to this child so that he may show compassion to the world."

Xaratuk looked to Najiir. Najiir raised his shoulders, his hands upturned. He repeated the word back to Mary. She offered a tiny nod of affirmation. He looked at Xaratuk.

"Sir, your native tongue has no similar word."

"Well," was all Xaratuk would say. He stomped to his advisors, gripping their shoulders. "Enough," he said. "I have been patient, but enough! I'm done with you, I'm done with her, and I'm done with this jumble of peasants. We are leaving—going back to Jerusalem." He shoved his finger before Merkis's nose. "This has been a fiasco, and I blame YOU!"

CHAPTER 33

The scream was wordless, knife-sharp—an urgent, intense shriek capable of piercing an eardrum. Everyone, including Mary, hastily surveyed the room, trying to pinpoint the source. Another whoop erupted, injecting even greater alarm.

One by one, faces turned toward Topur. He gawked into their gathered stares. All eyes were upon him, as though the others were convinced he was the cause. Another prickly surge shot from his hip into his torso, then burst into his chest. It left his body accompanied by a third unrestrained bray. "This cannot be!" Topur gasped, struggling for control. "What? What is happening?"

Dumbfounded, he returned the incredulous stares of the others. "It's not me!" he shouted. But it was him!

"What is happening?" he repeated, his voice rising in confusion. "Why am I shouting?" Instinctively, he darted from the sound. He jerked forward, vainly seeking some escape. Springing to his hands and knees, Topur pivoted, looking behind at a blank, unassuming stone wall. He pawed at his blanket, hoping to dislodge a rat, an insect, or maybe a snake. He jumped to his feet, chucking the ragged covering as if it concealed a pox.

"Topur?" It was Mithrias.

With tentative fingers, Topur raised his blanket to peer underneath. He shook it with outraged vigor, then abruptly stopped.

There should have been pain.

Aghast, mouth open, he searched for Mithrias.

"You moved," Mithrias whispered.

"I moved," said Topur, eyes growing wide. "I'm standing!" He lifted one hand, touching his sodden bandaging. No pain. He stroked the course of his wound up and down. Again, nothing. One final animal bark burst out. Topur leaped away from the cot.

"What is happening? What is happening!" He bunched the blanket and threw it against the wall. Nothing. Mary rushed from her stool to his side. She and Najiir reached Topur at the same instant.

"Master! You are on your feet!" cried Najiir. "No, you shouldn't be!" Najiir grabbed the abused blanket and tried coaxing Topur back to the cot. "Please, lie down. You'll make this worse!"

Topur stood rigidly in place. He looked at Mary on one elbow and Najiir on the other. "No pain," Topur said softly, despite his frenzied face. He waited for the words to sink in. "The gash—there is no pain." He moved the elbow where Mary had grasped. She released her gentle grip. Topur raised his arm over his head, then back to his side. He deliberately, but gently, patted his wound.

"Master?" said Najiir.

"Pull up my robe, Najiir. Pull it up to my bandages. Why do I not feel any pain?" Najiir kneeled to the ground and rolled back the purple hem of Topur's robe. Fold over fold, he raised the regal garment higher until Miriam's bandages were exposed.

"Cut them off, Najiir! Cut them!" Topur said. The soppy bandaging clung to Topur's torso. Simon handed his dagger to Najiir.

Najiir's hands shook. "But I'm afraid. Miriam has helped you so much. I'll damage her work. She would disapprove."

"I know, I know. Cut them."

Mary held the robe as Najiir used both hands to search for

a proper place to begin. He found a gap and ran the blade between the rusty brown bandaging and Topur's skin.

"Please, master, tell me if I am hurting you—"

"Cut, Najiir!"

Najiir made a long, straight cut through the linen bandages covering the sticky salve. Topur grabbed the hem of his robe and held it beneath his chin while Mary and Najiir gently pulled at the gummy covering. Mary looked at Topur for any response. He gave a nod of approval. She removed the bandages, handing them to Najiir. She put her hand on Topur's chest. Her palm was unexpectedly warm upon his skin.

Gone. The wound was gone. The maimed skin, separated by his attacker's blade and then held together by Miriam's balm, was now a faint, thin, roseate line. An unpresuming scratch was the only evidence of the attack that had left Topur struggling for his life.

His eyes darted. Topur pivoted, his hips following a circle as he turned to show the others.

"Ha! I am healed!" he shouted. "I am restored! Look here! Look at this!" Everyone looked on in amazement, their mouths open. Simon and Caleb scrambled forward for a better view. At the height of his exhilaration, Topur paused. "What is this? What has just happened to me?"

"May I touch it?" asked Najiir.

"I think you may—yes!" answered Topur. Mary helped Topur steady his robe as Najiir gently ran two fingers down Topur's side.

"No scar? The skin barely rises," Najiir said. "I don't understand. It has to be more than Miriam's salve, doesn't it?"

"Yes, Najiir," Topur replied.

They turned to Mary. As if the incident was nothing out of the ordinary, she smiled.

"May I, as well?" Simon asked Topur.

Topur was exhilarated. "Yes. Yes. See for yourself. You don't realize how badly I was—"

A new, piercing shriek erupted, one of panic and shock. But this voice was unmistakably that of a baby. The infant was bunched in Xaratuk's left hand, propped awkwardly high above his head. Mary gasped.

"King Xaratuk!" blurted Merkis.

Xaratuk glared, his arm outstretched as he grasped the child clumsily around the neck and shoulders, displaying him as if he were a trophy kill. The baby's body was rigid, enduring the mistreatment, his forehead mere inches from the ceiling. Grinning, Xaratuk stepped away from the crib.

"You foolish, gullible people!" he snorted. "You can't see your own noses! And you expect me to be as stupid as these peasants? I'll show you! This baby is no different." Holding the infant high, Xaratuk used his right hand to search for his short sword's hilt. He looked up at his quarry in triumph. He fumbled for the jeweled handle.

It wasn't a jeweled handle he grasped. His hand patted the hand of another, a hand already locked onto the short sword's grip. Xaratuk felt himself being pulled backward. Unable to regain his balance, he stumbled. He felt an arm tighten around his neck, abruptly forcing his chin to the side. He couldn't breathe. He groped for his short sword again, still holding the child aloft. He heard metal-on-metal as the blade scraped from its sheath.

Xaratuk blinked, struggling. The arm around his neck tightened, fingernails penetrating below his ear. He needed air. He had to breathe. He made one last attempt to regain his balance. A foot kicked his own out from underneath. Xaratuk fell back farther, the arm cutting off any hope of breath. A cutting pain tore into his side. The short sword's tip nipped through his tunic into the flesh over his ribs in the gap between his armor pieces. Any movement, any struggle, was met with overwhelming repression.

Xaratuk strained to look about the room. Who had him in an unrelenting grip? He looked for Simon, but Simon was scrambling for the dagger he'd given to Najiir. Joseph was beside Mary as they both advanced toward the child. Where was Caleb? Topur?

"Put the child down." Surrendering their own strategies, the others stopped, deferring to the commanding voice behind Xaratuk. "Give the child to his mother," the loud voice ordered.

Xaratuk hesitated long enough to feel the sword's point poke again. He winced as a thin, warm rivulet trickled over his ribs. He had lost his momentary advantage with no plan for regaining it. His lungs screamed for air. His cry of pain was stifled as the arm around his neck pulled his chin farther than it was designed to move.

His opponent had quickly and thoroughly bested him. His face, mashed and contorted by the powerful arm around it, failed to exhibit his gnarled hostility as he lowered the baby to the outstretched arms of Mary.

"Najiir, go to the door—keep it closed! Everyone else stays exactly, and I mean exactly, where you are! Do not approach us!"

Reunited with her baby, Mary rushed to the opposite side of the room, Joseph with her. They stared back at Xaratuk with an accusatory glare. No one blinked.

"Release me, Mithrias," ordered Xaratuk through his immovable jaw. "You have beaten me. I need to breathe." Xaratuk felt a tiny release in the pressure on his neck. But, instead of reprieve, he felt the sword make yet another poke into his side. "Mithrias!" Xaratuk shrieked.

Once more, Mithrias countered, dislodging a foot, forcing Xaratuk to swing and fall off-balance.

"I said release me!" gurgled Xaratuk.

"You coward! A child, Xaratuk! A child!" Mithrias screamed.

"I wasn't," Xaratuk choked out, but a quick pull from Mithrias's arm silenced any protest.

"How could you!" Mithrias's words clumped between his heaving breaths. "You imbecile!" he shrieked directly into Xaratuk's ear. "You have five words with which you explain yourself to these people. Five words or this sword goes through your ribs. Choose wisely."

"Mithrias!" pleaded Xaratuk through Mithrias's arm.

"One!" spat Mithrias. "Four more!"

All of Xaratuk's resistance and strength dissipated like sand through a sieve. Lacking both air and will, his body went limp. Mithrias's arms no longer restrained Xaratuk so much as propped him up.

"Nothing," Xaratuk began in a whisper, "makes any sense."

Mithrias eased his grip.

"There you are," Xaratuk managed. A stifled sob followed what little breath remained. Only after several deep breaths could Xaratuk say more. "You may as well kill me because I'll never understand."

The frantic energy that fueled Mithrias's defense of the baby abandoned him. He released the stranglehold around Xaratuk's neck, allowing Xaratuk to stand upright. Withdrawing the sword from between the armor plates, he pushed Xaratuk away. Mithrias bent forward, his hands on his thighs, head pointed to the ground. "You believed," he rasped. "You believed in a star, Xaratuk." His words came in short bursts between his panting. "A Temple, a palace, a star...those things speak to you...those things you understand."

Mithrias threw the sword at Simon's feet. Simon snapped to retrieve it. "Why should we not consider you as daft as you consider those in this house?" He straightened, placing his face immediately before Xaratuk's. "I say Mary isn't the only one hearing voices. It seems you hear stars talk. What did this star tell you?"

Xaratuk turned away.

"Why is some star to be believed but not a young woman?"

Mithrias turned to Joseph and Mary. "In a thousand lifetimes, I could not apologize enough to you, to your son, and to your friends, for all the mischief and distress we have placed upon you. You have done nothing to deserve such foul treatment. It is best we leave. I will tell Regulus."

Xaratuk's shoulders sank. "I am undone, Mithrias." Xaratuk swayed, his legs no longer willing to support him. He stumbled, falling to his knees. He covered his face with his hands. Mithrias dropped to his knees as well. Now, he placed an arm of consolation rather than restraint around Xaratuk.

"At one point, you believed so strongly," said Mithrias, consoling the friend he had just condemned. "Your expectations did not match what you found here, but you can't ridicule this woman, this man, and this child because of that. You came expecting to find a prince in a suit of golden armor, and you discover a child wrapped in a tattered blanket instead."

"I am ruined. I am ruined." Tears slid down Xaratuk's cheeks, each lugubrious one hastening the next. "Mithrias, what am I to do? My country is strong, but if the Romans have a mind to, they'll come for us. And what then? And what then?" He gulped back the tears. "I don't want our sons to die. I don't want to be king of the dead! What legacy is that?" He fell into Mithrias. "Generations lost! I merely wanted someone to help me."

Glassy-eyed, he glanced about the room, though he could not withstand the scrutiny of Mary or Joseph.

"I thought the star would lead me to our protector." He bent his head and could do little more than mumble through his tears. "The heavens...they did speak to me, Mithrias. It seemed so believable. The closer we came, the more certain I felt I was right. What else could it be?" His hands anxiously, thoughtlessly, pawed his rigid breastplate. "I understand what Merkis and Khartir are saying. I see it now."

Those in the room remained motionless. Raising his head, his face drained of emotion, Xaratuk finally spoke as if he was exchanging a dread secret. "The voice I have listened to is my own, telling me exactly what I wished to hear." He focused back on Mithrias. "What a way to learn, my friend. What a way to learn."

He rose from his knees, rubbing the tears from his cheeks. Mithrias rose with him. Summoning his courage, Xaratuk looked about the room. "I admit it." His chest heaved. "I saw this as a once-in-a-lifetime chance to align myself with the most powerful prince ever. I convinced myself that is what we would find. I was wrong—wrong about that."

"No one is saying you are wrong," said Mithrias. "You still don't understand, do you? It is time to listen, my friend. Time to listen."

CHAPTER 34

For the first time in his life, Xaratuk felt shame. He felt base and ignorant, qualities previously absent from his self-image. But apologize? To a household of peasants? He fought within to suppress any consideration of such humiliation, but failed. He knew he must account for his behavior. His powerful legs still shaking, his head still bowed, he crept toward Mary and Joseph. Mary drew her child defensively closer to her chest. The baby remained remarkably peaceful.

Xaratuk's voice cracked. "You may find it difficult to accept my apology." His words emerged slowly, separately, with great strain. "I never intended to harm your child. If you don't believe me, I understand—I do, but it is true. I am not the best of men, but I am no child killer." Xaratuk stretched his neck. "I simply wanted to show he was human. But, in fact, I don't know why my actions would have proven that. It was madness, and I am grateful to those willing to counter it. That madness is gone. It shall never return. Please believe me when I tell you this. I am not used to apologizing, but I apologize to you."

"What happened?" Mary said. "Why? It was so frightening. But God protects us." She cocked her head, staring at the child, and drew his face closer to hers. "Forgiveness," she said in Aramaic.

"I'm sorry. I don't understand." Xaratuk slumped even more.

"Forgiveness," said Joseph in Greek.

Mary spoke again while Joseph translated. "Practice forgiveness in this house, so he may show others how to forgive." With that, Mary's scrutiny of her child broke. She rested him in her lap.

"Forgiveness?" Xaratuk murmured through a bewildered smile. "You heard that again? We must love and forgive? I feel unable to comprehend it, but within these walls, I am alone in that ignorant condition."

"We have been instructed to practice forgiveness in this house." Joseph looked for Mary's affirmation. She gave it. "And so, we offer forgiveness to you."

For once, Xaratuk could not look another man in the eye. Were he to speak, it would sound feeble and faltering. He craved a pause with which to gather himself. He drew a deep breath, blinking back a tear. Another long moment passed before he could muster the will to look directly at Joseph.

"Joseph, Mary, my actions were inexcusable, and your forgiveness has touched me."

Defeated, disgraced, the object of others' pity, it was evident he should leave. He moved toward the door. Merkis stepped forward. "Much has happened tonight, my king. There is more to understand, more to discuss."

"It is best to go on without me. I am clearly outmatched by all this." Xaratuk kept moving.

"Please stay. It is important." Merkis stood before the door, blocking it. "So little has been revealed. So much remains."

"Do you still believe the star signifies someone remarkable?"

"I do, sir,"

"You do," mouthed Xaratuk, utterly deflated.

"I don't claim to understand everything shown tonight, but I am convinced we are part of something meaningful. I'm sure of that. "

"Well, for the first time, I am listening." Xaratuk turned away from the door. "We are all listening, Merkis. What should we know?"

Merkis possessed the measured voice of experience. His audiences invariably realized that listening to him and being included in his thinking was a privilege. "Whatever I might say at this moment," he began, "we must agree that it is too soon to draw conclusions. Our visit has been brief and has proven we have much more to learn. I cannot yet confirm the breadth and depth of the impact of this child. If you heed what these loyal shepherds declare, his identity and purpose are already established. But I ask all of you to consider what his devoted parents have made clear. We must wait. His time will come, and he'll demand our full attention. Use the interim to prepare for a message that goes beyond that of any previous scholar, priest, or prophet. If tonight is any indication, our expectations might be wrong, maybe useless."

He turned to Mary and Joseph. "This house has hosted many visitors, am I correct?" They, with Simon, nodded in unison. "Yet during that time, the star continued to shine. The bright light that for months beckoned us here, to this exact place, shines no longer. That beacon is gone. The gravity and importance of that alone shakes me to my core, and it should shake you to yours." With a raised hand, he gestured above. "My friends, the star *was* a signal. The star *was* a sign. It was intentional, with a mission and a purpose."

He paused long enough to ensure his message had been understood.

"I conclude the star's mission was fulfilled. This can only mean one thing. Someone, some few, or perhaps all of us, were meant to be here. There is no doubt that the star was a guide to usher someone to this room."

His grave gaze stifled any thoughts of contradiction. Merkis moved from person to person. "Each of you, absorb what that means." On to the next. "Is it you?" His focus was penetrating, as if able to bore into each man's soul. "Ponder this. Is it you?" he repeated. "If you believe it is, then why? If not, justify that as well. Each of us must search inside for this answer. Remember, the very heavens were altered to alert you to come here, to this place, to be with these people. Now, you are here. What will you do?"

Merkis stopped in front of Topur. "There's more. Besides the star's departure, we see the wonder of healing with our own eyes. Topur has been made whole. I am certain we all share with him our gratitude for this—for what else could it be, sir—this miracle."

Topur could barely speak. "It is a miracle," he whispered, looking at the baby.

"I don't carelessly use the term. Miracles are, by definition, extremely rare. I have always been skeptical about such things, I'll admit. But look at you." Merkis floated his hand over Topur's torso. "You have risked so much. I was alarmed when I saw you on a cart, lifeless, being hauled from that canyon. I thought we had lost our guide—for good. Only tonight have I appreciated how you were trying your utmost to protect us."

For the first time since joining the journey, Topur felt understood.

Merkis continued to step about the room, his attention shifting from person to person, giving each one their own audience. He came to Simon. "Forty? Am I correct, Simon, in recalling it was forty of you shepherds who witnessed the announcement?"

"That's right. It spoke to us."

Merkis paused, stroking his long beard, deep in thought. "Simon, you and the other shepherds feel steadfast loyalty to this child, knowing that when the time comes, you will follow him to far greater things."

"He is our savior, sir," said Simon, "our Messiah. He will free us from those who persecute our people and will reign over a righteous kingdom."

"You have been called. I see that." Merkis became somber,

looking almost sad. "If it is your grievance against Rome you expect he will correct, you will need your own miracle. If Mary's words are any indication, love and mercy and forgiveness may require of you a different strategy than swords and spears and armies. Listen closely, my new friend, so you understand your king's message completely."

Simon cocked his head.

Merkis stepped to Mary. "Mary hears a voice." Merkis's tone grew stern. "Someone hearing a voice denied to the rest of us is not novel but rarely genuine. I do not deny that among us are the rare few who display unique powers and abilities. Many—too many—claim they possess special gifts but are outright frauds seeking to prey upon the vulnerable." He paused. "To which group does Mary belong?" He gave a slim smile. "I believe Mary is genuine." Tipping his head to Khartir, "I assume you agree?"

Khartir grinned.

"I shall explain. First, the obvious reason. Look around, all of you. Mary and Joseph are not people of means. They have not exploited this situation to become wealthy. Indeed, they may be more destitute and without prospects than they were before. Frauds seek to enrich themselves or enhance their prestige. There is none of that here. And consider this: Mary does not boast of her gift. She is, if anything, reluctant. She wishes to keep her information guarded, if not secret. Charlatans almost uniformly do the opposite."

Merkis walked about the room. "There are more subtle indications, as well. Mary told us she couldn't summon the voice at her command. She doesn't spend hours in deep discussions or present personal wish lists she expects to be addressed. She is genuine because the voice of a supreme spirit is unlikely to be excessively available and so suggestible. And what Mary hears are prophecies and ideas that are not her own, expressed in words she would not choose."

Merkis stood next to Xaratuk, their shoulders touching.

"Mary, the words you relayed to us earlier: love, charity, forgiveness—were those words you heard from the voice? Were you relaying words spoken to you?"

Mary nodded.

"I am perplexed," Merkis said, "because those are not words I expected to hear tonight. They are words nearly absent from our minds and mouths." He looked at Xaratuk. "I wonder, like you, my king, if they can flourish in a world such as ours— a world that is clearly bent upon their suffocation. We don't hear appeals to act with these words in mind or—"

"Ashoka," Khartir interrupted.

"Yes! That is so!" He reached out to Khartir, shaking his forearm. "Ashoka. A profound observation!" He turned to the others. "Only a tiny few mention these words. We are rarely asked to consider them. But to deny that these should be our true goals and guideposts, to continue to ignore and revile them, will only hasten humanity's downfall.

"King Mithrias," he said, "last night, at dinner, I couldn't follow you and the points you made. But after hearing Mary's words tonight, I believe I understand you better. Like you, Mary reminds us that our better nature is within each of us. It is there, waiting to be summoned if only we would choose."

"Might we at least try?" said Mithrias.

Merkis gestured to Mary. "I am learning to expect to be amazed—even dumbfounded—by the events that surround and involve you. Are you prepared for a lifetime of this? Joseph, Mary, I confess I feel overwhelmed when I ponder your future. So many challenges await, and there is no one you can look to for advice. You prove to me that being from humble circumstances does not prevent one from being thoughtful and capable. But this?"

Merkis's eyes narrowed as he moved to the table. "My friends, can you think of anyone as eminently suited to this grave task as Mary? If she was indeed chosen, her selection was obvious. Might we understand more if we tried to listen as Mary does?"

Merkis sat on an empty stool. "Forgive me. I'm tired, but I'm not done."

Outside, Salnassar moved away from the window. He and Regulus had stood together outside the home in clandestine observation. It was easy to remain beyond the dim lamplight, their inclusion easily concealed.

But earlier, two soldiers had run to the house and had met Regulus with an urgent, whispered message. "I have to attend to this," Regulus said, looking grim. "Can I trust you?" Salnassar nodded. "Stay out of sight." Regulus sprinted away with the messengers. He was far from the house, well beyond earshot, when Xaratuk made his move for the child. Salnassar had a perfect view from which to watch his father.

He would never be the same.

He was as enthralled with Merkis's observations as the others. His mind began to spin with ideas and perspectives he'd never considered. Listening to Merkis, Salnassar noted an irritating ringing in his ears while a lump formed in his throat. Why? he thought. *Why am I crying?*

He stumbled away from the house, bewildered, intending to return to camp and find refuge. He met Regulus hurrying up the hill along with two hooded figures in dark cloaks. They walked more slowly, despite Regulus's urging to quicken their pace. Passing Salnassar, Regulus murmured from the side of his mouth, "This will be unsettling." He stopped to position the two figures well away from the house. "Stay," he commanded.

As Regulus proceeded alone, Salnassar moved to inspect the cloaked figures.

Arriving at the rough-hewn door, Regulus inhaled, then knocked.

CHAPTER 35

Inside the house, everyone turned toward the rapping. Dagger in hand, Simon lunged to be the first at the threshold. Preparing to open the door, he breathed deeply, puffing his chest, his thin arms rigid and taut. He unfastened the wooden bolt.

Regulus's martial frame filled the entrance. Eyeing past the much smaller shepherd, he moved a half-step through the doorway, treating Simon and his dagger as a mere nuisance. His face was grim as he evaluated the room. His deep baritone resonated. "My king, I must first ask this. Is all well with you? I apologize, but I had to leave my post briefly to attend to this matter."

"Thank you, Regulus," said Xaratuk, clearing his throat. Uncharacteristically, he stood hunched, his back to Regulus, negating any chance of revealing his discomfort. "I am fine. Thank you, but all is fine."

"Very well, sir," said Regulus, sounding unconvinced. "Then I am sorry I must disturb you once again."

Mary grabbed Jesus from the crib, clutching him. Joseph inserted himself between his wife and the door while Caleb rushed to stand with Simon. After an uncomfortable pause, Regulus waited for his king to respond. "Sir, are you quite sure you are well?"

"Regulus, what? Go on." Xaratuk remained with his back to his captain. "Why did you knock?"

Looking puzzled, Regulus announced, "Sir, two women claim they have come from Jerusalem. They say they are from the palace. They insist upon seeing you or the other kings."

"Women? Two women?" Xaratuk swung around. "We aren't expecting any women." He strode toward the door. Mary reinforced her firm grip on her child.

"They both have passwords, sir," said Regulus. "Independently, I might add. I presume you wish to question them further. They seem quite upset and claim this is an emergency."

"Emergency? You have done the right thing, Regulus." Xaratuk turned, facing the room. "Passwords? Who gave out their password?"

"I did." Mithrias and Topur spoke in unison. They looked at each other, then back to Xaratuk.

"I gave mine to Miriam," said Topur.

"I gave mine out, too," Mithrias blinked uneasily at the ground.

"Well, this had better be an emergency." Xaratuk recaptured his regal tone. "We'll see them, Regulus." He quickly turned to Joseph. "This may be important. Regulus will ensure there is no threat to you and the child." He checked with Simon for his approval.

"We will make room. Yes, bring them in," replied Joseph. Regulus left to summon the women and allow them inside.

Hoods concealed the heads of the two figures as they crossed the threshold, prohibiting any quick assessment of their identity. What the hoods did not cover, veils did.

"Please, come in," beckoned Joseph. Once inside, one of the women removed her hood.

Topur's heart banged in his chest. "Miriam, it is you!" Miriam turned to the familiar voice. Topur saw her initial relief switch to alarm. He was not some prostrate patient, barely able to move. He was striding, unhampered, directly toward her.

"Topur?" Miriam's eyes grew wide.

"Miriam, I have something wonderful to show you."

"Yes, yes. Apparently, you do." Her head moved up and down, repeatedly scrutinizing Topur.

"But you first. What has brought you to Bethlehem? Why are you here?"

"Oh, Topur, I am so sorry to come to you like this, but we are fleeing Jerusalem. We can't stay there. We can't stay here, either—none of you can. You must listen to me. We have time, but not much."

Mithrias moved to Topur's side. He inspected Miriam, then looked at the other hooded woman, probing for any cue.

"I remember you, Miriam." Mithrias frowned. "When we left the palace. You attended to Topur, correct?" Miriam nodded. "But what? What has happened?" He resumed his scrutiny of the other woman. "What made you leave…and so suddenly?"

Miriam touched the arm of the cloaked woman whose hood remained in place. "Herod has lost his mind—again." She raised her hands to pull the hood back. The woman halted Miriam's progress.

"It's all right," Miriam reassured. "We can put it back up." The woman ceased resisting. "Dear, they must see."

Fold over fold, Miriam eased the hood past the top of the woman's head. Mithrias stooped, seeking a better view, squinting as the face hidden by the veil emerged.

He saw a blackened eye forced shut from the swelling. The other eye was unmistakable. He rushed toward the woman, but she raised her hands. On her bared forearms were several long, straight red cuts and numerous crimson welts. Wide-eyed, Mithrias halted. "No! Rizpah! What is this? What has happened to you?"

"Just give us time to adjust, please," ordered Miriam. "She has been through so much, poor thing. It was all she could do to get here. I don't know how she did it. She insisted. Look at what they did to her." Miriam finished removing the hood. The veil was still in place. "Only a beast, an animal, would do something like this—and to one so lovely." Miriam stood back, her arms limp at her side. Mary gave the child to Joseph, then stood before Rizpah. She took her by the hand.

"I am Mary." Mary studied Rizpah's face. She floated a hand before Rizpah's forehead, then gently touched her brow. Rizpah swooned. "Please, can you walk with me to this cot?" Mary enfolded both Rizpah's hands within hers and, walking backward, guided her to the cot where Topur had once rested.

Rizpah, head bent, stood before the cot. "I am...I am..." Her chin pressed upon her chest. "I am ashamed to be here, before you, like this."

"Shame does not dwell in this house," said Mary.

"I am Rizpah. My name is Rizpah. Thank you for allowing me to come in, Mary," she said. "I thank you all." Mithrias moved with the women, assessing the gravity of Rizpah's injuries. Next to the plum purple of her swollen eye, her temple, peppered with crimson dots, revealed thin puffy welts. There were cuts above her other eye and over her nose. Hair had been pulled out by the roots.

"She is hurt. Seriously hurt." Miriam was on the verge of tears.

Mithrias tried to touch Rizpah's forehead, but she checked his hand with hers. "I can't let you," she said. "I hurt so."

"I examined her as much as possible before we left," said Miriam. "Nothing broken. I can give her something for the pain, but she would want to sleep. I couldn't let her take anything before coming here. And we need to hurry from here, so I shouldn't offer it now." She propped pillows on the cot. "Rizpah, you must be in agony. I wish I could do more, child."

"I will get some water and bandages," said Mary.

"You are most kind," said Miriam.

"Rizpah, can you sit? Can you lie down?" asked Mithrias. She nodded, then searched for his arm to help steady herself as she struggled to find the cot.

"I can't lean back," she said. "It hurts too much."

"Whipped," Miriam said.

"Whipped?" Mithrias mouthed, his eyes switching between horror and shock. "Rizpah, can you tell me who has done this to you?"

"You haven't guessed?" Miriam said. "That is the work of Herod."

"Herod?" blurted Mithrias.

"Herod?" echoed Xaratuk.

"That figures," said Topur, head shaking.

"Herod beat her, and when he was no longer strong enough to do her more harm, he had others beat her as well." Miriam beckoned Rizpah to sit on the bed. Wincing, Rizpah finally sat. Mary returned with the bandages and water. Miriam placed a moist cloth upon Rizpah's bruised and swollen forehead. Rizpah's eyes closed. A long exhale of relief pushed past her swollen lips.

Xaratuk maneuvered his way to Mithrias. "Mithrias, how do you know this woman?" he whispered. "I have never seen her. The other one—she was with Topur. But her," he nodded toward the bed, "how do you know her?"

Mithrias pulled Xaratuk with him away from the bed. His voice was hushed. "She was in my room, Xaratuk, after dinner. Your girls with you last night?" Xaratuk nodded, his focus preoccupied with examining Rizpah. "Well, Rizpah was in my room. She spent the night with me." He paused, waiting for Xaratuk's attention to return. "Herod expected her to collect information from me."

"Another spy? With you? But why would he beat this woman, Mithrias?"

"She didn't extract the information he believed she should have," said Topur, entering the conversation uninvited. "You are finally seeing Herod the Suspicious, and this time he is suspicious of you. He will not tolerate those working against his desires." Topur turned to Rizpah. "He hurts women, my friends. He has no misgivings about that. He'll hurt or harm or kill anyone he chooses."

"So you've said," said Xaratuk, nostrils flaring. He moved to stand before Rizpah. Head still bowed, her eyes closed, she struggled to stifle her pain. "I need to hear it from you. Was it King Herod himself who did this? Was it Herod's hand?"

Rizpah looked up to Mithrias. "Tell us," he said, "if you are able."

"It was Herod's hand," she said, "and the fists of others, too. It was Herod's hand that whipped me and blackened this eye, but it was a stronger hand than his that knocked out this tooth." Rizpah released her veil and used a finger to reveal a missing molar underneath a cut, swollen lip.

Mithrias gulped a hard, dry swallow. "There were more?"

"It's easy to make enemies within the palace, King Mithrias. You can make them by doing something, or...by...not doing something. You understand." Her breath came in abbreviated spurts. "There are those who resent me for my mere presence and relished the opportunity to address the wrong they felt. I now know I have more enemies than I had realized." She began to cry. "And I have lost some of those I considered my friends."

Mary dropped to one knee.

Stunned, Topur stared at Miriam. "Killed?" he mouthed.

"Yes," her whisper confirmed. She wiped away a tear. "Many."

Mary spoke, her voice choking. "Joseph, don't we have some wine we can offer Rizpah?"

"Of course." Joseph placed the child in the crib.

Mithrias moved back to Rizpah, kneeling next to Mary. "What would Herod hope to learn from us that hadn't already been discussed at dinner?" he asked. "I don't see what Herod believed you were withholding from him."

"You see why I gave my instructions to tell Herod nothing of our mission?" interrupted Topur. "It has lit a fire within the man."

"I'm sorry, Topur," said Mithrias in a hushed monotone. "So

sorry. We didn't know what else to do."

"If Herod heard from anyone—any of you—that you suspected a new king was in this house, then the life of every single person here is in danger."

Khartir and Merkis looked at each other with confused surprise.

"I told you he is a jealous and unstable man," Topur continued. "The man killed his own sons, suspecting they wished to be king—and they were legitimate heirs! Think of what he imagines this to be!"

Joseph returned with the wine. Rizpah took a small sip, then a larger one. "It hurts to swallow," she said, "but it feels good inside. Thank you for this." She emptied the cup.

"You are most welcome to it," said Mary, "and anything else we can provide."

Joseph refilled Rizpah's cup.

"Miriam has saved my life. I owe her everything," Rizpah said.

"Is this because we sent the musicians out of the room?" asked Mithrias. He grabbed a vacant stool and sat upon it before Rizpah. "Had they reported you to Herod?"

"What could they say but confirm Herod's fears to save themselves? Herod questioned them in front of me. They told him I had whispered to you in your language. They made certain Herod understood I had made it impossible for them to report anything." Rizpah closed her swollen lips. Tears slid. "But I didn't want them there, King Mithrias. And I would do it again." She tried to smile but failed. She touched his face with a light finger, tracking from cheek to chin. "I had told you to speak words only I could understand. I loved hearing your voice. The spies in our room also failed to give Herod what he wanted." Rizpah's gaze moved to Xaratuk. "But your girls told him all he needed to know. When he realized I wouldn't offer more, he had me bound and ordered his men to fetch his whip."

Miriam stepped forward. "I had gone to the front of the

palace to do laundry, but I was more interested in what others were saying about the priests. I arrived well after poor Rizpah's agony began, but I heard shouting and screams. Before I could reach her, the screams stopped. I could not find her. Going in room after room, I found no one until one of Herod's chamber servants found me.

"Luckily, this man is more loyal to us than to Herod. He was crying in despair. Between sobs, he told me of a woman beaten in Herod's bedroom. I knew right away it was you, dear." She gently patted Rizpah's shoulder. Rizpah took Miriam's hand, clasping it. "I might have left anyone else to bleed. I am not proud to say that, but there are scoundrels among his spies, evil plotters as ruthless as he. You've remained so different from the others. He thinks you're so pretty—always has—ever since you were a girl. But he wanted to hurt you, Rizpah. Your beauty probably kept him from killing you. He doesn't want a second Mariamne haunting him."

Miriam removed the moist compress and resumed her story. She had reasoned that she couldn't go into Herod's room and remove Rizpah without first disabling the demented king. So, she slipped back to her room to concoct a potion guaranteed to "keep Herod in his chair." She smuggled the mixture to the same bedchamber servant who had informed her of Rizpah's plight. He eagerly agreed to slip it into Herod's next drink.

With Herod comatose, she untied Rizpah. Courageous friends helped Miriam smuggle Rizpah back to the leper rooms. Miriam began her work, tending to the myriad of injuries she uncovered.

"I was surprised to hear you insist upon leaving," Miriam said. "Such a big step, but there were no other options."

Miriam returned the used compress to Mary, who had a fresh one waiting. "I asked Rizpah where she might go, and she told me she had to find the kings on their way to Bethlehem." Miriam studied Mithrias. "She told me about you. She said she had a password guaranteeing she would get through to you. It reminded me I had a password, too—from Topur. I began to prepare her when Kauib interrupted us. The poor boy was struck dumb with fear. Friends had informed him Herod was looking for me."

Miriam rose, touching Topur on the arm. "Among everything else, Herod was furious you were allowed to leave. To him, it was an escape, and that meant I helped you. Soon, he'd realize I had taken Rizpah from his room." She closed her eyes. "I have spent a lifetime fearing that man. It was time for me to escape the palace as well. I gathered Rizpah, a few belongings, some of my supplies, and found help to bring us here."

"This is an astonishing story, madam," Xaratuk declared. "You took great risks."

"Yes, we both did. They pale compared to what still awaits. Herod intends to kill this child. He made an announcement before my tonic took effect. To be certain this child is killed, Herod ordered his palace guard to kill every infant boy in Bethlehem—every—one! You can flee, but what a penalty for the other innocents to pay!"

Hands on hips, Miriam stepped to Mithrias and Xaratuk. "And if either of you kings figures to return to Jerusalem, you will never leave it alive. Herod does not view you as friends anymore, if he ever did. But I have made sure Herod will sleep a long, long time, and when he wakes, he'll not feel like traveling. That gives us just enough time for a head start."

Merkis cried out. "But we are not done! We need weeks— months! I need to know so much more." He reached behind, unsteadily, propping himself with the table. "Please, we cannot stop our discussion this soon."

Joseph grasped Merkis by the arm. "Regrettably, we have little choice, sir." He turned to Miriam and Rizpah, bowing. "Bless you both. You risked your lives to get word to us. We need to prepare for departure—immediately." Joseph scrutinized Simon, whose face slackened with dread. "And we must tell every family in Bethlehem with sons that those lives are in desperate peril."

Caleb stepped forward from the corner. "I will take care of that, Joseph. We're a small village. It won't take long."

"I will go with you, Caleb," said Najiir. The boys slipped out into the darkness.

An irrepressible impulse seized Xaratuk. He had obsessed over Merkis's words. If each of them had some purpose behind their presence in Bethlehem, he believed he understood his.

He placed both hands on Joseph's chest. "I have something I want to share with you and Mary. But it must not come to the attention of others. You need to trust me on this. It may appear suspicious at first, but please..." His voice was comforting, not commanding. "My advisor claims we are here for a purpose, and I know mine."

Joseph smiled.

"The fewer surrounding us, the better," Xaratuk added. "Don't be alarmed as I find tasks for others to accomplish. You and Mary remain inside."

"Understood," said Joseph.

Xaratuk moved to Regulus. "Bring my tent's center pole to me to place inside the house." Confused, Regulus tipped his head back. "Do it as inconspicuously as you can. Use three of your most trusted men to assist you."

"As you wish, sir."

"Good. And clear the shepherds from around the house. Find something for them to do. I don't want them at the door or by the windows. What I'm about to accomplish needs the utmost secrecy. Make something up. Tell them our people need help packing, or say Caleb needs help to warn their neighbors about Herod's plans—anything to get them away from the house."

"I understand."

"If anyone asks you about the pole, say it is being evaluated for Mary and Joseph's next situation."

With a salute, Regulus left to fulfill his king's orders.

Xaratuk turned his attention to Simon. He persuaded Simon that he and his fellow shepherds must prepare for Mary and Joseph's departure. He gave Simon permission to pick items from the caravan's supplies that the fleeing family might need. Simon was agreeable until he realized the implications.

"No. I will not leave while—"

"Simon, you have every right to be suspicious of me," said Xaratuk. "You do. But I am a changed man. Keep my sword. It is yours. You may need it more than I do."

"No," said Simon grimacing. "I must stay—"

Xaratuk removed his sheath, then took his short sword from Simon's hands. He sheathed the sword, held it out, and positioned Simon's reluctant fingers around it. "It's yours." Xaratuk led the wary shepherd to the door. "You have to tell your men something. They are unprepared for this news and the next step. Joseph and Mary are in danger, and your men look to you for what they must do. Go to them."

With Simon gone, Xaratuk surveyed the room. He could vouch for all but the new arrivals, Miriam and Rizpah. Removing them was unthinkable. He'd had enough confrontation for one day. If Joseph allowed for blind faith, so would he.

CHAPTER 36

Miriam inched her way to Topur. "Do you have something to tell me?"

"You must see this!" Topur gathered both her hands in his. He led her to the back of the room, away from the others. "I can show you this, but I have no words to explain it."

He opened his robe to expose his torso.

Miriam scrutinized the delicate pink line with her critical eye. She traced the scar's course with her finger. "I do fine work. I know that. But this is beyond anything I can do. Was some balm placed upon it? Some herb? Did someone do chants over you, say anything?"

"No, no. Nothing like that. It was just a series of sensations. They came over me suddenly, and to my amazement, the wound was gone! I could stand...move—without pain!"

Miriam studied Topur with a bewildered smile. "What I have been hearing is true. Unbelievable, marvelous, and unexplainable things happen in this house. There is something about this child Herod *should* fear. And we will be the better for it."

"Marvelous, indeed. It isn't much to show my wife, though. I nearly died from the attack. She'll look at this meager line, think it is nothing more than a thorny scratch, and accuse me of concocting stories."

Miriam smiled. "That's preferable to leaving you half-dead in agony." She pulled Topur closer. "What do you make of this?

Look at you! Look at Herod—he's ready to murder the children of an entire village because of this child!"

"Miriam, my thoughts are a jumble. The star is gone. What do we make of that? The family seems so genuine, the shepherds so devoted. After what happened to me, how can I not believe there is something unique about this child? Perhaps he is the one we've been waiting for. I know this: the family does not deserve the injustice that awaits them. I must help them protect this child however I can."

"We all must," said Miriam. "Tell me, where do you live? Is it far?"

Before Topur could answer, Regulus came through the door with three brawny soldiers, the ornate center pole balanced upon their shoulders. Noting the room's limitations, Merkis suggested he and Khartir follow in Simon's footsteps to assess how the shepherds were adjusting to the news.

"Remind them we are not the enemy," Xaratuk said as his advisors stepped past the door.

Those remaining made adjustments as Regulus and his men eased the center pole onto the dirt floor, then headed for the door.

"Regulus," Xaratuk whispered. "Remember to keep everyone away from the door and the window. Post your men outside. You stand by the door. No one is to see us."

"None shall." Regulus's deep baritone conveyed certainty. His men withdrew to their assignments.

Mary placed her son in his cradle. Her hands traced the geometric patterns and shapes carved into the wood. "This is exquisite. The colors are so rich."

"This is fine workmanship, King Xaratuk," added Joseph. "I have worked with wood and appreciate the skill required to fashion something like this. If you are proposing we use this fine pole after we leave Bethlehem, I should tell you we have only the one donkey—"

"No. I don't suggest you take it with you, Joseph," Xaratuk

interrupted. He maneuvered the pole, positioning an oval-shaped design on top. "I have something you will need. If you please, I am ashamed of what I did and said earlier. It was wrong. I realize that. But I am trying to follow Merkis's instructions. I am looking into my heart, asking why I may be here before you tonight. With that in mind, I have brought this pole inside. Joseph, you said you have worked with wood. Do you have any hammer and chisel?"

"Yes, I do." Joseph left the room and returned with the tools.

"Topur, can you and Mithrias hold the pole steady?" Xaratuk asked. "Hold it steady while we loosen this." Xaratuk stood astride the pole. With his finger, he traced over a thick, ornamental black line at the margins of the oval near the exact center of the pole. "There, Joseph, follow that line with your chisel, but be gentle. I don't want to break it or splinter it. I want to put it back."

After a few taps of Joseph's chisel, a crack appeared underneath the outline. He was breaking a seal that had fixed the oblong shape in place. Joseph traced a complete lap around the oval once, then worked the chisel to coax the decorative plug from its home. With a few quick taps, it was free. Xaratuk reached for the plug with both hands and gently placed it alongside the pole. He looked up to Regulus. "Are we completely alone?" Regulus peered out the window, one direction, then the other. "Yes, Your Excellency. We are alone."

"Good," said Xaratuk. He reached inside a hollowed pole. Xaratuk pulled out a crumpled rag and then another. After three more handfuls, he pulled out a leather purse. He held it in both hands, slowly straightened, walked to Mary, then kneeled before her.

"It would be my honor if you would take this and use it for whatever you find necessary."

Mary placed the purse in her lap. From his crib, the baby made lurches with his arms. Mary lifted the baby. Jesus' arms continued to move, this time toward Xaratuk.

"It seems he wants you to hold him," said Mary, eyes aglow.

"May I?" asked Xaratuk.

"Yes," said Mary. She handed the baby to Xaratuk. With eyes like dark moons, the baby stared intently upon the face of the man who had terrorized him—terrorized the entire house—hours earlier.

Xaratuk's mustache stretched to his ears to accommodate his smile. He had not lovingly held a baby, ever. The baby smiled in return. Their eyes did not part; neither blinked. Feelings of peace and contentment, feelings entirely foreign to him, welled from Xaratuk's chest, filling him, engulfing him. Finally, he said, "Yes. Yes. I am sure this is the right thing. Mary, Joseph—this child..." Xaratuk could not form the words.

"We understand," said Joseph.

The baby was close enough to touch Xaratuk's face. One hand, bobbing, reached Xaratuk's cheek. Xaratuk closed his eyes. The baby's hand lingered. Xaratuk kissed it. Reluctantly, he held the infant up to return him to his mother. He felt one more brush of a baby's hand upon his cheek. "This is a moment I shall never forget." Xaratuk raised his head, wiped his eyes, and whispered, "Please, Mary, open the satchel."

Mary placed her baby back into the crib and reached for the purse still in her lap. She unknotted the leather string that secured the top, parted the opening, and peered inside. Still unsure, she put a hand inside.

"It's gold!" she gasped.

Xaratuk held a finger to his lips. "We must keep this quiet."

"But this is gold!" She held the purse up to Joseph. He looked inside.

"This will help us—truly, it will, King Xaratuk," Joseph said. "We will put this to good use. Please get up." Joseph helped Xaratuk to his feet. "Thank you. Our most sincere thanks to you."

"There's more," said Xaratuk. "Mithrias, Topur, would you reach inside that pole for me, please?"

Mithrias and Topur reached inside the hollowed pole and

alternately pulled out more stuffing and seven more purses. They placed them before Mary and Joseph.

"Each one is filled. Some are larger than others," Xaratuk explained.

"I have never seen so much gold in one place in my life," said Topur.

"Nor have I," said Joseph, stunned.

"No, no, you haven't," said Xaratuk. "That is a great deal of gold, and many out there will wish to separate you from it. You shouldn't take it all with you at once. We are all too familiar with the bandits roaming the roads around here." Xaratuk moved closer to Joseph to whisper in his ear. "Gold has its own magical power. It is known to turn friends into enemies. That is why I wanted everyone else out of here. No one needs to know about this beyond those here in this room. The fewer people, the better. Joseph, do you know where you can safely hide some of this?"

"There has been little work for me since this began, and I have had ample time to explore the area. There are some excellent places that no one will bother. I can return for it when it is safe again for us."

"Good," said Xaratuk. "That is why I have Regulus here to help you. He'll take two men with him, and the four of you can quickly hide what you won't need to take. Use one place or several—whatever you think is best. But you know that Regulus and his men will not return to Bethlehem. There is no reason to distrust them."

He turned to his captain. "Regulus," he ordered, "make absolutely certain you are not being followed. Hide these satchels under your garments and go out as inconspicuously as possible. You must not be seen by villager or shepherd." Regulus, following Joseph, stepped out into the night.

Inside, Mary touched Xaratuk on the arm. "I don't understand such generosity."

"Mary, you have enough gold to support you, no matter

what direction you believe you must go. You don't need to stay here under Herod's nose if you don't wish to, and who knows how far you must go to be free of him."

"That gold is not mine, generous King. It is God's. He will direct us on how best to use it."

"Somehow, Mary, I believe you." Xaratuk reached for Mary's hand, and she willingly gave it. Her diminutive fingers looked almost childish inside his.

The post was prepared for removal. The door was opened. Simon was the first to enter. His gaze found Mary. She gently nodded, indicating all was well. The purse of gold she had held was now secreted below her child at the bottom of the cradle.

"Simon," Xaratuk said. "We've determined Joseph cannot use such a cumbersome item. Could some of your men help us return this to our camp?" Simon collected five men who moved in, hoisted the post, and returned it to the camp.

CHAPTER 37

M ithrias watched the shepherds depart. Every aspect of the journey had changed. Sighing, he knew he could not avoid facing what he least wished to do. His chest felt hollow. He kneeled beside Rizpah.

"Rizpah, what are your plans? Where are you going? I must know."

Rizpah's punished forehead wrinkled. She shook her head. "I was hoping you would tell me. When we first arrived, I met your son, Salnassar. I didn't realize you had a son. We spoke briefly. I sensed he thought I was intruding. I don't wish to come between you and your son. I'm sorry. I don't know what I should do." She turned from him.

"Rizpah, don't look away...please." Mithrias took both her hands in his. "I want you to come with me. But I had better explain myself." His throat tightened. The words he needed to say were thorny. They were caustic words, expressions that opposed every urge he felt thriving inside.

Their new situation was nearly perfect—no need to beg, plead or bargain with Herod. Hand in hand, they might slip the king's clutches forever. But Mithrias's inconvenient conscience overruled romantic fantasy. Such an escape was unjustifiable. Mithrias's mouth tightened. He licked his upper lip. "We should not leave together."

"What?" Rizpah pulled her hands from Mithrias.

"You must trust me, Rizpah." Mithrias felt his aching heart

pound. "I vow to you we will be together. But our best chance for that future demands we leave apart."

"I am frightened, Mithrias. This scares me."

"Herod will secure his borders to prevent our escape." Mithrias predicted that if he and Rizpah were captured together, Herod would portray them in the foulest manner. He would paint Mithrias as an ungrateful, lascivious thief; Rizpah as a lustful pawn. "Herod would have grounds to treat us severely. He'd be within his right to kill us both, and most people might agree. I'm sure the Romans would." Mithrias explained that if he died at the hands of Herod, his country would feel compelled to avenge his murder, ultimately setting the stage for war with Rome. "I think of my generals having to inspire their soldiers with a basis for their sacrifice. Would those men give their lives to revenge a king whose selfish desires led to his murder? I can't bear to think of our young men rallying to the memory of a dishonored king. No. I must be more responsible to them than that. My people will come to know you and know I love you under my terms, not Herod's. "

"I would never ask you to risk your kingdom."

Confused, Mithrias tried to conjure more options for escape, but his mind felt clumsy, incapable of formulating a viable solution.

"I have nowhere." Tears ran across her swollen cheeks.

Mary rose from her spot beside the cradle, then kneeled next to Rizpah's cot. "You are coming with us." She gathered Rizpah's hands in hers. "I don't yet know where we are going. That will be clear in time. But you are coming with us—with Joseph and me and the baby."

Mithrias's mind raced with the implications of this new idea.

"Oh, Mary, Mary," cried Rizpah, "I cannot go with you. Why would you have me? I would put you in as much danger—"

"You will come with us. We will trust God to protect us. Please."

"Perhaps this would work," Mithrias said. "Mary and Joseph will be far less noticeable, and with only a donkey or two, you'll be quicker, more mobile. We'll prepare a cart for you as we did for Topur. If you are stopped, you'll be recognized, which won't bode well for any of you. But you can take measures to avoid that. You would be a help to Mary once you are better."

"Mary, you don't know me. You don't know who I am—what I am. I don't deserve such kindness. You are a good woman, Mary, and people don't use that word when they think of me."

"We are exactly alike. We are both in terrible danger because of a vengeful and hateful king. We must escape from his evil. We will do it—together."

Rizpah looked upon Mithrias. He nodded, still absorbing the idea.

"And what about Miriam?" Mary asked. Miriam turned at the mention of her name. At that moment, Joseph, Regulus, and Najiir returned. Khartir and Merkis were next.

Regulus turned to Xaratuk. "The items are secure."

Xaratuk looked about the room. The best minds to plot their escape were assembled. "Regulus, we must plan. We must think clearly and act quickly. The stakes are high. We are confronting a treacherous, powerful man. We are too few to stand and fight. Joseph, our caravan is slow. As our venture into the canyon showed, any protection we may offer is woefully insufficient. Fleeing with us gives you no advantage. You may feel we are abandoning you, but splitting up increases the chances of any specific group's survival. I suggest we make our separate, independent escapes. We give Herod many targets, not just one. If captured, we can truthfully claim ignorance of the other's whereabouts. Joseph, have you given any thought to where you might go?"

"I have not. This has happened so quickly."

"Egypt," interrupted Khartir.

"What?" said Joseph.

"Where?" said Xaratuk.

"Egypt," repeated Khartir. "It was a region we studied as we traveled here. We thought the star might signify Egypt's renewal—Cleopatra reborn. Obviously, it wasn't. Nonetheless, Egypt is south. Since we are already south of Jerusalem, we have an advantage. Going north leads us toward Jerusalem and into Herod's waiting arms. To the east is a desert with limited, if any, provisions. Within three days of reasonable speed, we could be at the southern fringes of Herod's realm, and from there, we can proceed to Egypt. Alexandria has a large Jewish population. We could easily blend in."

"We?" said Merkis.

"What?" said Khartir, startled.

"You keep saying 'we.' Are you planning something you'd share with the rest of us?"

Khartir bit his lip and kicked the ground. "I didn't realize I said it that way."

"Oh." Merkis could say nothing more.

Xaratuk examined Khartir with a wary eye. "Egypt is far away." He turned toward Joseph. "Do you think you can make such an arduous journey—with this baby?"

"We will have help." Mary grabbed Joseph's hand. "Joseph, I asked Rizpah to come with us." Mary moved to Miriam. "And I would like you to come with us as well."

"I had not considered where I fit into all of this," said Miriam.

"I could use your help. You would be a comfort to me."

Looking at Jesus, Miriam smiled, "I don't know what I can offer that he isn't able to do better than I could ever hope to."

Mary smiled, then turned to Joseph. "They will be looking for three people: a man, a woman, and a child. It may be better to have more than three. We could claim Rizpah and Miriam are my sisters."

"Getting people to believe I am your sister may be your greatest miracle yet." Miriam snickered. "I am flattered, Mary, but I'd be more convincing as your aunt." Miriam frowned. "This is so sudden, and I don't wish to be a burden."

Joseph spoke. "I would welcome you gratefully. We need all the help we can get. We will be among many strangers—it is friends we lack."

Xaratuk stepped toward Khartir, surveying his youthful advisor from head to toe. "And you, Khartir, are you saying you wish to go with them? Your role as my advisor is secure back home. You are more important to me—to your country—than ever. I need you. What if I should order you to stay with us?"

"I will always obey, my king." Khartir frowned. "Returning with you was my only consideration until moments ago. I am still struggling with what is best."

He touched Merkis's arm. "You have always told me to look for the truth—no matter where it may lead. You urge me to press on, believing truth exists or that, at a minimum, we can try to understand more." With hands folded and head bent, he stood before his mentor. "You asked each of us to consider what we can do, what we ought to do. That made me think my calling is to bear further witness. When the child is ready to speak, I must be there."

Merkis closed his eyes as the first pangs of loss registered. "You are my family, you know. I am trapped. If you go, I surrender my aid, my comfort, and my inspiration." His voice choked. "But it is to a calling I, myself, endorse."

"If heaven wills it, I will return to you and King Xaratuk and tell you what I have witnessed. I will tell you that the child has spoken, and this is what he has said."

"I do want to know," mumbled Xaratuk.

"By the time there are words worth telling, I fear my presence here on earth will have passed." Merkis's frame shook.

"I know," said Khartir softly. "Were you younger, would it not be you who would press to go on? If there is this opportunity, shouldn't someone take it?"

Merkis, his eyes glistening, looked away from Khartir, then

nodded.

"How can I spare you, Khartir?" said Xaratuk, watching Merkis struggle. "I don't want to lose you."

Khartir closed his eyes. "You have not lost me, good king. I will not be away forever—far from it. Your kingdom is my home, and you are my king. I remain, as always, in your service. But you said it, and you were correct. The child has yet to say anything. Shouldn't I act as your eyes and ears and be there when that time arrives? I believe I serve you best by being with them." He looked over toward Joseph. "That is, of course, if they'll have me."

"And Merkis, you agree?" asked Xaratuk. Unable to speak, Merkis nodded.

"And you assume it must be you, Khartir?" asked Xaratuk. "Isn't there anyone else in camp I can send in your place?"

"You put me in a difficult spot, Your Excellency, but—"

"He is the one. No other." Merkis turned, placing his hands over his face.

Xaratuk put both hands upon the young magi's shoulders. "I will miss you. You are like a son to me, too. Know that. Return just as swiftly as you can—for his sake," he said, nodding to Merkis, "and for mine."

Xaratuk gently squeezed Khartir's shoulder. "Write everything down. All of it. I'll relish the time we'll spend together as you explain all this to me." Xaratuk placed his index finger on his lips. "And one last thing: tell him about us. Tell him about his visitors and how people from a far-off land came to see him and know him but were forced to leave much too quickly. Tell him he had a star above him. Perhaps you'll skip the part where I lost my temper?" Khartir smiled. "May heaven watch over you."

Khartir bowed to his king, then took Merkis by the arm and directed him toward the door. "We have much to discuss and little time to do it. Please pack with me." They left the house and headed toward the camp.

"That young man may be of more value to you than the gold," Xaratuk told Joseph, his voice thin and strained. "It pains me far more to part with him. The world has more gold." With a deep breath, he changed the topic. "Good. We need to get your belongings together right now. Put those things that must come with you on the doorstep. We'll pack them onto carts. Do you have any animals to take with you?"

"We've already gathered much of what we must take," replied Joseph. "I have only the one donkey. I sent Najiir for it."

"One donkey may have been enough for the three of you, but now you have, what, six people in all? You'll need more animals."

"Seven. Make that seven—or eight." Simon took Joseph by the arm, leading him away from Xaratuk. "Mary and Jesus must have some protection. You've got none. Not one of those strangers can help. Caleb and I are ready and willing to go with you. You need us, and we need to be with our Messiah."

He pulled Joseph closer, whispering. "We can find refuge much closer. Why Egypt? Surely we can avoid Herod's grasp without having to go that far. You should listen to me, not those foreigners. You can't leave us so suddenly. We have been faithfully by your side since the very beginning. He is our Messiah, Joseph. We understand whom we are protecting— what this means. Those foreigners don't—can't!" Simon's voice turned insistent. "I'm not convinced we can't make a stand here in Bethlehem. Look what Jesus did for that stranger over there! Herod has no power against something like that!"

"Simon, I have been considering all this, too. It weighs heavily on my mind."

Hands on hips, Simon tried to block Joseph's view from the others still in the room. "It would be better, Joseph, if we stayed with you and Mary. And if it isn't Bethlehem, there are many other places. I can convince most of the shepherds to move with us. Wherever you go, we can be there to protect you. You're not better off with strangers than you are with us."

"Simon, please listen. I can never fully express our gratitude. All of you have been patient, generous, and faithful. Your sacrifices have allowed us to survive."

Simon shuffled in place.

"Understand me, Simon. Please be patient while I explain. I believe it would be better—our purposes would be better served—if you remained behind. I am not saying stay in Bethlehem."

Simon looked away, his jaw clenched.

"Simon," Joseph continued, "you are a wanted man. You came to Bethlehem because it was too dangerous for you in Jerusalem. Herod's men know you. The Romans know you. There are men out there whose job it is to find you. Having you travel with us brings every danger upon your head to be upon Jesus's as well. Bringing you adds more danger, more risk."

"I could be in disguise, or what about Caleb, then? Have at least someone from the original group go with you."

Joseph put an arm around Simon's shoulder and spoke softly. His eyes searched for Simon's, but Simon stared at the far side of the room. "What I need—what we need—is a home to return to. This is the second time Mary and I have been forced to leave our home. At Nazareth, no one would accept us. Now, Judaea's king wants to kill our child. We must remain far away from Herod until he is no longer a threat. But what will we return to, more of the same? No, we hope for a more tolerant, if not inviting, situation. Who better to prepare for our return than you? Who has more ability, more conviction? Simon, it is you who will help others realize what has been revealed. I think we have the proper people in place for our flight to Egypt. But after that, who else could make Judaea home for us again? It's you, Simon—you."

Simon softened.

"We won't stay in Egypt," said Joseph. "We are not meant for that. So, if not there, where? With your help, we can make a new home. Truthfully, I would prefer to stay away from Judaea.

I'd rather return to Galilee. But we must stay away until Herod dies. I don't know what to think about his sons."

"He's killed off the clever and ambitious ones already." Simon snickered. "Those left are stupid and lazy, but stupid and lazy can be dangerous, too."

"All the more reason for someone I trust to find the best location for this blessed child to thrive. You would be doing God's work."

Simon nodded reluctantly. Joseph continued. "Don't lose your faith, Simon. It will be all you have hoped for. I am counting on you to tell the others they must be patient and wait for our return."

"I still wish you would let one or two of us go with you," said Simon.

"The others you say are strangers are the ones chosen for this next portion of our journey. You and I know the star meant something, but until tonight, we didn't know what. They arrived, Simon, strangers to us, but God meant for them to be here. Without this group of new friends, our flight to Egypt—or anywhere—would be far more difficult."

"If they hadn't come, hadn't aroused Herod's suspicions—"

"Word was bound to reach him, Simon. It was only a matter of time. You recognize that, too. I see God's hand keeping Herod away from us this long."

Simon pulled back his shoulders and stood erect, as if at military attention. "I shall do as you wish, Joseph. I shall prepare Galilee for your return and the return of our Messiah."

Joseph looked into Simon's eyes. "Simon," he said, "he shall always need you. Believe that and believe in him, even though we may be far away. Never lose what you know is true in your heart."

"Come home—quickly." Simon's eyes turned glassy. He clasped Joseph's arm. Kneeling before Jesus in his crib, Simon gave him a light kiss on the forehead, then looked up to Mary. "God is with you, but please, return swiftly. Your home will be ready." He rose, then strode through the door into the night.

Topur, watching it all, left Miriam's side and moved to Joseph. "Joseph," he said softly, "I arrived here, stuffed in a cart, nearly dead with pain, losing blood. I don't need that cart anymore. It's yours." Topur struggled for words. "But what do I say? What can I give? How does one repay a miracle?" Topur strode to a corner of the room and returned with the satchel of myrrh Miriam had packed. "Though in life I am a trader, I brought little to trade on this journey. I was more guide than merchant." He grabbed the satchel and dropped to one knee before Mary and Joseph. "Please, I want you to have this myrrh. My life is changed because of you, and I have so little to offer in return."

"Please," Mary said, "repayment isn't—"

"But you could use it along the way—for food, or fodder, or lodging. It trades easily. You'll see."

Mary spoke. "But why not use our—"

"We thank you for this gift." Joseph interrupted. "We can make excellent use of it. As Jesus grows, we will remind him of your kindness and generosity."

"My kindness and generosity?" An ironic smile crossed Topur's face. "A bag of myrrh, and now we're even? I leave Bethlehem a healed and whole man, thanks to this child. I shall forever and always be grateful, if not confused, about what has happened. It is all too incredible—every bit. Who will believe me?" Topur rose to both feet. "But whether others believe me or whether they don't, I know what has happened, and I will testify to it, and to you, until my dying breath."

"With that, any debt you may feel is then fully repaid, friend," said Joseph.

A wan smile crossed Topur's face. "And for you, this is just the beginning. What awaits, Joseph—miracles or otherwise?"

"There's no telling."

"The Messiah." Topur stood above the cradle. A look of profound sadness crossed his face. He looked first at Mary, then at Joseph. "This world, as it is, may not be ready for such good news."

"We understand. Though unbidden, he is now here."

"Every time my heart is elated as I think of all he can and will do, I feel such an ache," Mary said. "Why should that be?"

"Don't be in a hurry to grow up, dear child," Topur kneeled by the cradle and put a finger on the baby's chest. The baby held Topur's finger in his hand. Topur smiled. "I will be watching and listening, dear boy. I trust we are worthy of this. Not all of us are like mean, old Herod. Remember that, even when we make it difficult to believe." He turned to Mary and Joseph. "I hope this will not be our only meeting. I travel often, so I will listen for word about you."

"I hope that, too," said Joseph.

"God willing, then." Topur rose.

"God willing."

CHAPTER 38

Xaratuk seized command, organizing the expedition to Egypt, packing, or compulsively adding items from his caravan to augment Joseph and Mary's meager supplies. Soldiers and servants raced to comply with his directives until all that could be packed had been packed.

Outside, Rizpah clutched Mithrias's arm. She lowered one hand, slipping her fingers through his. She felt his gentle squeeze back. He pulled her closer. Her hooded head fell upon his shoulder. Together, they slowly stepped toward the camp.

They found Xaratuk trotting from cart to cart, inspecting and assessing. When he saw them, Xaratuk called out and motioned for Mithrias to join him. Edging Rizpah to a collection of carts laden with supplies, Mithrias asked, "Are you able to be on your own?"

"Yes. Maybe it's that wine. I feel so much better."

Mithrias evaluated Rizpah as she found a comfortable seat at the cart's edge. "Your face—it's not so swollen."

Rizpah touched her eye. "It doesn't hurt." She reached for Mithrias's hand.

"Something is happening." He surveyed Rizpah's shadowed face again. "Stay here. I won't be long."

Rizpah reluctantly released her hold. She placed her hand back on her brow.

Xaratuk had finished lashing his center pole to an oxcart as Mithrias arrived. The kings stood on opposite sides, their hands braced on the wagon's rim. Xaratuk frowned and spoke in a hushed voice.

"You know," he began, "I was not going to kill the child. That was never, ever my plan."

Mithrias stared blankly, concealing any doubts. "I was not going to kill you, either," he replied.

Xaratuk grunted. "Well, I am glad of that," he said, still whispering. "I don't know what came over me. I had no intention of hurting the boy, but I couldn't see why everyone was so enthralled. It seemed to me he was just a boy—a baby boy like any other. I thought we had all lost our heads. A king? From that shack? Pure speculation!" Xaratuk looked back toward the house. "I do see now that we have encountered something—someone—extraordinary. There is no denying what I saw tonight. I will count on Merkis to make sense of it for me." His hand passed to his brow, and he looked deeply puzzled. His voice cracked. "What is happening here, Mithrias?"

"It's all so wonderful, so mysterious. Merkis can help you far better than I."

Xaratuk spoke after an awkward pause. "That woman, your friend, she's not coming with us?"

"No. Not now." He looked squarely at Xaratuk. "You agree, don't you? We must heed Paris and Menelaus. We remember how that turned out." He stopped, then added, "But don't mistake me. I will reunite with her later."

Xaratuk shrugged. "I suppose the threat to that group is equal with or without her. They all face harm. No one is spared. I simply can't make myself feel good about Khartir joining them."

"Based upon what we've seen tonight, Joseph and Mary have advantages we are unaware of. I estimate their chances are better than we realize." Mithrias moved around the wagon. He put a friendly hand on Xaratuk's shoulder. Slowly, Xaratuk placed his hand over Mithrias's.

"That was a great deal of gold you gave them," Mithrias

said.

Xaratuk backed away from the cart, searching for anyone nearby who might overhear. "It is enough to last seven people seven lifetimes or more. It was meant to bribe a king, or a prince, or an army. I saw no point in withholding any. It is theirs, and I'm happy about it. They will never have to worry about money." He looked about suspiciously once more, then continued in his hushed tone. "That said, even with all the gold, I don't think they'll have an easy time of it. I don't see how. They'll never fit in, no matter where they go. How can they? My gift is a gamble. If they are not worthy, they will be exposed. To me, they seem deserving."

"You still believe you didn't find your ally? The child is not your partner in defending against Rome?"

"Mithrias, how can he be?" Xaratuk tittered. "Yes, I have given up on that hope. He isn't the guardian I had hoped for. The son of peasants amassing a formidable army? Very unlikely. I don't foresee soldiers from Jerusalem or Judaea ever offering me any defense against those Roman legions. Do you?" Xaratuk did not look back for a response. "And I still don't believe you can hug a Roman into submission. Mercy? Comfort? I'll need that explained because I still don't understand any of it."

"Don't underestimate this one, my friend." Mithrias chose his words carefully. "So you found he doesn't have an army at his disposal. But you witnessed the shepherds' intensity and willingness to do anything for him. Who is he to inspire such devotion? And from this little house, in this tiny town, you see how he can agitate a king. All this turmoil, without an army, never leaving his crib, never speaking. Imagine what unrest he may arouse once he can! The disturbance he might generate may keep the Romans so busy they won't have the stomach to consider adding to the empire. So, maybe you found your ally after all. Who is to say?"

"I had never thought of it like that."

"Xaratuk," Mithrias resumed, "do you not find it odd that,

during all this time, considering the places we've been and the people we've met, we have yet to be confronted by a single Roman—not one? How should we interpret that?"

Xaratuk jerked his head to the side, his mouth open. Before he could respond, Mithrias added, "If you doubt this child's power and influence, merely consider yourself." He paused. "You. Without the ability to speak one word, this child summoned the great King Xaratuk to appear at the doorstep of a shack and donate a fortune. If that isn't a power to pay homage to, what is?"

"This is a great deal to consider, my friend."

"Will you have enough gold left over for our return?" asked Mithrias, changing the subject.

"The other tent poles have gold in them, too, more than was in this one. I thought I had to bring enough gold to buy allegiance from a mighty kingdom, but all I needed was enough for a small family. It seems like a bargain." Xaratuk smiled, then turned serious. "But back to that woman, Mithrias. It was just one night. Are you seriously considering...because, I admit it, I was swept up in a fervor over those girls sent to me, but—"

"You are right to be concerned, my friend. It was just one night. That kind of passion can warp one's judgment. The deaths of Deioces and Doria left me broken. Topur had a bandit's knife tear his body. Losing my wife and son had torn my soul. I need to be open to miracles. Topur had his. They do exist. Can't Rizpah be mine?"

Xaratuk tried to speak, but Mithrias quickly interrupted. "My head is full of questions and doubts. But I also hear a faint but determined voice coming from my heart. Should I not pay heed to it? Is it my enemy, a voice of deceit? Or, like Bethlehem, might it suggest insight beyond what is obvious?"

Mithrias put his hand on Xaratuk's shoulder. "I won't listen to inflamed arousal. That voice is not complex in its desires. I listen for the voice that encourages those things Mary spoke of: love, mercy, charity, and compassion. When I listen, I hear that voice telling me to trust this."

Xaratuk's eyes narrowed. "On top of Herod's tower, you were convinced you moved about in a world devoid of heavenly attention. Now this. You talk of love and miracles and the rest. So much change in such a brief time. It seems too much, too quick." He pointed a finger. "Don't allow these voices to convince you of things that are not there. Heed my example, my friend."

"She is not a conquest. She is my healer. I was rendered a shattered man. So far, she, and only she, has given me the will to put myself back together."

"I hope your kingdom, not to mention your son, can come to feel the same and understand her as you will."

"Yes, Salnassar. This may be a problem. I need to find him and attempt to explain this. Have you seen him? I don't know where he has been or what he has—"

"It looks like you will find out sooner than you thought," Xaratuk broke in.

Salnassar emerged from the darkened shadows on foot, leading his horse. He held the reins up to Mithrias.

"This is your horse," he said meekly. For once, his face did not strain to flaunt his resentment. His eyes were soft, his brow inviting.

"Salnassar, I was going to look for you to tell you—"

"I saw everything. Everything," Salnassar said. "Regulus let me watch from outside through the window. I saw everything."

"Salnassar, I should explain—"

"I watched you. You helped people. You say it is important to help people, and then you do it. I watched you help a poor baby. I met that woman, Rizpah. I saw what Herod did to her. We spoke. She needs your help, too." His chin dropped. He blinked, then raised his head back up. "You saved my life in the canyon, and I never thanked you. I see you better now for what you are. You save people. Hearing Merkis made me think." He paused. His breath came in brief spurts. "I know why you are here. But I don't know why I am here, and I fear there is no reason. No one—nothing needs me." His chin quivered. "I want there to be a reason. I must find out. Maybe you'll help me." He held the horse's reins back up to Mithrias. "You should ride, sir."

"Huh," snorted Xaratuk, "A boy has just become a man right before my eyes—another miracle."

Mithrias blinked back tears. He placed his hands firmly on his son's shoulders. Salnassar pulled his father close to him. "I am ready to prove I can be the next son you are proud of."

"Finally." Xaratuk walked away, slapping Mithrias on the back.

CHAPTER 39

Topur stepped from the house with Miriam, placing the few remaining objects ready to be packed on the doorstep. They stood together, facing the dark hill that led to camp. Torches were tiny stars lining the way. "I must find Rizpah," said Miriam. "The poor dear. She has suffered so. All these changes— her prospects—such uncertainty. Come with me."

"I should find Najiir first," Topur said. "We must gather our belongings. I don't know where they are. After that, I should tell Joseph what I remember about the route to Egypt. It's been years. And this time, we must consider both Herod and the Romans. So much to do."

"Come get me when you are done." Miriam scurried down the hill, but Topur remained, hands upon his hips. He searched vainly into the night for Najiir. Not knowing where to begin, he stepped toward camp. A whispered voice called out his name. He looked around. No one. The voice called to him again from beside the house. Najiir stepped from the shadows. The lamplight through the window back-lit his slender frame as he emerged. "Master," he said, nervously clearing his throat. "I need to speak with you."

Topur, relieved to discover the boy so quickly, moved toward him. "I was looking for you. Where is our tent, my donkey? We need to plan our route home. Should we go with—"

"I have to ask a favor of you, master."

"Yes, yes," said Topur. "Go ahead, but you don't have to call me 'master' out here."

"I don't know how to begin. I don't know how to say this."

Topur cocked his head. Najiir never had trouble speaking to him. Topur drew closer and put his hands on the boy's shoulders. "What is it, Najiir? You can talk about anything with me. What is bothering you? Is it something to do with what happened to me inside? Because if it is, I—"

"No, nothing like that." Tears welled over Najiir's eyelids, trickling down his cheeks.

"There now, dear boy. There is nothing so bad, is there? Talk to me."

"I think—I think I should go," Najiir blurted.

"Go?" asked Topur, stepping even closer. "Go? We're all going. No one is staying here, and you're coming home with me—"

"To Egypt. I think I should go to Egypt."

"Oh," Topur stepped back. His lungs held fast. He felt dizzy. An ache surged from within, one distinctly different from the pain of his wound. It was an ache beyond the purview of miracles. This ache was from the soul, not the body.

The dim light reflected off Najiir's bowed head. Topur had never considered a future without Najiir. They were a pair. They were father and son in every respect but one. His immediate reaction was to say no—of course, no—what a ridiculous idea! He stifled that response before it could emerge.

Najiir stared at his feet, unable to look at Topur. "You gave me a life I know I don't deserve. I worry you'll think I abandoned you." Najiir sniffed. "I should just ignore this—the feeling will go away. I can't just run out on you." He pounded a fist into his thigh. "Not after all you've done for me." His words became more garbled. "Not after all you mean to me. You saved my life."

"I see," murmured Topur. He gathered the boy inside a firm embrace. Najiir's featherlight frame shook with sobs. Topur pushed away slightly, looking into Najiir's eyes. "You believe you must do this?"

Najiir nodded, still shaking. Topur's breathy exhale found its way past the lump in his throat. Life would be so different. Business would be so different. All the advantages he'd bragged about to Mithrias would be gone. What would he need to do to regain his competitive edge?

How selfish! Topur admonished himself. How utterly selfish! Moments ago, he was the beneficiary of a God-sent miracle. Yet, here he was, assessing whether losing his spy in the bazaars might make his business life more difficult. He chastised himself, then offered God a short but earnest prayer, begging forgiveness.

But Topur did not ask forgiveness for wishing that this boy, whom he dearly loved, might instead remain with him.

"You believe you can help them?" asked Topur, using the cuff of his royal robe to wipe away Najiir's tears.

"Yes, sir," Najiir could not complete a sentence without a sob interrupting. "What Merkis said about listening, and about being here, each of us, for what purpose."

"Merkis was right. With all my being, I believe that."

"Only," he sniffed, "being a boy." The pace of tears quickened. He could barely squeak out the next words. "Being just a slave…"

"Oh, my." Topur realized his heart had not hit bottom, for it was plunging again. His tears came too freely. He bit his lower lip to no avail. "Don't think that, my son. Don't think that."

"I thought since you won't be there to show them the way, and they still need someone to help, maybe I could."

Topur gripped his adopted son as if he might never have this chance again, burying his face in the youngster's hair. He was surprised to hear Najiir muster such confidence. "It is such a long journey, and there will be danger—"

He suddenly thrust Najiir at arm's length. Topur's eyes grew wide and intense. His chin lowered, leaving his mouth agape. His scrutiny flew about the boy—head to toe—as if he'd never seen him.

"No!" he gasped. "No. No, no, no!" Topur's shout was so alarming it shocked Najiir out of his misery.

"W-What?" Najiir stuttered.

"You? The star meant to bring *you* here?"

Najiir recoiled as though he'd done something wrong.

"You, Najiir!" Topur clasped the boy's shoulders. He gave them a shake. "This—all this is about you!"

"The star? No, no. It was for the kings," Najiir protested. "The star was a beacon for the kings."

"No, I see it now." Topur scrambled to organize these new thoughts. They flew wildly, like grit in a sandstorm. "I thought this was about me," he whispered. Topur placed his hand to his head and grimaced. He gripped Najiir's chin. "Back home. Atarah. I wanted no part of this. God's will. She said it was God's will that I come with the kings. No, no." Topur's head vibrated. "No. Bless you, Atarah, but God was not working to get me here." Topur stepped back, releasing Najiir. "God needed me to make certain *you* would arrive. And to think I nearly ruined it!" He pounded his fist upon his forehead.

"The kings," Topur said, "that was you, wasn't it? The kings came for me at your suggestion—*you* volunteered my name on the Trading Road. I see that now." Najiir made no move. "And, and, and through you, Herod's army knew the kings were headed to that canyon and came to our rescue. And God sent you ahead to Bethlehem to prepare Mary and Joseph and the shepherds for the kings. Only you could cultivate Joseph's trust to allow such suspicious foreigners into his home."

Najiir stared at the ground. Everything Topur had asserted was true, but never subjected to this interpretation. Until now, only whim and circumstance had guided Najiir.

"And you're not done," Topur continued. "This family needs to escape Herod. Who will help them? Who will find the safest way to Egypt?" Topur's words sounded like an urgent secret. "It's you, Najiir. This is about you! Mary and Joseph speak only a little Greek. How are they to cope in Egypt? Only you can help them understand and be understood. You'll be their pathfinder—the lead, gathering information and making friends, just as you have faithfully done for me. I can't go on from here, leaving Atarah and the girls to fend for themselves. The kings can't go, nor the advisors, not even the shepherds. You must go! This family needs you. You were brought here to do this!"

"But master, I don't see how—"

Topur collapsed upon a stool at the base of the window. He motioned for Najiir to sit on the empty stool next to him. "Don't you see? The kings could have made it here on their own. They didn't need me." He blurted a humorless chuckle. "My knowledge and experience were immaterial. Despite me, not because of me, everyone reached Bethlehem. I am here only because God wanted you here, which wouldn't have happened unless I came with you." Topur's hands softly cupped Najiir's face while he placed a long kiss upon his forehead. "Though I dread your absence from my life, I know you must go!"

Inside the house, near the window, Joseph turned away from the voices outside. He looked over to Mary. "I feel much better about reaching Egypt safely. We have all we need. This night has revealed why the star was placed above us." He turned to look out the window. His eyes filled as they gazed upon the sight of a man and boy rocking, weeping, locked in a loving embrace.

Mary put her arms around Joseph's waist. "I think that is everything. All we can move is at the door. The rest we don't need or can replace." She looked at all four walls, clasping her husband. "I can't say I will miss this place. So much has happened, Joseph, but it was never home."

"I wonder if we will ever be able to think of any place as home," Joseph said through the lump in his throat. They lingered. "I will summon the others and prepare them."

"Then I will stay here with Jesus until you are ready for us to leave."

CHAPTER 40

Mithrias carried a plain, dark sack slung over one shoulder. Rizpah clung to his side as they stepped toward the house. Topur and Najiir were still seated near the window under the lamplight's dim glow. Topur's arm circled the boy who had buried his head in his hands. Mithrias called out, "Topur, is something wrong? Is Najiir ill?"

Startled, Topur looked up but smiled. "On the contrary, King Mithrias. Najiir is very well. It has been an overwhelming day for both of us."

"Understandable, if not understated," replied Mithrias. "Topur, we left Miriam down at the camp. The caravan will come past the house as we leave Bethlehem, but she said she needs to speak to you before it moves."

"Then we should go to her at once. We have much to tell her, as well."

Najiir stood, using his sleeve to dry his eyes. "Thank you, King Mithrias. Thank you, ma'am. It has been an incredible privilege to be with you." Mithrias cocked his head. He looked to Topur.

"Topur, is there something I should know?"

Topur placed a hand over Mithrias's wrist. "Yes. Later, I promise to explain, but Najiir must follow the reason he is here, just like the rest of us. First, we must go to Miriam."

Mithrias could only nod as Topur and Najiir collected themselves and hastened to the camp.

Joseph was at the doorstep, but upon seeing Mithrias and Rizpah, he invited them inside. Mithrias gently placed his sack on the floor. As they came within the lamp's soft light, Joseph said, "Rizpah, your face. It's far less swollen."

Rizpah moved a hand to her battered eye. She dabbed and pressed. She removed her hood.

"Rizpah, your blackened eye!" Mithrias exclaimed. "The bruising—it's gone, and the cuts are gone, too!"

"I don't ache anymore." Rizpah staggered, reaching to Mithrias for support. "Oh, Mary!" she whispered. "What is this? What has happened?"

Mary scrutinized Rizpah's face, then nodded her approval. Showing no sign of surprise, she said, "If soldiers stop us, they will be looking for a woman who bears the marks of a brutal beating. No one matching that description will be with us."

Mithrias stood mute and stunned. Rizpah's enchanting beauty was restored. He offered both hands to her. She took them. "You..." he managed. "You must go to Egypt. This is the right decision."

Rizpah's eyelids dropped. Mithrias felt her hands grip tighter. He turned to Mary and Joseph. "These things never happen. My mind fights with what my eyes see. First Topur, and now Rizpah." His gaze scrutinized every aspect of Rizpah. "You have been accepted."

Tears trickled down Rizpah's cheeks. "Mary, I have not lived a life deserving such beneficence. I am not worthy."

"Your life is not completed, dear friend," Mary answered. "Perhaps all this is to prepare you for what you have yet to accomplish."

Rizpah released Mithrias's hands, moving to Mary, wrapping her in a close embrace. "With all my heart, I thank you." She hugged Joseph. "I am so grateful." She kneeled before the cradle, kissing the baby on the forehead. The infant's arms rose. A hand touched Rizpah's chin. "I will walk with you," she said tenderly, then slowly stood, her gaze never moving from the cradle.

"I am thankful as well," Mithrias began, "but anything I can give is so inadequate. I brought little with me. I joined this journey hastily, and it wasn't to investigate your star. I thought I could flee from my troubles." He stroked his brow. "They only grew worse. I felt I had lost everything I ever cared for. I even lost belief." Mithrias's forceful shoulders sagged. "Or, I say it better when I confess I adopted a new belief—a belief in nothingness. My life was no more than a solitary imprint in the middle of an empty desert, without distinction, without purpose, soon to be erased by the winds that blow upon every man. I determined it was best to reject the heaven that rejected me, if it existed at all." His head straightened. "But being with you, with him, has restored me." He kneeled on one knee to open the sack. "Rizpah, will you help me?"

"Of course." She kneeled next to him.

From underneath the benign covering, Mithrias pulled a jeweled chest of azure blue marble streaked with white lines. Oval-cut stones of vivid green marked each corner. A much larger crystalline red stone was perfectly centered in the middle.

"I don't have a tree of gold like King Xaratuk, but I do have this." He removed the lid, then lifted the chest.

"Frankincense. An entire chest of frankincense!" Joseph gasped.

"This is the most beautiful chest I have ever seen!" exclaimed Mary. "The fragrance of kings!"

"King Mithrias, we are humbled by such a rich offering, but—"

"I brought it in case Salnassar and I needed to bribe our way out of some misfortune." Mithrias smiled. "All of it is yours, but this is so insufficient. I can't begin to offer anything meaningful as compensation for all you have given to me."

"King Mithrias, you acted to save our child, and—"

"You restored my will. And the words you spoke, Mary.

We Three

Those are among the words most dear to my thoughts and my heart, but I felt alone. I was too isolated, fearful, and ashamed to speak those words, even among friends—caring instead of hatred, compassion instead of conquering, words that honor and support people's lives. Words not considered kingly. But for the first time, I see they can be—they should be. Can this child become a king, teaching and living by those words? I feel a world set against it. I'm compelled to help give him that opportunity."

"The world will know this child better because of you, sir," said Joseph. "We are sincerely grateful for this gift, but even more grateful for your support and faith. Your faith in us, in this, in him, matters most. That faith, and the faith of those like you, will sustain us." Joseph moved to Mithrias and stooped to touch him at his elbow. "Please rise, King Mithrias. You have brought uncommon honor into this house."

Mithrias helped Rizpah to her feet. "And you, Rizpah. My miracle began before I stepped into this house. I was certain I would remain untouched by love for the rest of my life. Feeling that left me bitter and desolate. But in one brief night, you swept all that away. You erased the darkness, the emptiness that surrounded me. You took such risks. You have paid a dear price. Can you know, in your heart, how deeply you have touched me, how much I yearn to be with you?"

Mithrias turned to Joseph. With his jaw clenched, he spoke through his teeth. "Every muscle in my body is straining to take this woman with me. I must do what I least wish to. I must let her go. It is best for her, best for my people. But my anxious heart will not rest until I hold her again. Joseph, it is my queen who goes with you."

"She goes with us, and we go with God," said Mary.

"If I didn't accept that with all my being, I could not do this."

Rizpah locked her arms around Mithrias's neck. "Being with them will help me become the queen you deserve." She drew his chin to her mouth and kissed him.

Kerry Ames

CHAPTER 41

Miriam stood alone, inspecting the packed cart she and Rizpah had seized. She had taken inventory, noting Xaratuk's overwhelming generosity. The provisions he donated would handsomely equip those heading to Egypt. Looking up from her assessment, she spotted Topur and Najiir.

"Why such gloom, you two?" She did not wait for a response. "Topur, where shall I go? I can't decide. How can I abandon Rizpah? She still needs care and would welcome a familiar face, wouldn't she? Where else can she go? But me? To Egypt?"

Miriam moved to the far side of the cart. She called into the shadows. "Come here," she ordered, waving an arm. "Come here, where they can see you."

Kauib emerged into the flickering torchlight. "What am I to do?" Miriam asked. "Kauib didn't want to leave the palace, but we all know he couldn't stay. I wouldn't leave him behind. Once they realize I have gone, they'll surely presume he had some knowledge about me." She took the boy's chin and directed it to her face. "They would hurt you, Kauib—very, very badly. I won't let them do that."

Kauib refused to look back at Miriam. She turned to Topur. "He doesn't believe me. He would rather I had left him there. That wasn't possible. But now, what am I to do? Do I tell Joseph and Mary to add one more to their growing list? And a young boy, at that? It doesn't seem right, but where else can I go with him?"

"He can go with Topur."

Stunned, Miriam shuffled. Topur's back straightened as he considered the prospect.

"Yes, he can go with Topur," repeated Najiir. "It makes sense." His eyes brightened with enthusiasm.

"Well, that is one solution I had not entertained," said Miriam. "Creative, I'll admit, but Topur, can you even consider it?"

"It would keep my master occupied since he won't have me along." Najiir's confidence inflated. "Kauib will fit in with the family as I did, and I will feel better knowing someone is looking out for my master."

"Wait," said Miriam. "Isn't Najiir returning home with you? Where is he going?"

"Egypt," said Topur tersely. "With you. God's will."

"God's will? What does that mean?"

"Najiir must go to Egypt. He'll have time to explain. He will be with you." Topur eyed the young boy standing close to Miriam. "The lad would come with me? I was dreading the loneliness. Najiir cannot be replaced, but this seems like a good idea. Do you think he'll agree?"

"I think he'll agree with whatever I tell him he has to." Miriam smiled with relief. "Kauib, you know Topur."

"He was the man in your room." He eyed Topur up and down. "You made him better."

"Yes, well..." Miriam stammered, "I may have helped. But you know Najiir, too. You trust him. He lives with Topur but isn't going home just yet. You could go to Topur's home and wait until I can come for you later."

"You'll come for me?" Kauib's frown wasn't permanent after all.

"I will come for you, dear." Miriam bent down to hold the boy. "I will come for you."

"Topur is a great man, Kauib. Trust me," added Najiir. "I will come back, too, as soon as my work is done."

Under his breath, Topur told Najiir, "Be careful. He'll expect that."

"You will see me again, master. You will."

A column of torch-bearing archers led the caravan approaching the tiny village. The slaves, servants, and handlers followed, conducting their depleted supplies. All extraneous gear and livestock were left behind, unexpected bounty for the villagers. As the caravan climbed the short slope leading into town, they were met by the shepherds assembled by Simon and Caleb.

Joseph stepped from the house. In moments, a semicircle formed around him in the exact location previously illuminated by a star.

"So much has taken place tonight—this unforgettable night," Joseph said. The air was crisp and cold. His breath was visible in the lamplight. "God has put this in motion, and each of us has been called to it. May He always guide our steps." There were universal nods of agreement. "Where do I begin? We want to thank all of you for the uncountable blessings, for the food and shelter, for the protection, for the endless help, and for your faith." He stepped to Simon and Caleb. "We thank you first because you have supported us from the very beginning. Your presence has sustained and defended us. May it ever be so. We need you to spread the word of what has happened here so that the seeds we are about to sow land on fertile ground. Everything that grows will have you to thank." In unison, the shepherds instinctively dropped to their knees with bowed heads. "May the blessings of God be with you."

"We will prepare the way and await your return," said Simon. "We are your servants forever."

Joseph turned to the advisors, who were linked arm in arm. "I thank you for your wisdom and stubborn desire to understand. There is so much I, myself, do not understand. But I am encouraged by your willingness to find meaning here. You are strangers to this. You could dismiss us outright. But you try to understand when it may be far easier not to. To recognize that God has stirred the thoughts and the actions of those so far from us, so estranged from us, so foreign to our ways, is an important lesson we will reflect upon. I am grateful you realized there was something to explore, something to discover, something that roused you to action. None of the others would be here without your prompting and encouragement."

"So many questions remain, Joseph. So much more to learn," said Merkis. "I thought we would have far more time together. When I ponder what might be, this thought persists. Mary, alone, hears a voice of prophecy. An astounding vision was displayed before these devoted shepherds. But the star was in the sky, visible not to just one, or two, or to an exclusive group, but to anyone who would bother to look. We who have traveled from so far away are evidence this message is, I believe, for everyone."

He turned to Khartir, placing his hands on Khartir's shoulders. "Joseph, Mary, the one I treasure above all others, goes with you." Merkis's eyelids were red. "May we be happily reunited soon." Khartir put an arm around his mentor.

Joseph bowed before proceeding to Xaratuk. "We seem a disappointment to you. We are not what you expected—"

"Please," said Xaratuk. "I leave with more questions than answers, but you are in charge of something undeniably wonderful, and I shall be proud to say I was here. Someday people will ask me, a king, about what I know of some man named Jesus, born in Bethlehem. That day will come, I'm certain." Then, in a softer voice, he added, "And thank you for your forgiveness. I shall always, always remember this night."

"You are most welcome, great king. You are a generous man," said Joseph.

Joseph stepped before Mithrias, who had one arm around Rizpah, supporting her. "Thank you for your faith in us. You knew nothing about us, about him, yet you were willing to come to our aid at the likely cost of your long friendship. I didn't expect that. I hope others can feel such faith as quickly as you."

Joseph looked to Rizpah. "You will find comfort, protection, and meaning with us for as long as you wish to stay."

Rizpah bowed her head. Mithrias cleared his clenched throat. "Joseph, my lost soul found a reason to live, a reason to hope, and a reason to act. I have meaning and purpose once more. I will see you again soon."

Joseph moved to Topur. "I overheard what you told Najiir—about how you think the kings could have made it here without you."

"Oh?"

"That isn't so. They had no realization of the evil inside Herod. You alone told them they needed to question his motives and his actions. Without you, they—or we—would not be standing here now. Maybe both. Thank you for getting this group to Bethlehem. And thank you for aiding our escape. We owe you so much."

"It is I who owe you."

Joseph patted Topur on the shoulders and bowed his head. Moving to the doorway, he lifted the cradle with the baby inside. He turned to address those assembled one last time. "All of you, each of you, go with God." A chorus of "Amens" rose from the shepherds as they stood. Joseph placed the cradle at the end of his cart. Mary sat alongside. Seeing this, Regulus ordered his troops to prepare for departure. Simon stepped forward.

"Captain, we shepherds are dividing into three groups. The first group will leave with you and guide your people to the swiftest way from here, heading first to the east and then to the north. We will scout the area ahead of you to ensure your safe passage until you are beyond the reach of Herod. The second group will move with you, Joseph, and do the same thing heading south. The third group will stay behind in Bethlehem. We have alerted the town. Once Herod arrives—if he arrives— we will know and send word ahead."

"That is a sound plan," said Regulus, "and quite unexpected. It is the very thing we need for a successful escape. I admit to you, sir, that I have misjudged you. You and your men have proven to be brave and earnest friends. Please accept my gratitude."

Simon stiffened. With a tilt of his head, he accepted the compliment. "We must go—now."

With those words, the ancient sands felt moist, human tears once more. Movement now prompted separation. Lives that were intertwined, disentangled. Hearts fell. Throats choked. Eyes shut. Hands trembled. Hugs. Kisses. Soft words. Sincere oaths. Expressions of deep and abiding love.

Miriam released Kauib. Khartir's arms loosened from Merkis, then he grabbed his king's hands one more time. Mithrias held Rizpah, released her, then held her again. Crying, she could not utter the words she wanted him to know. He kissed her forehead. "You are my queen, and we will be together."

Rizpah's chin trembled. "Yes" was the only word she could form.

Topur kneeled on one knee before Miriam. "Oh, get up," she said, mixing her crying with a stifled laugh. "I didn't fix you."

Topur kissed Miriam's hand, then looked up. "If not for you, this child would have had to raise a dead man. That might be beyond even his ability." He smiled. "You are a most amazing woman, and you must—absolutely must—meet my wife. If nothing else, I need you to confirm my alibi."

He stood and gave Miriam a long hug, which she willingly accepted. Tearfully, she placed Kauib's hand inside Topur's. "Be good to each other," she said. "You know I have ways of checking."

Najiir stepped before Topur. "Once this is done, I will return. I will come home."

Topur's mouth widened, expressing his uncertainty. "I don't know where or when your calling will end, Najiir. I only know how precious you are to me. They need you. If someday you can return, satisfied your deeds are completed, our door is open, and we will welcome our son back into our home. Loving arms await you there." Topur thrust himself around Najiir. Holding him for what he knew to be too long, Topur finally pulled away. "Take care. Be smart." He paused, holding a finger in the air. "And be careful whom you talk to."

Through his tears, Najiir was able to smile. "Forever yours," he said, then stepped to the front of the cart.

The procession was moving. Shepherds were at the lead. The road split just inside the village, separating those on a path to Egypt from those headed east. Regulus, followed by men marching with torches, had already turned past the humble dwellings, disappearing from sight. Mithrias, riding next to Xaratuk, was not far behind. They were followed by Merkis, who looked surprised to see it was Salnassar who had touched his arm and was now walking by his side, already peppering him with questions.

Khartir, leading a donkey and cart laden with supplies, followed the shepherds on their initial leg to Egypt. Caleb led the next wagon. It was packed with additional supplies and carried Miriam, who scrutinized Rizpah's renewed face. Joseph, leading the cart with Mary and the baby, was the last of the group.

One lone cart remained fixed before the humble dwelling. Topur reluctantly urged Najiir to get underway.

"I am trying," Najiir said, pulling on the donkey's halter. "The donkey. She won't move. I can't make her move." Topur stepped to the side for a better look. Sighing, he recognized the donkey. It was his, and she was now headed to Egypt.

"Rub her ears," he said softly.

"What?"

"Rub her ears." He cleared his throat. "She likes her ears rubbed."

Najiir shrugged, then made a fist, using his knuckle to rub

at the base of the donkey's ear. The donkey gave him a headbutt. "Yes, like that," Topur affirmed. Still, the donkey did not move. She looked back to Topur, her large, inquisitive eyes blinking.

Topur inhaled. His chest heaved. Overcoming his misgivings, he nodded. "Go. Najiir will be good to you." The donkey looked forward. Najiir gave a gentle pull. Together, they began trotting to catch up with the others. Topur stood fast, showing no more movement than a stone, watching until the last of those headed to Egypt had gone from someone, to silhouette, to shadow.

Mary smiled. She looked down at her baby, then twisted forward to watch those fleeing Bethlehem split in two directions. Slowly, she turned back, looking beyond Najiir and his cart, on to Topur standing motionless, shoulders stooped, holding a boy by the hand. Her gaze moved to the dwelling in the little village she had called home for many months. Thoughts of stars and shepherds and scars and gold and voices and kings and frankincense and even Herod cascaded relentlessly. It made her dizzy. Her baby, safe for now, felt small and warm.

Mary tightened his blanket, pulling him closer. He did not wake. What a serenely beautiful face, she thought. How unaffected by the evening's tempest he appeared. Unexpectedly, a wave of peaceful contentment coursed through her. She felt renewed, assured. She felt comforted and capable as she pondered all that had come to pass.

The End?

ACKNOWLEDGMENTS

Might Matthew have given us more details? With respect to his Nativity story and the visit of the wise men, there are gaps—large gaps. How many travelers arrived at Bethlehem? Matthew tallied gifts, not people. What happened to the star? Who else could see it? Why would men from the East detour to visit King Herod rather than go directly to Bethlehem? And, what would suggest to these foreigners that this child, who had not said one intelligible word, was the culmination of Jewish prophecy?

I felt compelled to create an alternative account to address some of those gaps. I'm not the only one. Over centuries, Matthew's original story has been changed and embellished in print, song, and theater. Initially, I could barely form the words to explain the subject of my story. I felt my contrivance might offend those who don't tolerate any reinterpretation of established Biblical accounts. Or, secular readers would be dismissive, certain I was evangelizing. My target market appeared to have a population of zero.

Or, maybe, my audience was almost everyone. People are drawn to familiar stories reframed with a new, unique, and challenging perspective. Hollywood believes that.

First, I had to learn about writing a novel. Over seven years, my story has been subjected to numerous filters and edits. I stopped counting after the twentieth draft. At some point, I needed to stop. Improvements could continue, but could I? All shortcomings are attributed to me. Two editors, Susanna Daniel and (especially) Lisa Lickel, did their utmost to refine my efforts and break my stubborn habits. When I veer from polished and intriguing storytelling, the fault is mine. They tried. They did.

As I summoned the confidence to speak about my efforts, encouragement arrived. Chris VanAlstine affirmed my initial inspiration to write. Elizabeth Caulfeldt-Felt provided lists of resources and sage advice. She and Karen Bezella-Bond, Nicolas Kubley, Christine Sommers, and Mark Thwait gave needed critiques in our pre-Covid writers' club. The enthusiasm of my first beta reader, Dee Leyshon, was oxygen for a fragile flame. I had additional help from Cathi Dziedzic and Sharon Holy. Jeanette Santoski and Inez Krohn offered unexpected affirmations that meant more to me than I can convey. You made me believe I had a story worth telling and that people from any background or orientation might appreciate it.

Don Santoski gave me editorial support and encouragement.

Dr. Kathy Krohn-Gill and Dr. Gregory Gill expand the definition of friendship. They did so much on my behalf. Thank you for exposure to your Bible Study group and the encounter with Christopher and Kathleen Graham, Alan and Carol Crevier, and Chris and Evelyn Lee.

Heartfelt thanks to Jeanette Ames and Lynn Kincaid for their financial support giving me the time and space to spend endless hours without compensation. Your investment made this happen.

I thank Dr. Arthur Herman and Dr. William Kirby for the inspiration of lifelong learning. I am grateful to Dr. Michael Hakeem, who developed the lens through which I view the world. I wish I could sit with you again, drink another mug of Hamm's beer while Bill Evans plays in the background. Your commentary would likely be scathing, but insightful.

Thank you, Paul Ruane, for the exquisite cover art, and to Rita Ann Powell for her talents and support.

To The McMillan Memorial Library of Wisconsin Rapids: Thanks for being a top-shelf resource in a small town. The entire staff is beyond helpful, and you are a tribute to what a public library can and should be.

To Ron Harris and John Berg my inexpressible appreciation to you for being, well, you. Your presence, support, and insights are vital to my intellectual and personal happiness.

Finally, to my wife, Donna. What happened to your innate skepticism? There was no reason to suspect I would carry this out to fruition. You never questioned my time, my commitment, or my goal. You didn't flash a single eye-roll. There's no justification for believing in this or me, but you never faltered. Time will tell whether I deserve your confidence. The odds are not in our favor. But without you, there would be no odds to consider. I dedicate this book to you.

Thanks.

And thank you all.

ABOUT THE AUTHOR

Kerry D. Ames is a product of the Midwest, born in Wisconsin. He received degrees in Psychology and Sociology from the University of Wisconsin – Madison, then a master's degree in Sociology from The Ohio State University. Graduate school convinced him he'd make a poor and unhappy professor, so he abandoned the academic track and worked in both the public and private sectors. He currently lives in Central Wisconsin, among the jack pine, deer, cranes, and turkeys, mulling over history, genealogy, science, and religion. During good weather, he can be spotted in his bright jersey bicycling long, flat stretches of rural roads. He is sustained in rare comfort by Donna, his wife, after she first attends to the demands of their two cats, who remain oblivious to their pampered circumstances.

Printed in the USA
CPSIA information can be obtained
at www.ICGtesting.com
LVHW041608171223
766712LV00012B/445